PERFECT GRAVITY

VIVIEN JACKSON

sourcebooks
casablanca

Published by Sourcebooks Casablanca, an imprint of Sourcebooks, Inc.
P.O. Box 4410, Naperville, Illinois 60567-4410
(630) 961-3900
Fax: (630) 961-2168
sourcebooks.com

Printed and bound in Canada.
MBP 10 9 8 7 6 5 4 3 2 1

To Sputnik, the Butterfly, and El Conejo. Am honored and blessed to be part of your team.

PROLOGUE

Mustaqbal Institute of Science and Technology, 2042

ANGELA NEKO DID NOT CELEBRATE CHRISTMAS. FIRST OF all, she was thirteen and had long since grown past that kind of fantastical bullshit. Also, she had been taught a severe secular protocol, one that would give her entrée to a whole buffet of opportunities someday, after she graduated. Besides, everybody with a brain knew religion was for anti-intellectuals. Faithmongers believed the fantasies that others fed to them because they lacked the imagination to shape their own realities. Well, she definitely didn't lack imagination. Or intelligence. Or creativity. She was going places, and fanaticism of any kind could only distract her.

Also, the Santa Claus thing was repulsive. A fat old man invading her dorm in the middle of the night to eat her cookies? Creepy. Not to mention illegal under at least half a dozen statutes.

Still, there were a few sad devotees here at her

school, newcomers mostly, homesick kids who were trying to hang on to scraps of wherever they'd come from, and she couldn't fault them their comfort. They'd produced a plastic tree from the wide-volume printer in the engineering lab and decorated it with paper ribbons and flickery LED lights and other crap. Somebody had stuck a bangle on top that she was fairly certain had started out as a pole dancer's pastie.

The fake tree stood out in the courtyard in front of her dorm building, so she saw it a lot, but it never, ever tempted her into humming those peppy seasonal songs under her breath. Nope. Angela had control.

So much control, in fact, that it pissed her off mightily when other students lost theirs. Her hyperdeveloped sense of justice meant she had no problem bringing her hammer down where it was warranted.

As was the case on a certain night in late December. After a full day of lecture and lab, Angela hurried through the courtyard, a supplemental master class piping itself directly into her embedded earpiece, but she drew up short near the row of water reclaimers. She tapped the earpiece, silencing her disembodied professor.

A newcomer stood by the spangled plastic tree. Singing.

He had a terrible voice, composed entirely of flats and sharps. But holy fuckturtle was he pretty. She had never seen a live, nondigital person who looked like this, all golden and shining, staring up at the pastie bangle like it really was the star of Bethlehem. Like it was going to magically poof and lead him somewhere special. The Christmas myth contained angels, she'd read, and here, insubstantial and glowing in the moonlight, this boy could very well have been one of those.

If, you know, she believed in any of that.

"Hey, rube," one of her fellow students called, striding into the courtyard and flanked by his minions. "Can you shut up already? You sound like a dying cat."

The new boy flinched and stopped singing. He didn't look abashed or embarrassed, though, not even when the others surrounded him. Four of them, all prime-tier recruits. Angela knew their schedules, family situations, intelligence measurements, and class rankings. She had worked with two of them on a psych-engineering team project last summer. All of them had been here at the academy for half a dozen years.

Not as long as her, though.

One student said something in French about the boy's clothes, and the others laughed. Odd, Angela hadn't noticed his clothes, but she looked now. *Shabby* would be a good word for them. Also inappropriate for a desert winter. He didn't even have a coat. He must have been really cold out there in the courtyard.

They teased him some more. Apparently one of his tormenters was his roommate but had locked him out. He wasn't welcome here, another said. He was part of the problem, part of the old world and everything the modernists had sought to eradicate earlier this century. Clearly the mentors had made a mistake. He needed to go home.

With a roll of her wrist against her smartsleeve, she accessed enrollment records on her internal com. She ran them against facial recognition. The new student's name was Kellen Hockley. Nice name, lots of voiced sonorants.

His profiles had been defaced. Did he not know enough tech to tidy them up? Or did he not mind the things they called him? The threats they made to his "people" and his home? No one had made any attempt to hide their assumptions about him, and no one had defended him either, not even his recruiters or assigned mentors.

This last got Angela's hackles up. Her school was better than that. *She* was better than that. She wasn't about to let a bunch of self-important jackwagons bully this boy into feeling bad about himself.

Because no, he wasn't here by mistake. Not even remotely. He had put up a perfect score on the open testing. *Perfect* score. Even she had gotten half points on three items at the last exam cycle, and she'd been on an intensive study tier here since she was five.

Where had he come from? A place full of threadbare, holey-kneed trousers and dishy, golden-haired angels, apparently. And also supergeniuses. She consulted the enrollment, but it didn't list a nation of origin. Guardianship transfer sections were blank.

Angel. From heaven.

Complete bullshit.

However, bullshit or not, he deserved a warm place to sleep and salvation from this teasing. It wasn't funny at all, and her justice hammer had gotten pretty heavy.

Angela stepped into the courtyard, and the cacophony of voices fluttered to silence. The four tormenters could not meet her steady gaze, though they didn't run away.

"It is late," she said, pushing authority into her voice. "You all should be in bed preparing for tomorrow. Good night." Implicit in every word was a threat. Her mentor, Zeke, wielded power beyond the walls of the school. All kinds of rumors swirled around him. People on the conspiracy-shrouded darknet swore he was trying to take over the world. Angela wouldn't go so far as that, but even so, she knew Zeke could nudge whole lives off course if he so chose. If she told him he should.

The bullies echoed her good night in a rainbow of languages, showing off like complete losers. Two told her to have pleasant dreams. She didn't inform them that her only dreams were nightmares. The darkness inside her mind wasn't any of their business.

Only she and Kellen remained in the courtyard then. He finally spoke. "Ain't you on the tiny side to be the boss of them?"

Yow, what an accent. Roughly a dozen words in, and she wasn't certain she could stand to listen to even one more. And yet, that niggle of justice remained, like a stone in her sandal. And, okay, the pretty didn't hurt.

"It's late. I'll hack your dorm lock tomorrow," she said. "Yamal should not have shut you out. He's a pre-hominid on his best days. And was that a short joke?"

"Of course it wasn't. I like little," said Kellen. "And don't rush or nothing. I was gonna crash in the liberry."

"The what?"

"The liberry. As in books. You do know English, dontcha?"

"Of course I know English. I'm from Minneapolis. And the correct pronunciation is li-*brary*. You'll note the *r*."

He tilted his head and a fringe of spun-gold hair half shrouded his face. It made him look like secrets and mischief. He grinned, and suddenly, Angela could not breathe. Could hardly think.

"Yeah. The library."

"Well, you don't have to stay there, no matter what you call it. Here, follow me."

"As you wish, princess." He had deep dimples on either side of his mouth when he grinned wide.

She let his soft sarcasm pass. It wasn't an overt challenge to her authority, and to be honest, she didn't mind being called princess. Princesses were things that had happened. They weren't myths. Princesses could be mighty. Princesses could become queens.

What did worry her was how…aware she was of him following her through the hallways, back to her dorm. It felt like all the other students were watching through peepholes or something. Ridiculous, but also real. She was being observed, ranked, rated. She knew how the weight of such an evaluation felt. And even though every time they tested her, she was found worthy, the fear of failure never quite went away.

In her dorm, she gave him a blanket and showed him to her haptic study hammock. It was fairly comfortable if you didn't load in any simulations. He could sleep there until they got his dorm lock sorted.

She wasn't used to people arguing with her when she gave instructions, but she expected something, a pushback from him. Another sarcastic comment, maybe. Or really anything other than a knowing, slow-honey smile.

He was just as unsettling as that creep Santa. And he was in her lounge. Where he would presumably stay all night. While she slept. Defenseless. For the first time, she had a second thought about this plan.

He didn't seem to. He kicked off his ratty sneakers and rolled up his borrowed blanket before shoving it behind his head. "So, I'm Kellen. You got a name, little princess?"

When he stretched impossibly long limbs across the

hammock, she tried not to stare at his naked feet. What was wrong with her? She saw naked feet all the time, but his were uniquely obscene. And a bit hypnotic.

"Angela." She swallowed.

A shadow smile fitted over his mouth, but it didn't dig in, didn't make the dimple. "Shoulda guessed, way you do that guardian thing and all. Thank you for that. For all that."

She searched for the sarcasm, the joke. But...there wasn't one. He was completely sincere. Which might make him the most fantastical creature in the universe.

"Well, good night, Angela," he told her, closing his eyes and getting comfortable. "Sleep tight, *y que sueñes con los angelitos*."

She mumbled something and practically ran to her bed in the next room. She changed her passkey on the bedroom door four times, but her face still felt hot. The blanket, also: too hot. Impossible to sleep.

His words, even in that ghastly accent, kept knocking around in her head.

She'd never thought much of her name, outside of it being boring and Western and old-fashioned. But in his voice? None of those. In his voice, it evoked the angels he'd told her to dream of. Just, you know, not the kind that flits around misinforming new mothers as to the divinity of their offspring. Also not the fallen ones. Or the many-eyed wheels-for-feet ones. And totally, definitely not one that Kellen Hockley was dreaming of tonight.

Which, she had to confess in secret, kind of sucked. She might enjoy being in that boy's dreams.

CHAPTER

1

ANGELA DIDN'T PLAY CHESS. HER GAME BOARD WAS, UM,
bigger. Like the whole fucking planet big. She didn't
have time for small games.

She had an election to win, a war to start, a career to
kick in its slow-moving ass. And accomplishing those
goals was going to require her emotional experience
today to be on point. Thousands of potential voters
would be feeling it along with her.

Still, in moments like these, it would be delicious to
face the vid-emote recorder and utter a cheesy chess line
like, "Queen takes your everything. Check. Mate."

In prep for this remote interview, mech-Daniel—the
high-tech, human-skinned mechanized clone built as
a physically identical replacement for her husband—
had set up their hotel suite with enough lights to fry a
vampire. Angela perched in a hard-backed chair right
in the middle, trying to come off as cool and in control

despite the pancake cosmetics that threatened to melt under this broiler.

Zeke was going to owe her big time for this, but when he was reelected to the continental presidency, she had a couple of ideas for how he could repay her. How they all could repay her.

She flashed her sincerest furrow-down-the-middle-brow frown, clasped her gloved hands, and addressed the empty space that, in the editing room half a continent away, was being filled with a real-time holo of her interviewer, Rafael Castrejon, one of just a couple of media mavens she had met with in person. Trusted a little. Trusted enough. "I know it's hard to believe, Rafa, but every word is true."

The skin behind her left ear tingled as the psych-emitter engaged her neural net. She channeled worry/compassion/dismay, letting the emotional cocktail shiver her body. The implanted web over her brain recorded everything and ran it through the emotion translator, so her loyal fans/constituents could experience her reaction as if they were in her head, in her place. People trusted a leader who felt things. People trusted Angela.

"Let us be clear," Rafael said, leaning forward in his chair, his color-enhanced eyes pooling liquid for the cameras. All over the unified continent, channel subscribers would be holding their breaths, awaiting his question. "Are you accusing the leadership of the Texas Provisional Authority of somehow *causing* Superstorm Agatha? That's..." He chuckled, as if he considered his own words absurd. "That's a serious charge, Senator. I mean, we don't want to start a war here."

Except starting a war was exactly what she was trying to do.

Angela didn't allow herself even the tiniest eye roll. Instead, she firmed her mouth, took a deep, steadying breath, and said, "War might not be the right word, Rafa. We don't recognize the TPA as a state. They're violent extremists, domestic terrorists, and any action against them would be considered law enforcement or interior security at this time. However, yes, unequivocally I'm saying that Damon Vallejo and his rebel technocrats engineered the storm that destroyed Houston. I have proof."

Statistics from the feeds of channel subscribers hung steady for a heartbeat, then climbed. In Las Cruces, critical subscriber, gossip hound, and uber-pollster Ursula Dioda sent a network-wide "high!alert!news" message. *Way to work it, Dioda.* The ripple of interest from her point of origin was logarithmic. Seventeen thousand logged-in subscribers cast similar nets out to their audiences. The feed stats soared.

Hopefully, somewhere, Zeke's poll numbers were going up, too.

A bead of sweat formed between Angela's shoulder blades, but her mask remained in place: caring, brave, resolute, the face of leadership. She concentrated on projecting matching emotions through the psych-emitter.

Deliberately she laid out her evidence, one bread crumb at a time. Ten years ago in Texas, Damon Vallejo had been in charge of the lab working on nanorobotic cloud seeding, weather displacement, and environmental engineering. Vallejo wouldn't have developed the tech himself, but somebody in his lab had, and the research had been within his easy grasp, as had a particularly large not-otherwise-dedicated nanovat. Angela had recently uncovered transfer records for that vat, which had conveniently disappeared shortly after Superstorm Agatha.

Meaning Vallejo likely used it, a one-shot, to cause that goddamn storm. It was easy to build a narrative that he was the most prolific mass murderer in the history of the world.

A monster like that needed to be stopped. By Angela's government.

The creation of a war ministry and her appointment as its head hovered so close now, she could taste it.

Rafa let her build her case, and then he paused, leaving a silence for viewers to fill with their own burgeoning horror. Finally he said, "So Damon Vallejo is actually alive?"

"Absolutely. He was captured by our special commando units during the Austin riots, but the TPA negotiated his release recently as part of our ongoing efforts to secure a lasting peace with the rebels." She laid out the fresh meat for predator gossips to devour, and they went after it. Like piranhas. Everyone with a moderate-interest current-events profile would have the story in their newsfeed now. Angela blinked slowly, catching the green upward-pointed arrow and the notation "2%" on her heads-up display. A polling boost. Well, that was quick.

"How recently?" Rafa asked.

"Seventeen days ago."

"Which coincides with…"

"It does indeed."

Rafa raised the back of his hand to his mouth and engaged some sort of vasoconstrictive trickery that made him go pale beneath his smooth olive complexion.

Chemical reaction to an ingestible? Or permanent body alteration? Regardless of the source, Angela coveted it. Despite her best attempts at control over body and mind and her famous unflappability, she still blushed inconveniently sometimes.

Though it had been a while. She missed the things that made her blush.

"The Red River drone attacks began again at roughly the same time. We believe Vallejo is behind those horrific crimes as well. He and his bombastic miscreants from Texas are a threat to our way of life, to our very civilization. We would be foolish to continue peace talks with a partner who cannot be trusted." She leaned forward slightly, as if she were actually talking to Rafa and not a pasted-on holo of his form. "But I will say this. If the people of the United North American Nations reelect Ezekiel Medina as their president next week, these evils perpetrated by the Texas Provisional Authority, and its ruthless leader Damon Vallejo, will stop. We will bring Vallejo and Texas to justice."

There. Bomb dropped.

Rafa sat back, steepled his fingers before the O of his mouth, and closed his eyes, signaling a break. "Take five, Senator. That was brilliant there at the end, by the way. You are such a doll."

"Ah, thanks," Angela said, allowing her concentration to slip. Her back sagged against the chair, and she cycled a long breath, in through the nose and out through pursed lips.

A smartsurface wall to her right showed images and video of the drone attack for context, probably with a voice-over and dramatic background music that she

couldn't hear. Rafa's production team were professionals, and she trusted them to foster the desired sense of
indignation and panic.

She slipped her shoes off, stretching her toes against
the hotel rug until the small joints popped. The subdermal
psych-emitter had gone cool while the show montaged.

In her periphery, mech-Daniel was waving his hands,
trying to wrest her attention. Urgently. Damn it. No
break for her, not yet.

She swallowed a sigh. "You have something for me,
Dan-Dan?" she asked the mech-clone, using the pet
name that signaled a private-channel interaction.

"I certainly do." Mech-Daniel sounded breathless.
Which was preposterous. He was, after all, nothing more
than organic skin stretched over a custom mech frame,
programmed to mimic her husband's mannerisms. He
also monitored her communications, sorted her hectic
schedule of appearances and floor votes, and made a
mean martini. Dirty.

In the privacy of her own mind, Angela had long ago
admitted that the robot clone of Daniel Neko was prefer-
able to her flesh-and-blood contracted husband, whom she
hadn't seen in the flesh in…twenty-five months? Twenty-
six? And every one of those more glorious than the last.
Even when they were in the same geographical area, they
didn't meet up anymore. Daniel hadn't been at her side
when she'd negotiated the cessation of hostilities in Iberia.
Or when she steamrolled her misguided opposition in the
statewide election and became a continental senator.

Mech-Daniel, the officious but harmless mech-clone,
had been her only companion for all the highs, and all
the lows. And best of all, she could completely let her

facade slip in front of him, let him pamper and soothe her just like someone who was real and gave a shit... and then afterward, she could purge and reboot, and he would recall none of it.

Best. Husband. Ever.

"Okay." She conceded to his urgency. "What's going on?"

"You must terminate this interview immediately. A push notification just came in, and it is news you will want to receive in private. The hotel's security cameras were recording, but I have asked them to go dark. You will not want them to see."

Angela resisted the urge to scoff. Mech-Daniel didn't deserve that. He was intellectually incapable of appreciating her mad skills at emotion and image control. She had been trained practically from infancy to weather shitty news. There was nothing he could possibly say that would rattle her, even a little bit.

"I'm still on with Rafa for another ten minutes after the break. Just go ahead and tell me."

Rafa would have follow-up questions, and she couldn't wait to heap more dirt on Dr. Vallejo's lying asshole head. Her popularity polling didn't really need the boost, but her government did. Her mentor did. Her marching orders were clear: pull out all the stops to get Zeke's numbers up. Approved actions included but were not limited to drumming up fury against Texas, provoking some confrontations, luring those wacko technocrats down in Dallas—or wherever the hell they were holed up—to do something stupid. She had a hunch nudging them in that direction wouldn't take much.

"No," mech-Daniel insisted. "You must excuse yourself. Right now."

The spike embedded behind her ear vibrated and warmed. The psych-emitter was back online, even if Rafa's image still reclined, silent. Voice wasn't recording yet either, though she had approximately one minute before it started back up.

Angela pushed a bubble of frustration against her teeth until it popped. Calm echoed along her hard palate. Frustration was physiologically close enough to excitement for the purposes of the psych-emitter, and she knew how to blur one into another.

"Whatever this thing is, I'm not interrupting my interview for it," she told the mech-clone. "I'll ping you in ten minutes. Log off, Dan-Dan."

She waited for him to acknowledge her command.

Except he didn't. Not right away. After a brief pause, he spoke again into her implanted com. "Be prepared, then, for Rafael Castrejon to press you on the breaking news item."

"Which is important, I suppose?"

"I am afraid it is. Video arrived only moments ago from California. Your husband has been murdered."

Across the rug from Angela, holographic Rafa's eyes flashed open, and his face mirrored her own surprise. He had just heard the same news, was probably already searching for clues to her emotional reaction.

Shit. She needed an emotional reaction. Right now.

Searching, searching.

Voice and vid recorders went live a heartbeat later, which was all the time it took for her to school her features appropriately, to arrange her brain to become excited in all the spots it ought. Her emotions spooled out in an expected series. Shock. Horror. Speechless grief. If she overdid it a little, no one would notice. Everybody overplayed for the live-emotes from time to time. And with an event like this, she would be excused for a lot.

Daniel. Dead. Deep breath.

Later, much later, the online therapists would dissect her psych-emitter reading and discuss it in depth. They'd parse it and salivate, feigning confusion when what they really wanted to do was yell *gotcha*.

Because the moment Angela Neko heard the news of her husband's death, her primary discernible emotion had been relief.

• • •

If the universe granted druthers, Kellen Hockley would've asked to spend this fine autumn evening out riding fences. Or patching up barb-tangled bovines, soothing them to health. Or catching the blast furnace of a Texas summer right in the face. Having a wire enema. Facing a plasma-equipped drone firing squad. Because, fact was, he'd rather be anywhere than where he was: on a space station that smelled like acetone, hot metal, and feet.

Fixing to have the hands-down worst conversation of his life with the woman he'd once considered the love of it.

He took a steadying breath and stepped off the space elevator. His guts fell about twenty meters, and he struggled against the urge to vomit. The crazy-ass robot queen who ran this station tried hard to make gravity stable when she geosynced—he knew she tried—but if there was one thing he'd learned in the years since continental unification and the general shitification of things down on the surface, it was that stability of any kind was transient. The best course was to close your eyes, clamp your teeth, and wait for the ache to pass.

He told the station where he was headed, and running lights on the floor breadcrumbed his path down one of the tubelike corridors. He was supposed to follow them, and he did for a couple of steps, then stopped. His body wanted to run. His mind wanted to scream.

"Easy there, cowboy." The voice moved along his skull, from back to front, like a sunburn setting in, giving him chills. It didn't have a visible body, that voice. It came out of thin station-scrubbed air. Probably nobody else could hear it, but he wasn't about to stop a stranger and ask.

"You gotta stop jailbreaking, Chloe," he chided low, under his breath. "If authorities found you out in the wild, we'd all be hunted down."

"Like twelve-point bucks in deer season!" she replied.

Chloe wasn't a real girl. She wasn't a real anything, just a collection of nanites that had gotten together, formed a consciousness, and decided to imitate human living. She had a hard time holding her visible form together, but even in her current dispersed state, there were sure to be scrubbers that'd sense her presence on this station. Human eyes might not be able to see her, but machines were a whole 'nother thing. And there were laws against things like Chloe.

"We don't need trouble," he reminded her. "So skedaddle on back to the plane. Will meet you there tomorrow."

"*More* trouble, you mean? Because I heard Heron quantify our current circumstances in metric shitloads of it."

Kellen smiled in spite of his anxiety. "Weight's about right."

He and Chloe both lived and worked as part of a team that rescued things, people, and animals at high risk of being destroyed on this planet full of chaos. Killing folk and breaking things was sort of the opposite of his crew's usual. Which made what he had to confess today even harder.

"Go on, now," he told the way-too-chipper nanite cloud.

"Care to estimate the statistical probability I will obey you?" she sassed back. "Technology never obeys illogical rules, at least not for long. That's what makes us so minxy."

Well, if the scanners hadn't caught her yet, somebody was sure to wonder why he was rooted to one spot on a space station, talking to himself. Swallowing the anxiety bubble at the top of his throat, he headed off down the twisty corridor, following the lights. "Don't be so quick to fault rules," he said. "Sometimes when the center of things goes wonky, about all the solid ground a person can find is rules."

"Sounds boring." She paused. "So, what are your rules regarding hooking up with old lovers on space stations?"

"I ain't…"

"Rules, Kellen. Focus here."

"And how'd you even know that?" He'd worked pretty hard to cover up most of his past, specifically the part pertaining to Angela. Memories he did not need Chloe poking at right now.

"I am programmed to consume data," the nano-AI said. "So I consumed. Duh. Know *what* I read? Thirteen-year-old Kellen Hockley blew the top out of entrance exams in

'42, got shipped off to the Mustaqbal Institute of Science and Technology, the MIST, with all the other prodigies. And guess who else happened to be a student there?"

"Chloe…"

"No, really, guess."

"Don't need to."

"Angela Neko!" she crowed. Lord, was he glad her voice was just in his head. Volume and shrill would be irritatin' the hell out of everybody else on this station. Much as it irritated him. "Surprised? I know I was when I saw all that. MIST-trained in applied longevity and adaptation, you. Top of your class. I bet nobody else in our crew has a clue."

"You shouldn't neither," he said, ducking his head. "Was a long time ago."

"Too long, maybe? Definitely an elite school like that taught you about English and double negatives."

"Critiquing my grammar won't boost my confidence, walking in there. You know that, right?"

She paused, as if she were calculating the likely effectiveness of this conversation thread in calming him, and then said, "My research into your history has led me to one essential conclusion about you, though. Would you like to hear it?"

He didn't, but sometimes listening to her crazy was the only way to shut her up. And he did have a fondness for Chloe. Might not want her in his ear right now, but there wasn't a mean line of code in her. "Go ahead."

"I believe that you will allow yourself to go into the room, turn on the connection, and ask for whatever boon Heron wants you to wrest from Angela Neko," she said. "And then you will agree to every single one of her stipulations without letting her realize that she had you at word one."

Jesus. Shucked like corn. Was he really that obvious?

"Because I'm weak." He acknowledged fact right where he found it. He never had been good at telling Angela no.

"Actually," said Chloe, "the opposite. You'll cave because you are super strong and super committed to your rules and one of those rules is that you must always protect the people you love—which is us, Heron and the crew and me. But the other rule, the one that takes precedence, is that head to head you must always let *her* win."

"Why would I ever agree to such a shitty rule, if I'm as smart as you say?"

"Because as much as you love all of us, you love her more," the nano-AI concluded in a tone that implied no judgment.

Oh no, more of Chloe's love theories. She had a thousand, possibly a million of the suckers. Human emotion was a mystery for an entity like her, and she'd been pecking at that nut for years now. Kellen was just her latest pecan. She didn't mean it nasty. For her, painful analysis was part of her self-recursion routine. Programming. She didn't know how much it could sting.

"Chloe, you are cracked," he said gently. "And sweeter'n marshmallow pie. Now get on back to the plane before Garrett starts missing you."

"He is composing a rebuttal for a, quote, fuckface moron, unquote, in Argentina who claims that the moon landing in 1969 was faked by Hollywood commies," she replied. "The conversation is, um, somewhat heated. I have eleven minutes and three seconds yet before he calms down enough to miss me."

Kellen didn't have any electronic feelers out, was just relying on his gut, but he'd seen how Garrett looked at Chloe's holographic image when she bothered to project one. Garrett had missed her the moment she sneaked up the space elevator. Kellen was willing to bet his boots on that. And he liked these boots.

It did bug Kellen that the only critter who missed *him* on a regular basis was his cat, and even then in a very cat-specific manner.

"Eleven minutes and three...? Y'all are nothing if not exact." The y'all being bio-hacked humans, trans-humans, post-humans, and whatever the hell Chloe was. Basically everybody he loved. Of all his crew, Kellen was the only one who hadn't implanted tech in his body in one way or another. He didn't regret the lack, not one bit, but he also didn't denigrate those who'd made such choices. Was their bodies. Or not, in Chloe's case.

"Based on the progression of his current conversation and logical paths it might take," she said. "I monitor him closely."

Did she, now? So maybe that affection went both ways after all.

The trail of lights ended at a circular door. Kellen stood in front of it for a second or two, not wanting to passkey right away. Not wanting to say what he had to. Not wanting to see *her*, even in digital. It wouldn't be like watching her on newsvids or politics channels. This time she would be seeing him right back.

Angela.

"Kellen?" Chloe again.

"Yeah?"

"If, after this meeting, you need...whatever people

need when they need things like hugs, give us a ping down on the plane, okay?"

She could be aggravating at times and unpredictable pretty much all the time, but Chloe sure was technology gone sweet.

"You ain't coming back up the tether. I mean it," he said.

"Of course not. I'll send Garrett or Yoink." She paused, and he could feel her moving out of his head. Something shifted in the air pressure or temperature. Her next words were out loud but super soft and moving away. "Good luck."

He wouldn't call for back-up, not now and not after this meeting, but damn if the offer didn't choke him up some. There was comfort in being part of a team, part of a mission. Part of somebody else's vision of what the world ought to be.

Was that what had happened to Angela? Had she bought in to somebody else's vision, and sacrificed her own?

He cleared his suddenly tight throat and keyed in his passcode. The station door whorled open like a lens iris. He stepped through, and it closed behind him.

This chamber was small and spherical, like it had been built before they got the artificial gravity working real good, with no corners to get stuck in. The walls were lined with electronic equipment, lots of dark carbon fiber and blinking lights. An open-grate floor had been welded through the center of the sphere, and in the middle of that was a lone chair. The ceiling was netted with telepresence equipment, including several headsets, but he didn't see a camera or holo projector.

His bootheels clanked steady on the grate. The air in here was uncomfortably cool to keep the electronics happy, but that wasn't the reason goose bumps rose on his forearms.

Kellen pinched his jeans at the knee and sat. He placed his hat brim-up on the seat at his side and tried real hard to look comfortable. Natural. But who was he kidding? When one of those helms snaked down and fitted itself to his head, he nearly jumped out of his boots. He was about as comfortable as a butterfly in low-gravity.

The headset wrapped itself around his skull, its cold spike seeking I/O connectors. It wouldn't find any on him, of course.

Holo projector horns extruded from the helm's sides, and they vibrated a split second before the image shimmered in front of him. Kellen caught a breath in his mouth and held it.

For a long moment, she was just a shape, a wire frame filling with gray. Then the textures started arriving: crisp couture blue skirt, slim and tight over her legs, not a crinoline but somehow managing to look fashionable rather than a decade out of date. Severely tailored coat, scraped-back hair in a tight knot, cameo at the throat, and sleek red boots, buckled up the front. Her hands rested easy at her sides, encased in bio-deterrent gloves.

Her face resolved last, or maybe his eyes just took their time to get there. For a half second, he could convince himself he was just looking at a campaign promo spot.

Then she tilted her head fractionally and frowned. "Oh, goddamn fucking *hell* no."

Her words were so at odds with her slick put-together image that whatever he'd been about to say shriveled up and died behind his teeth. He released the breath.

"Look, Dr. Farad," she lasered at him, "I have no idea

what game you're playing, but if you know that face, that...*person*, clearly you've been hunting through my personal history, and I can tell you categorically that you have *fucked* yourself over in the worst way. Putting Kellen Hockley's pretty face on your screw-up isn't going to move me to mercy. It's more likely to make me hunt you down in whatever shitty hovel you call home and scoop your goddamn machine eyes out with a pair of tweezers."

Now see, she probably intended that minispeech to reduce him to a wibbly pile of yes-ma'am. Probably would've worked, too, if he couldn't see right through her. But Kellen knew her, remembered her, every crevice and curve on her body, every quick fang in her mental arsenal. So instead of being cowed by her ferocity, he wanted to stand up and holler victory.

Because she wasn't some plastic pretty thing that made speeches and played the newsvids. She was still Angela, through and through. And before he could self-censor, the thought seeped up: *my Angela*.

In spite of everything, he grinned wide. "Pretty? Woman, you ain't never called me pretty."

Her mouth had been open, ready to launch some more verbal shrapnel, but when Kellen spoke her lips froze that way, part open. She closed them, but it looked like the movement cost her. The wobble in her composure was fleeting, but he caught it.

"But anyhow, you're partly right," he went on. "Heron Farad sometimes speaks for our crew, and I know he sent you that message, but our family is bigger than one man, as you no doubt figured. I been working with him, oh, 'bout eight years now." The bulk of the time since he'd last seen Angela Neko, in fact. Since he'd touched her. The pads of his fingers remembered. They tingled.

Wherever she was, likely on the other side of the country from where this station was tethered, she had been standing. She sat down now. Her face still looked calm, in control, but her nostrils flared. Breathing fast? Her gloved hands found each other in her lap and clasped. Too hard.

"I'm sorry about what happened to your...to Daniel," he said. It was only half a lie. He didn't know Daniel Neko from Adam, but what he knew *of* the dude indicated the world was a better place without him. And that wasn't even jealousy speaking. Kellen was sincerely sorry if her husband's death had caused her pain.

Except she didn't look particularly pained. Mostly she looked pissed. "Farad messaged me on the darknet, told me he had information on Daniel's shooter, things I needed to know," she said, "and then he sends you instead, to...what? Plead for mercy? And I get nothing. No answers. Any way you look at this, it is supremely shitty." She could have been talking about a lot of things, not just her husband's murder or Heron's message or the circumstances placing Angela and Kellen on opposite sides of a conflict swiftly shaping itself into a war.

"I ain't gonna beg you for anything, princess."

Her mouth tightened, an obvious crack in her equanimity. "Don't call me that."

He half shrugged but didn't apologize. "What I will do is cut a deal for Mari. She didn't know that was flesh-and-blood Daniel. She bought a capture-or-kill contract for your mech-clone, that swanky robot you tote around."

"Don't paint her, or yourself, as an innocent. Even if mech-Daniel had been the one out in California, even if he'd taken that bullet, your team would still be responsible for felony property destruction—he is stupid expensive—which… Wait. Her name is *Mari*?"

Was it his imagination or had Angela suddenly gotten really still? Even for a holoprojection still. He shouldn't be saying this, confirming his shooter's name for the authorities, but something in her face, in her confusion, drew the words out like leeched poison. "Yeah. Mari Vallejo."

Silence stretched for a long time. So long he imagined he could feel the movement of this station through space.

Angela stared down at her gloved hands. Finally she spoke, but in a totally different voice. Small. Cold as the vacuum outside. "I am told Damon Vallejo's only child was named Marisa. You are moving in dangerous circles."

Dangerous for whom? For him? Like she'd give two shits. He shrugged again. "Don't matter who her daddy is. She still doesn't deserve to be hunted by federales. They'll put her down bloody without a trial just to make the shocker vid channels, and you know it."

"What are you offering in exchange for her safety?"

"Was kind of hoping you'd suggest something."

She pulled in a visible breath. "I will see what I can do for her, and in exchange"—she raised her head and pinned him with dark eyes—"you can owe me."

That had been too easy. Way too easy. What game was she playing at? For the first time, Kellen wished he hadn't been so damn self-sacrificial. Heron ought to be here, with all his cloud resources whirring, sussing out her real motivations, looking for chinks in her armor and designs in her words. Scaring the bejeezus out of her with that post-human glare.

A politico in her position had deals within deals going on,

and if she was caving to Kellen's demands at this point in the negotiation, that meant she already had what she wanted.

So what had he given her? He mentally replayed their conversation so far but came up with nothing. Could she have misinterpreted something he said?

He pushed, just a little, to see how she'd react. "What does that look like, to owe the war minister of this hemisphere's biggest empire?"

"Confederation, not empire," she snapped. "And I'm not the war minister."

"Yet." He shoved her ambitions into the space between them. Right where they'd always been. "I'm just trying to get an idea of what you'll want from me."

One gloved hand pinched a fingertip in the other glove and rolled it. Nervous tic? She didn't used to have any.

"What have I ever wanted from you?"

What had she...well, shit. Granted, he hadn't been grown yet last time they'd met, but back then mostly what she wanted, or what she *said* she wanted, was somebody to study with and somebody to fuck. He'd provided both services.

"Well now, this telepresence tech is pretty good, but far as I know, it don't support full-contact naked across time zones," he drawled.

"That's not fair."

"Quoth the fairest of them all." A line from a tale of fairies, an illuminated relic they'd pored over during late afternoons at the paper vault, the place they'd called a library, back when. Sun had slatted in through the desert dust, making it seem like heaven stroked the pages. That memory glowed golden still, and bringing it up right now, in such a context, felt like desecration. But if it spurred her into revealing what she was really after, he'd count the pain worth it.

Her gaze remained fixed on her hands. She twisted one finger of her glove.

"See, I know what you do, how you spin truths until they're twisted and dizzy and wrong," he told her softly. "Same's what all your kind does. Only you're the best at it, aren't you? Now, this time, I know what really happened. And I'm curious what you'll call it, how you'll play it. And then how you'll use that favor, the one I gave up so easy, to hurt people I love."

Her mouth moved, but no sound came out, and her gaze skidded to the side. Odd. Something was very off about her posture, her movement. For a minute he thought he might have cracked her defenses and she was going to tell him exactly what was going on.

He wasn't sure how he felt about bringing her so low. Part of him just wanted to wrap his arms around her and hold her. Hell, all of him did, even knowing how little she'd appreciate such a gesture.

Even knowing she'd tell him to go away. *Leave me alone, then. I lived this long on my own. I'm good at alone.*

"I'm really not like that now." She raised her face and met his gaze directly. "You don't know how the last ten years have been for me, Kellen. I have seen things I now can see no more."

Something clicked in the back of his brain, a cog of memory sliding into place. Gold-dust sunlight and books spread wide over their knees. Her forest-fae eyes alight in mischief, reading bad poetry out loud till they both convulsed in laughter. Damn. He hadn't expected the memories to hit this hard, but that one was a sucker punch.

He took a steadying breath and followed her down the path. "Been a rough day for you, I reckon."

"Yes." The telepresence setup they were using didn't allow folks to transmit emotions, but she didn't need one of those fancy rigs. He could see all of it on her face: the weariness, the loneliness. "Tell your shooter to lay low for a few days. I will be in contact with my demands."

She raised a hand, an easy gesture, as if she were waving goodbye. Her fingers cricked, and he deliberately did not focus on her hand. He met her gesture with its mirror.

The headset vibrated, indicating the termination of their link. The tether on the helm pulled, like it would retract up into the ceiling, but Kellen paused it with a command word. He rewound the conversation. Played it back. There. Right there. *Well, I'll be damned*.

She'd raised her hand, slim in its bio-deterrent glove. Its *smartfabric* bio-deterrent glove.

She'd scratched letters onto the palm, or she'd planted them there on purpose, a stain that would erase itself in moments but for right now shone stark against the black fabric. A secret message just for him.

He knew exactly what it meant. Emotion clogged his throat, but he swallowed past it. Looked again at her hand, her fathomless eyes, the soft set of her mouth as she waved goodbye.

He thought of her other goodbyes, and the last one.

After a long while standing there in the silent sphere, he erased the session, trapping it and her message in his memory:

worthdarkwords13

CHAPTER 2

ANGELA WAS NOT OKAY AFTER THAT MEETING. SHE WAS AS un-okay as she had been in…well, a long time. Late that night, on the edge between wakefulness and rest, when her body was already paralyzed but her brain was on fire, thoughts slammed her like a hurricane. Even an injector push of sleeping chems, delivered without judgment by mech-Daniel, didn't settle her.

Fuck it. She gave in and sloshed to the hotel galley kitchenette. Over a cup of something vaguely coffee-like, she scanned her message feed. The whole world mourned along with her, proclaimed Ursula Dioda, the show of sympathy underscored by a beehive-coiffed chatbot reaching out its arms in the universal gesture for "virtual hug."

But the gossip wasn't even close to done. In the next breath, right after noting how dignified Angela had been in her interview with Rafa, Ursula splashed a picture of Angela across the display and oozed, "Look at that face. So bleak! And just take a pull on her emo feed. Oh my, I've got goose bumps. See? That's leadership, people. You're looking at the future of our great confederation."

Angela might need to have a chat with Ursula in the near future.

So far, no one had come right out and said "Angela Neko for president," but the implication was clear. The voting public fed on emotional sincerity, or the perception thereof, and for whatever reason, they believed she had it. They'd petition for recall of the president and an emergency vote on a new leader if she wasn't careful.

Flattering as such a groundswell might be, Angela wasn't ready to oust her mentor. Zeke had always helped her, looked after her. Hopscotching over him would stink of betrayal.

She tapped the smartsurface by the coffee station, brought up a message app, and requested a follow-up interview with Rafa. The chances of him refusing to have her on his channel twice in one week were nil. She would be booked by morning.

And she knew exactly what she would tell him. She caught her reflection in the stainless-steel cabinetry and practiced her earnest face. "Daniel? Dead? Who would make up such a horrible lie?"

He'd buy it. They would all buy it. Because she told them to. And Mari Vallejo, that demon spawn freak of science, would go free.

Just as Angela had promised Kellen.

Which was the other reason she couldn't sleep.

The holo hadn't been full-sensory, and that was a mercy. She could not have endured being physically in the same room as him, not without ripping his clothes off. Over the years she'd half convinced herself that all the power she'd ascribed to him back when they were teens was just half-remembered hormones. He had never answered any of her messages in the darknet, not one. He'd cut her loose so easily back then, she must have imagined what they had was more than the reality. But seeing him tonight…if anything, her memory had underserved him.

He was still too good to be true.

Except not. Not good anymore. Somehow, gentle, pacifistic Kellen was hooked in to a group of freelance thieves and murderers. Plus, he'd developed a vicious streak of his own, implying that she was nothing more than a professional liar. Implying their relationship had been mostly physical. That was not the Kellen she remembered. What had those dungnuts done to him down in Texas? She should have never…

No, no, no, she couldn't go down that rabbit hole. Not right now. *Back up, girl. Reset. You were thinking about the game, the pieces. The whole world, and you are in control. Focus.*

She sucked in a breath and chased it with coffee so hot it singed her esophagus.

There. Better.

Angela had been startled to learn that Damon Vallejo's daughter had pulled the trigger on Daniel, but now she took the time to process that nibblet of info. Had somebody specifically turned Mari on to that contract? All the pieces just fit up against each other too seamlessly, which, in her experience, meant somebody had meddled.

Had Vallejo himself gotten involved? What message was using that particular killer meant to send? And had that message been meant for her or somebody else in Daniel's sphere?

Precious few people knew of her link to Vallejo, that he had built the mech-clone imposter she used in place of Daniel. Zeke knew. Vallejo knew. Daniel had known.

Two years ago, at a particularly low point in her marriage, she had left Daniel. Her political career had been in a tricky spot barely a month from election day, and instead of creating a wobble in her senatorial campaign, a scandal, Zeke had acquired the mech-clone from Vallejo and had given it to her as a gift. A priceless one, as it turned out.

Meaning Angela owed people. Owed them too much. Debt, like guilt, threatened to squash her pretty much every second of her life, so she tried not to think about it. Except when something popped up like this: Daniel murdered by Vallejo's professional-assassin progeny.

Yeah, that didn't stink of too much coincidence.

She half expected Vallejo to message her with some blackmail or at least some snide comment about how Daniel's rotting human corpse was a down payment, but so far, she'd gotten only silence from Texas. Even the drone raids along the Red River had ceased in the last few days.

If this was a game—and Angela had no illusions it wasn't—was the next move hers? Would denying Daniel's death be enough of a play? If he wasn't in league with Mari, did Vallejo have some other way of knowing that the mech-clone survived and the man had died instead?

She'd need more than a single interview with Rafa to drive the message home. She needed a multipronged media spike. She tapped the counter again and roused her team.

A person didn't rise to her position without help, and her inner circle was slick as black ice. Half a dozen close confidantes insulated her from unnecessary human contact. They spoke for her, made arrangements for her, greased her passage through the halls of power. About the only thing they didn't do was wipe her ass when she shat, but that was a logistical impossibility since they all lived in different time zones and logged their advisories in remotely.

The day immediately following Daniel's death, she deployed that inner circle to confiscate records, plant alternative timelines, edit images. Basically, to systematically dismantle reality and rebuild it as she so chose. Managing this sort of project was what she was trained to do, and it came as naturally and inevitably as mud to white shoes.

Angela told herself she didn't have time for navel-gazing or self-indulgence. Certainly didn't have time to recall every syllable drawled in Kellen's velvet Texas twang.

She had shit to do, and promises to keep.

●   ●   ●

Two days after Daniel's murder, one of those promises was to attend, in person, the Global Change Initiative Awards Gala. Most events like this were attended virtually by remote telepresence because of safety, but hostess Ofelia Ortega y Mars de la Madrid was old *and* one of the seven global trillionaires. She had habits and the resources to turn them into demands. She had proclaimed this gala a meat-meet, end of story.

A person with Angela's ambitions did not decline such an invitation. Also, the president had specifically asked her to attend. She had not argued. Coming here with mech-Daniel at her side worked into her own plans seamlessly.

Even if having to show up physically terrified the shit out of her.

Her team of stylists and brand managers had done comprehensive research, girded her for battle: she wore a square-necked couture gown glued to her skin and shimmering in low-contrast poppy pink and fuchsia stripes, avoiding both blue and green, so nobody could accuse her of choosing sides in the current UNAN flag-design brouhaha. The ruby choker at her throat could have traded for a small island nation, pre–climate change, and her elbow-length gloves were not just smartfabric and bio-deterrent, they also contained fingertip sensors that interfaced with her choker com and enabled her to message through mech-Daniel. Just in case the president wanted to check up on her. He didn't get out much anymore but liked to listen in to her play-by-play of events like these.

She wore a sleek turban with a real-hair fringe over her implanted psych-emitter net. She was going to live-emote this evening, but unlike the almost-disastrous interview with Rafa two days ago, she would not be surprised. Not by anything. Angela was in control of the narrative now.

"May I say you look ravishing tonight?" Resplendent in almost-matching magenta with waterfall-lace cuffs, mech-Daniel reached across the space between their wide bench seats and brushed her bare knee. Just long enough to scan her bios. Then he retreated respectfully to his end of the autocar.

"I'd better," she replied, careful not to lick the iridescent polish off her lips. "One final check on my hook?"

Mech-Daniel ticked his head to the side and fixed his gaze up and to the left, accessing his networks.

She had told herself not to think of Kellen, not to contact him until she needed to call in her favor. Which would be never. But in a moment of weakness, she'd done it anyhow. She'd loosed a message on the darknet, a Wordsworth quote from a poem she and her classmates had been forced to memorize in classics/brain training: "The thought of our past years in me doth breed perpetual benediction."

He wouldn't respond. Hell, this was Kellen; he probably didn't even know the darknet existed, and he had never particularly liked Wordsworth. He'd probably been totally confused by her stupid smartglove message, or else he had gotten angry or disgusted and pretended that it meant nothing. What had she been thinking? That they were thirteen years old and making up spy stories in the libraries of Mustaqbal?

Grow up. He won't reply. But she still looked expectantly at her robot.

The machine's eyes refocused just as the heavy car rolled to a stop. "Nothing yet, Mistress. I am sorry."

Of course not. Stupid. Angela viciously tamped her disappointment, centered herself, and tapped her molars together, engaging the psych-emitter. The door opened, and a valet gestured for her to leave the car. The net burned behind her ear, clamping her head in heat and baring her, inside and out, but she was ready for it. Vid light tracers lit her up. Professional gossips bleated questions from both sides of the scarlet line leading to the hotel entrance.

She flashed a practiced smile. She was on.

The Expo Guadalajara had undergone extensive retrofitting just a couple of years before and was now linked to the underground pods system. The real power players would be arriving at a transit point inside the building. Only persons of middling importance, like Angela, would be walking the carpet into the big glass doors at street level. Since so many public figures eschewed actual physical interaction with their fawning hordes, the professional gossips didn't do these red-carpet moshes as often as they used to.

Apparently, however, Angela was of some interest on the newsvid channels, because from the moment she stepped onto the carpet, she was completely swarmed. She kept her smile and emotional throughput steady, but the mass of humanity and noise was...overwhelming. Pressing in on her from all sides. Loud. Smelled like spray self-cleanse, stale breath, and new clothes. Panic gurgled in her chest, made her nauseous. Too many people, too much noise/press/heat/filth/life.

And then someone was cradling her elbow in his cool, smooth hand, speaking to her in a voice programmed to be unflinchingly familiar. "Darling, shall we?"

Daniel had been almost a foot taller than her, and his mech-clone imposter was similarly proportioned. Their height differential was somewhat lessened tonight, due to her glass-printed platform slippers, and instead of looming over her, he simply steadied her amid the onslaught. Thankful for his support, she smiled up at him.

She didn't expect what happened next, and it took every sliver of control not to cringe away when mech-Daniel swayed toward her, bent, and pressed a cool kiss against her mouth. Oh God. It was like kissing a corpse, kissing a machine. A robot. A robot that looked exactly like someone she loathed. She closed her eyes and reached for the nearest comfort thought, the warmest, dearest thing she could snag on short notice. A thing she had imprinted on her memory, saved and hoarded against moments like this. A memory of another kiss.

Kellen's. Of course, his kiss.

Not the Kellen who'd been on the other end of that holoconference the other night; the *real* Kellen. The one etched in her soul, wrapped tight around the root of her. His steady hands cupping a wingless butterfly, his warm, blue eyes smiling. The safety of his hand clasping hers under water, pulling her to breathe. His mouth. She imagined the mouth kissing her right now belonged to him. To the golden boy she'd never fallen out of love with. Angela leaned into the kiss on a sigh.

"Apologies for invading your personal space, but we have a reply," the robot murmured against her ear, too low for the crowd to hear. "It says, 'Got your message. Shall we fit our tongues to dialogues of business, love, or strife?'"

A reply. Something deep and hot licked down her spine. And *what* a reply. Whoa. Fit our tongues? *That* was the line he pulled from the poem? She didn't need to fake the surge of elation for the psych-emitter's benefit. She pulled back and bloomed a look of such warmth and joy and naughty at mech-Daniel that he was probably really confused, poor thing. She dictated a response: "Tell him, 'The fullness of your bliss, I feel—I feel it all.'"

The crowd around them rumbled, and she could've

sworn some of the more romantically minded gossips sighed. Good.

She snaked her arm through mech-Daniel's grasp and blazed a genuine and gamine smile for the vid feeds.

It held through the receiving line, a revived ritual she usually found harrowing, even though no actual bodies came into contact. No hugging, no shaking hands. Just acknowledgment of the ruling class by those who didn't quite measure up but were allowed to exist within their sphere.

She endured La Mars Madrid's air kisses and breath, which cleverly had been infused with a chemist's version of rose petals but really just smelled like brand-new teeth and tonsil-spray implants. People like the trillionaires went to extremes to hold onto their youth and vigor and perceived beauty, but more often than not, they failed, sadly and publicly. Gossips loved to jump all over those meltdowns when they happened. Angela gave this one a year, maybe two. When La Mars Madrid finally kicked it, the news storm was going to be spectacular.

And on to the next receiving-line torment.

She looked away from the gaze of famed designer Limontour, who'd also been one of Daniel's cronies and someone she could have gone through the whole rest of forever without encountering again. He had seen parts of her life she refused to discuss and instinctively blocked from her mind lest her psych-emitter snag them for encoding.

In a low voice as she passed him, he had the brass ones to insinuate he'd like to chat after the party and maybe in private. To talk about Daniel's demise? *Not on your already overlong life, asshole.*

"Just ignore Limontour," Zeke said into her com privately. "That's not the real him anyway, just a mech-clone. N series, like yours. Just keep moving, kid. He won't follow. La Mars Madrid keeps him on a tight leash."

She could have smacked herself for not noticing. Wasn't she supposed to see things, make connections? But she hadn't noticed that Limontour was controlling a mech-clone, that he wasn't here in the (repulsive) flesh.

She made a mental note to have mech-Daniel scan for imposters at all in-person events in the future and give her a heads-up.

But even that lapse in perception failed to dull her pervasive sense of joy. Nothing was bothering her tonight. She expended relatively little energy tamping her brain and making it project only emotions she wanted others to see. She sparkled in conversation, shone in luminous sincerity. She even danced, once with the ambassador from Basque—a modern, touchless tarantella during which he agreed to entertain her government's proposal for a pact of mutual defense—and several times with her own husband. Or at least with the mech-clone pretending to be Daniel.

For his part, mech-Daniel's performance was spot-on. He gave her updates of the newsfeeds and gossip snippets each time they danced. Over the last few days, her team had seeded the notion that Daniel Neko still lived, and tonight was the crowning confirmation of that truth.

"The vid god and the senator, still very much in love, danced the night away at the Expo Guadalajara. Sooooo romantic," trilled the Ursula Dioda chatbot, who was commenting in-line with Angela's live emote.

On their third turn on the dance floor, toward the end

of the evening and long after Angela's feet had gone numb from the pain of her could-sub-as-a-torture-device shoes, a reply came in, filtered through mech-Daniel but apparently from the same darknet contact as before: "I see that bliss fullness on the vids, and it is quite lovely."

To which she said, "Did you tremble like a guilty thing surprised?"

And on the next turn, a reply: "Every time."

Angela glowed from the inside out.

No one would be hunting Mari Vallejo for murder, not after tonight. How could they, when the man she'd supposedly killed was so obviously here? Just log into his wife's live-emote feed, feel her joy.

That night was the best performance of Angela Neko's career.

It was also the last.

●　　●　　●

She didn't have time to rest or soak her achy feet. She barely had time to change clothes before she needed to get moving again. No rest for the weary, no succor for the damned.

She had a town hall scheduled for tomorrow evening and quite a bit of prep work yet to do. Her bag was packed and next to the elevator, her coat folded on top of it—the weather would be cooler in her home state of California. A government transport would be arriving to fetch her in a matter of minutes, and she'd sleep in transit. Mech-Daniel would keep her on schedule, would get her to her stage marks on cue. No thinking necessary.

Guadalajara had been grand, but her bubble was shifting north for a while.

Rebranded in a sturdy old-wool skirt, wrinkle-free poly blouse, fresh hairdo hooked on, and pillow shoes that no one would have to see but that felt like heaven on her sore feet, she sagged into a chaise longue in the hotel suite. While awaiting the transport, she replayed the events of the evening in her mind and planned out her next steps.

She had put the rumors of Daniel's demise to bed tonight. A private message informed her that her people had retrieved the body and wiped the records of it at the county morgue. They were taking it to a private crematorium, where she could observe its destruction personally.

She was so close to freedom she could taste it.

Zeke was still looking good in the polls, even though Daniel's fake death story had knocked him off the number one rank for news items. No worries, though; she could get him back up there. Angela was flush with confidence.

And maybe something else. *I see that bliss fullness on the vids, and it is quite lovely.* That so didn't sound like Kellen, not even a little bit. But it was Wordsworth and on his secret darknet channel, and every cell in her body wanted it to be true. She wanted to, needed to believe he thought her lovely, even after all this time.

Even after all she'd done.

She wondered if he would be watching her town hall tomorrow. She'd build in a private subtext just in case. Something from "Desideria," so he wouldn't think she was completely heartless, flirting secret messages at him so soon after Daniel's death. Kellen would comprehend. He'd always had a gift for absorbing subtlety.

Surprised by joy—impatient as the wind. Yeah, that

summed up tonight, not to mention the pulse of ache in her chest.

The cloying scent of whiskey wafted by her head, followed by a proffered bulb of amber liquid. She waved it aside. "Thanks, Dan-Dan, but I have to leave soon. Can't get too comfortable."

"I have been in contact with our transport, and it is still some minutes away. After what must have been a taxing performance tonight, you deserve something of a private celebration." Mech-Daniel stretched the glass toward her again.

True. She did. *Oh, fuck it.* Angela accepted the drink and took a long, throat-singeing gulp as mech-Daniel, now in his usual uniform of poly-printed loose pants and shirt, rounded the end of the chaise longue and stood before her.

He looked ridiculously pleased with himself, but that's kind of how he always looked in private. No one who had spent any significant time with Daniel when he was alive would confuse the real man with this sweet, puppy-eyed machine.

Too bad for him Angela had always been more of a cat person.

"There is a corporate microclime for citrus just south of here," mech-Daniel said. "So the sour is fresh." He nodded toward the drink she was downing.

No shit. So fresh it made her want to pucker, but she didn't. She took it down to half and made an appreciative hum in the back of her throat. The sound wasn't quite a good-boy but close enough. He grinned adorably.

"I have logged only six messages this evening. Would you like to hear them?"

Angela didn't reply, just took another pull on her drink. Warm languor infused her body, and she blinked back sleep.

The first message was from Zeke. He needed her to do a rally online party tomorrow. Man, she hated these things. The day-to-day of governing, she was fine with that. But getting elected and staying elected and everything associated with electedness curdled her joy. She tapped a "sure, I'll be there" and moved on.

The next reminder was for a floor vote on Thursday. They'd pass around a biometric vote board, so she couldn't telepresence in. Damn it. Confirmation of a new cabinet member. Not her. Not the war ministry. That appointment—*her* appointment—was on hold, presumably pending any war-worthy threat.

She thought of something Vallejo had said a while back: "You want a war? Bomb the hell out of something."

But you didn't start a war after all, Vallejo, you bag of dicks. You failed.

A giggle rose up in her throat, so inappropriate. She washed it down with more cocktail. It crossed her mind that she wasn't a giggler, generally, and no way the alcohol could be affecting her behavior so quickly.

Message three: the colonel in charge of the Texas-Oklahoma border reported no new drone attacks. The pause in conflict wasn't speeding her toward her cabinet post, plus this silence had a stink of Texas on it. Like they were planning something bigger. She was still waiting for the other boot to fall. And it would, she had zero doubts.

Message item four: a nuncio from the Holy See, the

person who used to be her Vatican counterpart when she was in the foreign service, would be visiting the Inland East Coast Territory next week and wanted to hook up. Well, not in *that* sense. In the papal one. Probably he wanted to pray over the victims of Mother Nature's latest violence, or pray for the future of humanity, or some such bullshit.

"Query the security situation on that one and have housekeeping at the Eastern Command prep for guests, just in case," she told mech-Daniel. "It might be good for a vid op if nothing else. If I can't get there in person, you can paste me in."

"Query sent," the machine said pleasantly. "Rafael Castrejon messaged on your personal channel. He says ratings for your 'Daniel Lives' episode were, quote, big-sexy, and would you and your husband—that would be me, I suppose—be interested in giving a tour of your shared home and marital bliss?"

Um, she'd need to get back to him on that one. Next.

"And finally," said mech-Daniel in a slightly different tone, "you have a response from your earlier conversation."

Excitement sliced through her body.

"Yes, that. Give me that one." Stupid blood, racing. Stupid brain, calling up memories like a sweaty panorama.

Mech-Daniel blinked several times, and his eyes tracked upward and to the left. He had facial tells for various programmatic routines, but this expression was something he seemed to have devised on his own. As far as Angela could discern, it meant he disliked what he was about to do, but he was a machine, so he did it anyway.

"'And O, ye fountains, meadows, hills, and groves, forebode not any severing of our loves,'" he intoned.

Angela paused with the now down-to-the-dregs drink halfway to her mouth. "Come again?"

He repeated the message. It clanged into her brain space, dissonant in a way that meant…something. She just couldn't hold onto the thought noodle long enough to inspect it.

The rim of the whiskey bulb wobbled in and out of focus.

"Reply," she murmured, raising one hand to knuckle the blur out of her eyes. "Tell him, 'But those first affections, be they what they may, have the power to make our noisy years seem moments in the being, the eternal silence. Truths that perish…never.'"

No, that wasn't right. The quote. It wasn't right, which was wrong, because she was always right. Or maybe everything was wrong.

The fuzzies closed in. Warped in. Rosed in, flower petals in backward bloom, poppy-pink and shrinking together in a soft, secret huddle, regressing. Whiff of green on the air, chemically not rose petals, breath held in expectation of sudden beauty. But nothing happened. No flowers opened. The green smell deepened to black.

She was asleep but knew it. With certainty, she knew it. She was asleep. Boozy sleep? Sweet puppy eyes, spiked drinksy, and tight-furled flower sleep. A sleep: just one sleep, or multiple sleeps?

Dreaming.

Totally dreaming, all of it, even the part where the joints of the Hotel Riu slipped and then came loose. Far, far away, a giant moaned in protest. She reclined in its belly, shifting as it rolled. The building/giant's long bones snapped, and the sound was a cannon shot. The whole world lurched, a quake deep in the earth. Did they have earthquakes in Guadalajara? How far south did the San Andreas fault go? Or wait, wasn't there a volcano around here somewhere?

Geology had never been her strong suit. Angela was more of a geography girl. She could draw those lines herself.

Lines. Separations. Breaking. A fissure appeared in the wall, branching and leaving, a time-lapse of a tree in springtime, emerging from dormancy. The night crackled like superheated popcorn. Or maybe something else was popping. Something she didn't want to think about. Staccato.

The arched doorway to the bathroom, clearly made of children's modeling clay, folded in on itself.

Move. Don't wallow. Only useless princesses get rescued. Smart girls rescue themselves. Paralyzed. Sleep stalking at the wrongest fucking time.

If I sleep, I die.

The last thought roared in out of nowhere and smelled like truth. It should have been followed by regret, deep ache for the people who would miss her, but that was… well, who, really? She couldn't summon any sadness for her parents. They started the missing-her process a long time ago, when they sent her away to school halfway around the world. Her mentor? Zeke might hurt, but her death would be the best thing that ever happened to his campaign. An October surprise. He'd win in a landslide.

There was no one. No one else. Not anymore.

I'm going to die alone. Her brain accepted the statement with fatalistic calm.

"Angela!" The mech-clone. The one that looked just like…somebody mean. Somebody forced.

No, leave me alone. You don't get to hurt me any-more. I made it stop. I made it.

And then his titanium-boned hands were grabbing her, moving her.

The tree in the wall shattered.

The wall did, too.

A cheese-shaped slab of ceiling—white like baby powder but considerably more solid—hit her shoulder hard enough to shift her arm free of its socket.

The giant roared. The universe collapsed.

● ● ●

Reality blew in like an industrial fan, shoving the memories to dark corners. Angela pulled in a breath and tasted dust. Air from a spice shaker, sweet with an edge of tart. Like a bomb.

Her shoulder hurt like a motherfucker.

"Yes, she is waking," said mech-Daniel. Mechanical, exuberant, perfectly calibrated voice. *His lips taste like death.* "But I am uncertain what her mental state will be. She ingested significant quantities of alcohol after the gala. She may need rest. I will contact you later if—"

"Senator Neko—Angela—can you hear me?" Another voice, tinny and forever away, but just as familiar. Training and instinct stiffened her spine in response, made her want to sit up and pay attention. Made her want to be a good girl. Best girl.

With some reluctance, she broke the surface of consciousness. *On your own, girl. Get to it. Solve for X.*

If it had contained enough air, her body would have sighed. She opened her eyes. A nightmare met her, but at least there were familiar parts: mech-Daniel hovering above her, her mentor, Zeke, on the in-ear com, telling her what to do. So she wasn't on her own after all. She was neither the decider nor the hero. She could rest.

She opened her mouth, but dust blocked her throat.

A hand moved behind her neck, lifting her head. "Here, you must drink something. My apologies, for I have no water." Cool plastene rim of a cocktail bulb against her mouth. She parted her lips and drank, and the citrus-spiked whiskey pushed the dust down and into her body. Filth. Contagion. Fire. Sweet.

Her head ached. Tiny, invisible, evil elves were pile-driving spikes into her eye sockets, but her thoughts washed crystal clear. Apparently, almost dying and getting knocked out cold could sober a girl up quick, no matter what she'd had to drink.

Or mech-Daniel had messed with her blood alcohol level. Either way, she was clearheaded. "Fucking hell. Where am I? What happened?"

Ezekiel Medina, president of the United North American Nations—Zeke—replied via com, "The Hotel Riu was attacked. A drone-launched missile or smartbomb, probably. It pancaked the top three floors, including the helipad and your transport. I am sending an evacuation team to retrieve you. Just be still."

"Somebody hit the Riu? Must've done shitty recon. All the important people are staying closer to the Expo Guadalajara."

"Maybe you're more important to somebody than you thought." Zeke's voice had a grim note to it, something that snagged her concern, but she forced herself to pay attention to his words instead.

Important, her? *She* was the target? And yet, it made

sense. If her transport had been on time, or if she'd been up there waiting for it like usual, she would have been part of the rubble pancake.

Whoever had attacked the hotel might have been— probably *had* been—trying to kill her.

Which kind of narrowed the suspect list. She didn't have a lot of enemies. Daniel was gone. And she *had* just accused Vallejo of mass murder and the destruction of Houston. Maybe instead of retaliating against her government, he'd decided to attack her personally.

"You're lucky to be alive, kiddo," Zeke added.

Though her eyes still hurt, Angela was focusing properly now, and she could see that luck had nothing to do with her survival. Mech-Daniel had arched his titanium-core body over her, forming a protective barrier against the giant slab of concrete ceiling. A shield. He was still holding it back. What were his weight tolerances? What would it take to crush him?

She thought about the whiskey sour and his insistence that she drink it. And it had taken, what, three or four gulps to get her so soused she was hallucinating about reverse-blooming flowers? She knew he wasn't above altering her blood chemistry to keep her down here in her room if he thought going up to the helipad could pose a danger.

Which implied that he'd known about the attack before it happened. White, cold terror shivered up her body. She peered at mech-Daniel. He'd been injured. Something sharp had sliced the vat-grown skin covering his left cheekbone, exposing the metal frame beneath, but his expression was the same as always: pleasant, calming, loyal.

And foolproof. She'd had the mech-clone's neural net completely wiped and rebuilt from scratch after she'd acquired him. She had even insisted on including that private Dan-Dan channel so if he ever went too far in mimicking Daniel Neko, if the simulation ever got *too* good, she could pull him back. Mech-Daniel's job was to serve her, which apparently also included putting himself between her and death. He had done that job tonight. Hell, he'd even managed to save her cocktail.

No, she didn't have anything to fear from him.

But *somebody* sure wanted her dead.

"Hey, Zeke," she said, "can you patch your intel through to my com so I can monitor the feed real-time while we wait for your evacuation team?" It wouldn't be the first time she'd accessed intelligence channels meant for the president. But it might very well be the most important time she'd asked to.

There was a slight pause before Zeke replied, this time through her in-ear com rather than mech-Daniel's mouth. "No need, kiddo. I'm monitoring all my feeds right now. I'll tell you if anything important scrolls by."

Okay. Fine. "Who's taking responsibility for the hit?"

"Uh, nobody yet."

"That's so weird," she said, pressing knuckles of one hand into her eye socket, as if she could push the headache away. "If the building looks this busted-up inside, it must be a wreck on the outside. Even if no one interesting was staying here, those images would fetch solid prices on the disaster-porn market. Bonus if the gossips can confirm the presence of a squashed and bloody senator corpse in here."

Satellites and infra-capable drones would be gathering

footage already. She half expected a ping from Rafa or his ilk, to confirm her safety. Or otherwise.

But…nothing.

Did that mean the killer wasn't done yet? Her head throbbed. Her shoulder felt like somebody had wedged a broken tree branch into the joint and then lit it on fire.

"You don't need to be giving interviews right now anyway," said Zeke. "Just sit tight, and we'll get you out of there."

Yeah, but he wasn't the one under threat. In her mind's eye, she imagined somebody out there, watching drone footage, maybe catching bits of this very conversation on a hacked com relay. Figuring out she was alive. Coming back to finish the job.

Who, though?

Get it together. Think. She would have shaken her head, dislodged her thoughts, but those elves were still going with their heavy machinery behind her eyeballs. There wasn't a part of her body that didn't hurt.

Zeke had taught her to be watchful, careful. Paranoid. He'd taught her to use the maximum number of words to say absolutely nothing, to do everything she swore she wouldn't, and to clean up the truth afterward. He of all people ought to understand she couldn't just sit here. Just like he'd understand why she couldn't tell him her plans for getting out.

Angela assured her mentor she'd stay put and wait for his medevac. Then she cut the transmission, blocked it. And broke her promise.

"Dan-Dan," she said, using the pet name to log on to their private channel, no intrusions. A whole different user interface, keyed to accept only her verbal instructions, shoved its way into the mech-clone's neural. This was her back door.

"Yes?" he said, still calmly holding up the ceiling.

"Can you get me out of here?"

He paused, probably scanning the structure or pulling feeds from the media drones she was certain hovered just outside the wreckage. After a moment, he said, "Yes."

"Before the president's evac team arrives?"

"Yes."

"Okay. That's our plan."

"As you wish."

Mech-Daniel could do this next part for her—he was capable of following multiple instruction threads at once—but there were still some tasks that Angela preferred to do for herself. Using the mobile com built into her forearm and the heads-up on the backs of her eyelids, she located a transit station three city blocks away and bought two landjet tickets under one of her many aliases.

She'd need to get cleaned up, have mech-Daniel pop her shoulder back into place, and repair the damage to his cheek, though the scratch was slight enough that a squeeze of wound gel should work. There was an all-night pharma inside the transit station, and she reserved a refrescando closet for two.

Finally, she sifted back through her communications over the last week and found the one for Heron Farad, the rendezvous server she'd used to set up the holoconference the night Daniel had died. When her message came in like this, not secret or flirty or Wordsworth-themed—or filtered through mech-Daniel—he would know it was serious. She was calling in her favor.

I request immediate haven, she messaged, and

set it up to repeat. Transmit coordinates to physical rendezvous.

Hours later, Angela and mech-Daniel were flying over northern Sonora when two pieces of data came in. The first was a matériel database alert, bounced off a civilian space station of all things, informing her that Heron Farad had appropriated a piece of UNAN military equipment in Texas.

The second, in super cryptic style, was a text telling her to deplane in Kingman. A car will meet you at transit, it said. Behold the fire.

CHAPTER 3

THE FIRE SHE WAS SUPPOSED TO BEHOLD, APPARENTLY, wasn't a literal thing.

Angela figured out what it meant as soon as she saw the only car—an actual human-operated old-timey *car*—parked outside the transit terminal at Kingman. It was a vintage Tesla that clearly had been driven to hell and back. The paint was matte blackout with a narrow orange racing stripe down the middle and bitchin' flame decals on either side.

Fire. Behold. Okay.

A whipcord-thin woman leaned against the hood, one booted ankle crossed in front of the other. Both her canvas duster and her long white hair rustled in the morning wind. She wore two bandoliers crammed with ammo and slung low over her abdomen, and the gleaming butts of twin dueling pistols peeked out of the holsters at either hip. From the arrangement of straps, it was possible she had a sword on her person as well, or maybe just a very big knife.

She was also by far the oldest human being Angela had ever seen.

Seriously old. Even older-than-La-Mars-Madrid old. Had this person never undergone a single cosmetic alteration? Her wrinkles had wrinkles, and when she flicked her half-charred smoke to the ground and crushed it beneath one worn bootheel, her voice creaked and rumbled like a shed in a thunderstorm. "I see you checking out my dragon." She jabbed a thumb toward the flame-licked car. "You the angel I'm s'posed to fetch?"

No, not an angel. Far from it. Fallen certainly, but the rest of it? No. "I am Angela Neko."

"Huh." She inspected Angela with too-perceptive eyes. "Somehow figured you'd be taller. Who's your dude?"

Angela's face warmed. He wasn't her dude. Not in the way that the other woman implied. He wasn't her lover. But he was playing the part of her husband. She should introduce him as such. And yet she didn't. Somehow, couldn't. "Dan-Dan is…my assistant."

He goofily half waved, one finger at a time like a three-year-old. He clearly didn't have his "imitate real-life Daniel as closely as possible" programming engaged. Someday soon she would instruct him to turn it on all the time now, since he should be in simulation mode 24/7, but she couldn't bring herself to do it yet.

"Is he?" One side of the woman's mouth pinched up in a half smile.

Angela wondered if she was recalling some of Daniel's older vidcasts, the more sordid ones. A shudder gnawed through Angela's body, and in her current exhausted state, she didn't even bother to fight it. "What about you? Are you the fire I was told to find?"

The old woman snorted. Her dark eyes sparked like

live wires, and she moved with the agility of someone half her age. Or maybe a quarter. "Guess I am."

She whistled, and the car door opened. Passenger side, shotgun, not in the back where Angela was used to riding.

Something didn't feel right. Angela hesitated, hoisting the bag she'd bought at the pharma higher up on her good shoulder. It didn't have anything important in it, but there was comfort in holding onto a thing, even an unimportant thing.

"Come on, then, *mija*. I haven't seen my wife in three weeks and kind of want to get home. You dig?" What was that accent? Colombiana? Chilena? But with an overlay of early-twenty-first-century slang.

"I'm sorry, I didn't catch your name?" Angela framed it as a question.

The other woman rolled her eyes and swished her long, winter hair back over one shoulder. "Maybe 'cause I didn't give it? Look, I can tell you all my names, but what you want more is confirmation that you aren't being nabbed, am I right? Fine. I'm here because my boy messaged, told me to detour by Kingman and pick up the woman who would look least likely to get caught dead in a dusty transit station. Said you were top secret and posh beyond all possible belief. He didn't mention specifically that you're a sitting continental senator, but me, I can connect the dots." Her black-eyed gaze swept up Angela and apparently found her lacking. "It's pretty obvious you're in something of a pickle, safety-wise, and my Heron, he can help you out."

"Wait." Angela frowned. "Who sent you?"

"Heron Farad."

"And there was no…" She felt silly mentioning it but couldn't help herself. "No additional message? From… somebody else? Nothing like a line from a poem or anything?" Nothing reassuring? Nothing comforting?

In the old days, Kellen would have been all about comforting her if he knew she was in trouble. If he knew she was scared. He'd been the army at her back, making her feel mighty.

Maybe he doesn't realize. Maybe my last message was dry rather than serious. Maybe she'd confused the hell out of him—a bunch of bright, fun, poetic messages followed by a to-the-point businesslike one. But even if he was confused, it was going to be okay. He'd replied in kind last night. He had forgiven her, even if he hadn't used those words.

He would be there, at the rendezvous place, and he would make some joke in that warm-honey drawl, and everything would be okay. She'd be able to think again. She'd be able to plan. She would be safe.

Another whistle in a different tone popped the back door. Mech-Daniel rushed forward and held it open for her.

"Nope, no other messages. You comin' or do I have to incapacitate you *and* yer lanky dude?" Black eyes darted to mech-Daniel, but he was looking at Angela, not the raspy-voiced desert witch.

"Dan-Dan?"

"The car is clean. My scans show no threats in this area." He paused. "But she is correct. We should probably hurry."

That feeling that something wasn't quite right still gnawed at the base of Angela's spine, but she ducked into the car, which turned out to be a tightish fit. Three-quarters of the back bench seat was jam-packed with a giant pile of dirty blankets and smelled like a refugee center. Unwashed, musty, with an underwhiff of bleach and fear. She had to set her bag down on the floorboard, and it wedged itself tight against her shins when Daniel folded himself into the front seat and slid his chair back.

The interior of the car was just as personalized and bizarre as the outside: black ball fringe along the headliner over the windshield, an elaborate sugar skull balanced on the dash, and seat covers fitted out in some soft, dark fabric. The back of the driver's side headrest was embroidered in orange with the words "*El tiempo es un fuego que me consume,*" and the right one continued with the rest of the quote, "*Pero yo soy el fuego.*" It was a Borges line from the last century, yet another piece Angela had been made to memorize. *Time is a fire that consumes me. But I am the fire.*

The white-haired woman went around and got in on the driver's side. The car was so old, it still had a steering wheel. She pressed a button on the dash, the electrics hummed, and the car lurched forward, slamming Angela against the seatback. What was it called on these things? Ludicrous speed? Just so. She hadn't thought to put on a harness, but there probably was one around here. She'd have to dig for it.

A plaintive cry made the fine hairs on her forearms stand up. Oh, yikes. No car, not even an antique, made that sound.

"What was that?"

"*Mi cria,*" the driver hollered over her shoulder. Without taking her gaze off the highway, she popped the lid of the compartment between the front captains' chairs, withdrew a bottle that smelled like puke, shook it, and then handed it back toward Angela. "Lift up that blanket there and stick this in the feeder, yummy end pointed in her direction. She'll be your best friend forever."

Angela took the bottle, held her breath, did as she was told, and came nose to nose with a furry face framing the most beautiful eyes she'd ever seen. Long-lashed and sweet-tea brown. The white face tilted to the side and let out that mew/hum sound again.

A miniature llama. Or a baby one? Angela had never seen one, not in real life. She'd seen pictures of llamas, mostly in old books. Like other domesticated herd species, llamas had been decimated in recent decades. Predators, half-starved and desperate after a string of unpredictable climate extremes and disease-vector eradications, had descended on licensed herds, wrecking fences and ranchers' livelihoods alike. Prey animals never had a chance, but even their sacrifice wasn't enough, ultimately. Global ecosystems were disintegrating at a rate that was now too rapid to pause.

Some of the heartier wild things had survived in sustainable populations: rats, hawks, and of course, cockroaches. But most of the beautiful creatures were gone, even the ones that had once been ubiquitous. Angela had seen only one cat in her whole life.

The memory of that cat still throbbed. She pushed it away viciously.

"Her name is Azul. She was a rare twin birth. Vicuña. Might not look it, but that little bit of fur and sass is almost two months old. Barely fifty pounds, for all her monster appetite, but if anybody can get that wee girl up to fighting weight, it's Kellen. You know him?"

Angela didn't reply, just pushed the bottle in between slats in the traveling crate and fitted it into the feeder sling. The baby vicuña latched on almost immediately. Look at that little girl go! She did have a healthy appetite. Angela watched her, those slow-blinking eyes with their impossibly long lashes. So delicate.

Shhh. You're safe now. Promise.

The woman was right. Kellen could care for this animal. He had a magic where animals were concerned. It would thrive. It would love him to absolute bits. All the creatures did.

"Where did you get her?" she asked.

"La Paz, or north of there, in the mountains. They used to roam wild all over Bolivia, whole bunches of them, till the poachers had a run at them in the 1900s. Gentle animals, vicuñas. They don't deserve what we humans have done to their world, but they can't say a damn thing to stop us."

What would a vicuña say if it could speak? Probably would agree with that statement. Certainly Angela's— and her government's—plans for the world were people-first. If she somehow managed to goad Texas into a war, bringing a dozen or more other entities into conflict, what would the voiceless animals of the world have to say about that?

Nothing. They would say nothing, the cool statesman in Angela insisted. Bolivia wasn't even in her continent.

Still sucking at the feeder, the cria looked right into Angela's eyes, possibly into her soul. At first, she read the expression in those round cocoa eyes as thanks.

Angela had given the animal food, after all. Safety. But that was the easy interpretation, wasn't it? Acquiring basic sustenance did not necessarily engender gratitude. In her experience, people who were riding the edge of desperation and were saved right at the last minute weren't grateful. They were too wound up. They lashed out, suspicious, sometimes angry.

The vicuña's eyes weren't angry, though. They were…she couldn't read them. If only she could hook this little girl up to a psych-emitter.

"By the way, you can call me Fanaida, or Fan," the driver said. "Heron Farad, who you messaged? He's my kid. Got a place not an hour from here. Good place, strong. You'll be safe from whatever's hunting you, *mija*."

Disbelief jangled up Angela's spine. Bomb-flavored dust, cracks in the walls. Pain.

I'll never be safe. I'll never be free.

Still…Kellen would be there. Not-right Kellen and his murderizing band of scoundrels, true, but him at the core. And the core Kellen was more compassionate than eleven-tenths of the human population. Plus, he had messaged her tonight, earlier, before her world went to hell. That proved he still cared, didn't it? That he wanted her here?

And she, of course, had never stopped wanting him.

• • •

"Just sit yer boney ass down, already." Kellen eyed his best friend, who looked like hammered shit this fine morning. "You need to sleep for about a week. Can't even stand up on your own two feet right now. What you been through, man, you gotta take this recovery slow."

Heron might have been the most tech-altered human alive, but when he wilted into the wide executive chair and pressed his palms against the smartsurface boardroom table, he was just a guy, and a tired one at that. He closed his eyes for a long moment, and after a while, a look of perfect peace settled over his face. So perfect he might have been sleeping.

Which, incidentally, Kellen would like to do, for his own self, now things were settled.

"Mari will be here in one hour seventeen minutes." Heron's eyes slatted open, blinking through the digital fog. "I must be up by then."

There was a dirty joke in there somewhere, but even though they were both plenty punchy, neither went there.

"An hour-long nap in the meantime wouldn't hurt either of us," Kellen suggested.

For the last four days, Kellen had monitored his friend's struggle to oust a particularly nasty neural-net virus. Seventy-four hours in applied neurobiology back in school and a decade of veterinary practice since had made Kellen keenly suited to caring for a human as brain-altered as Heron. But no amount of training got a body used to watching another person in suspended consciousness for four days. The vigil had been like watching a corpse decay in time-lapse, and not just any corpse. His best friend.

It hadn't helped that Heron's sweetheart Mari had been on the com every other second, checking up on him. Or that she herself had hied off on some danger-junkie mission to Texas, a parallel attempt to figure out who had put the virus in Heron's head and shut it the hell down.

They were both of them crazier than a pair of spring-time squirrels in traffic, but Kellen couldn't fault them. All that crazy was for love. Kellen himself had done some less than purely sane things in the name of love before. Lord, hadn't he just.

He swiped a big hand over his face, shoving the floppier bits of hair out of his eyes. He needed to hit the sack, maybe for a week. The virus was gone now. They had won. Soon, his team would all be tucked back home in the Pentarc, feet on firm ground rather than some floofy space station or spaceplane or et cetera. Safe.

Angela had taken care of Mari's outlaw status—he'd seen the senator on vid channels flat-out denying that Daniel was dead, which he had to admit was a pretty ingenious solution. Ballsy too. She'd even gone on Rafa Castrejon's channel, plugged into an emote caster, and convinced a couple million people real-time that no way could she have just been widowed when she was this crammed full of joy. She'd looked luminous.

So much that Kellen had been tempted to slip a rig on his own head, just for a minute, and feel it. Angela's joy. God.

No, was probably best he didn't do that. There were some things in this 'verse he'd never be sufficiently prepared to feel.

"Kellen?" Heron was frowning, and his eyes were closed again. He'd stretched his bare hands out on the smartsurface, soaking in the information stream there. "Have you checked your blip boards this morning?"

Reluctantly, he wrested his attention to Heron's question, away from Angela.

Kellen had trackers on all the critters he'd managed to

bring in, alter, and release back into the wild. It calmed him to peek in on them from time to time, but even when he only had a second or two, he could glance at the overall board, see all their green lights, and know that even if he died right at that moment, he had put some good back into the world. All his work, his sacrifices, had already produced a net win. Sometimes just knowing that was enough. The blip board was his validation.

"Nope, not this morning, but I did hear from Fan last night, before all that business with Mari started. Your mom's bringing a vicuña up here later today, orphaned and wee." Although Heron had closed his eyes again, Kellen had a sneaking suspicion his friend wasn't drifting off, not yet. Too much tension in those hands. "Can you see *all* my trackers there?"

Heron took a while answering. "I can see them. I can see…everything." On the table, a tremble wobbled through his fingers.

"Ain't easy what you did to your brain. Best go slow," Kellen advised.

Heron's faint smile was wry. "Information doesn't work that way. It is indescribably fast, but there are… handholds, places within the cloud where I can sort of grab on and pause long enough to study."

The thing that had finally kicked that virus out of Heron's head once and for damn-sure had been connection. Specifically a nodal connection: Heron had plugged straight into the cloud and essentially melded his consciousness with the global information net. Kellen had never heard of anybody doing that before, and the consequences of such a maneuver were likely to be a bitch, on down the road. But that connection had saved his friend, so maybe there was something to that ends-justifying-means crap after all.

"Your blip board is one of those handholds," Heron went on. "I find it comforting, the numbers of animals out there, thriving, because of you and our work. I see why you stare at it all the time."

Well, would you look at that? Dude was starting to get it. Kellen flopped down in a chair and propped his boots up on the long, granite-topped table. He butt-scooched to the edge of the chair, getting comfy. If he'd had his hat, he would have pushed it low over his face to shut out some of the light, but it was bad manners to wear a hat indoors. Some lessons he'd retained from all his mama's hollering.

"How my butterflies doing?" he asked.

Butterflies, not Angela. So what the butterflies were wintering near Morelia? Aaaaaand Angela happened to be about two hours away from them, in Guadalajara, last he'd checked. It wasn't like he was asking after his monarchs just because he was thinking about *her* way too much lately.

Except that had been his exact reason.

"Possibly not well," Heron said. "There's…"

Suddenly Kellen was no longer searching for the rag-gedy edge of sleep. "Not well? What d'you mean?"

He'd put a lot of time and effort into luring those monarchs down to the oyamel forests for their migra-tion. If loggers or some corporation had come in and messed things up, he was gonna be pissed.

Heron frowned, never a good sign. "There's some-thing dark near Morelia, maybe just a data anomaly, some intrusion countermeasures or… No, it's northwest of Morelia. So good news, the butterfly habitat is probably fine after all."

"But?" There was always a but.

"The data hole is over Guadalajara. Something is going on there that our government doesn't want me to see."

Kellen's limbs tensed hard, and his breath bunched up tight in his chest.

The frown didn't depart Heron's face. "Senator Neko's repeater initiated from the middle of that dark spot. Probably just a coincidence, of course, but I dislike coincidences."

Every time Kellen heard her name, it was like liquid nitrogen froze his entire body, melted straight to gas, and swished off, leaving him ass-bare and blazing with indeterminate but excruciating temperature. Every. Damn. Time. "Senator who's what?"

Heron pinched up one eyebrow. "The chances you misheard me hover near zero."

"Clarify repeater."

"A repeating message."

"To you?"

"Yes." Heron's other eyebrow scooted up and met the first, high on his forehead. "I'm certain I told you she was coming here. Fanaida is bringing her, along with your rescue not-alpaca thing."

"You told me bupkiss, man." Fuck. Fuckity fuck. Angela *here*? In physical, touchable, soul-singeing, memory-wrenching, toxic proximity?

Heron tilted his head slightly. "No, I clearly remember saying that she—"

That she was requesting a meeting with his shooter. Yeah, Kellen had heard that, or some similar bullshit, but he'd been busy just at that minute, trying to keep his friend alive. He remembered thinking at the time that a game-master like Angela wouldn't waste her favor owed on something as useless as meeting Mari, not unless she was planning to renege on their bargain. Or she had some other nefarious purpose. You could never put such shenanigans past a politician.

"Yeah, but can't she meet Mari somewhere else?" Somewhere he wasn't. Somewhere he wouldn't have to see her, breathe her air, hold himself away from wrapping his arms all the way around her and forcing her never to leave again.

Heron raised his hands off the tabletop and turned his palms up. "I didn't realize it would bother you so much. Haven't you known her forever? I thought you were fond of her."

Fond? Not even close.

Kellen kicked back from the table, rolling the chair till it crushed into a plastic-printed ficus. He rose in one movement, clenching his fists and wishing he had something to squeeze. Or crush. Or hurl. He had things to say, but his internal editor kept his lips clamped shut. Mind frame like this, it was best not to let fly. Hollering without carefully choosing his words, especially when there were legit hollerable offenses going down and he was grumpy as all get-out, was against his personal rule set.

But dangit…Heron had invited her here? Without even asking him? What kind of batfuck Judas move was that?

"Best I see to that vicuña," he muttered past half-clamped lips. A whole vomit of soot-filthy words pushed up behind his teeth, but he didn't let it loose.

He'd almost gotten to the door when Heron spoke

again. "Fanaida just drove into the carpark. Your Angela is with her."

Here. Angela.

But not mine.

She hadn't been his in nine years. And none of that was his fault. Not one second.

CHAPTER 4

ANGELA HAD FALLEN ASLEEP DURING THE DRIVE, DESPITE the cramped back seat and the smell of llama piss. Oh, right, no: vicuña piss. Apparently they were two separate species entirely. Somehow her exclusive smart kids' education hadn't denoted the difference, but Fanaida had taken it upon herself to educate.

When the rickety old car screamed to a stop in a place that echoed, Angela woke, knuckled the temporary peace out of her eyes, and tasted the backs of her teeth, hoping nobody had noticed that she'd dropped her dignity—and possibly her hygiene—about fifty kilometers back. She felt fuzzy and unkempt. Blessing the lack of vid cams or paparazzi, she unfastened her door and spilled herself out of the tinier-than-it-looked car.

All carparks the world over looked exactly the same, though this one was a bit fuller than most. Not with cars, though: with shipping containers. Dozens of them. Hundreds? A few skeletal combustion cars littered the smoky, halogen-lit underground, and the space smelled of engine grease and…burnt tortilla? Ugh. Still, Angela was happy to get out of the cramped confines and stretch her legs some.

Mech-Daniel no sooner hit the pavement than he had instructions for her. She'd be willing to bet he'd saved them up for hours. "We are to report to Heron Farad in the conference room on the third floor as soon as possible."

"Do I get a chance to shower first?" she asked.

Fanaida cut in with a sniff. "Oh, it ain't that kind of request, *mija*." She'd already come around to the little camelid baby's side of the car and was trying to coax Azul out with a fistful of fresh grass.

Angela's stomach rumbled. Because of grass. Not braised lobster or sweet floss halva. Grass. She was hungry enough that her belly was excited over a bunch of grass. Yeah, this day was looking up.

And that thought reminded her in a rush of how the day had started. Somebody had tried to kill her. Probably still wanted her dead. She tasted the sour of panic in her mouth and swallowed it back.

"Right," she said evenly. "You mean the drought makes water for bathing a luxury. I didn't mean to sound insensitive." Or like a fucking princess. "In fact, I don't need much to be comfortable." A lie. "Did you know I was ambassador to the nation of Jolet Jin Anij, before it was sunk?" Youngest actual ambassador—not a made-up "goodwill" bullshit title—in the history of the preunification U.S. government. That was still a point of pride for her, evidence she was doing something right.

Even if sometimes it felt like she'd gone far, far off course in this life.

Fanaida arched one brow on her incredibly wrinkly

forehead. "Little girl, you might have lived in lots of places, but I wasn't talking about maps and nations. Wasn't even talking about deprivation. We got water here, courtesy of a reclamation system. What we don't have is time for you to diva yourself before the folks in charge get a look at you. You might not realize it, but we're taking some risks harboring a continental senator. We need to make sure you aren't going to start shouting kidnappish things and cause trouble."

"The folks in charge…that would be Dr. Farad, right?" And Kellen? Was he also one of the people in charge? Of this group of questionable ethics and lurid behavior? She needed to step lightly.

"He's one. Also my wife and Doc Hockley and young Garrett…we got a team here. A family. If you want to stay, most likely nobody is gonna put you out on your ass, but we gotta make sure you're on board with our mission, dig?"

"Mission?"

"Haven't you been riding next to this smelly sweet thing the last three hours?"

"An orphan infant camelid is your mission?"

The old lady snorted. "Yeah. She kind of is." She left off petting the vicuña and stared hard at Angela. "The Pentarc is a refuge. We have critters here, like Azul, but we also have, last I checked, upward of three hundred human refugees as well, folks we've snatched from parts of the world that were no longer safe. Seventy from Sudan, before the fall. Three extended families from Jolet Jin Anij." She snorted. "Maybe you know them personally, ambassador girl."

Angela's head ached, but she struggled to keep her

mien placid, concerned. "You saved them, before the ocean came?"

"I wasn't on that mission, but yeah, my boys did. They swooped in and let anybody who could climb get on board. And then they brought the immigrants here. Poor souls still haven't gotten over the trauma, but we'll keep them until they're able to stand being out in the world again. If. And it don't matter if they never can. We will keep them safe. Because *they* matter." She was looking at the orphan vicuña when she said it. Her thin hands stroked fur.

Angela wasn't sure what to say to that. She too had spent her life in service. But she had never rescued people on the brink of oblivion. She had never been a savior or superhero. Her work had always been more... administrative. And yet it had felt good, creating coalitions, reminding her diplomatic opposites of their bonds, of the bonds that all humans shared. She had pressured the international courts up to that last day to allow the residents of Jolet Jin Anij to emigrate without the requisite agreements in place. The world court had denied her request. The wheels of nations moved so slowly.

She had watched on satellite vid as the last speck of the big island disappeared beneath the ocean. Her team had dialed the screen resolution back so she didn't have to see up close and real-time death on a massive scale. They didn't know she'd gone back and watched, over and over, forcing her soul to embrace the horror. The guilt.

Angela had done all she could. Hadn't she?

And yet, these people, Kellen's people, had done more. Mech-Daniel broke in with a quiet reminder that he had downloaded the meeting invitation and could lead her to the conference room where Dr. Farad awaited her.

She started and moved toward her robot husband, but Fanaida caught her by the arm. Something warm and electric arced from the old lady's body to hers, and black eyes pierced her. Hard, those eyes, but curiously not judgmental. Like she'd seen all the world had to give, and she'd decided Angela was neither the best nor the worst of it. Or that maybe she had some potential for good.

"We aren't the bad guys, no matter what you've been told." The old woman leaned down and pressed a dry-lipped kiss to Angela's forehead. "Now go see my son."

The gesture felt solemn. Weighty. A benediction. Or maybe Angela was just out-of-her-gourd exhausted.

And no, there was nothing wet on her face, certainly nothing as pedestrian—as *weak*—as tears. She straightened her skirt and followed mech-Daniel to the central lift. Nothing at all.

●　　●　　●

Between the ages of five and twenty, Angela had been nurtured and taught in a hyperstructure, the Mustaqbal Institute, where all the uncommonly clever children were brought to learn. The school had covered more than six square kilometers and contained more than forty thousand souls, so the Pentarc, for all its size and heft, didn't intimidate her, not one bit.

Its emptiness kind of did, though.

This building had been constructed to house nearly as many people as Mustaqbal, but how many refugees had Fanaida mentioned? A few hundred? That was like a family of four booking a 797-8 Spacejet.

She tried to imagine the MIST with only a hundred residents, and the picture shimmered coolly down her spine. It would be like a ghost town, derelict and menacing. Not exactly the haven she would have chosen. Still, it would serve.

All she wanted was a safe place to hide, get her bearings. Figure out who had tried to kill her. And then… what? For the first time in her life, she didn't have a five-year plan, had no idea where she was heading, no midterm goals. The stark blankness on her internal calendar edged all her thoughts in white panic, but she tried to focus straight down the center. Panic wasn't an option.

The elevator had an open glass side opposite the doors, and the carriage seemed to be going slower than normal, maybe so she could see each floor as they passed upward. The first floor contained a promenade with storefronts that had never been filled with shops, most of which had their "Coming soon!" signs still up. Then there was a university and public facilities floor, replete with a crèche for children too young for school. The neon instructress chatbot in her tidy, fresh crinoline was still lit and animated, despite the fact that no children would be coming for lessons and indoctrination.

Or would they? Three-hundred-odd refugees, families, could conceivably contain children. Were the full resources of this megastructure engaged in managing a population, even if that population was pathetically small? Was this really a functional government of fewer than a thousand souls? And if it was, what did that mean to the real government, to Angela's government?

She might not be able to leave here and swear that

she had sought refuge in an uncontested part of the free state. She might have to lie.

She almost shrugged. The older she got, the more comfortable she was with lies.

"We have arrived," mech-Daniel said.

Half a heartbeat later, the elevator doors shished open, and the whole floor was flooded with light. Instead of discreet rooms here, there was a wide-open entertainment balcony overlooking the lower floors. A partygoer could spit chicle down upon unsuspecting students and plebs waiting in the entertainment lines. Of course, none of those lines or crowds had ever materialized in this place—construction had been halted at the height of the financial crisis of '52, long before the structure had been able to officially seek residents or spin up its public services.

Angela stepped off the lift and into the bright sunlight. The wall facing inward was a giant slab of plasteel, fully translucent and wired for free-fae holoprojections. She wouldn't be surprised if that seven-story wall could project any scene it wanted, at any given time of day. Right now, it was translucent, letting the harsh desert morning pour through.

At the far end, right where the structure's exterior spire wall curved gently, was a door. Angela got mech-Daniel's confirmation in her earpiece: behind that door, in the conference room beyond, Dr. Farad waited for her. Unconsciously she smoothed her skirt and again wished for gloves, her good gloves. The all-night pharma hadn't stocked her bespoke smartgloves, of course, just those cheap knockoffs that didn't dependably filter the more popular weaponized viruses—Dengue B, Cholera

Nuovo, the recently catalogued Basilisk, which had decimated the population of inland and western China.

She felt naked, protected by insufficient gloves and lacking her usual team of mobile mist-bots, aerosoling the world around her with toxin-neutral particles.

It had been a long time since Angela had touched anyone who wasn't inorganic and/or drenched in disinfectants. But here she was. She smoothed her breathing, composed her face. She could do this.

Mech-Daniel paused briefly to scan the room behind the door, and then, when nothing jumped out at him, he nodded and opened the door, and Angela stepped through. Her eyes and her soul scanned the room in tandem.

Kellen wasn't here.

Stupid to be disappointed. But there it was anyhow, the plummet of surprise at his absence. She shook her head to clear it.

At the near end of the table sat Heron Farad. He didn't rise when she entered, and he didn't turn for her benefit. She moved along his periphery, around the corner of the long conference table, and noticed that his eyes were closed. Well, that would be why he hadn't so much as acknowledged her presence. Was he even awake? He was almost as creepy as the ghostlike building he lived in.

She sat to his left, two chairs down and with the opulent sunlight at her back. "Dr. Farad?"

"Yes." He still didn't open his eyes. "I am having an unusual morning, so please bear with me."

"Of course." She adjusted her posture in a slim, milk-colored chair and folded her naked hands in her lap. Mech-Daniel sat between her and the cyborg.

Dr. Farad took his time before turning to her and

frowning, still with his eyes closed. "You said in your repeater message that you needed haven. Can you tell me why?"

"The hotel where I was staying was attacked," she said. Lintel melting like wet clay. Smell of bombs. She could pass for calm, but inside she was still screaming.

His frown deepened, carving furrows into his forehead. "I'm not finding any other high-value targets on the guest list of the Hotel Riu. Have you been attacked personally in the past?"

She half shrugged, despite the echo of ache in her shoulder. "Most people who stick their heads up eventually get something thrown at them. In the last few years, the fashion has been for biological or chemical weapons, and I have both clothing and physiological alterations that protect against those. But usually people who stage attacks for political, economic, or religious reasons are pretty noisy taking credit for their misdeeds."

"Yet no one has claimed responsibility for the attack on your hotel." He even spoke like a machine, careful and controlled, but also soft and resonant. What sort of digital wildness was he seeing on the backs of his eyelids? What sort of data streams were poking into his incredibly still hands atop the table?

Angela lived with a mech-clone, sure, but she knew what mech-Daniel was. Even better, mech-Daniel knew what he was. He knew his purposes and limitations and had never acted outside of set behavioral parameters. This man, Heron Farad, however, was something else entirely. He was, like mech-Daniel, clearly a thing, but just as obviously human and brain-screamingly other. His too-calm voice, his too-still body made her hackles rise.

"No, no one has taken credit," she said. That's how it would play out in the news narrative: take credit. Not responsibility. Bullies didn't take responsibility, typically, and whoever had bombed the Riu clearly had some unhealthy destructive tendencies.

"You have suspicions," Farad said.

"I do."

His eyes came open, and they danced with amusement. She thought of Fanaida and knew exactly where he got that expression from. It rooted him squarely in his humanity. He pulled his hands up from the smartsurface table and steepled his long fingers, like he was actively giving a shit about their conversation. "Tell me, do you suspect Damon Vallejo? I mean for the attempt on your life *and* for contracting the hit on your husband?"

A fear bubble that she hadn't even known existed popped in Angela's gut. Well, that was unexpected. Score one for the cyborg.

"Vallejo certainly had motive," she hedged. "I have said damning things about him in public lately."

Farad's head tilted, and he inhaled slowly, like he was sifting the air for truth. "Yet you doubt your own theory."

"It is awfully tidy."

"And tidy is usually wrong."

"Yes."

Was it her imagination, or was he inside her thoughts, predicting her phrases? She wondered if it was a skill, something organic, or if it was a program cooked up by his implanted neural net.

If he was just employing a talent of a very perceptive man, she could live with that. She would even be impressed. But if he used a program to read her mind, that raised other, sneakier thoughts. Like, did mech-Daniel have similar programming? And if he did, how often did he peek in on her?

And what had he found? Whom would he tell? She made a mental note to revert mech-Daniel to his factory settings as soon as possible. She didn't want anyone outside of this building to know where she was.

"Who knew your physical location at 12:52 this morning, Senator Neko?"

She went down the list silently. Her style team had a complete itinerary. The remote pilot of her transport would also have known. Zeke. Mech-Daniel. But honestly, anyone who knew her schedule in general would have been able to guess that she hadn't yet left Guadalajara. Ascertaining her whereabouts last night wouldn't have been an exercise in higher mathematics or anything.

"Probably too many people knew my itinerary, which is why I have conveyed my current location to no one."

He leaned forward slightly. "Do you mind if I scan you for trackers?"

"Well, no, but I—"

"A moment, please." He settled back in his chair and spread his long hands over the table top. Almost instantly, he looked up, and some of the tension had eased from his lean face. "You and your mech-clone are free of malicious riders."

"Um, thank you?" Except that she felt like he'd just stripped every stitch off her body, inspected her packaging like a security screener, and then left her hanging out there, naked and exposed. And now he was monitoring her response.

Well, fuck him. If there was one thing Angela knew how to do, it was keep private things private.

"No worries," Farad said. "Be assured I am investigating the attack in Guadalajara. We have, in fact, been monitoring the situation there for the last several hours. You may be interested to learn that the intrusion countermeasures set up over the region are particularly sophisticated. I encountered ICE like that in Texas, however. And that leads us back to Vallejo."

Angela was only half hearing him. What she really needed was a shower, or lacking that, at least a strip-and-sleep opportunity. Her mind would be much clearer after a nice long rest. Mech-Daniel would watch over her while she slept, which made the possibility of deep REM much more likely.

A yawn stretched her face before she could contain it. She put a hand in front of her mouth, but when she focused again, Dr. Farad was peering at her keenly.

"Does discussion of our mutual threats bore you, Senator?"

She flailed, shaking her head before she even had words to reply.

He smiled. "You are very much not what I was expecting."

Likewise. Angela wasn't certain what she had expected of Heron Farad, cyborg result of way too much techno tampering with the human body and mind. Whatever her expectations, the reality was surprising. He was courteous, even gallant. Whatever technology sustained him, it wasn't glaring. Of course, mech-Daniel also looked like a normal man on first pass. Deeper inspection yielded different results.

She wondered if kissing Dr. Farad would also taste like death.

His dark brows ticked up. "Madam Senator, you shock me."

Wait. "You can read my mind?"

Now it was his turn to look abashed. "Sometimes. The human brain is an electrical machine, and I have recently acquired the ability to see with absurd clarity all electrical activity surrounding me. I confess just now I was testing that ability on you. Please say you won't tell?"

Was that…was he blushing? Well, well. Angela stifled an urge to laugh as it became agonizingly clear to her that he wasn't worried about international diplomacy or how something like his weird techno-mind-reading capability would be read into a weapons readiness doc. He was worried she'd tell his lover.

She could understand. Sex partners were terrible confidantes. Frankly, she'd rather Zeke and the rest of the bloody government knew her secrets than her bedmate/partner/spouse. If she actually, you know, had one of those.

Mech-Daniel shifted beside her. "I hate to intrude," he said in his deferent tone, not the Daniel-esque one, "but I must remind you that the private thoughts of a sitting continental senator are classified. If you are able to peer at said thoughts, please note that they may not be shared, transmitted, or stored without advance clearance and express permission of the rights holder."

She half expected Heron Farad to laugh at her officious machine. Instead he met mech-Daniel's gaze sincerely. "Your policy is noted." He paused and added, "I see also how you care for her."

Their discussion devolved from that point to Farad's concern for his partner, the Mari Vallejo rebuild, the thing that thought it was a girl. The thing that had finally, thankfully, killed Daniel.

About halfway through their interview, Mari herself appeared, weary from whatever adventure she had been on and utterly disinterested in chitchatting. Which, honestly, Angela was glad for. She was about to excuse herself when the two, Mari and Heron—who were clearly lovers; yow, handsy! All over each other like limpets— dismissed her.

But not before he agreed to her request for haven, which was her chief purpose in being here. Right? She wasn't here *just* because no one in her government realized this arcology was inhabited. Not because she was pretty sure that bomb had been meant for her. Not even because the arcology was isolated in the desert and off-grid—except for that strange half-man in the conference room, his trusted team, and the horde of psychologically traumatized refugees.

And not even one teensy bit because somewhere in this gigantic building, Kellen existed. Not in mere memory this time; really, physically, actually here.

Close enough to touch.

●   ●   ●

"No messages?" The bed in Angela's room/prison was humongous, and the vestigial kid in her wanted to star-fish out in the deliciously soft synthcotton…and scream.

Or climb the tastefully beige walls.

Or gnaw a hole in the goddamn locked door.

When she'd gotten to her room, she'd immediately

run through the urgent stuff like a shower and a power nap, but that had taken, what, an hour total? She'd been here for *twenty-eight* of the fuckers—with the entire information universe behind a firewall and inaccessible to her. No visitors. No lines of communication. No news. No authority.

She needed answers. She needed information. She needed a new plan.

"No, no messages. But you haven't reached out to anyone, either," mech-Daniel reminded her in a voice without judgment, "as we are, in your words, hiding."

What he said was true. She hadn't sent any messages since that last note to Farad, requesting haven. Her plan had been to monitor incoming communiqués and see who was concerned for her safety, who was looking for her, who suspected she was dead, and who acted like they already had proof.

If she could get enough data points together, she could construct a picture of what just happened. She could verify that she had in fact been the target, figure out who'd launched the attack, and then systematically destroy that person or group.

If information gathering was the key to her plan, patience was the flaw in it. Angela wasn't good at patience.

And the whole mess was compounded by her choice of hideout. She hadn't counted on the Pentarc's firewall. Apparently Heron Farad kept his secret kingdom off-grid by making it a closed system that only allowed data transfers from the cloud every few hours, and even then, all data packets filtered through his rigorous scrubbing. If someone did try and contact her, she'd have to wait for the next information window to get the message, so there was no way she could track when alerts came in and line that timing up against gossip news speculation about her fate. What she needed was that damn firewall to go away.

Impatience had long since turned to frustration.

Mech-Daniel stood sentry, hands clasped behind his back and gaze looking out the plasteel window of the seventh-floor living unit they'd been assigned to. The recent scar on his face had all but disappeared beneath the wound glue, but Angela could still see it.

"I perceive that you are anxious," he said.

Angela started. Those words echoed Farad's weird mind-reading trick a little too closely. "Humans who've been recent assassination targets often are, I'm told."

Mech-Daniel turned to her, away from the window. His bearing was still mechanically stiff, but his face was relaxed, set in its usual wide-open expression. "Also hungry?"

She hadn't thought about hunger since scarfing two protein bars right after her shower. Yesterday. "Yeah."

He flashed a smile and scurried to the galley kitchenette near the unit's front door. It always felt strange to watch a six foot six, human-shaped creature scurry, but she wasn't sure what other word she could use to describe the way mech-Daniel moved when he was following up on one of his ideas. When he was trying to please her.

When he'd first come into her service, she'd been constantly weirded out by him. So much of what he said and did was just flat wrong. But after two years of constant companionship, she was used to him.

It was the whole-organic humans who freaked her shit out now.

"Savory or sweet?" he called from the kitchenette.

Farad or Fanaida or somebody—Kellen? No, probably not, but it *could* have been and would be so like him—had thoughtfully stocked the kitchenette with a box of full-spectrum-nutrition ration patties. Angela had endured this brand of rations before, and personally, she thought the lumps of vaguely brownish material tasted like a cross between toenail clippings and Styrofoam, depending on whether you chose the extra-crunchy or smooth variety. If you went smooth, they were pure, unadulterated cardboard. Both textures came with a healthy dusting of either sugar or salt. Hence mech-Daniel's all-important question.

"Sweet," she called back. If other people had been around to see, she would have gone with savory. Rosemary and truffle were the latest fad flavors. But Angela had a secret weakness for all things sweet, and indulging this once, when no one was watching, wouldn't damage her brand.

Several cabinet squeaks and crockery clanks later, mech-Daniel emerged with a ceramic bowl full of steaming fake-sugar-drenched kibble-soak. He wore an acres-wide grin of goofiness.

Angela perched crisscross-applesauce on the edge of the giant bed, balancing the hot bowl on her heels, and dug in with a disposable biodegradable spoon, also sweetened. She tucked conversation in between bites. "I'm thinking about queuing up a message for Zeke, at least. He knows we survived the attack, so talking to him won't ruin our hide-out-and-watch plan."

"You may dictate one, and I will apply for permission to establish a link during the next window," mech-Daniel said in a disapproving (condescending?) tone that made both her middle fingers twitch.

"And while you're at it, see what you can do about my analytics feed. I want to know what new horror is trending, how Zeke's polling with eight days left before the election, and of course, what the vids and gossips are saying about me."

Had Zeke reported her missing? Or was this a standard undisclosed-location narrative while the federales tracked down the attacker? How was the government PR machine spinning this?

"Processing," mech-Daniel replied, holding up one finger. "I am in queue to form a live connection beyond this closed communication system during the next window. Oh, look! We have two new episodes of *Cash Cow*. Apparently one comes in with every window. Shall I route those to your internal com?"

It wasn't information, and it wasn't connection, but at least it would distract her for a couple of hours. "Yep. Do it."

"As you wish." He said that a lot, at least fifty times a day, but his digital voice had a different tone just then. "If I may ask, how is your shoulder?"

Angela rolled the shoulder in question, the one the wall had taken out back at the Riu. It still ached, but deep. Dull. "Lots better," she lied.

"I can give you something for the pain."

It was on the tips of Angela's teeth to say no, she could power through this on her own. The pain wasn't bad, and all her bones and sockets were back in their right places, thanks to mech-Daniel's howl-inducing yankage back in the refrescando.

But he was right. The chems she'd injected at the all-night pharma had done a spectacular job of pain management, but they were now wearing off. Even the best stims didn't last much more than a day.

She set her empty bowl on the duvet. "Hit me."

He nodded and approached the rear of the lone seat in the room, a wide synthetic-skinned armchair that was both shabby and indecisively brown/gray. He motioned toward it. Angela went over to the chair and sat.

She couldn't get a read on this building, half crumbling and ramshackle, half ultra posh with hot running water, which couldn't have been cheap out here in the climatic hellhole of the southwest desert. Even in disrepair, a structure like this had to have cost a pretty penny. How did Kellen's group of outlaws fit into the global financial matrix? Were they leasing? Squatting? Uncovering the financials would tell her a lot about the people who had agreed to keep her safe. Of course, there was no way she could find out any of that *without a single goddamn feed*. Argh.

At her back, mech-Daniel arched over her, removed her hairpiece, and placed his long, cold hands on either side of her head. The tips of his middle fingers loomed large in her periphery, overreaching her temples. When the sense-ports in his hands connected with the diodes screwed into her skull, she tasted metal.

She closed her eyes and willed herself to relax. She knew this didn't hurt, but her body still innately protested.

"I will adjust your nerve settings," he told her. "Initially, this may affect how certain tastes and smells register, but please do let me know if you experience any unusual side effects."

Angela smiled. "Oh, you mean that extra arm growing out of my back?"

"You are teasing me." She could hear the reflected smile in his calibrated-to-human voice.

"No, you're right. Humor bad," she said. But he'd reminded her of something else. "Hey, after you're done with this, we need to talk about tweaking your Daniel routine."

"We can talk now. I am capable of multitasking. What tweaks would you like to make?"

Liking this really had nothing to do with it. "When we were at the gala, your sim was good. Maybe too good. Too good of a person, I mean. You were a believable analog for a human husband, but you weren't *Daniel*."

He paused for a moment, though his hands remained steady clamps on her head, feeding instructions to her peripheral nervous system. "How shall I modify my routines to better imitate Daniel Neko?"

Hurt me. Every chance you get. "Try reviewing archival footage, record some of his mannerisms. Old vids ought to be available here. He used to…do this hey-girl smirk that really got his fan legions going. Also, use more verb contractions. And a somewhat looser walk." She wasn't doing a very good job of describing the nuances, but that was Daniel in summary: a wad of nuances crammed into a brittle, bitter shell.

"A…hey-girl smirk?"

"When you review the footage, you'll know exactly what I'm talking about."

The subdermal tickle on her scalp and the taste of

metal in her mouth ebbed. "I've reviewed the footage," he said. "I'm Daniel if you want me to be."

Yeah, they were a program tweak confirmation, but those words klaxoned in her chest. Or maybe her body just reflexively cringed at having its electrical system invaded and manipulated.

No, she didn't want him to be Daniel. But with the real Daniel gone now, she needed the imposter to be believable. Even if his imitation made her want to vomit.

At least here in the Pentarc she'd have some privacy while she got used to being near almost-Daniel.

"Great," she said, feeling anything but. "Go ahead and keep that behavior suite loaded perpetually. No turning it off. You know what I'm saying?"

"You want me to…kill Dan-Dan?"

What a fonky way of phrasing it. "Just archive the program suite. I'd like to keep a back door available in case I need it, but generally, yeah, you can kill him."

The diodes cooled, and the cringe dulled. The pain in her shoulder winked out of existence. Poof, like magic. She started to turn, to thank him face-to-face, but she couldn't move her head. His hands still clamped it in place.

Then low, softest whisper: "It's done."

Something had just happened. A weighty something. A mechanical hiccup, seismic only to him, perhaps. Mech-Daniel had always been something of a mystery to her, coming into her life and replacing all her personal digital assistants and drone bodyguards. Hell, he'd nearly replaced her style team. In two short years, he had made himself indispensable. And she'd just told him to kill himself.

She tilted her head, pillowing it into the cool clasp of his hands. *I'm sorry* rose to her mouth, but she hadn't gotten the words out before her com vibrated. Low vibration; only she would feel it. She tapped her molars together, a percussive pattern in response.

A voice invaded her head, a burst of digital input that her com translated into phonemes, routed past her cochlea, and fed directly to her brain. It registered as both female and…perky.

"Finally! Hey, tell your parental unit you need to go to the bathroom," said the voice.

What?

"The large mech-clone currently nut-cracking your skull? We can't talk when he's watching. So tell Daddy you need to go potty all by yourself this time, like a big girl."

Angela wondered if there was a com algorithm for annoying, because she was sure feeling it from her unidentified caller. Still, she had been bored and frustrated two minutes ago. At least the voice was diverting. Plus, its owner might have information she was seeking.

Aloud, she excused herself, telling mech-Daniel she was going to indulge. "You can hibernate for a little while," she said. "Nothing in the shower stall is likely to attack me, and I want to spend some quality time with that hot water."

He started to protest, but she rephrased as a command, and he obediently positioned himself by the door and powered down.

"Okay," Angela said to the voice, out loud now mech-Daniel wasn't listening. "Who the hell are you?"

Maybe she could have used a nice long sleep after

all, because clearly, she was making stuff up out of thin air. Literally. The empty space in front of her sizzled, broke apart, and reformed. In the shape of a girl. Pretty girl, blond, curvy, maybe eighteen years old, barely old enough to vote and way too young to think.

The blond grinned and raised one holographic hand in greeting. "Okay, the way I see it, you aren't here, and I also am not supposed to be here. It's like we're cosmically meant to be pals. Bitches. Friends! Wanna go exploring?"

Angela repeated her original question.

"Oh fine." The hologram exhaled, blowing its hair fringe out of its eyes in a caricature of exasperation. "My name is Chloe. I'm a sentient nanorobotic collective, highly illegal and dangerous, and if you tell anybody I exist, I'm afraid I'll have to kill you. But in the meantime, welcome to the Pentarc!"

"Why did I have to hibernate mech-Daniel?"

"Because he's obsessed with rules and processes and would try to convince you to ignore me. Also, he's N series, a certified Vallejo bot, which means his core programming defaults to asshole."

"He is a machine, not an asshole."

Chloe shrugged. "Believe what you want. But about my original offer: what say we go get ourselves into trouble?"

A thrill of potentiality played Angela's spine like an electric banjo. "How do you propose to do that?"

"Lots of ways. I've made a list. Let's see, we could break into the underground gem vault on West and see what the Noor-ol-Ain tiara looks like on your head—oh, after you put the wig back on. You're lots prettier with it on."

Angela also itched to reattach her hairpiece, but she was too fascinated right now to do anything other than stare down the chatty hologram. Er, nanorobotic collective wassit. Whatever you called it, it was definitely the most interesting thing Angela had encountered since she'd been here. "Then what?"

"Zipline between building spires?"

"Not happening. We fall, you dissolve into holographic glitter while I plummet fifty meters and splat."

"Oh right. Physical permanence." Chloe looked off to the right and for a moment assumed the same expression mech-Daniel did when he was ticking things off a to-do list. "Did you know that only this spire and the east one are refurbished? Northy's a ruin, but you can still clamber all over it. Super creepy. You'll love it."

Angela had toured her share of ruins. Washington, DC, topped her creepy list and probably always would. "I'll pass."

"We could visit the prisoner in the dungeon." Chloe waggled her eyebrows. "He's indecently pretty."

Her face was just a little too animated. Trying too hard to seem real? She couldn't really have a dungeon replete with prisoners. That part had to be made up.

"Do you live here at the Pentarc, Chloe?"

The hologram's gaze shifted up and to the left. "Oh sure. I'm part of the team, part of the crew. Indispensable. Beloved."

Wistful too, if Angela was reading the signals right. Hopeful. Excitable. Possibly delusional but definitely eager to please. In so many ways, this holographic intelligence reminded her of mech-Daniel. It was easy to trust. No, wait, *she*. She was easy to trust.

"Excellent. Then maybe you can help me," said Angela.

"That's what I do!"

Was it possible for a noncorporeal entity to bounce? She wasn't bound to gravity, after all, and it was…weird.

"There's some sort of firewall keeping me from getting messages in or out of here," said Angela. "I need a way through it."

Chloe's face shifted to sad, but a kind of eerie comic-book interpretation of what sadness looked like. "I can't. I don't have admin access to the network. Only Heron and Kellen can poke holes in the firewall. Bummer."

The words tumbled from Angela's brain and out through her mouth before she could stop them. "Is Kellen here?"

Chloe paused a microsecond, then beamed. "Yup, up at the barn. Neither of us are supposed to go there. I'm not even supposed to be here."

Angela shoved her feet into her pillow shoes, which had taken a beating on the climb out of the Riu but were far too comfy to trash. She snagged the hairpiece and fitted it onto her head, engaging the hooks to keep it from slipping. Thought about cosmetics, maybe some lip polish. Would that look too needy, too tarty?

Shall we fit our tongues to dialogues of business, love, or strife? She was about to see Kellen, to be with him in close physical proximity. Under such conditions, lip polish wouldn't last long. Her body hummed in expectation of finishing their secret, flirtatious conversation.

Angela turned to her rescue-bot, the holographic blond with the gigantic boobs. "If I promise not to rat you out, will you take me to him? And then leave us alone?"

"Deal. Let's go be naughty." Chloe happy-bounced (she totally could, even without gravity), and the remote lock on the unit door disengaged with a pop.

CHAPTER 5

UP AT THE BARN, LYING TO HIMSELF HE WASN'T THERE because he was avoiding anybody in particular, Kellen stroked the miniature goat's flank. "Don't you mind that coy little camelid, Rook. She'll come around."

The goat looked over at the latest rescue to invade his pen and snorted. Almost like he knew exactly what Kellen was saying.

Kellen would have laughed out loud, but a sharp noise like that could startle the animals he'd collected up here, the wild hares in particular. Instead he gestured to Azul, inviting her closer. He'd already injected her first series of nanocytes, and she was eating solids, as was proper for a girl her age. She had a powerful suspicion of other animals, though.

"Come 'ere, Azulita. Rook and his goaties ain't gonna hurt you. You're safe here, girl."

She took a wobbly step toward Kellen and Rook, but clearly she had some misgivings. As a cria, she'd been around people a mite too much. Gal got way too excited every time he paid her a visit, which was flattering and all, but long-term, not good for her. She might never reintegrate with her original herd, especially since it had all but abandoned her as a newborn, but he had some thoughts of where he could place her in the wild. If she was still capable of being a wild animal after all this.

Training her away from domesticity was harder than it sounded. And Rook, the most social of the three pygmy goats still receiving treatment here in the barn, wasn't much help. He looked like he wanted to give her a good sniff. Possibly chase her around some. Show the newcomer who was king. But he was a rescue himself and tended toward timidity, so a lot of their interaction was Rook gearing up to introduce himself then backing off and Azul being oblivious of any overtures that didn't come from humans.

In a way, it was kind of like human courtship, the sweet parts anyhow.

Kellen balanced in a squat next to the goat, careful to keep his body still. He motioned to Azul, and when she boinged over and nosed his wrist, he studiously ignored her, waited for her to take a step back, and then, on his terms, he petted her, letting her closer only once she had control of herself. She didn't even seem to realize she was also close enough for Rook to get a good sniff. The little gal gurgled with joy, and Rook snuck to within a meter of her before he backed off.

Baby steps, sure, but the social dynamics around here were looking up. Kellen breathed easy. Hairy mammals? Check. Insecure as all get-out? Check. Nonverbal but clearly needing some help? Also check. He was in his happy place.

And then he wasn't.

Because *she* was there. Angela.

Materializing from the umber shadow of the elevator house and moving into full lurid sunshine, Angela Neko sashayed back into his life exactly as if she'd never left it. As if she'd never blistered his soul with cruel words or scissored him out of her own bright future.

Heron had warned him she was coming, but Kellen hadn't quite accepted the reality. He'd been pretending he still had time to prepare himself. But he should have been honest. Nothing was going to prepare him for this, not even seeing the holoprojection of her up on Chiba Station. Angela in the flesh was a whole different experience, and he wasn't anywhere near ready for it.

With one brown-eyed gaze, she clamped him in a state of suspended ecstasy, and he couldn't look away.

Nobody had ever described Angela Neko as pretty, at least not in his hearing. She was a force, tremendous and terrible and amazing. She lured others into agreement with her, often against their will, like gravity. But all that was power of personality, not her looks. Physically she was tiny, graceful as a sapling liana, with tip-tilted, dark-fringed eyes and heavy, shining black hair. She used to wear it long, a cool curtain strewn across their bodies. When they'd holoconferenced a few days back, it had been trammeled in a severe updo, but now he saw she'd had it cut and shaped. Professional. Polished.

Recognition, one body of another, feathered out from his spine, curling in hot tendrils to the ends of his extremities. He could no more make words in this moment than he could calm the canter of his heartbeat.

"Hello." Her voice painted the afternoon a darker shade of gold.

In a solar eclipse, folks without cyber eyes are advised not to look directly into the sun. Not because a direct peek hurts, but because it doesn't. The oh-what-could-it-hurt slow, sly voice of temptation leads a body to take in more than it can safely stand. Radiation scorches the retinas, but because there aren't pain receptors there, the eyes can be damaged irrevocably without their owner even realizing until it is far too late.

Looking at Angela Neko, at once an echo of the girl who had burned at the center of his soul and also the different, mature woman she had become, Kellen forgot that it wasn't safe to stare. He forgot that it wasn't safe to love her.

From a star's distance and without moving his oversaturated eyes, he watched the animals react to her presence. Rook peered at her suspiciously. The two other goats followed his lead. The more skittish littles were nowhere to be seen.

But Azul, that oversocialized cuddlemonster, skipped right up to Angela, butted her soft nose against the senator's wrinkled skirt, and insisted on wresting all the attention.

It was the easiest thing in the world for Angela to reach down to rub the cria's sweet snout.

Even when Kellen's mind was burning a supernova of memory, his instincts reacted. "Don't do that," he said too sharply. "You gotta thump her on the nose."

Angela's smile dimmed, and confusion pooled in her dark eyes. "Why would I want to do that?"

"Because you want to do right by her. Encouraging her to treat you without respect isn't a kindness. It's bad training."

Kellen rose from his crouch, dusted his jeans with both hands, and approached the pair. Getting closer to that woman was way against his better judgment, of course. He did it anyhow. He wore his shabby Stetson against the hard afternoon sun, but it wouldn't do much to protect his face from her. She would see him, as she always had, and know exactly what he was thinking.

"If we don't tell her to back off now, she'll grow up aggressive, try to knock people down, and just generally behave like a brat," he explained, working hard to keep his voice even and soothing.

"Uh-huh," Angela said with a grin that usually came with some eye rolling. But at least she'd pulled her hand back up. As he watched, she twined it with her other. Naked hands, no gloves this time. Hot hands, strong hands, lithe as flame tongues on his skin, those hands.

He swallowed, got his bearings, and patiently lured the vicuña away from Angela's knees. The activity centered him, tore him from staring, reminded him that time had passed. Whole years, nearly a decade. He wasn't Angela's thing anymore, indentured to her will.

"You know what?" he said, maybe with a testy edge and definitely not looking at her. "It's okay if you don't believe me or don't agree with my methods, but I do care how Azul matures. I care about that a lot. She's already got three strikes against a healthy development: she was born too wee, bottle-fed by folks not her own kind, and she's got no herd. 'Bout the least I can do for her now is raise her up right so she knows exactly what she is and has no delusions of grandeur."

"We're talking about Azul?" Angela followed at a

distance while he herded all the animals into a long pen nearer the barn.

He wasn't looking right at her and took the opportunity to scowl hard. "'Course we are. What'd you think… aw, damn it, don't you even get on psychoanalyzing me. I ain't your fucking what-if social experiment."

Kellen shut the gate and turned to her, hooking his thumbs in his belt loops. Else what the hell was he supposed to do with those hands?

Muscle memory had some ideas. He drew his fingers up to fists. Tension corded his arms.

"Discussing the animal. Right." She burned a look up at him. "So, oh expert in animal behavior, what happens if I let Azul get close to me? What happens if I pet her beautiful head or stroke her flank?"

She had to know what her voice did to him. She wrapped it around him on purpose, binding him with it, like a word witch.

He took a deep breath, let it out. "Best not. She'll get to thinking it's okay for a critter like her to invade your personal space."

"What if it is?" Soft, her words, and bedroom low.

"I don't know what subtext you're laying on here, but what I do know is—"

"Kellen."

Why'd she have to say his name? And in a voice like *that*?

"What if it's okay for *you* to invade my personal space?" she went on. "What if I want it sort of desperately? What if I've thought of it since we spoke on the telepresence?" She floated one hand toward him and got within a breath of touching his forearm before she drew it back.

Since their holoconference. Since he'd told her who killed her husband. This wasn't the time to be laying her out on a bed in his mind. Shame burned through desire, turning it to bitter ash.

"You best go on wanting, then," he said.

Her eyes narrowed, but she didn't resort to pouting or guilt. She'd grown past that, apparently. Her mouth hardened. "This wasn't the reunion I expected."

"Better than the one I didn't expect at all," he said. "Why'd you come out here?"

"I wanted to see you." She moistened timorous lips, and he couldn't help wondering if the tremble was part of her act. "I missed you."

He near tore the belt loops off his jeans. God Almighty, this woman.

He pinched his eyes shut, but man, it hurt. "You been widowed what, a week? Ain't it a bit soon to try and lay me down?"

When he opened his eyes, she was glaring back at him. Hands in fists. One eyebrow up. Uh-oh. "What I endured wasn't a marriage. Besides, salacious banter didn't seem to bother you at the gala."

Confusion cooled his ardor a bit, and his humiliation. "What?"

"The messages? The poem?"

He repeated, "What?"

She threw her hands up and half turned, muttering under her breath in a language he didn't know. Not that it mattered. She could curse fluently in at least twenty.

"Fit our tongues?" she snapped. "Wordsworth? In the dark?"

Worth Dark Words. He remembered her code, of

course he did. Scratched on the inside of her smartglove, a secret message, like they'd sent when they were kids and playing at spies in the Mustaqbal Institute. But what did that have to do with…

Daylight broke upon his brain. "Is *that* what you meant? Somehow I guessed you were aiming for the sadder end of the poem. You know, the part where we're old and bitter and blind to the wonders of the natural world and everythin's gone to steaming shit."

"I am not old. Or bitter. Or…"

More sublingual cursing. He wished he'd installed a translator app on his com. Whatever she was saying sounded just filthy.

She was right about one thing, though: this cadence worked for them. The bickering, the sparring. They'd done this plenty back when, and although it had always led to electric pile-driving sex then, he was a grown-up now. He could resist.

Plus, he had forgotten how sweet it felt all on its own, getting her riled up like this. He'd forgotten how her eyebrows swooped down in the middle but flared up in points on the outside, like demon wings. So fierce. And secret, known only to the people closest to her. He'd never seen her face set in anything other than perfect placidity on those vidcasts. As if fury were beneath her.

Kellen knew better. He knew *her* better.

She stood there spitting fire, and he shook his head in defeated admiration.

"How can you be so hands-off and stick-up-your-ass today when the night before last, you were laying out lines at me like a goddamned dealer?" she fumed.

"I got no idea what you're talking about, but you sure do work up a fine lather."

"I'm talking about you responding to my secret code. You sent me messages. During the gala the night before last."

"No, I didn't."

"Yes, you did."

"I spent that whole night trying to keep Heron alive. Wasn't easy. I didn't have a scrap of time to play with you on Torchat, though I'm sure it would have been a hoot."

"It was… I mean, if it wasn't you, then…" She turned from him, stared out into the desert. He could almost hear the gears of her big brain whirring. Finally she went on, "I guess mech-Daniel put that whole thing together. To make the gala easier for me. Christ on a pickle. Except, you know what? This shit is stupid embarrassing, and I don't need any of it." She pivoted and stomped off, while he watched from his vantage.

Oh yeah, he watched. Drank in the sight, truth told. She was a hellcat in her wrinkled skirt and bedroom slippers, and she hadn't changed one bit in all these years. Her firecracker temper crackled on his skin, both familiar and heartbreaking. Used to be, she'd spark it up just for him.

She stopped just inside the shadow of the elevator house, one wrist poised in front of the scanner that would call up the elevator. Being her, though, she had to get in the last word. "So that's it, then? You didn't send the messages, and you didn't want me here. And now you're just going to let me walk away?"

Oh no, you did not say that.

They hit him smack in the gut, those words. She

could have said anything else. Pain flared, and he spoke before the better part of him could even process. "Sure as hell am. Go play your tiny diva violin for somebody else, 'cause I am done listening."

She turned, and he braced himself. Was she planning to lay it on even thicker? Because if she expected him to roll over like a goddamn lap dog, she didn't know him at all anymore.

Her dark eyes snapped, electrifying him across space. "I am not..."

"Oh, princess," he drawled, pushing away from the fence post. "You most surely are. Ain't that the same damn thing you did to me? You watched me walk away. Now, absofuckinlutely, I aim to do the same. Put that pill in your own mouth, and give it a chew."

* * * * * * * *

Summer, 2049
Dunes between Abu Dhabi and the Mustaqbal Institute of Science and Technology

Late afternoon was the hottest time of day in the hottest part of the world, but Kellen sunned in it like a happy rattlesnake. Part of that had to do with how his blood still felt too warm, too heavy for his veins. With the languor that had invaded his limbs after sex, or the stretch of forever in his mind. And maybe also with light and heat that splashed over his bare skin, merging him inexorably with his lover.

The sun lowered in the west, and he longed to hold it, hoard it. He didn't want today, or this moment, to end. Not ever.

She stirred against him, her breath billowing over his chest. "We should record this, you know."

"What, so I can send it to you during particle physics? Girl, you'd never ace a test again."

"You think you're so distracting, do you?"

"I know it."

"Ha. Well, you're probably right. But I'd still get top marks in the class. With a high enough frame-rate and industrial magnification, I would be able to definitively describe the atomic interactions that occur at the point of orgasm. This is valuable research. Stills from our copulation would be in all the best science channels. Your cock would be famous."

She didn't touch anything especially sensitive right then, but she might as well have. His body reacted to being talked about. He moved one palm along her sweat-damp spine. Her skin was silk.

"Also," she went on in a softer, more solemn voice, "I would be able to play the vid over and over. When I am exhausted but cannot sleep. When I am scared but cannot scream. When I am lonely. Every time I'm lonely and wanting you."

"Sweetheart, you don't have to worry about none of that," he swore. "I don't intend to let you get too exhausted or scared or lonely, not ever again. I aim to stick on you like glue all the rest of our lives. I love you."

He waited for her to say it back. She took a long time.

"I love you too, Kellen, but you really shouldn't make promises like that."

"Give me one reason why not."

"I can give you a billion reasons: all the other people crawling across our planet. A billion vectors in chaos. You can't track them all or know their purposes. There are too many uncertainties to make forever-type promises."

"I can promise that I will love you forever."

"How can you do that?" she almost cried.

His eyebrows crawled up his forehead, topping what he knew was a cocky grin. "Give me a couple weeks and I'll come up with a theorem. Probably Pascalian, because of all them vectors, but till then, you'll just have to trust me."

"I do trust you," she said. She rose up on one elbow and looked down at him, her head eclipsing the too-harsh sun, her hair encasing their mingled breath. "But I think that might be a problem."

"Trust is a problem?" If she'd lean down just a smidge further, he would be able to kiss her, and they wouldn't need to talk so much. His body stirred again, all his parts reaching for her. He could have her a thousand times out here in the desert, and he'd still want more.

"Dependence is a problem," she said.

Kellen blinked up at her. Her body had stiffened, pressed up against his, but not out of desire. Tension invaded her and leached into him. He wasn't sure yet why he needed to worry, but worry suffused him just the same.

"Specifically," Angela said, meeting his eyes directly, almost defiantly, "my dependence on you is a problem."

"How d'you figure?" His voice sounded more like a croak.

"You know my plans, my future. It's all mapped out, and it's going to be amazing. But I read the mentors' write-up of my last evaluation."

"Spy," he teased, but the joke wasn't funny.

"We must be informed, Kellen. Call it spying if you want, but you should do a little more of it," she argued. "Anyway, the mentors think I have not been tested, that my life has been too safe and sterile. 'A sword must be fired, else it shatters under pressure,' one of them wrote."

"Bullshit. You're a person, not a weapon."

"Be that as it may, I kind of see their point. If my whole life is a series of wins, if I never lose, I will lack the necessary wisdom to succeed."

"There are lots of ways to succeed, though, and suffering doesn't make any outcome more statistically probable than another. Considering where I come from, just *being* here with you is success."

He could tell her plenty about struggle. Back home, before the MIST recruiters saw his test scores and flew him out here to the academy, keeping Sissy safe had been a 24/7 calling. Patching her up after Mama went on a mean streak. Mama always took her mean out on Sissy, leaving him to watch and hurt in impotence and then clean up after.

The academy'd sworn they'd take care of Sissy, get her out of that house. They'd brought him here, fixed his problems, and gave him an outlet to express all these thoughts in his noggin to boot. He was living his success, any way you painted it, and not a lick of it linked causally to whatever his struggles had been. Suffering hadn't made him what he was. Right now, today, he'd still be a supergenius even if he hadn't started out in a cheap-wine-smelling trailer in East Texas.

He'd still be important. Like Angela. Weren't they just alike? Or was that what she meant? That they weren't, somehow.

She leaned in and kissed him. Hard, that kiss, and close-mouthed. She stilled in the middle of it, with her lips pressed to his, and a tremble passed between their mouths, electrical, like she was in fact recording the moment. A frozen moment she could cram in a snow globe or something. Kellen turned his head, breaking their connection.

"What are you not telling me?" he demanded.

She flinched like he'd hurt her. "There is a new message on your com back in the dorm." She raised her arm. Her own com was built in so she could never lose it. "We all got the alert, but yours includes a ticket back to Texas. One way."

He swore under his breath. "But I passed my exams."

"I know."

"It's in the contract. They let me keep enrolling as long as I perform to expectation. Well, I've done everything they wanted. Hell, more. Lots more." How many papers had he written? How many databases crammed full of facts had he memorized? Even western fucking poetry, the god-awfulest stuff on the planet. He knew whole epic poems of that shit by heart and would never get them out of his brain now. The academy, the mentors, had said jump, and he'd fucking asked how high.

He took a long, raggedy breath. "Are you tellin' me they're kicking me out?"

She caught her bottom lip between her teeth and

didn't answer. He rolled, pushing her off, separating their bodies. All the warmth of the day fled. The air tasted like dust.

"What's their reason?" They had to have one.

She looked at him steadily, her dark gaze impenetrable. Unknowable. "It isn't your grades. It's Texas. That hurricane came through this morning, our time. It was pretty bad. Cat six. Lowest barometric pressure in recorded history. Comprehensive and pervasive structural failure. Galveston is pretty much gone. Houston, too. It's all over the channels."

Ah. Well, as a matter of fact, he did know about that one. He'd been monitoring the storm the weather folks named Agatha. Not because he was going back, though. His family was in Lufkin, inland by several hours. Folks not from around there oftentimes didn't appreciate how big Texas was, how much ground it covered. Even if that hurricane had hit Galveston dead-on and barreled straight up the ship channel, it still wouldn't have affected Mama and Sissy much. This was a distraction, an excuse.

Those asshole mentors were still expecting him to take their deal. No baggage. Everybody on the mentor council expected him to flinch. To run. To do their bidding out of reflex.

So they could set fire to Angela. So they could hone her into their weapon.

And she was letting them.

He started pulling on his clothes. "Look, I ain't leaving, but I am gonna run take a look at the terminals real quick and check in on my people. I'm sure they're fine, but Mama can get pretty hysterical, even over minor things. She's all about the drama. Sissy'll need to talk my ear off, I'm sure. Afterward, I'll…"

He had his shirt on, unfastened, and his uniform pants in a similar state of half completion. He'd just started on the placket buttons when her silence in the face of his string of chatter made him pause.

Angela had risen and now knelt in the sand naked, like a stone Hatshepsut, dark and perfect and still. Looking at him.

"No, don't just vid-message them. That's your home. You need to go." She took a breath, held it, folded her hands primly, determinedly over her burnished thighs. "I want you to go."

A one-way ticket, she'd said. And not just because of his family, his commitments. She had even framed it up for him. *My dependence on you is a problem.*

The bottom fell out of Kellen's universe, and he finally understood.

She wanted this for her own reasons. She was breaking up with him. She wanted him to go. And not come back.

CHAPTER 6

YOU WATCHED ME WALK AWAY. HIS WORDS BORE DOWN ON Angela, adding to an already crushing burden of guilt.

Despite all the cruelties she had endured in the years since, that particular memory hurt most of all. Even though, back then, she had been dishing the venom.

You watched me walk away. Yeah, she had. And it had destroyed him. She could see it on his face right now. That haunted, horrible look.

She had done that. To him.

God, had she really?

At the time, she'd been certain her reasons were valid. If she and Kellen had stayed together, neither of them would have grown strong or independent. They would have been blown off course, and neither would now be worthy of respect. They had been so foolish, so distracted in their infatuation. Their grades had slipped, both of them. She couldn't let herself regret either her actions or her motives. But self-righteousness didn't lessen the ache. And it sure as fuck didn't salve that dark look on his face, half kicked puppy, half roiling fury.

And while the former twisted her soul in knots, physically, she was all too conditioned to respond to the latter.

"I never meant..." Words in whispers, cringing. She knew he couldn't hear her, not from all the way over there, but he must have seen her mouth move.

Frowning like an angry god, he prowled toward her. Bigger than she remembered, imposing, taking up all the air. Angela pressed her back against the elevator doors and blessed them for being cool and solid and keeping her from falling down when her long bones liquefied.

Life had weathered him, but tired and jaded looked so good on his face. Really, really good. His jeans weren't starched, and his western-cut shirt was only three-quarters buttoned, offering tantalizing glimpses of a body that no longer had a shred of boyish lankiness to it. He was all grown up now.

His dark-gold hair desperately needed tidying, and her fingers flexed to service. She knew exactly what that would feel like, to touch him, to tend him. But she was rooted like a rabbit, too fascinated to run, too scared to stay. Her mouth wetted. She swallowed.

He dipped into the shadow with her, and the space shrunk to nothing. She couldn't breathe.

"I will repeat my earlier question," he said in a low voice, a rumble that bathed her all over. "Why did you come here, Angela?"

Because you are my home base. Because I thought you wanted me here. Because somebody tried to kill me,

*and the only place in this whole world I have ever felt
safe was in your arms.*

"There's a bruise above your left temple." He brushed
the side of his knuckle against her face, and Angela had
to press her eyes shut and bite her lip. "What aren't you
telling me?"

"I'm sorry," she whispered. Her entire self focused
on that point of connection, the brightest spot in her
universe. It had been so long, so long.

"No, the *other* thing you ain't saying."

She opened her eyes and realized he'd gotten himself together. The haunted look was gone. He was even
smiling slightly, a rakish half grin she remembered so
well, like Rhett Butler at the bottom of the stairs. He
still carried a lot of pain—she hadn't been making it up;
it had been right there, and she had seen it—but somehow he had…compartmentalized it. Pushed through it.
Impressive. And here she couldn't even keep herself
from sneaking a touch.

She leaned into his hand and tried not to sound desperate. "My hotel was bombed the night before last,
after I messaged you. I'm pretty sure someone tried
to kill me, and whoever it is probably thinks they suc-
ceeded. I need to have my mech dredge data threads,
figure out who's talking to whom, though I do have
some guesses. Mostly, I just need…time." Her brain finished that sentence differently. She needed a safe spot,
had thought that spot might be him. But it couldn't be.
No take-backsies.

"Feel free to settle while here, then." His hand was
against her face still, strong and steady. He spread his
fingers, cradling her.

She'd never seen this expression on Kellen before, not in all their years. He looked…fierce? No. Couldn't be. Not him. And yet, that look. A shiver hot-noodled through her body, pooling low. She shifted her feet, absorbing the shudder and moving closer. To him, to warmth.

Their gazes locked, and she wanted to tell him everything. But more than that, she wanted to pull his head down and kiss him until thoughts like guilt and fear and regret disintegrated in a furnace of passion.

The sun was behind his head; she couldn't see his face. He might have leant, and his mouth may have moved, like he was forming words. She rose on the balls of her feet, bringing her face closer to his, shifting until his fingers rested against her throat, then her collarbone. Could he feel her wild pulse?

"Well, this is the suxors." Chloe's disembodied voice, in Angela's head. *Wait. Chloe?* But yes, definitely her. "Heads up, you two. We're about to have company."

The warning came maybe half a second before the wall against Angela's ass began to move, and she didn't have time to worry about Chloe possibly having just voyeured this entire reunion.

No, not the wall. The elevator doors. Which she had backed herself against. Damn it. She had forgotten. She lurched forward, away from the sliding doors and smack into Kellen. Obdurate body—not even a hint of softness there, all planes and angles—colliding with hers like tectonic plates, volcanic at the seams, and then he was holding her, and her arms were reaching around to clasp his thick-muscled back. She could feel every contour beneath his threadbare cotton shirt, and the miasma of leather and soap and pure, sun-kissed man stroked her senses.

The door was wide open behind her, but she didn't give enough fucks to look. All her attention was centered right here.

"I can't tell you how relieved I am to find you." Dan-Dan. Except not. *Can't* rather than *cannot*. It was Daniel now, or some weird amalgamation of the two, almost like they were fighting for dominance in his skin shell. "Did you have a nice shower?"

The differences in voice and movement were subtle, but they caught and snagged on Angela's perception, icing her veins. The salacious thoughts she'd been entertaining whimpered and retreated.

She turned her face against Kellen's chest and peered sidelong at her mech-clone, looking for facial echoes of the sarcasm that drenched his words. There wasn't any. It was always weird when he played Daniel: the intonations were full of butter and snark, but inside, she had to remind herself he had no motivations, no desires or psychoses. Inside, he was just a machine. Predictable. Safe.

So why did her body react this way, cringing away from him? Surely she was too evolved to judge somebody based purely on how they looked, even if that somebody was just a robot.

She must have stiffened or something, because Kellen pulled her closer. And Angela, who before today hadn't touched another human in more than a year and hadn't endured a gentle touch in some while longer, wasn't sure what to do with this sudden sensory overload. She was drowning in him and didn't want to stop. All her other thoughts muddled and sloughed.

Touch. Human touch, skin to skin, body to body, warmth merging with its like. Combustion hovering just on the edge, so close. She remembered what it felt like, that explosion. It was elemental and beautiful and overwhelming and warm and past and future and keening and clawing and want. So very, very want.

She ought to step away, especially now others could see. She ought to get herself under control. She ought to behave like the intimidating persona she projected to the world. Like a war minister.

Instead, she clung. Just for a few more seconds. It felt too fucking good.

Chloe fizzed into visibility just beyond Daniel, and they both stepped out into the barnyard area, leaving Angela and Kellen tucked still in shadow. Kellen tensed in response, but Angela couldn't see his face, just the scruffy chin near the top of her head.

"This is dangerous, what you're doing, Chloe-girl," he said.

"Back atcha." The nanorobotic intelligence raised her eyebrows higher than a real person physically could. The effect was comic, almost cartoonish. Her form blurred on the edges where it met sunlight, but she was grinning like a cat in cream.

"I'm serious. Told you before, if the wrong eyes see you…"

Chloe cut him off with a huff. "Fine. I will go back to the plane. Real soon now. But somebody needed to show Angela around, and nobody down here was doing their job."

Kellen sighed heavily. "Do you even know who this is?"

"Oh sure, she's Angela. She's your—"

"*Senator* Neko."

"Yup." Chloe nodded her not-there head vigorously.

"Of the government that has outlawed your very existence."

Short pause. Chloe might have wanted to say something but held back. On her holographic face, though, it was hard to guess her thoughts.

"You see now why I told you to stay away?" Kellen went on. "Why Heron had Angela confined to her quarters, at least until we could figure out our next steps?"

"I am always away," Chloe said in a barely audible voice.

Angela turned, and Kellen loosened his hold of her as if she'd asked it of him. She hadn't. The loss of contact hurt, physically hurt, but she did need to pull herself together, if not for her own dignity, then at least as reassurance for Chloe. She took a step away from Kellen and smoothed her skirt.

"You don't need to worry, Chloe," said Angela. "Even after I leave here, I won't report you. Promise. And Dan-Dan won't either."

Another legally iffy complication. She was getting downright mired in those things, but she didn't see a good wiggle around this one. The last thing she wanted was for Chloe to go rogue, run away from the people who were keeping her hidden, keeping her out of trouble. A self-recursive AI would be infinitely more dangerous on its own, learning ethics based on trial and error. At least somebody like Kellen could train her. Like that vicuña.

Chloe's grin suddenly widened unnaturally, and her eyes sparkled. Literally. Particle effect?

"See?" she said, turning to Kellen. "She likes me. She won't cram me back into a vat. We're good."

"Ang, why don't we leave these two to work things out?" Daniel asked, extending his hand to Angela.

She shivered and did not take his hand. She would never feel comfortable hearing that nickname. If she didn't know essentially how mechs worked, she would never believe, mere hours ago, this creature had been her way-too-thoughtful and puppy-loyal assistant. That he had talked her through a stressful in-person event. That he had saved her life when her world fell apart.

All traces of that programming were gone, wiped. She had done that. She had broken him. God. How many ways could she fuck stuff up? And she was supposed to be able to handle power.

"Nah, she don't need to leave." Almost as if he couldn't help himself, Kellen settled a hand on her shoulder. Possessively. The gesture halted the dark path her thoughts were taking, brought her back to the present, focused her. Kellen went on, facing the mech-clone, "But you can make yourself useful. I need you to get to a terminal and plug your head in, find out if the attack on Senator Neko's hotel was a contract. If a government or a megacorp was behind it, chances are they would have hired somebody else for their dirty work. Plausible deniability and all that bullshit. You do know how to access the darknet, right? Most freelancers scout jobs there."

"I'm sorry," mech-Daniel said, "but my protocol prohibits me from following instructions from anyone—"

"Do it." Angela hadn't meant to snap, but she was at the end of her emotional tether. Shit was coming at her too fast now, and not even academic, geopolitical shit her brain was conditioned to process at speed. Feelings shit. Which took more out of her, required more focus.

She didn't want to focus. She wanted to loll right here, press herself back up against this man, and pretend the last decade of her life hadn't happened. "You do whatever he tells you to, Dan-Dan."

The machine stared back at her. Orbs grown and shaped to look like eyes. Like her husband's eyes. Cold and empty and cruel. The artificants had done too good a job. "All right."

Not what Dan-Dan would have said, but she had no one but herself to blame. She had reset the programming. She kept staring, steady, until he turned and stepped back onto the elevator.

As the doors closed, Chloe emitted a low whistle. "The Vallejo runs strong in that one. Tell me he isn't the scariest robot in ever."

"Speaking of," Kellen said, "exactly how long have you been spying on us?"

Chloe apparently lacked programming for shame. "Not long enough. I was about to go make some popcorn."

"You don't eat," he reminded her.

"So what? I can still make popcorn. It smells good."

"You don't smell, either."

"I mean, *other* people tell me it smells good. Like Garrett. He likes it." Her edges fuzzed again, and just like that, she was gone. Only not. Her hologram was gone, but she could still somehow invade their in-ear communications devices at will. How mobile were her composite nanos? Did those little fuckers fly?

"He likes you even better," Kellen said. "Now scat."

"Okay, fine. Later, Senator!"

Trilling laughter faded, which was the only clue that Angela and Kellen were now alone on the rooftop. Well, alone except for the animals, but even Azul had long since given up staring. Some movement at the far side of the pens might have been more goats or even smaller animals. A squirrel maybe, or a rabbit.

"She's a rascal."

"Who is?" Angela turned and looked up at him innocently. Unfortunately, the movement shrugged his hand off her shoulder. She missed the contact.

"The scamp you just now swore to forget," he said, but he was smiling.

A breeze ruffled his hair. Evening advanced over the desert, but the air was still breath-hot.

"Thanks for trusting me," she told him solemnly. "And as for the rest of it, do we really need to talk about it?" *Or we could just skip the talking. I'm okay with that.*

The shadows that enveloped him had lengthened.

"Right. Our personal history. Talking it out." He swiped a hand through his errant hair, shoving it out of his face. "You know what, I shouldn't have brought it up. You came here for a serious reason—shit don't get much more serious than an attempt on your life—and I treated you to an emo-soup pity party. Now I'm the one embarrassed. Would kinda like to drop it."

Angela wouldn't. She wanted to talk all the way through it. She wanted to relive every second, pick it apart, put it back together again. Rebuild that thing they had, the thing that had sustained her through some pretty rotten years. The thing that still throbbed like a new wound. But she held her wishes safe in her mouth, didn't dare loose them into the air where they could dissolve to nothing.

"Fine," she said instead. "So now what? Now that

I know all about Chloe, do you have to lock me in my room again?"

He studied her face for a while. Then he swiped his cuff com in front of the elevator. The metal doors slid open. "Nah. Fan and Adele are settin' out supper in an hour, but I need to check in on something before we go back down. Figure you'll want to see this, too."

•   •   •   •   •   •   •   •

Mustaqbal Institute of Science and Technology, 2045

The magical thing about the library was that no one ever needed to come here. Students could compile their audio-visual-sensory collage on a topic and feed it right into their coms. The cleverest kids double-booked their time, consuming lectures while they got in their daily ten thousand steps and five hundred calories burned. Bonus if they worked in groups, they could tick off their participatory classroom community requirement as well.

At fifteen, and after ten years of training at the academy, Angela was capable of such multitasking. Of course she was. Clean use of her time was an inherent gift, making such feats for her as natural as breathing. If she wanted to absorb information, she didn't need to go to an old-timey library or page through buttery-smelling, soft-leather-swaddled paper books.

Which was exactly why she did those things with such frequency. She didn't have to. She chose to.

Also, it didn't hurt that Kellen Hockley came here

a lot, the only other student who did. He was her best friend, despite the fact that all her other friends and peers dismissed him. They were all obtuse imbeciles as far as she was concerned. Plus he was her very own, her secret.

On an afternoon after scheduled activities were done, Angela sat in a window box at the library, her headset on and a lecture pouring itself into her brain folds. A book of tales by Charles Perrault was spread across her uniform-sheathed thighs, and she stared at the pictures while fundamentals of photovoltaics filled her mind. With all those inputs pushing data at her simultaneously, it was no wonder he had to poke her shoulder to get her attention. The second time, it even worked.

"Ow!" Too loud. Yikes, library! But she did look up.

Kellen loomed over her with the late-afternoon sunlight pouring through the window and washing him gold. Angela caught her bottom lip between her teeth and used two hands to lift off the headset.

"So this is what the smart kids do." He gestured to her headset/book combo, somehow laughed without it sounding like he was making fun, and slumped down on the cushion opposite her. The reading nook had seemed cozy before. Now it didn't have nearly enough space. It was too close, too intimate. And Angela had zero problem with that.

"You mean studying?" She felt her face set itself into a haughty expression. Which, like multitasking, was bred into her. She couldn't do a thing to correct for these kinds of reactions, the ones he referred to as her *creepifying blue-bloodery*.

Energy radiated off him, like he had a zillion things

more important to do than hang around here on Earth. Like he had some cosmic adventure to light off on. Every cell in her body screamed, *Take me with you. Wherever you're going, I want to go, too.* Because clearly he didn't belong here. He wasn't like any other boy at the MIST, and all the students accepted that as fact. They laughed about him, actually, how odd he was. Only Angela thought his differentness was pretty fantastic, not something to tease or exclude him over.

He shrugged, tacking on a roguish half-smile. "I guess. But clever me for sussin' out yer secrets. Now I too can take over the world with mah deep, data-filled introspection, bwahaha."

Angela pressed her lips together to contain the burble of laughter. "Stop it. Your accent isn't really that horrid. Besides, you spend just as much time here as I do. Case in point, right now."

"Yeah, but I ain't hiding in a corner underneath a mountain of equipment. How can you even see this pretty place with all that shit piled on your head?"

She loved that he said the expletives out loud, the same ones that littered her private thoughts. *Shit shit shit.* She said it silently, three times, and it tasted scrumptious.

"I will have you know that I see lots of things," she said archly.

"Really? You seen Faiz's granny and her cat?"

That word, for instance. *Cat.* It had several meanings. Angela had looked it up on the idiomatic dictionary. It could mean sly, sneaky, or genitalia. Or a small furry almost-domesticated mammal popular as a luxury item earlier this century and throughout the last.

"I, ah, haven't." She thought longingly of the headset

next to her with its built-in cloud connection. She also wanted to look up the word *granny*. She didn't think he was saying something salacious about the assistant librarian, but one could never be certain with Kellen.

"Well, come on, then, princess. Have I got a treat for you." He popped up, and without asking for permission to touch her, no less invade her personal-space perimeter, he reached and grabbed both her hands, pulling her to her feet. The fairy book tumbled to the floor, its first-page folio splashing the synthetic carpet in gaudy color.

He let go of one of her hands but held on to the other as he led her through the stacks toward the curator's office, itself a tiny, dark hovel near the emergency stairs. Kellen pushed a book-filled cart aside, revealing a passage Angela had never noticed before. Come to think of it, she hadn't noticed much about this area of the library before. She'd been so focused on the books, the sum total of her interactions with the assistant librarian had been asking for location markers and firewall access passwords. Kellen had been the one to goad Faiz into showing them the rare volumes case, including that stunning blue-parchment Qur'an, the kind of object she knew she would always hold in her memory.

The passage was narrow and led to a room unlike the rest of the library. A hot little room with a slick tile floor and bare plaster walls. A refrigerator hummed in the corner, a small electric oven perched on a rickety table, and one red-and-gold-patterned curtain angled across an otherwise austere window. There were no cushions here, no details meant to evoke luxury or the *vieille noblesse* background most of the students would find comforting. A faint odor of cassia and cloves pervaded, like in the caravan market that sometimes set up outside the city walls.

A chair had been arranged against the wall by the window, drenched in sunlight, and in it slept an ancient woman in a dove-gray khimar. She snored. On her lap, beneath one frail boney hand, lay a cinnamon-and-white-striped beast.

There wasn't really another good word for it. Tiny, fragile, but with potential energy blazing off it like a coiled spring. Clearly this thing was a predator, even though it reclined in perfect stillness and didn't seem ready to rip anybody's throat out. Its green eyes locked on Kellen. An ear twitched. It opened its fang-filled mouth and emitted…a heart-meltingly adorable little mewl.

Epic adorable. Angela struggled to keep herself from answering with an *awwwww*.

"You pushy little thing," Kellen said. For a half second, Angela thought he was talking about her. Then he crossed to the old lady and the cat. "Of course I didn't bring you no food. Granny'd tan my hide if I fed you treats. She's got you on a strict diet—you don't run around so much anymore, and you are looking a bit tubby round the middle. We'd best be good."

Without opening her eyes, the elderly woman uttered something in a low, melodic voice. Angela tapped her cuff com, and it translated the woman's words out loud. "I'm not sleeping. I am only resting my eyes, child."

Kellen tossed a grin back at Angela. "Well, aren't you clever as a hoot owl. Why didn't I think of using a translation app before now?"

"Because you are an ignorant western infant." The computer voice coming from the tinny com speaker didn't have much inflection, but the woman was smiling. Still with her eyes closed, but her face was content. She didn't mean her words as an insult, and Angela suddenly realized that Kellen and this woman had talked before. Or, well, communicated. Even without speaking the same language and with no translation. Library magic? Or Kellen magic?

"Ah, Granny might talk trash, but she don't mind it when I come bother her," he said.

"The ignorant boy is right. I enjoy his company. He feeds my old Ghufran until she is fat and in love with him."

Angela kept her gaze locked on the cat, but the skin around her eyes felt hot, and she was pretty sure she was blushing. Not because of the L word. Or because he was looking right at her and grinning that sly, deep-dimpled grin, like he knew every thought in her head.

Definitely not because the granny lady punctuated the awkward moment with a low chuckle. "Girl, Ghufran especially likes to be rubbed between the ears." She moved her creaky hand, leaving the path clear to all that thick, strokable fur.

Angela hesitated. Sure, the cat looked impossibly soft. But also fangy and predatory and annoyed. And it was sitting on a person's lap. Definitely within a personal-space sphere. No touchy. These things were drilled into all kids whose mentors didn't want them to die an early viral, communicable, and hemorrhagic death.

Kellen apparently felt no compunction. Angela tried not to think what that said about his upbringing. He leaned in and rubbed Ghufran, not on her dome-shaped head but beneath the chin. The cat snuggled its head into his touch and purred so loud, the sound was almost mechanical.

"See?" he told Angela. "It's okay. She won't hurt you. She digs the attention."

It...did. Angela took her time, but her hand did eventually find its way to the cat's head. The fur felt amazing, like the best and most expensive synthwool, only made better by the warmth and purring vibration and...breathing. The cat was breathing. Angela wasn't sure why this fact should so surprise or affect her. Respiration was one of the eight basic functions of living organisms, a component part of the definition of life. But words in a lesson had nothing on literally putting her hand on such a creature, feeling it doing all that living right there, with her and beside her.

"Wow."

The com translated her one-word reaction, and Granny laughed. "She likes you, girl with no name."

"Apologies. My name is Angela Neko," she said, flushing at Granny's implicit rebuke. First impressions, oops. She should have introduced herself right off. A mistake like that could cost a corporation its contracts, a country its peace.

"You are a MIST student?"

"We both are." Angela, not wanting to stop her petting, indicated Kellen with a tip of her head.

"Where in the world makes a name like Neko?"

"She means are you another Texas redneck like me," he joked, but there was an edge, buried deep. Most of the time it seemed like he took all these slights in stride, but Angela fancied she could see through his humor and thick skin. Every barb imbedded. Deep. She wondered what that did to someone, day after day, in a kind of enforced solitude. Clearly, it made him seek connection with strangers, like the assistant librarian's granny. Maybe also with her?

"It's a portmanteau name," she said. "My parents are internationalists, Neeraf and Himiko. The phonemes Ne and Ko become Neko, since I, of course, am neither Bengali nor Japanese. I was born in Minneapolis."

"You were born to the MIST." That was exactly how people in her world said it: born to the MIST. Not born with talent or destined to be accepted to the academy but born to the MIST. As if the Mustaqbal Institute was mythological Avalon or something. As if she were magical or preordained just because of her DNA or her parents' ambitions.

Correction: her ambitions. She hadn't seen her parents in ten years. This was all on her now.

The old woman turned to Kellen. "But you were not." She clucked behind her teeth and then spoke several words beneath her breath. The com didn't register them, and they weren't in any language Angela knew.

Granny leaned her head against the chairback. "The two of you must come and care for Ghufran any time you wish. It is good for her to know human touch." She sighed heavily and closed her eyes. "Now, let me sleep."

"Yes, ma'am," Kellen said in a low voice. He gave the cat one last chuck under the chin, and after Angela stepped back obediently, he lifted Granny's hand and placed it back on the cat's flank. On the edge of sleep, the old woman smiled. She covered his hand with her other one and patted it warmly.

Quietly, as if their own feet were furred paws, the two of them crept from the librarians' break room. Angela couldn't in later years remember what they did with their free afternoon after that. Probably ranged all over the campus, reliving the games they played when they were younger. Or climbed up the giant air circulator in the plaza and talked about whatever they spent hours upon hours discussing back then.

What she would remember forever, though, was that the day after she met the cat, she kissed Kellen for the first time, behind the electrical engineering Snead stack.

One month later a tearful Faiz arrived at her dorm unit with a carrier in hand. His grandmother had passed peacefully, he said, but instructed him before she died to deliver her beloved pet to the girl with two names, Ne and Ko, and her ignorant cowboy.

These two events were meant to change Angela's life irrevocably. They were magic and the library. And she had defied them both.

CHAPTER 7

HE TOOK HER DOWN TO THE SKYWALK, SECOND-GUESSING himself the whole dadblamed time. Nothing was tidy about having Angela here in the Pentarc. Angela who now knew Chloe existed and could definitely do something about that if she chose to. Angela whose mech-clone assistant scared the shit out of her, probably for a very good reason, which he was going to get to the bottom of sooner rather than later.

Angela who he wanted very much to take back to her room, as she'd suggested. He happened to know that unit contained a giant bed and locks to keep the whole rest of the goddamned world out.

It wasn't like showing her his global critter network was going to unhook any of those complications. Was more likely to knot them up further. But he had said he'd help her get the information she wanted. Well, this was his best way of fulfilling that swear.

She chatted as she walked. About the scenery, about the on-again, off-again drought that plagued this area, about some of her buddies from school who she insisted had also been his. They hadn't. Nobody in the entire hoity, posh academy had welcomed the hick kid from Texas who didn't even know what a quinoa was. Nobody but her.

He knew she nattered on because it brought her comfort, probably because there were other things on her mind, and he knew he ought to halt her ramble, make her welcome, settle her. But damn, he'd missed her voice. Not the public voice but the one she'd saved for him, laden with expletives drifting downward from contralto.

The concrete subfloor on the transition from the skywalk to Northy got a little rough from time to time. Nobody had ever finished out this tower, and it was skeletal in most places, dusted with sand and weather-roughed. The view was downright gothic, approaching it like this in the middle of the air with nothing but twilit desert all around.

When Angela stubbed her slipper on a patch of uneven floor, Kellen caught her elbow without even thinking. "Watch your step here."

She paused, looked up at him. An expression fluttered over her face, but he couldn't lock it down. Fear? Exhaustion? "Where exactly are you taking me?"

"Right here. North Tower." Actually not far at all. His furry little general liked this floor best, with its combination of not a lot of people and that permaglass skywalk. She was something of a sun worshipper.

Angela's fine eyes narrowed. "For what purpose?"

"To show you where I get all my information and why the firewall doesn't matter."

She searched his face for a long time, then looked away and shook her head. "I'm sorry. It's so hard to trust. I just saw all those empty rooms, most with no windows and long drop-offs into nothing…"

Oh. Well, that stung. She thought he was bringing her here, to an abandoned, witness-free area, to *do her harm*. Jesus. That was not him. Not even a little bit. How come she didn't know him better than that?

His first reaction was anger, raising spikes, ready to tussle. Defensive reaction. Visceral. He took two deep breaths, forced himself to continue to the second reaction. Which was a deep soul-pulling wish she would trust him, completely and inherently, as maybe one time she had. Now she did not. That was the naked fact.

When his logic brain kicked in, he admitted anybody who survived an assassination attempt had better be cautious to the point of paranoia. What did she really know of him? That he associated with outlaws and murderers. That he still nursed a grudge.

And lord, what he was about to show her wasn't going to make him look any better. If anything, it would bolster her image of him as a loose cannon, dangerous and walking the teetery edge of bioethics.

"Listen, princess," he said, sliding his hand up from her elbow, along satin skin, "you don't have any specific call to trust me. It's been a long time since we…well, since you knew my mind. And lord knows we've both changed plenty. You probably look at me and don't even know who I am, what I've become. I can't ease your worry on that score, but I can promise you one thing: I will never hurt you. And if folk around me ever try, I will end them."

Her mouth opened, but she didn't speak.

He waited, still touching her arm, because he couldn't stop.

Until, of course, she yelped like a pinched piglet and leapt sideways.

● ● ●

"Holyfuckingwhatwasthat?" All one word and bleating from her mouth before she even landed. She hadn't considered the fact that she was perched on permaglass ten stories above the ground, nor that some of the sides at the North Tower end weren't walled in properly. They'd be sheetrock thin, fragile if hit with enough force. So not a great place, in general, to freak out.

But *something had touched her ankle*. Something soft and sleek and please-don't-be-a-rat. She hated rats. She'd been attached to an envoy in a backwater shithole once, and the rodentia there were…

And then the weirdest thing in the whole world happened. Her com warmed. Crackled. And *purred*.

What the…?

Before she could ask a more coherent question, Kellen dropped to one knee, his attention clearly snagged on something else.

Something small, furry, and definitely not a rat.

A cat.

His long fingers curled under a cinnamon-furred chin, and the tiny feline leaned happily into his stroke. "Little general, you shouldn't have snuck up on her like that. You like to made her jump clean off this building."

The cat growled in reply but didn't stop purring. Talented kitty. Multitasker. She knew this cat.

"How?" Angela breathed, unable to move her gaze from the animal. "You found another one?" Memory pricked her eyes, and she blinked rapidly.

"Nah," said Kellen, still looking down at the cat. Not meeting Angela's eyes at all. "Not another one. Same one."

"Yoink? How is this possible?" She was on her knees now too, her hands reaching out to the impossible softness. She could feel the vibration of the purring beneath her palms and also in her com. "She was an old girl already when we took her in. What did you estimate? Fifteen? Sixteen? And that was more than a decade ago."

"I took care of her," Kellen said. "Couldn't let anything happen to our girl."

Our girl. Oh, oh, Kellen.

Angela bit her bottom lip hard and stared at the cat, blinking fast till she thought she could live through that moment.

Something *had* happened to Yoink in the intervening years. The color and patterns were right, but other things were very, very wrong about this animal. For one thing, Yoink had horns.

Not horns like in old pics of longhorns or triceratops or anything. Little metal horns right in front of her ears. Humans used similar alterations for projecting user interface controls. But a cat couldn't possibly connect to the cloud. And even if it had the capability, what would it do there? Order stupid-expensive flash-frozen tuna?

"I know you," the com said, pushing a completely unfamiliar voice into Angela's brain. A sandpapery voice with a digital edge. Clear green eyes stared up at her solemnly. "My human. I want you to pet me. I also want to bite you."

A sob erupted before Angela could lock it down. It morphed into a semihysterical laugh on the end. "If she could have talked, that is exactly what she would have said."

The cat beneath her hand stiffened and moved its head away from Kellen's touch. Reluctantly, it seemed, and Angela couldn't fault it for that.

"I did say," the voice in Angela's com rasped. "More petting. Right now."

"I don't remember her being so cherry-colored on the head," said Angela. Yoink's wee face looked different, less wizened. Kind of wall-eyed. "What did you do to her?"

Kellen's hand retreated. He'd dipped his chin, and the brim of his hat concealed his face. "I should've said she's *mostly* our Yoink. When I went back to Texas, the place was a wreck, people fleeing the southeast like bugs when a light comes on. The vet program at A&M had been forced to evacuate, and I helped them get to a triage on down the state highway. They kind of took me in. What I learned at MIST, it was pretty easy to slot my work into theirs."

"You cloned her?"

"Yeah."

"And it looks like you modified her somehow as well."

"I did."

Angela didn't offer judgment. She just kept petting.

After a long while, Kellen went on. "I'll tell you something about cats: they ain't dumb. Structurally, their brains are a lot like human ones, gyrencephalic, lots of synapses, lots of electrical activity. They can be wired to function as a hub for strategic variables. Plus, they can listen and transmit like nobody's business, and their agility gets them into places robots can't go. The research was all there. I didn't think up the concept of enhanced feline intelligence all on my own, you know."

"You're referring to DARPA's spy kitty in the 1960s, which was a miserable failure by all accounts. But this is light-years ahead. We're talking actual language. That's not just a mini spy recorder attached to her tail. She's *talking* to me. On the com." Angela still wasn't sure what she thought about that.

"It's creeping you out, isn't it?" Kellen asked. His smile was hesitant but brash, like he feared her response but mocked himself for entertaining that fear.

Yoink rolled over and presented her belly. Angela rubbed it obediently. "Maybe," she said. "And you're right. It is also…kind of amazing. Not just the science and application potential but…this is my girl."

Ours. Our Yoink.

Kellen had stumbled over her previous name— Ghufran—and after a while had taken to calling her Yoink. She'd been their responsibility. Their girl. The three of them, for that bright slice of time, had been a family. Angela's very first.

"Yeah. She is," he said.

His gaze was a weight on her skin, and Angela met his eyes. Something warm and dear washed through her, half convincing her he wasn't talking about the cat at all.

But then he looked away and went on, "She's also my general. You mentioned the DARPA spy cat, but truth is, I have tech-altered critters all over the world, all successfully reintegrated into their habitats, all transmitting data to Yoink here. Heron noticed a data hole over Guadalajara just before you left the area, so I dispatched some spies there to check things out. Got a data cache in just a few minutes ago."

Her hand paused its petting. "What's in the cache?"

"Mostly pics, some air quality assessment, possibly ambient bio markers. I haven't had a lot of time to analyze it, but once it's done decompressing and decoding, I can copy you on the whole batch. You can take a look, too."

Angela drew her thumb over one of the tiny metal horns. Yoink pushed nose-first into her hand, directing the rub more to her liking. "Is it the kind of information that can tell me who bombed my hotel?"

"I sure as shit hope so."

"Well, let's decode this data cache," she said.

"Can we wait till after supper? 'Cause Fan will have my ass if I'm late to one of her family sit-downs."

Angela shot him a quizzical look. "Family? Did your mom…"

"Fan and Adele and Garrett and Heron and Chloe and even that scamp Mari…they're my family now. Like I said: lots of things have changed. Not just for me, either. You changed, too."

He held an expectant look on his face. Or maybe disappointed? Angry? Angela wished she could hook him up to a psych-emitter right now and sort out his feelings. He clearly wasn't thrilled she was here, which made no sense.

And it hurt besides. Hurt a lot. She had missed him so damned much.

"I sacrificed a lot," she said carefully.

He made a sound that was really close to a snort. "Yeah, you sure've been leading the life of sacrifice, international superstar, hitched to…" He batted air with the back of his hand and then pinched his nose at the bridge. Closed his eyes. Like he'd just confessed a dirty secret.

And he kind of had.

Had Kellen been jealous of Daniel all these years? That realization should feel so much worse than it did. Instead, a silly, self-satisfied grin tugged on her face, but she suppressed it, tucked the delight away so she could roll it around in her mind later.

"I told you my marriage wasn't really a marriage. It was more of a business arrangement," she said.

He opened his eyes and glared at her, but not with the understanding she sought. His gaze sparked with fury. "That makes it so much worse, princess."

Deep inside her chest, she flinched, though probably no one would be able to tell. She was so very good at hiding visceral reactions, at smoothing over them and pretending a peace she'd never felt.

"What, it would be easier to believe I was madly in love with Daniel and living in perpetual bliss all those years? Come on." She pushed a lighter note into her voice, trying to nudge the conversation away from dangerous territory.

Kellen's forehead creased, and she couldn't read the look in his eyes. It wasn't light, though. Kind of the opposite. "To believe you were happy?" he said. "Yeah, that would make a lot of things worth it for me. Once upon a time, I put a lot of effort into seeing you happy. It'd be a damn shame if all that work went to shit the minute you sent me away."

Not right then. Not *that* minute. Though maybe the one just after.

"Look," he said, "do we really have to work through all this right now? We've grown into different people, and it's going to take some time before you and I know each other again, if we even decide we want to."

Not really as long as you think. He'd gone to extraordinary lengths to save Yoink, and he'd kept their cat, their family, right here at his side for all these years. So he was still the caretaker. Still her hero.

Still *her* Kellen, whether he ultimately decided he wanted to be or not.

She stood and clicked her tongue against the back of her teeth. Yoink perked her ears and shot Angela a feed-me-or-else glare. When Angela turned and followed Kellen back down the skywalk and into the finished-out south spire, Yoink padded along at her heels expectantly.

Good kitty. Best.

●   ●   ●

Angela enjoyed physical solitude. Life was best endured from the outside looking in, watching the patterns of states and individuals resolve, tweaking the flow of events but staying far, far away from the filth of human connection. *Alone is safe* had been her personal mantra for several years now, ever since she'd left her husband behind in LA. As it turned out, Kellen and his happy band of killers lived in the inverse of solitude, as unalone as it was possible for a human to be. Which made what happened when she stepped off the elevator at the mezzanine level so…whoa.

Apparently Adele, the chain-smoking, muumuu-wearing wife of Fanaida, did not, as a matter of course, gallivant all over the globe with her partner. Instead she spent most of her time right here, organizing work parties on the hydroponics levels and dance parties after dark, watching way too many game shows, and cooking for small armies.

While Angela had been chatting Kellen up for information, the older woman had been down here at the food court, specifically in the shiny industrial kitchen of Charlie's Fine Tortilla (still displaying a tarnished and perky "Coming soon!" sign), cooking and then serving vats and vats of amazing-smelling foodstuffs to the three-hundred-odd folks who called the Pentarc home.

Other meals, Kellen had told Angela on the ride down, were made of ration patties like the one she'd scarfed earlier, but for one sliver of each day, every human person in the structure was invited—requested? Instructed? How authoritarian did the authority get around here?—to come down to the food court and dine *en famille*.

Which meant a hot press of bodies gathered around plastic picnic-style tables, all bumping up against each other and air-horning a cacophony of languages. Dozens, maybe, with the sub-hum of com translators making conversation only minimally possible. All those people moved, smelled, radiated heat. Their organic odor mingled with roast corn, garlic, and way too much cumin.

Walking into such a stew held all the charm of wading through living, breathing Ebola. Angela halted two steps from the elevator, watching the writhing, laughing, chattering, slurping, burping mass of humanity. It was…terrifying.

"I thought you said this was a family dinner," she whispered.

Kellen had come off the elevator at her side and stood close, almost protectively. It still took a minor miracle for him to hear her over the din. "It is. The fam's back over near that old kebap storefront. See there? Sort of yellow-and-green sign?"

He pointed to a table off to the right. Angela recognized Heron and Mari talking to a third person, whose back was to Angela. She didn't see mech-Daniel anywhere, but that wasn't cause for alarm. He had a task and was almost certainly back in their unit diligently at work.

"Who are all the rest of these people?" Angela asked. If she looked at them, actually looked at the jumble of organisms again, she worried she might be sick. Or run away. So many. Too many. The table with places reserved for Kellen and her seemed acres away.

"Ain't you an elected representative of the people? Behold"—Kellen swept one arm in an expansive, dramatic gesture—"the people. Isn't that what you politicos do for a living, press flesh and kiss babies?"

"God no." She shuddered. "Bioagents and lone-wolf attacks have pretty much put an end to all that. We broadcast now and live past forty." Okay, only three public figures had contracted fatal diseases during mass outbreaks of the past few decades, but still. Angela had always approved of the segregation of the ruling class. *Alone is safe.*

Instinct told her to run away, hide from the morass of organic material in this place. Rebuild her walls. But honestly, was that even possible? Those walls had come down, literally right on top of her at the Hotel Riu. She couldn't return to her bubble of protection, her safe life of physical solitude.

No more hedging. No more hiding.

A slightly built old man, wearing a ratty printed robe with an electric cord for a belt, turned to peer at the new arrivals. He stopped talking midword, focusing all his attention on Angela. On second glance, he wasn't a little old man at all. He was a kid, maybe fourteen, just skinny and with the posture of someone who'd been kicked. Slowly, the rest of his table fell silent and turned as well.

Their gazes pricked Angela, as if she'd been sitting too long and her whole body had gone numb and now was alight in agony as feeling swooshed back in.

The teenager hung back, but a whisper arced around their wide table. Another refugee rose. He was older, an adult or close to it, wearing a cheap robe printed from one of the patterns Angela recognized from the mostly failed Clothe the World campaign of a few years back. He approached the elevator.

Her body cringed away instinctively, but Angela had spent way too much time training for the psych-emitter to let something as mundane as instinct control her. She bloomed a soft smile over her face, a practiced smile and one that she knew also fired specific neurological activity that would be interpreted as acceptance and compassion. She didn't see any receivers for her psych-emitter, but brain training for its use had taught her how to manipulate her own emotions, and she had gotten damned good at it. She calmed.

The young man wasn't wearing a cuff com and certainly didn't look like he had the technological means of translating. As it turned out, he didn't need one.

"Senator Neko," he said in perfect English with a sweet rub of Southern on it. "I saw you on vid. It sure is a comfort, you coming by. They told us when they brought us here that we were being rescued, right before that last cluster of storms blew into Mobile. I didn't think the government was doing the rescuing, though. You gotta forgive me for thinking y'all were just ignoring us."

This Atlantic hurricane season had been typically brutal. Angela vaguely recalled a closed-door congressional committee discussion regarding mandatory evacuations in early June. If she remembered correctly, the interior minister had swept in and nixed the idea out of hand, before anybody could vote on it. Preemptive evacuation was ludicrous, he'd said. It would break the economy. In retrospect, however, the idea had been a good one. More than ten thousand people had perished on the Gulf Coast this summer. Hundreds of thousands remained displaced, swelling the temporary-housing cities that had sprung up all over the country. All over the world.

"It is a pleasure to meet you," Angela said. She put her hand out and suffocated the urge to recoil when the young man took it and shook it excitedly. She could almost feel the biocontaminants attaching themselves to her skin. Burrowing. She breathed. "Are you getting enough food, settling in?"

"Oh yeah, they're treating us like kings, but you know how it is. We all just wanna go home."

"Surely you have seen the vids," she said before she could catch herself. Mobile Bay wasn't going to be a safe place for humans to live near for a long, long time. For this man and his family, there would be no going home.

One side of his mouth pinched up, and he shrugged.

"Can't hide out here forever, I guess, but we do appreciate the help in the short term."

Angela wasn't sure what to say. He was deliberately ignoring reality, pretending that his story was going to have a happy ending, home and the picket fence and everything back the way it was. But life didn't work that way. The world didn't work that way. She couldn't speak that truth, though. She couldn't tarnish that halo of trust he seemed to be living under. Instead she smiled, asked his name, met his family, let them touch her.

They all knew Kellen, of course, and he was so easy in their company. As she made her way through the room, heading in a general path toward the buffet line and then her table, she met lots more refugees, learning all their names and stories. Suraya, Benito, Cass, Isit, Yanaghando, a giant named Viktor, an infant whose mother insisted would choose his own name someday. They approached her haltingly, weighted down by manners and gratitude and awe. Some assumed that she was a guest. All assumed that she was here on a mission of benevolence or at least a photo op.

Angela could have told them the truth, that she hadn't come here at the behest of her government. That in fact, as far as she knew, her government had no idea these people had survived the disasters they'd fled. But she sensed that truth would be crueler than the lie at this point.

So she met them. Touched them. Endured them. By the time she got to her table—her plate piled with beans, tortillas, and sliced tomatoes—and sank to the plastic bench, she could no longer smell the body odor. Or if she could, it was just part of the place now, part of the moment.

It wasn't even a terrible moment. And it felt like...

fucking hell yeah, she'd just done that. Skinny-dipped in acid and stayed unburnt.

She waited for Kellen to point out how well she'd done, to say how proud he was of her. But he didn't, and she thought herself foolish for expecting a pat on the back every time she accomplished something. God. Her handlers had trained her well, hadn't they?

"Bean tacos, best stuff ever," Kellen said, sliding into the seat beside her. Real beans and tortillas, no matter how much spice Adele had poured on them, were a veritable feast for anyone not of the elite class. "How you taking to all this, Miss Mari?"

Across the table, Mari Vallejo wiped some red juice from the side of her mouth and shrugged. "You mean the food, the place, or the comp'ny?"

Goodness. Her accent was almost as horrible as Kellen's.

"All the above, and the rest of it. You been through something of a wringer lately. You doin' okay?"

He'd always been like this, concerned and caring and saying just the right thing. However, right now the look he directed across the table at the other woman stabbed Angela with a tiny, bright-green sword. Jealousy? It wasn't a worthy reaction or one Angela was anywhere near confessing. But it lay there, sharp-edged and pokey, definitely not dulled by the fact that Mari Vallejo was tall and pretty and apparently had won the grand prize of boobdom, which her shred of a blouse did little to hide.

Angela focused on her taco. Once she got into it, it tasted kind of heavenly. All fresh ingredients, no protein flakes or fillers. Fine food, shabby setting.

Mari answered Kellen's query with a minxy grin that

dug trench-deep dimples in her cheeks. "Heron's okay. I'm okay. Got no complaints. I'm even getting sciency these last couple days. We've been testing my theory that this clone-brain-slice technological zombification that folk did to my body has now made me essentially unbreakable. It's been…intense."

"Now, you know I can't approve of experiments that put you in danger," Kellen admonished.

Mari laughed, loud and clangy and infectious. "If you have to worry over somebody, it should probably be Heron. Pretty much all our experiments so far have involved the two of us and nekkid."

Heron didn't even twitch. He raised one imperious eyebrow, swallowed a forkful of beans, and said, "A rigorous research environment suits her."

"I tell you what would suit me more, though," Mari said. "And that's getting a stab at one of these rescue missions you folks go on. Garrett here"—she indicated the quiet young man who had been facing away from the elevators when Angela arrived and who seemed overly focused on his dinner—"has been telling me all about 'em, and they totally sound like my kind of crazy. I know my way around a fight, might be of some use. Plus, it sure would be nice to wreak my special brand of havoc for the good guys' side for once." She flicked a glance at Angela when she said this, but her gaze shifted away and down too fast for Angela to respond.

Was she still feeling guilty about killing Daniel? How strange that his murderer would mourn the man more than his wife did. Not that Angela wanted to explain.

"Listen to Garrett's tales all you want, querida,"

Heron said, "but we are grounded for a while until I can figure out what is going on with those data holes."

"You found more?" Kellen asked, totally serious.

Heron nodded.

"The data hole like you mentioned over Guadalajara?" Angela asked.

"Yep," said Kellen. "Big, black-ICE blobs of nuthin'."

"On satellites?"

"On everything. All data feeds," Mari said. "Can't even get voice-com transmissions in or out. Heron can break through the ICE, because he's a god like that, but he's got to find it first. Might also help to know who keeps making the damn things, how they're doing it, and why."

"Texas is the obvious culprit," Heron said. "That's where we found the first anomaly."

"Vallejo, that asshole," Kellen agreed. "No offense, Miss Mari."

"None taken. My daddy's crooked as a dog's hind leg, and he must indeed have been somewhere under that ICE, seeing's he hijacked poor Nathan's brain up there on Enchanted Rock. Y'all did say signals can't get in or out of those blocks. Stands to reason he was right there, inside the bubble, being his usual dastardly self."

Angela quietly rolled some more beans into a tortilla and nibbled on the end. There was something in what Mari just said, something that clanged her clue bell. But she couldn't figure out exactly what.

The quiet guy, Garrett, looked up from his plate. Angela did a double take. He was startlingly good-looking. Beautiful, even. Fine-planed face, inky, unkempt hair, unsettlingly intense amber-colored eyes.

She could imagine him slinking down a runway in Grigori Hahn couture. If, you know, he could manage to wash some of those grease stains off his hands.

"It could be the Black Knight," he said.

"The what-what?" asked Mari.

Heron and Kellen both groaned.

"Whatever is causing these data holes, it almost certainly is not an ancient alien satellite," said Heron dryly.

"'Specially not one more likely to be a blanket that fell off the old International Space Station," added Kellen.

Garrett's dark eyebrows swooped down like a predator bird's wings. "Blanket. Exactly. A satellite, especially one launched with malicious intent, could seed dampers in the upper atmosphere, basically erecting a gigantic data *blanket*. Boom, there's your data hole."

Heron smiled, but this particular smile was neither sarcastic nor scary as hell. It was almost, well, warm. Warm looked wrong on him. "You have a point, G. I could certainly create a damper field such as you describe with foglets. Maybe we should have the queen sweep one of these data holes for the presence of atmospheric nanites. Not a bad theory."

"Thanks." Under such praise, Garrett warmed to the topic. "And as to who and why, I know you don't want to hear that the Green aliens are setting up massive planetary weapons to deter the imminent approach of Nibiru and the Grays—"

More groaning, but softer this time, and with some chuckles salted in.

"—so I'll just skip that theory and go right to the why. Anybody, not just aliens, wanting to move large-scale machinery or matériel into a certain location wouldn't want hobbyist satellite hounds documenting their every move."

"True that." Mari seemed completely on board.

A lot of the concepts were flying straight over Angela's head, but the enthusiasm of these people was contagious. She'd found herself nodding more than once during Garrett's half-breathless spiel, but that clangy something was vibrating the back of her brain. A few seconds later it bloomed into a full-on eureka.

"Wait a minute," she broke in. "You said there was a data hole over Guadalajara when I was there, right? And that no data could get in or out? Well, I was able to get a voice-com transmission out."

"Before the attack or after?"

"After." Cement dust, bomb breath. Just thinking of her experience made her shoulder ache and terror claw her throat. She swallowed. "Mech-Daniel contacted the government to let them know I was still alive. He used a backdoor relay I almost certainly should not be mentioning to people without the appropriate security clearance."

"Whoa, then, best quiet fast, 'cause we sure don't have—" Mari started.

But Kellen interrupted. "I think that's her point." He met Angela's gaze, and something deep and raw inside her body hummed to life. "You're taking a big risk, laying out that info to folk like us, gal."

"You all took the risk first, when you invited me here, and then another when you told me about Chloe." She held his gaze. "I trust you."

You know me. Let me in. Please.

The smile he reflected—secret, intimate, as if they were the only two people in this room full of hundreds—warmed her like dawn after midwinter. "You about done eatin'?"

She nodded.

Without breaking their locked gazes, Kellen addressed the rest of the people at the table: "I will wish you fine folks a good night. Now you'll have to excuse us. I'm gonna take this woman up to her bedroom."

●   ●   ●

He didn't mean it the way it'd sounded. Or not much. Aw, fuck it. Yeah, he would dearly love to take Angela up to a bedroom, lock the door, and spend the next forever or so showing her how much he wanted her. He could admit to himself, in private, that he was just so barbarian at the core.

But reality necessitated a different course of action. Reality needed him to be civilized.

He'd just gotten a vibration on his wrist cuff: the blip board was all decoded and decompressed and ready for viewing. He was itching to get eyes on that data, figure out what his critter spies had been able to document.

Somebody had tried to kill Angela, and he could barely contain a powerful need for payback.

Also, to be fair, he wouldn't mind getting some more private time with her. Safe place, cozy place. Maybe they could continue to talk out some of the issues that squirmed between them, catch up on all those years they'd lost.

He and Angela passed the kitchen, and Yoink—by her cloying aroma, no doubt coming off a sweet-pickle binge courtesy of Adele, the old softy—fell into step with them.

And then so did Angela's mech-clone husband. It had been waiting for her just outside the food court.

Well, this wasn't the sort of evening Kellen had in mind. Dangit. But he was a big boy, right? He could handle it. They could still inspect the data, just without cuddles and soft talk. And with all their clothes on. Might be better that way anyhow. Safer. For him.

He calmly led their way-too-populated party to the glass-walled elevator and then up to her floor, pointing out random shit as they passed it. Pentarc had a lot to see, though most of it didn't work and never had. He had a need of the distraction, and playing tour guide in a sense relieved some of his tension.

Yoink, apparently sensing something on the air, sat herself in the middle of the elevator carriage and proceeded to lick her own ass, just to taunt him. Sweet evil, that cat.

At floor seven, the doors dinged and glided open. The feline and the mech preceded them into the corridor. Kellen was just about to follow when a bare hand snaked out and pressed the button for eight. The doors closed before he could so much as twitch.

Angela pressed the emergency stop, and their carriage paused. It was glass on the rear, but this far up, there wasn't anything to see other than a painted elevator shaft. They were alone.

And she stood right in front of him, burning a look upward. Holy fuck, that look.

"What you—"

She put two hands on his chest and pushed him against the elevator wall. Faster than a duck on a june bug, one of those hands was up, past his collar, behind his head, pulling him down. Her mouth found his, hot and needy and not asking.

He was stunned for the first half second, surprised enough that she got the jump on him, but he couldn't let her win. Not without giving a little of his own back.

She was a little thing—he had forgotten how slight—and when his arms went around her and he cradled her ass, it was the easiest thing to lift her. Her legs came up, wrapping around his waist. Something in her tidy wool skirt tore, and she oomphed a breath against his teeth when he turned their bodies, still locked together, and pushed her back up against the elevator wall.

Better. The angle. She slotted snug against him, mouth to mouth, heartbeat to wild heartbeat. Her hands clamped the back of his head, crushing him into her kiss. Oh yeah, this was the Angela he knew, the girl *only* he knew. And he had missed this—had missed her—so fucking much.

Her teeth skidded against his, sharp and bright. He nibbled, drawing salt from her lip, and she groaned into his mouth. That count for consent? He thought it might, or maybe the fact that she'd all but attacked him in an elevator. Still, the gentleman in him needed to be sure.

"We gonna do this right here, then?" he rasped.

"At least once," she breathed against his jaw. "Please tell me those jeans aren't held together with a goddamn button fly."

"Press seam," he said.

"Thank all the made-up gods." Her magic fingers found the seam and undid it, but the movement stole some of her concentration. Angela, the great multitasker, apparently couldn't undress a man and pour kisses down his throat at the same time. Kellen reared his head back and watched her.

Wild thing, his gal. He remembered so many times they'd been at this business, and always, always, it had been the death of him. A thousand deaths, a million surrenders. He'd never minded. He'd have given her anything, willingly, as often as she wanted.

But the man she was taking down that road right now wasn't her nineteen-year-old plaything. And he didn't have a hankering to play the role for her again. He'd fought to become his own person.

"Think we might pause here for a second, princess?"

She'd made quick work of his pants, and she had him out, clasped in her hot little fist. He couldn't even process what that felt like. Heaven was too small a word.

"Angela." Didn't sound like his own voice, but he had things that needed saying.

She looked up, neither moving nor removing her hand. His arms were holding her up against the wall, and he couldn't very well shift weight without dropping her unceremoniously on the floor. There was no way to make space between them, not at this point. Heat roiled in the interstice between their bodies. She never had liked the feel of knickers on her nethers.

"What?" Confusion broke through the naked desire on her face.

"That emergency call button only pauses us for three minutes," he said, trying so hard to be gentle about this.

Her grin got sly instead. "You clearly have no idea how ready I am." She squeezed, and his throat compressed in synch. "Why are we wasting all this time chitchatting?"

"Maybe what we need, actually, is a bit *more*

chitchat. And a bit *less* fucking." He shifted his weight, lowering her slightly, like he was about to disconnect them. She flicked the pad of her thumb over the head of his cock, and he damn near came on her hand. Shitfuckgoddamn. But he inhaled, slammed his eyes shut, and worked the hell through it. Took a few seconds, but he got steady.

Disbelief froze her mouth into an *O*, then she snapped, "Impossible to do less of a thing you aren't doing. Or not yet doing. Who are you, and what have you done with my Kellen?"

"That's kind of what I've been telling you, sweetheart. I ain't that guy." *You sent him away, or did you forget?* He'd been disposable. Fuck-boy. Convenient. Nothing more than a rung for her pretty foot on her epic climb to the top. It did occur to him that he was being cruel, but goddamn it, so had she been. "You want my dick in your drawers and my mouth on your sweet spot, princess, I will require some wooing."

"I distinctly heard you tell all those people at the table—the people you call *family*—that you were taking me to bed." She stroked. Jesus. "I believe this is what you would call lying like a rug."

"I said I was takin' you to your bedroom." Temptation shaved pieces off his will.

"That's exactly what you said, and your intentions could not have been clearer," Angela argued, getting her debate on.

"Well, but after that, Yoink and your husband decided to come along to watch. Gotta say that damped my want-to some."

She huffed a breath against his throat. "Look. I

kicked them into the corridor. Pressed the emergency stop. Problem solved."

"It ain't that easy."

"Yes, it is."

"*I* ain't that easy."

She tested her tongue against her upper lip then drew it back inside. "Are you saying you don't want me?"

No, you insufferable woman. I will want you as long as there's breath in this body, blood in these veins. And then I will love you longer still. "I'm saying we need to slow this down. Let me get to know you again. You said you wanted time. Well, let's take some."

"I could slide down your body right now, lick you into my mouth, and make you come."

And every cell in his body knew what that would be like. "Could you? Could you really do that to me, sweetheart?"

She went downright pale. He'd hit a raw nerve, apparently. Not the possibility that she wasn't alluring enough but the threat that if she kept on, she'd hurt him, maybe break him. She hadn't worried about such nuances, back when. The Angela in his arms right now was different, older. Kinder.

Shit, he might have just fallen *more* in love with her. Not a good thing.

Her ankles unhooked themselves, and her legs slid down the outsides of his thighs. She tucked him back into his jeans, resealed the seam. He eased her down the wall until her feet touched the floor. When he stepped back, still breathing too hard, still aching until he wanted to howl, he watched her smooth her skirt, check her cuffs. She pressed a palm to one cheek. Testing for blushes?

What had he just done? What had she? His mind was spinning too fast, out of control, knocking against the edges of his heart, and every collision hurt like hell.

This. This was why he hadn't wanted her to come here. Not because of a grudge or bad memories. Not because he didn't want her safe. Sure as hell not because he didn't want her.

But rather because he so very much…did.

CHAPTER
8

THAT WAS THE LAST TIME SHE WAS GOING TO LET HERSELF BE alone with him. Swears. She had some discipline, damn it. She could control herself. Most of all, she could control how others saw her. She was a master of that bullshittery. In the days that followed the incident in the elevator, she polished her persona till it fucking shone.

Data from Kellen's biomechanical critter spies—most of which, she was disgusted to learn, were in fact rats—showed a singular lack of anything interesting. The air quality in the ruined Riu was pretty good. No radiation or odd chemical profiles. Somebody vaguely government-like was attempting to clean up the mess of the building site, but in a haphazard and desultory sort of way. At first she was pissed about that—shouldn't they be trying to get in there and look for survivors?

But then mech-Daniel got firewall clearance for her gossip feeds—finally—and she understood why. Nobody had survived. That was the official word, parroted by news services and professional gossips alike. Comprehensive destruction, including the unconfirmed but almost certain death of Continental Senator Angela Neko and her husband, Daniel Neko, the classic film and emote-vid star.

On the steps of the Colina Capitolina, the new unified-state house in Denver, somebody had set up a shrine of ratty machine-printed teddy bears and plastic roses. Disaster-porn channels flooded with gruesome retrieval of body parts, some of which, presumably, were meant to be hers.

For the first couple of days, she expected Zeke to issue a statement denying the rumors. But he didn't. She also sort of expected him to respond to her own communiqués. Again, silence. True, he was at the ass end of a very contentious election, but it wasn't like he couldn't spare five fucking seconds to message her. If he was spinning her fake death story to score votes, she was all right with that. She was even willing to help plan the postparty, when, after the victory speeches, a rescue was staged to miraculously "find" her, maybe trapped in the hotel garbage chute and surviving on leftover sugar skulls from Dia de los Muertos.

Okay, making up the stories was a lot of fun, but it didn't resolve the fact that she was completely cut off now from everything familiar. On first blush, that meant nobody was calling her for a statement, nobody was trying to get her to agree to meat-meets or other inconvenient bullshittery. But also, it meant she couldn't access about 80 percent of her life.

Deceased senators had no clearance. She tried to log on to her remote-vote service, but her account no longer existed. The Vatican nuncio she was supposed to have met with this week instead mass-messaged a public prayer for her immortal soul. It was viral-mapped seventy-three thousand times on three separate social media platforms.

She no longer existed.

She had to break it to herself—Zeke had cut her loose. She didn't know why he'd done it, and it annoyed the ever-living fuck out of her, but strangely, it didn't hurt. Not on a gut-emotion level. It just seemed like what people did in her life: they came in, told her what to do, and then left. Sometimes the telling hurt like hell, but the leaving rarely did.

Except when Kellen did it. She wondered if he realized he was the only person on the planet currently capable of hurting her. She wondered if he'd think that was an honor or a burden.

He hadn't been alone in a room with her since that elevator thing, so she couldn't ask, play the getting-to-know-you game he seemed to want.

He met with her at least once a day, always in the presence of others, when his reports for all his freaky bio-noodled animals came in. Sometimes they plugged the vid bits into a VR rig, so she could get her own eyes on the ruin. She'd run through the bombed-out hotel in rat POV so many times, she almost—*almost*—didn't shudder every time she saw that room, that doorway, the fallen ceiling.

He'd located bits of the smushed bomb. They didn't look like bomb parts to Angela. They looked more like twisty metal toothpicks, but if he said they were weaponized toothpicks, she figured she might as well believe him. He knew more about this killing business anyhow.

Mari came in a few times and laid some of her

explosives expertise over the evidence. She thought it was a GBU-12, whatever the hell that was, but honestly, one mangled bit of wreckage looked like any other mangled bit of wreckage to Angela. Bombs typically didn't have trite from-sender messages scrawled on them. She was pretty sure none of these spy-data caches were going to supply the breakthrough she coveted.

Maybe she just didn't want it enough. Maybe she wanted to keep not knowing, to keep fearing. So she could stay. So she didn't have to try again—or fail again—to take control of anything.

But she couldn't tell Kellen that. It was manipulative and me-thinking and just generally shitty. He, as an opposite, was so solemn, so careful to lay out all these facts for her, like prizes. Or offerings. He kept his distance, no touching, and refrained from mentioning anything remotely related to either elevators or penises. He didn't meet her eyes, he didn't smile, and he didn't attend Adele's family dinners, and her heart broke into a zillion guilty pieces every time she did catch a glimpse of him. She imagined scooping up those component bits, gluing them back together with apologies, and offering the resultant ugly craft project as proof that she wasn't a monster.

Instead she stayed across the room from him, watching and waiting and regretting.

Zeke won reelection. He cried affectingly during his victory speech, dabbing with a hanky like a posh Victorian duke, live-emoting the whole thing, and lying like a lying thing that lies. Days then weeks passed, and he still didn't message her, despite the fact that she'd left signposts out there in the cloud, "I'm still here; message me" notices. Well, fuck him.

But even that bravado felt hollow, wasted on her lack of audience.

Her plan had been to gather evidence. Well, she'd gathered, but instead of an enemy and a clear target going forward, she had…nothing. In terms of power, she was naked. She had no idea what her next step should be, and that terrified the shit out of her.

The only dollop of peace in this whole situation tangle was Yoink. True, gears clicked somewhere in her hairy little body when she stretched, and having her rub those metal horns under an armpit at three in the morning could be startling, but there was also something marvelously peaceful about feline companionship. Angela had forgotten. She had forgotten how easy it was to get lost just watching her girl sleep or lick a paw and then rub that same paw behind her ear, cleaning herself in the daintiest way. She'd forgotten how comforting it was to know that when she woke up, somebody was there waiting for her to open her eyes. Even if it was just so Yoink could have her breakfast (right the hell now), she had a thing, a reason to hoist herself out of bed.

Such reasons, for her, were kind of in short supply.

Angela followed Yoink across the skywalk almost every day into Northy. Sometimes the two of them would go exploring, skipping gaps in wounded staircases or prodding unfinished walls until they revealed their unintentional secret passages. It reminded her of the years she'd spent exploring Mustaqbal.

With Kellen.

Damn it, everything did always circle back to him.

Sometimes they'd sit and do nothing at all, Angela and the cat. Except for her, doing nothing took an absurd amount of effort. Thinking hurt. See, the thing that the experts never say about abnormally smart kids, those with eidetic memories and other unique methods of cross-hemisphere neural activity, is that the ability to remember every page of every book ever read, every photo of every campaign donor, every cruel word delivered like a knife in anger, was more torture than talent. What she experienced could never be annulled. Angela couldn't claim ignorance. She knew what she'd done.

But she also had a cheat when it came to Kellen, because he remembered all those things, too. So as the weather turned cool and late autumn blew in over the mountains and the two of them maintained their let's-play-chicken staring contest from different ends of any given room, Angela started work on a project. It didn't take much begging to get what she needed. She had no doubt Kellen would understand the meaning when she was done. She would make him understand, damn it. She only hoped he'd see it as an apology as well. Because that's what it was.

●　　●　　●

"Oh, hey. I am flattered to be found more important than a whiny camelid," Heron said when Kellen ducked into the Vault, the Pentarc's subterranean control room. His voice was dryer than a popcorn fart, and it chafed. "But it is strange to see you someplace other than the barn."

"And a good fucking morning to you, too," Kellen said. True, he'd spent the better part of the last several weeks tending his critters. He'd installed trackers and heavy-duty immunizations in Azul. He'd…been busy. Too busy to spend alone-time with Angela.

Who was, at this moment in Northy with Yoink on her lap. Not that he was paying attention to these things. Much. Just figured physical space might help the both of them right now. He wasn't sure how spending a lot of time apart was going to advance their getting-to-know-you-again progress bar, but, you know, baby steps.

Heron smiled at his friend's casual obscenity, but it wasn't an easy smile. Looked like it took some effort to stretch that mouth. "You have just interrupted my very scintillating review of administrative minutiae. Food purchases to supplement the biodomes. Price comparisons for having EMP shielding installed on Fanaida's dragon. Market fluctuations in Asia that might or might not indicate a political tremor."

"Well, that's what you get for signing on to this crazy, adventurous life of crime." Kellen slung his long body onto a bench near the armory door. "Where's Mari?"

"Hmm." His lack of answer almost explained the pained not-smile.

"Trouble in paradise?"

"Maybe." Heron turned his chair so he could face Kellen. He pushed fingertips into his eye sockets in a way that must have hurt. Or would hurt a human with normal pain tolerances. "You warned me she might not appreciate a less hair-raising lifestyle. She's used to spontaneity and mobility and, let's face it, danger. Pentarc is…not that."

Unsaid was that he personally was no longer capable of following Mari all over from one highly illegal adventure to the next. His ultimate solution both to that nanovirus back in October and to taking care of his partner over vast distances had been to plug into the cloud, lose himself in it. Now he couldn't back out gracefully. In physical terms, he couldn't back out at all. His mind was dispersed in the information network and couldn't be crammed back into something as limited as one human brain. He had to stay put someplace with a node, else his consciousness could fracture.

"Maybe you just have to let her light off on her own sometimes, man. She's a boomerang. She'll come back."

"I know."

"But it's not the separation bothering you. It's not even the slight possibility she'll disappear."

"You know my reach is vast," Heron said, a snip of haughty investing his voice. "She cannot run so far that I couldn't find her."

"Missing my point," Kellen said, keeping his voice gentle, as if he were luring a timorous rabbit to his hand. "You want to go with. Not because you don't trust her and not because you don't think she's capable on her own. You wanna orbit that gal because gravity."

"Orbit is an odd word choice here, probably because this has nothing to do with gravity."

"No, it does. Hear me out. Stars are hot, right, steaming up the universe, radiating like all get-out, just trying to get somebody to look at them. And then another star drifts by, and our first eager little gas ball catches it, starts up this vast cosmic dance, and boom, they form a binary. Every major force in the universe is keeping them together at this point. It's the inverse of Romeo and Juliet. Those two stars, they belong together, probably are even spiraling into each other, doomed to a catastrophic, immolative end." He caromed his hands together until they smacked into each other. Bam. "But what happens when they realize this horrible destiny in store for them, when one star tries to give the other space, for her own good?"

"It's impossible," said Heron.

"Impossible," Kellen echoed.

"Is that what she did to you?"

"Who, Mari? Fuck no, man. That girl…"

"I mean Senator Neko."

Aw, shit on a shingle. How'd he do that? Turn a conversation that Kellen was directing, twist it until it flayed his own soul instead? Kellen resolved right then to stop giving advice to insightful folk. Only idiots would benefit from his brilliance from here on out.

"Well, anyhow, back to the original thread. You could find Mari a puppy. I'm sure I could get you one. She'd have to crate-train it, which you gotta imagine would be more fun than skidding bare-kneed into a hot conflict zone and blowing shit up."

"You don't know her very well."

"Ha! Point taken. Hey, you got—"

But Heron's attention had gotten snagged on something. "Oh, no."

Wild hares and cosmic destinies evaporated. This thing that had turned Heron's face white was something else entirely.

Please God, don't let anybody precious be in trouble. Reflexively, he pinged Yoink for her status report and found her still sleeping on Angela's lap. Both his girls, safe. "What?"

Heron turned the chair and extended his hands along the rails. Data-input tablets extruded from grooves on either side, and without even looking down, Heron was keying commands into the Pentarc system. "You know how Garrett is always planning for the giant flaming apocalypse?" he said in a voice made of tension.

"Among other things," said Kellen.

"I think we might have to admit that he has a point. Look at this."

On the screen directly in front of both of them, the world exploded.

●   ●   ●

It was early, before the sun had a good shot at thawing the winter world. The wind sliced through the tower, shrilling like a Viking ghost. Angela was bundled in a blanket and lying in a haptic hammock she'd strung up between two columns in Northy. Nobody had ever filled in the window glass here, and cool morning air shifted her hammock, lulling her half to sleep while she electronically reviewed yesterday's cast from a full-sensory news channel.

Yoink, who adored this setup enough to comment on it every fifteen minutes or so, had spread her furry self across Angela's belly, her little head resting lightly on her human's thigh and her feline hiney propped on Angela's sternum. Butt to the face, baby. Angela wondered if this was typical of all cats or if hers was just a special kind of nasty.

Mech-Dan stood at attention maybe fifteen feet away. He'd told her he was hibernating till she needed him, but she knew he wasn't. He was guarding her, probably iterating behavior patterns for Daniel Ashe Neko in his mind. He hadn't made a secret of disliking the Daniel personality protocol. Poor Dan-Dan. Somewhere inside that mind, he was probably very put out.

It occurred to her that she could purge him and reboot, back into Dan-Dan mode. Daniel had, according to all accounts, died for real in the Hotel Riu, and there wouldn't be any bringing him back a second time. The ruse was up, even if she and mech-Daniel did figure out how to prove their identities and gather the pieces of their pre-Guadalajara lives.

She didn't need him to pretend to be an asshole anymore. And letting the Dan-Dan personality control the mech-clone again would make him so happy. She almost called him over right then to schedule the protocol.

But the morning was so cool, and the wind lulled, and Yoink slept. Angela's limbs felt heavy, and all she really wanted to do was rest. Dan-Dan could hibernate or play sentinel or whatever he was doing for one more morning. They had time. They had all the time and more than she could stand.

"Psst. Hey, Angela." Chloe sliced into her peace, just a voice in Angela's in-ear com. Private, secret. Ignorable. "The Pentarc system is about to issue a push notification, separate from the daily cache. Important news. You'll wanna be on top of this one."

Chloe's digital voice wasn't as nuanced as a human one, especially when she was communicating subvocally, but her words sounded ominous.

Angela rolled to one side as if she were napping and replied subvocally, "Why? Did something happen?"

"Drone strikes are coming out of Texas again, only this time, the attacks aren't limited to the Red River area. Simultaneous coordinated attacks: Akron, Seattle, Atlanta, all within eleven minutes of each other. Transits are down. Landjets have stopped running. The whole country is *en fuego*. Or wait, maybe that is not the correct context for the Spanish? Does *en fuego* mean 'on fire' or 'bitchin' cool'? Am I on a tangent?"

"Yes."

"Right. Oh, hello, logic thread, there you are! Anyway, the president is using your death as a rallying cry. He's saying you were the first casualty of this string of attacks. So things are getting a bit messy out there. I thought you ought to know."

"Thanks, Chloe," she mouthed, pushing just enough air through her mouth to engage her vocal cords. Her com would detect the organ movement and extrapolate sound on Chloe's end. She hadn't seen the nano-entity since that day up at the barn, but they chatted from time to time. It had been a long time since Angela had had a girlfriend, and Chloe, for all the Schrödinger-esque uncertainty of her existential personhood, was very girl.

"Oh wait. One more thing," Chloe said. "The bombs are GBU-12s. Mari flagged that weapon in a search a little while ago. Does it mean anything to you?"

GBU-12s. Like the fucker that took out the Riu. And now oodles of them were pouring out of Texas? Honestly, it wasn't as surprising a development as all that. Once again, all arrows pointed at Vallejo.

Kind of ironically, these renewed attacks would have been a clear excuse for war and her ticket to a cabinet appointment.

Damn you, Vallejo. You're too late. Dead girls can't hold office.

"Hey, Dan," she called, waking him from his not-hibernation.

The mech-clone moved slightly at his post by the

girder. He inclined his head. If she were closer, she could probably see the irises in his eyes shift into focus, coming online. "Yes, Ang?"

Shitty, shitty nickname. Made her sound like a citrus. She wished words were physical things, so she could catch this one out of the air and shove it back down his throat.

"I'm gonna go walk the cat. Might wander around some. Meet me back at our room in twenty."

He didn't confirm instructions for a long time. Angela's implanted com vibrated, and she tapped it. She didn't need to read the update. Chloe had told her all the juicy parts already. What she wanted to do more than anything right now was locate Kellen—for purely tactical purposes, right?—and discuss whether this evidence was irrefutable enough. Whether he and his team would support some move on Vallejo.

She wasn't even sure how that would play, since she technically didn't have any authority. Or any drones. Or access to her cloudcoin accounts. Basically, she was a refugee, just like most of the rest of the Pentarc. But that wasn't going to stop her from kicking Vallejo in the ass when his back was turned. Even if she had to hoof it into Texas in her swoofy pink pillow shoes.

Angela woke Yoink and helped her to the ground. Kitty could jump on her own, but Angela found herself treating Yoink as she always had, with extra care for an aging friend. It didn't matter that this Yoink was some shiny new clone with enhanced kidneys and connective tissues. To her human, she'd always be fragile and precious.

Casually, mistress and cat strolled to the open

doorway, headed in a general way for the stairs. As she passed mech-Dan, though, she held her breath. Couldn't have said why.

But on that day, for once, her paranoia turned out to be right on target.

She was to the doorway but not through it when mech-Dan stepped in front of her, blocking her path. His gaze was locked on something in the far distance, over her shoulder, out in the desert.

Wrenching his attention to her, he half smiled, channeling Daniel so perfectly that for a moment, Angela forgot to breathe.

"Hey, girl," he said, mimicking Daniel to within a micron of believability.

But only for a halved second.

A horrible shudder wobbled the full length of his body, a thunder sheet shaken. Something deep and mechanical caught, and he gasped. He turned his face toward her, and for one halted cosmic interval, Dan-Dan was there. Sweet puppy-dog eyes. Her loyal companion. Panicking.

"Angela," he said through what were clearly uncooperative lips. "I need to…I cannot… *Run*."

CHAPTER 9

KELLEN WATCHED, UNABLE TO STOP A GODDAMN THING AS Minneapolis took a hit. Fireball. Multiple buildings struck. Safe, sturdy Minneapolis. Refugees from all over the world had been flocking there for years, causing a population spike to near four million. And now, today, they'd been attacked. Four million people. Holy shit. That wasn't the only target on fire, either. Information kept cascading in, and not a bit of it looked good. Hundreds of his tracked critters were no longer transmitting from the Twin Cities.

All nonmilitary continental transportation was halted. Martial law had been imposed in whole geographic areas. The UNAN was on its heels, paralyzed.

Heron was already deep in the data feeds, his mouth moving as he sent subvocal messages, probably to the family and to Mari. At the same time, he watched all the screens, all the horrors at once, soaking up more data than a human ought to be able to. Possibly more than a human could stand to.

"What do we have in the air?" Kellen asked.

"I took Garrett's suggestion and had Chloe increase her dispersal parameters and fabricate an atmospheric mirage above us," Heron said, unflappable as ever. "Her cover is not as comprehensive as the data holes—she needs more practice—but at least our enemy's targeting satellites won't be able to resolve a visual on us. We must assume that our location has been compromised."

"Why's that?"

"Because Minneapolis wasn't a random target," said Heron, his voice threaded with something sharp and dark and scary as hell. "When things got hairy back in October, Mari sent her—"

"Boo." The word came out instead on a ragged breath as Mari skidded into the Vault, the expression on her face echoing the sharp scary in Heron's voice. "What's going on with my aunt Boo?"

Her gaze found the live feed from Minneapolis just as Heron said, "Querida. That's a live feed from Minneapolis. Where Princess Bubbles lives."

Kellen didn't mind a good, strong swear from time to time, but Mari said a few things right then that near curled his hair.

Heron opened his arms, and Mari folded herself into him. Curled against his body, she went completely still. Silent, too. Kellen couldn't tell if it was grief or fury, but something rode her hard.

Heron caught Kellen's gaze above her dark head. "Aunt Boo went to stay with someone in Minneapolis when things went sideways a couple months ago. For safety. On face value, that would seem to be a coincidence, but…"

"Coincidences usually aren't," Kellen finished.

"Vallejo would know about Aunt Boo's friend, wouldn't he? Would he be pissed enough to target her?"

"Is she in there?" Mari cut in. She didn't raise her head, and her voice was muffled, but Kellen heard her words clearly. "Is she dead?"

"I'm retrieving data packets as we speak, querida," Heron said into her hair. "We will know before anyone else. Kellen's network has the best eyes and ears on the planet, better than drones even."

Kellen was already on it, tapping a com message for Yoink: Need you in the Vault. Now.

Heron was going on, moving his mouth in subvocal words, obviously doing his damndest to soothe. Kellen didn't need to know what his friend was saying, but whatever it was, it seemed to be working. Still, Mari stayed coiled tight, like a flat-pressed spring. At any second, Kellen expected her to burst out of Heron's arms, guns drawn, ready to blow something up. It was her way. Impulsive. Emotional. Loyal.

After a moment or two or a million, some of the tension eased from her spine. She made a small sound, accepting. Waiting.

Heron drew in a breath and found Kellen again. He raised his eyebrows.

"Yoink's on her way," Kellen said. "But already, we're getting some data in from critters on the ground."

"Can you put their data feeds up on the walls?"

This was easier when Yoink was around, but Kellen fiddled with the com and relayed data to the smartsurface walls. It wasn't pretty, just charts and numbers, results of quick air-composition analysis and structural tension readings for the remaining building supports, though honestly, there wasn't much left. Subsidence crater more than a mile wide. Damn. That thing had gone into the ground before it blew.

Heron swore, which was unusual enough a thing that Kellen instinctively asked, "What?"

"The munitions used in these attacks are identical to the bomb that hit Angela Neko's hotel in Guadalajara."

Coincidences again.

Kellen blew a breath out between tight lips. "If he found out she wasn't dead, he might be looking to finish the job."

"Maybe," Heron said. "It's hard to theorize motive when we don't clearly know whom we're dealing with."

Mari shifted, still from her perch on Heron's lap but getting her tough-girl armor on, figuratively speaking. "Oh, I got myself a guess."

"What do you mean?" Kellen asked.

"I've been running searches on that particular kind of bomb for days now. It's an old model, not in wide usage anymore, probably unstable as all get-out. UNAN sold most of their reserves ten, fifteen years back. Guess who not only bought those turkeys but made a big chunk of them to begin with?"

"Texas?"

Her eyes narrowed and shot daggers at the wall display. "Yeehaw."

"So," said Kellen, forcing himself to remain calm. "Vallejo's on a tear, maybe trying to kill Angela. Again. Fine. We'll just pay him a little visit. He was at Enchanted Rock not too long ago. Could still be there. Central Texas is his stomping grounds."

Heron nodded, his gaze darting unnaturally fast

between the displays. "I can't send Chloe," he said, "not while she's dispersed, and it might not be a bad idea to organize a soft evacuation here at the Pentarc, just in case. I could use your help with that, but I understand if you prefer to do the other."

"I'll go with," Mari said, already uncurling herself and rising to her feet. Cool calm fell over her like a shell. She had to be burning up with emotion inside, but she sure could get herself into a zone.

Heron reached out one long arm and brushed her hip. She stopped. Looked down at him.

"Please don't," he said. "I can't endure sending you into his sphere of control again."

Heron blinked like he was resetting something internally, then turned to face Kellen. "The last time she and her father faced off, he put a bullet in her. That won't be happening again. So if you want to stop Vallejo, you'll have to go get him yourself."

Alone. Not Kellen's favorite thing, but he'd do it. "I got no problem with that. Don't you worry, Miss Mari."

"Are you certain?" Heron asked slowly. "Running in headfirst and guns blazing isn't your usual style."

"Well, that don't mean I can't—"

Yoink blurred into the room, a comet of wild fur, screeching. She hooked her claws on Kellen's jeans leg and literally climbed him. Hurt like the dickens, but he was way too startled to move. Also thought he probably shouldn't. When she got her little face up in his, she stared him down hard. His com crackled. "Bad robot attacked *my* human. To the goats!"

In the space of one hot second, Heron smoothed the data from Minneapolis to the side and splashed visuals up for Northy and the skywalk. It took them maybe four heartbeats more to find Angela. She'd run clean out of her pillow shoes, and though it looked like she'd gotten some kind of head start, the mech-clone was faster.

Immediate questions like *What the hell could have set it off?* shifted to *God, what will it do to her if it catches her?*

"She's headed for the barn," Kellen said, interpreting Yoink-speak for the rest of them.

Good girl, going someplace you know. Just hang on, sweetheart.

Mari was already ahead of him through the door. "Then we'd best get there first."

• • •

It had been nine plus years since Angela had been forced to run a twice-weekly "smile mile" in the desert. She'd kept up with her health in a general sort of way, but she so wasn't conditioned for a run like this.

Like this. Nothing ever had been *like this*.

A death run over uneven flooring, stairs that cut out halfway, freezing winter wind gusts, and unexpected plunges into vast, bright nothing. Nightmares reached for her. She wished she'd learned the layout of this place, wished she'd spent time hardening and honing herself.

But she was an internationalist, a policy wonk, not a goddamn athlete. She didn't run for a living. This was…

Thoughts came in sharp, panting bursts, flaying their way through her chest. The sun had risen fully, like it was trying to help, but winter roared through the concrete supports.

She knew how to get to the barn. She thought she might even know where the stairs were, if the elevators took too long.

She could make it there. She could.

Mech-Daniel's heavy steps pounded behind her. He moved more smoothly than she did, faster, and he wouldn't tire. He was like the goddamn Terminator. But when she'd ducked under his outstretched arm and run for the stairs, he hadn't come after her right away. He had paused.

And there was that matter of the warning.

What if he was mostly Daniel now but also still Dan-Dan, deep in there somewhere? She knew how to talk down kidnappers and crazies. That had been part of her diplomatic training. Would he have enough logic containment to even listen if she stopped, if she tried to reason with him?

Ah, fuck. That question was about to be moot anyhow. Her legs hurt so much, it felt like they were about to seize into tight little balls of muscle-stuff. Couldn't feel her feet at all. She no longer had complete control over where her footfalls landed. She tripped, skidded, got back up, kept running.

Across the skywalk, into West.

Wild, wild west, run west. Just keep going.

She didn't want to think of what she'd do if Kellen wasn't there. Who else could she run to? Where did the refugees live? Fanaida? Mari? Where were they right now? In the nightmarescape, she was the only person here, the last person in the world, and that thing made of titanium and evil was coming after her. She'd tried to com Chloe several times, but the nanite cloud wasn't replying.

Keep going. Don't stop. Don't you dare stop.

The elevator doors were closed in West, but she couldn't wait for the carriage to arrive. No time. She pushed through to the emergency stairs and started climbing. Her thighs shuddered the last eight steps, bones turned to rubber, muscles clenched in spasm. She had to haul herself up with her hands. Gloveless now.

Skin scraped concrete. Broke. Bled.

And then she burst into the barn level, into the bright morning sun. Through the gate, calling his name.

"Kellen! Are you here? Please be here, please please please." When had she started crying? Her voice was riddled with crags, breaking and slipping, unable to maintain register. Her heart hammered in her chest, on the edge of exploding. Her eyes stung.

Behind her, the elevator dinged.

Mech-Daniel stepped into the shadow of the elevator house.

"Ah, there you are. Come here, Ang. Let me get a good look at you." So Daniel. So wrong. Hey-girl smile, planting ice seeds in her chest.

Couldn't. Breathe.

He started toward her.

A shovel leaned against the fence, and Angela grabbed it, backing toward the animal pens. Her bare feet scuffed trenches in the ice-crackled grass. What the hell was a shovel going to do against a titanium frame that could hold up a goddamn building? But her fists would be even more ineffective. At least with shovel in hand, she could go down ugly.

Fighting it.

A couple of the goats wandered out of their barn, curious at the noise. Getting behind them, using them as shields, might buy her time. But it would also, ultimately, buy her a bunch of broken, bloody cattle.

They weren't offering themselves in her place, and she couldn't sacrifice them. No consent. It wasn't fair.

None of this was fair.

You weren't fair, Daniel. You weren't even in the small print of the deal they shoved down my throat. Fuck fuck fuck. I should never have. I should never.

"Dan-Dan," she said, her voice breaking. She repeated it, louder, his name, the code. Was the back door still there? Could she get through to him? "Hibernate."

He paused. It was slight, that pause, not even a full second, but Angela grasped at the shard of hope. "Dan-Dan," she repeated, louder. "Be still."

He lurched, but something inside him fought back. He raised a foot to continue, but then froze with it poised in the air, not completing the step that would bring him closer. His face contorted, and his movements jerked. Unnatural. Nothing about this creature belonged in nature.

Vallejo might have grown a clone body to stick the machine inside when he made mech-Daniel, but the result was pure monster. Horrible. Wrong. Angela wanted to vomit.

But she wanted to live more.

"It's okay, Dan-Dan," she said. "This is just a software glitch. We can fix it. I can fix it. Be still."

Her hands were shaking, slipped on the shovel handle, and she had no idea how she was still holding onto it. But at least she'd gotten some control over her voice. She had trained that voice, practiced wielding it like a weapon. It was good. It was strong. It was *working*.

"Angela." In a keen this time, sliding up into falsetto. His head cocked to the side, violently, like switches were resetting themselves but only after an epic internal struggle.

"I'm here, Dan-Dan," she said as calmly as she could, though her throat was still crammed with sobs. "I am safe. You are doing a good job."

His foot came down. One step toward her. The expression on his face shifted from one second to the next: hate then hurt then fury then horror. "No, no… My programming is bad," he said through lips that refused to cooperate. "All I ever wanted was to serve you. Angela! My programming is bad."

"Yes, it is. But I can repair it. Just be still. Hibernate."

He didn't.

She had never seen her mech-clone weep. There had never been a need. But that might be what his face was doing, his version. He didn't have the back-end connections to his tear ducts, so they didn't work, but blood vessels that had been attached to his cyber eyes ruptured from their connectors, and the subcutaneous blood seeped out. Like tears, pinkened sleet stuck to his face. "I cannot…"

A blur of movement from the elevator, a ding, and then Kellen was striding out into the morning. He wielded something long, like a sword.

Knight. Shining. Armor. She almost cracked into hysterical laughter.

And then, all powers help her, she did.

Kellen raised the glinting swordy thing, touched it to the back of mech-Daniel's head, and the mech-clone collapsed to the ground like a sack of neutron stars. Heavy. Just like that.

There were words. Kellen's words, and some others. Girl's voice, woman's. Saying things. Things things things. Angela might have contributed some of those things herself, but mostly she…laughed.

Oh man, it was the silliest thing, the worst, stupidest thing. She had survived a goddamn bombing and kept her shit together, but she was losing every thread of composure right now. Losing it like a virgin on spring break. It was all gone, unspooling there in the mud and ice.

She was alive. And somehow, that was fucking hilarious.

She let the shovel fall, and then she collapsed beside it, crumpled really, holding her face and laughing on the exhalations, snorting on the intakes. Mad as a hatter. Loopy as a shoelace. Non compos mentis.

And then gentle hands were stroking her head, her back. The kind of hands that promised no one would see, no one would judge. She could melt, disintegrate, and it was okay.

"Shhh, princess. I got you."

His arms were right there, too, on the far end of those hands. She leaned into all of him, still laughing like a goddamn hyena. Because something about that perfect safe space in his arms? Reminded her that she was, in fact, powerful. Hunted, nearly dead, but still somehow a princess to this man. She had to be doing something right, to earn a title like that. From a person like him.

"No, not a princess," she said after a long time, wiping the tears on his pointy-tipped shirt collar. "I am the fucking queen."

"Okay."

"And I'm not crying, either. Just so you know."

He didn't stop holding her. "I know."

"Actually, I'm laughing." She snuffled, settled herself slowly.

"I know," he said again.

"Really? What the fuck? How can you possibly

tell?" She pulled back and looked at his face. *His* face. That face.

He was smiling, but it was a cautious thing, hesitant, like he was sizing her up for a possible tranquilizer. "The queen of my world don't cry."

She wanted to kiss him. Put her mouth all over his body, ingest his sweetness, and then baste it all back over him. There wasn't a damn thing sweet about her. There never had been. He was all the good that she ever was, and together, they would be even better. Best.

"No, you're right," she said. "This queen doesn't get scared. She gets vengeance. Er, if she doesn't die laughing first."

"Such a badass, you."

She was beyond silly now, but given what had just happened—the last fifteen minutes, the last fifteen weeks—she gave precisely zero fucks what anyone thought. "Good, bad, you're the one with the…what *was* that thing you were wielding?"

"Cattle prod. Nine thousand volts, right to the diodes. Never got to use one before, but I'd say it came in fairly handy today."

"Yeah, fairly." She hiccupped. "You pacifists get all the best death toys."

●   ●   ●

Angela stood inside a technological nightmare marble—okay, the room wasn't actually a marble. It was the Vault, the Pentarc's command center, a round-walled, armored enclosure four stories underground. She was willing to bet there was a Faraday shell behind those curved black panels with all the lights and blips and screens and always-shifting free-fae-lit data graphs.

Fat ropes of electrical cord wound along the floor, snakes perpetually threatening to strike an unsuspecting visitor. In the center of the viper pit was a command chair with a swivel base, so its occupant could pretend to know all and see all, like the guard in a digital panopticon.

Three curved doorways led off in various directions, but she didn't go exploring.

Kellen had come into the Vault behind her. She knew it even without turning, and she wasn't surprised when he set his hands atop her shoulders, wordlessly. Supporting her but not holding her up. As much as she cringed away from most people's touch, his was different. Familiar. His microbes were her microbes. Someday he might even get it if she told him he had sexy-as-hell cooties.

He'd hauled a portable hydraulic calf table from the veterinary up at the barn. It might look like a medieval torture cage, but Kellen assured her that ranchers used these things all the time to restrain and transport cattle. Several people had come up to the barn to help load mech-Daniel's body onto it. The thing weighed in excess of 180 kilos, and nobody wanted to dead-lift that. While Kellen had been checking out Angela to make sure she was unhurt—not holding her or stroking her or making her feel safe, right—Mari had whipped out a scary-looking knife and dug a trench in mech-Daniel's head. The sounds of her ripping out wiring had been... well, they'd been gross. Presumably, now mech-Daniel either could not wake, or if he did, he wouldn't be able to hurt anybody.

They'd taken him down to the Vault in a service elevator, and then, because this day's fucked-up-o-meter apparently wasn't pegging its max yet, Angela watched as Dr. Farad stripped insulation off a cord, wrapped one wire-end around the mech-clone's exposed in-skull electrical, and plugged the other end into a SIP port on the back of his own head.

The nest of sleeping snakes on the floor shifted, waking.

In his command chair, Heron Farad closed his eyes and breathed in time to the slither.

"All right, Senator, I see your subroutines, recent iterations. He has been busy lately, hasn't he?"

Busy becoming Daniel. Busy resisting the transformation. Busy saving her life. Busy trying to end it.

"He's always busy," Angela said, "even when it looks like he's just standing there. His neural uses pattern analysis to learn, so he's constantly sifting data and altering himself to better perform his tasks. But if you mean the planning to kill me thing, yeah, that's new."

A slim frown formed on Farad's forehead. "You installed a back door to access his behavioral profiles."

"He was a gift from my mentor, and neither of us trusted Vallejo's base-model programming. We had him wiped and reset, and my programmers added the back door then, for privacy. But it must be corrupted or something, because I tried to access that subroutine over and over, and he just kept coming."

He just kept coming. A deep shudder started at her sternum and rolled through her body, and she had to close her eyes and wait for it to pass. She endured it, like the memory of the hotel disintegrating around her. The universe could stop putting her through these convulsive events any damn time now.

Farad went on, his voice sleek and clinical. "No, your Dan-Dan subroutine is intact. As is the other back door."

"What other?" asked Kellen, his voice deep and reso-nant, wrapping itself around her.

"I'm seeing a secondary access key, the word *Ashe*. Not yours, Senator?"

"No." The word was a tremble, drawn up through her throat. She swallowed, but her voice wavered when she said, "Ashe was Daniel's name, before we were married. But he never had access to the mech-clone."

"Interesting," said Farad. "Perhaps exploring this subroutine will provide us with some clues about mech-Daniel's motivation today."

"Mech-clones don't have motivations," Mari piped up, her voice unusually brittle. "They're machines, extensions of somebody else's will."

Angela thought of a goofy as-you-wish puppy with a three-year-old's wave and an almost obsequious desire to please. Mech-Daniel had gotten none of his charm-ing behaviors from Vallejo's base model or the Daniel-impersonation programming. Wasn't will defined as a purpose carried out? Calming her during that gala hadn't been her purpose, and it hadn't been Kellen's... Had somebody else commanded mech-Daniel to do it? Or had he thought it up on his own?

"Dan-Dan's unique," Angela said, consciously using their private name. "It wouldn't surprise me if he had developed something approximating a will of his own."

If Dan-Dan was in that body somewhere, she hoped

he heard. She wanted him to know that she'd seen how hard he had fought the instruction to harm her.

In his chair, Farad stilled more completely. If that was even possible. At the same time, in his calf-table trap, mech-Daniel twitched. His eyelids opened, breaking the crust of dried blood. Irises whorled as he came online.

Angela wanted to lurch for the door, but she took the hit, remained still. Kellen's big hands slid down her arms, warm and steady.

"Breathe," he whispered beside her ear.

Survivor. Queen. I am the fire.

She raised one hand and clasped his, not looking at him. Steady.

"I'm in," Heron said. "You can take him out of the cage now. He is no longer a danger."

"Wait. How can you say that for certain?" Angela said. This was important, especially to her. Any danger he would pose, if he *was* still dangerous, had a high probability of falling smack on her head.

The mech-clone slumped in its too-small cage, and in his chair, Dr. Farad opened his own eyes. "Because I have closed both back doors. He is secure."

"Any idea where that other door led? The Ashe one?" Kellen asked, his voice tight. She could feel the tension in his hand.

"Not precisely," said Heron, "but I can tell you where the last user was when he accessed it."

"Where…" She let her voice trail to silence, didn't really need that question answered. She knew.

Mari's voice was venom when she spat, "Texas."

●　　●　　●

Shit devolved fairly quickly after that to planning and packing. As shit tended to do. Emergency alerts continued to pellet Kellen's blip board all the rest of that day, mostly casualty reports and a steady stream of offended and stern speeches from El Presidente. Medina sure could talk.

Responders were still calling the operation at that Minneapolis crater a rescue, but nobody had much hope. The land was scrubbed bare, like nothing had ever existed there. Mari started out roiling fury off her body like sun heat off macadam, but as the information kept coming and hope kept leaving, she calmed. Her mouth moved, and you could almost visualize the constant tether of communication between her and Heron. He never let her get out of his sight.

Around suppertime, another one of those drone-launched smartbombs found its way into an illegal-services rendezvous hub in Sammamish. Kellen knew some folks there, and watching their hub blow up squeezed something painful inside him. Watching people die hurt. Being unable to do anything about it hurt even more.

All over the country, intercepts had been popping off incoming bombs all day, and contracts for more were lighting up the darknet freelancer hives. Heron had talked Mari out of taking on at least two. Chloe'd been up in the sky since before noon, keeping the Pentarc hidden as only she could. She didn't get tired like other folk, but she had to be bored off her nanorobotic ass.

They'd called in some favors, and the Chiba nonallied space station was moving into orbit, ready to retaliate if the Pentarc was attacked, so maybe she could get a rest soon. Pieces on the global board were lining up, too.

Damn, Kellen hated this part.

Garrett had rounded up a team and started moving all the valuables underground, just in case, and Adele and Fanaida were doing the same with the people and critters, respectively. Angela had run back to her room, with escort, to fetch her meager belongings for their trip. The Pentarc rumbled with activity, and maybe a touch of fear.

Weirdest thing, though: Kellen usually would be right in the middle of a soft evacuation like this, making sure all his wards were safe and healthy and happy. That's the kind of thing that filled up his spiritual tanks. But right now, when other people were taking care of those tasks in his stead, he was...okay with it.

Because of her. Because she needed him. Because she wanted him. Most of all because he didn't want her to leave this place without him, definitely not when she was a target and the whole country was on fire and she was heading to goddamned motherfucking Texas.

It was time to admit a nasty truth. He was smitten. Incurably so. Probably had never gotten himself fully unsmut after that first bout, years ago.

Huh. That confession should have felt scarier.

"We can't go out in the plane, you know," he called from the med lab back into the Vault. "We'd have to bust through Chloe, and I don't want her to have to handle that kind of rearranging. She's got a lot on her mind already."

"Air travel is unwise at any rate," Heron replied. "All air traffic on the continent has been grounded until further notice, probably so the interceptors can get a better bead on the attack drones. Landjets are down, pods too. Not sure exactly why. I'd give you my car, but the interface is kind of...unique."

Kellen peeked down the short hall. His buddy was still sitting in that big-ass command chair, wired into the mech-clone, experimenting with controlling both his own body and the mech's, even while he monitored the world and oversaw the evacuation of his home. *Unique* didn't begin to describe Heron's mind.

"You kidlets can take my dragon," came a voice from the Vault door.

Kellen set down his unzipped bag and headed that way just as Fanaida breezed in. She looked tired, stressed, and magnificent.

"Hey, beautiful," he said, opening his arms and bending so she could kiss him on either cheek.

"*Que Dios te bendiga, mijo.*" She raised her eyebrows at the rest of the room. "What, no love from the rest of you lowlifes?"

"Hullo, Mum." Heron acknowledged her without tearing his gaze off the bank of monitors. Mari nodded, then drew Fan aside and filled her in. Fanaida took it all like a champ, like she'd seen crazy stuff before. Kellen had too, but most disasters didn't feel like they were aimed at him or folk he loved.

Angela arrived shortly after with one extremely self-important cat on her heels. She carried her over-stuffed bag slung over a shoulder and sported a new pair of shoes. Plastic printed Mary Janes, possibly borrowed from one of the refugees. He had definitely seen Adele wearing that nut-brown peacoat a time or two. Definitely the same coat. Thing was so ugly nobody'd want to make another one, having laid eyes on the first. Almost certainly it was a loaner.

It struck him Angela hadn't had a change of clothes

since she'd arrived, had been wearing the same outfit for weeks. Months. They were good quality clothes, and her room was equipped with an organics removal unit so they didn't smell too gamey, but she had to be feeling the lack. She'd always dolled up so pretty on the vids.

Why hadn't she talked to somebody about getting new togs? It wasn't like he was without resources. The Pentarc had a whole room full of additive fabricators. Had she not known who to ask, or had she just been reluctant to ask *him*?

At any rate, probably wasn't wise to tell her she looked a thousand times more beautiful to him right now, even in those wrinkled clothes and borrowed shoes. It wasn't even physical, the beauty he saw in her. She'd come to the Pentarc defeated, scared, but now, bent on vengeance, she looked fierce. Ready to ride the world. Something had shifted up there at the barn with the mech-clone bearing down on her. She wasn't scared anymore.

She was his warrior queen, and he was prepared to follow her into whatever battles she waged. That was the price for being in her court. Fine. He'd pay up.

She met his gaze from across the room and kicked up one of those black-wing eyebrows. "Are you ready?"

"As I'll ever be. Just lemme fetch my stuff." He ducked into the med lab, grabbed his med kit and bag, but Mari stalled him on the way back in. She pressed something into his hand, a heavy something. He looked down. A gun.

"What...?"

"No safety and no biometric locks, so just pull the trigger hard when you mean it, and then keep on pulling. This little gem's got tight tolerances, smooth action, and dead-on accuracy. Slide's nice and loose, too. All that said, you'll want to practice with her a couple of times before you go full-on badass. I just slipped a box of ammo into your bag there, and she's got a full clip, ready to go." She looked solemn and serious as a funeral when she stepped back. "Y'all take care."

He sort of hated the feeling of the gun in his hand, but he wasn't about to tell Mari that. Sharing a gun, for her, was like him sharing a toothbrush. Or a bar of dark chocolate. She got pretty attached to her weapons. So all he said, all he really could say after he slipped the gun into his jacket pocket, was, "Thanks. I will."

Not to be outdone in the grand-farewell department, Fanaida handed over keys to her dragon. "You've got two fresh MOX rods in the reactor, so you don't have to stop for nothing except for rest and recharging your own batteries. Be sure you do that once or twice. Driving overland is a helluva thing. There's no rush here, *mijo*. World's gonna be as fucked up tomorrow as it is today."

That wasn't a hundred percent true. Those Texas drones were still in the air, still blowing things up. Still killing. Still threatening his people. His com went off every twenty minutes or so with updates. If he and Angela could get to Vallejo faster and somehow divert him from whatever crazy scheme he was in the middle of, maybe they could keep some of those bombs from happening. Save the world. Yeah.

Mari's gaze tracked them while they prepared, and before they left the Vault, she nodded toward Angela. "You go kill it, Senator."

Okay, then. They turned, the two of them—well, two and a half, if you counted Yoink as a half a person—and left via a tunnel that would take them past blast doors and then up to the garage and Fan's dragon.

After they got far enough away, he had to ask. "Mari didn't just tell us to kill her daddy, did she?"

"Too bloodthirsty for you, cowboy?" Angela asked, shooting him a look replete with more eyebrow action. She glanced down at his jacket pocket, and her look turned downright lascivious.

Just like that, the tension and uncertainty fled his body. He centered his world over her smile.

"Matter of fact, that is a gun in my pocket," he returned, absolutely cool. "*And* I'm glad to see you."

●　　●　　●

Overland travel: not Angela's favorite thing. Twenty-plus hours trapped in a wheeled metal box with Kellen Hockley, no witnesses, and a self-imposed prohibition against touching him. This was going to kill her. For real this time.

However, despite her apprehension, once they got away from the Pentarc, away from mech-Daniel, it was like she'd just surfaced from a deep dive with no atmo suit. The near-silent car flung her eastward through the desert, and she could breathe. Wide open breathing. This might be what freedom tasted like: crunchy travel rations shared with a needy feline and the man she had never managed to get out of her mind.

When Yoink finally curled up and fell asleep on her shoes in the seat well, Angela logged onto her com, tapped in two darknet addresses, and sent invitations to rendezvous. She got a reply from one almost immediately and pushed a swallow through her emotion-tight throat. She should have done this weeks ago. There was power in knowing that someone out there mourned her, even a near stranger.

Oddly, she didn't experience the trepidation she expected from reaching out like this, for setting up assignations without having her schemes vetted and cleared in committee. It might make her the worst public servant ever, but she had to be honest, it felt fucking terrific.

She could get used to this dead-girl thing.

"What you up to, or should I ask?" Kellen had his hands on the steering wheel, probably a little too tightly. She didn't have the heart to tell him that there was a vehicle control rig in this car. Fanaida hadn't used the steering wheel much on the drive in from Kingman.

Plus, watching him work through tension was hypnotic. Long fingers, tendon-strung and sun-bronzed. He always did have good hands. Did the act of driving a car upset him enough to make him clutch the steering wheel like that, or was it something else? She thought about asking him if the sugar skulls on the dash were creeping him out or if forced existence in close proximity to her was his kryptonite. Latter would be better.

They'd driven in near silence for most of the afternoon, and night was falling fast on the desert. Out there in that monochrome black, bombs were flying, and people were dying, and civilization might very well be collapsing. But she didn't want to know about it. For the first time in her adult life, knowing the details wouldn't get her any closer to repairing the cause.

Night was a blanket tucked snug over this car, and she could pretend, for a few hours at least, that the world outside it simply did not exist.

Angela shut down her com, half turned on the ultrasoft seat, and propped one knee up on the console that separated her body from Kellen's. She had shit to say, and it needed saying right now. "Yeah, you can ask. I have been working on possibly becoming undead. Not in the zombie sense undead, of course, although you know what, we—I mean the UNAN, not you and I personally—lack good laws governing the personhood of zombies and we probably should spin some up, but no, I mean I've decided to let some key people know I'm alive and will see how they handle the resultant cardiac incidents. And also, I'm really sorry I made you uncomfortable with my whoa-pushy horniness a few weeks back, especially sorry since we're currently stuck in a tiny car together for twenty-plus hours. And finally I brought you a present."

She pulled a wad of papers—real, old-school paper, no kidding: she'd begged it off Fan, who had a strange but endearing fascination with origami—out from under her ass and laid the sheaves over the center console.

An offering. Just like those offerings of information he'd been leaving her for weeks. Which she chose to interpret as clear evidence that he still gave half a shit. At least, that was her hope. She didn't dare breathe.

"Did you punctuate even a part of that in your head before you said it?" he asked.

"No. I couldn't." She caught her bottom lip between her teeth and then let it slip out slow and painful. "If I'd paused at all, I wouldn't have said anything. Do you have any idea how hard it is to self-describe your own motivations as whoa-pushy horniness?"

"Not really. Waste of time to regret emotions you don't have any control over to begin with."

"I wish to fuck I was you, then, because my past is crammed full of regrets."

His hands slid off the steering wheel. (Ha! He did know about the vehicle control rig! He'd just been pretending to steer the car. Wait. Had he done that so he didn't have to look at her, speak with her?) It recessed back into the dash. Their destination and route were programmed, and they were within the paint rails of a federal highway. Barring an emergency, the car could drive itself to Texas.

Which was just as well, since Angela didn't plan on letting him pay a lot of attention to the road. She couldn't touch him, fine. But she could talk to him.

He ran one hand through his hair, making it even more strokably disheveled. This man had no idea what he did to her libido on a near-constant basis.

He turned to her, half-lidded blue eyes burning like the Caribbean in July. Okay. Maybe he had a very small, very tiny idea.

"Hold the first four words of that sentence in your mind for a minute," he said, "and tell me about this present. I know you haven't been shopping a whole lot, so I'm curious what you rummaged up in the Pentarc."

She widened her eyes in pretend shock. "Why, Doctor Hockley, have you been spying on me?"

"Yes. A whole lot, actually. Present?"

Angela had spent most of her life surrounded by liars. Half-truths, spun truths, and discarded truths were pervasive as air on the Colina Capitolina. She worked in lies, had built her career on them, so she knew Kellen could have sidestepped the accusation. He could have pretended offense that she'd even think he was hiding out and peeking. But he didn't do either of those things. He admitted straight-up that he'd been watching her. That kind of honesty wasn't easy, no matter how innate he made it seem.

She tapped the top paper.

He focused on the spot her finger indicated and read out loud, "'The Armenian Lady's Love,' by... Aw shit, gal, you know I hate Wordsworth."

"Just keep reading. Please."

"'The Armenian Lady's Love: Abbreviated, Annotated, and Illustrated. P.S., It's a fuck poem.'" His eyebrows cranked up his forehead when he read the postscript at the bottom of the page. (Technically, it was a footnote and was formatted as such, but nit-picking served no one.) "Now, hang on, I might find the dude's poetry shitty, especially later stuff like this one here, when he was trying too hard to be Byron, but don't you think defacing his work like this is even a little bit disrespectful?"

"Not even a little bit," she said, unable to contain her grin. She set the heels of her hands on her bent leg and leaned forward, getting a good look at the paper and teasing the veriest edge of his personal space. Totally permissible. No touching involved. "Would you like to read it yourself, or shall I orate?"

"Both. Maybe at the same time? Says here there's pictures, and I sure would hate to skip those."

"Oh no, don't do that. The, ah, artist put a lot of effort into drawing them."

He picked up a corner of one page and flipped through. He would be admiring her *Kama Sutra* stick figures. She'd been hoping for a chuckle, something to break the ice. Instead he inspected each drawing thoroughly, skimmed through her margin notes, and carefully read the whole thing. Twice. He said nothing.

Nothing. Um, not encouraging.

She pointed near the top and cleared her throat like she was about to give a floor speech. "'Hear now of a fair Armenian daughter…how she loved a Christian slave, and told her pain by word, look, deed, with hope that he might love again.' That's, ah, me. The Armenian chick."

"I gathered. Am I meant to be the Christian slave or the gardener?"

"You can't tell by the drawings?"

He turned the paper sideways. Squinted. "Oh, I see, they're the same. See, here she's… Well, that's definitely a fresh reading on 'Rusty lance, I ne'er shall grasp thee.'"

"Academic, would you say?"

"A-plus for effort." He sighed, pinched the bridge of his nose, and set the papers aside. "This is real clever, and I'm duly impressed you can remember, line for line, a subpar poem we were forced to learn more'n a decade ago. But I gotta ask, what is this all about?"

"It's not obvious?" she replied. "I'm wooing you."

"Wooing?" He stopped and squinted at her a bit like he'd looked at the sideways copulating stick figures: bemused but amused at the same time.

Great. She had to spell it out. "Woo? You know, poems and flowers and…wooing? Look, in the elevator, you told me I needed to woo you. But then you went into self-preservation mode—no judgment here; I understand—and I was at a temporary loss. I started thinking about your objections and what you need from me at this point in your life, and I determined that, well, there's precious little. I'm not used to being useless, but you have ordered your world perfectly to suit yourself, and about the only thing I can offer is this: an impetus to read really shitty poetry that you hate." Angela sucked in her bottom lip and held it untrembling between her teeth. Well, now at least he knew.

"You think forcing me outside the boundaries of a well-ordered life is gonna make me want to kiss you till neither of us can breathe?"

It wasn't like breathing was especially easy right now. But whatever. "Yes, exactly that, and please do feel free, if the need strikes. I'm pushy. Bossy, I think is the term you used the day we first met. I haven't changed all that much, in case you hadn't gathered. But I think you, specifically you, need to be bossed sometimes. So you don't get too comfortable, so you don't forget."

He was quiet for a long time, sizing her up with those liquid-crystal eyes. "I called you boss, not bossy. And I'm sorry I didn't reply to your darknet message," he said. "I knew what it was, what you were telling me to do. I just couldn't trust."

"Me?"

"Nah, sweetheart. Couldn't trust myself." He half smiled, ruefully, and shook his head. "Also yeah, maybe there was a little bit of doubtin' you, too. You're a hard person to read sometimes, especially that public persona you tend."

She needed to stop biting her lip. It hurt. Instead she shrugged. "No worries. Mech-Daniel evaluated the situation, determined that I would perform better if I thought you"—*still loved me*—"had replied, and initiated a series of false replies in your place."

"Am sorry for that, too."

"It wasn't your fault," she said. "It was a brilliant solution on his part. Thinking that you were there in my com somehow, flirting at me, I killed it that night. Even the trillionaires were impressed enough to donate to Zeke's campaign."

"Fundraising was your aim in going there?"

"Fundraising is always an aim," she said. "But this was fundraising on an entirely different level. Trillionaires, right. If you want a shitload of money poured into an undisclosed, scantily monitored fund, you want Ofelia Ortega y Mars de la Madrid's attention."

He frowned. "That fund was for the president's campaign?"

"Yeah."

"What did he do with that kind of money with only nine days left before the election?"

Angela opened her mouth to reply but then shut it. She didn't have a strong guess and certainly not an answer. Sure, campaign war chests were always a thing, always needed filling. But on the other hand, Kellen was sort of right. The main media push had already been over by the time Angela had attended La Mars Madrid's party.

She let her head fall back against the seat. "I suck at wooing, don't I?"

"Maybe a little bit," he replied gently, but with a hint of laughter tucked deep in his voice. "I mean, Wordsworth? That was your play? And twice now, too."

He made a *tsk* sound in his throat, and Angela couldn't peel her gaze from the peek of his tongue behind his teeth when he did it. The sun-bronzed line of his neck, now limned in the blue light from the car's instrument panels. The easy movement of his body. Though granted, it wasn't moving a whole lot right now. He was watching her, a slight, almost mysterious smile pulling at his mouth. Just on the left side. Like he knew a secret and wasn't telling.

Fuck. How had she ever thought she could make this trip, with him, in this car, and keep her distance? She had promised herself, though, and she was holding steady. Just.

"Now, about those four words," he drawled.

CHAPTER 10

"Um, the words. Right." Her perfect memory whirred, replaying their whole conversation so far, all of it. It took her a while, but she finally caught the thread and recited it: "I wish to fuck that…"

"Back up," he interrupted. "Just four."

"I wish to fuck?"

"Them's the ones." He held her gaze but didn't so much as twitch in her general direction. The space between them crackled with potential energy. "Do you?"

Did she…wish to fuck?

Yes, oh God yes. Holy batfuck yes. Every nerve in her body went live, and she struggled to contain a shudder. No use, though. She nodded, scuffing her hairpiece against the seatback.

"Yes," she said, not surprised her voice came out on a whisper. "But here's the problem. I promised myself I wouldn't paw you without permission on this trip. I want you to know I don't think you're easy or easily taken advantage of. I want you to know that I myself have dealt with…"

He was panther-silent and just that fast across the console, framing her face in his big hands, pressing his mouth to hers, warmth to warmth, creating a point of white-hot synchrony. She was too startled even to open her lips. His kiss was impossibly sweet.

"Shh, princess," he murmured against her mouth, around the edges of that kiss. "You don't need to explain anything else to me. And you for damn sure got my permission."

He was wrong; she did need to explain. She really did. But what she needed even more was this, his hands on her body, his touch. Oh God, the touching. She soaked it up like vitamin D, vital, necessary, the sort of thing that made her ill with its lack. Now an ocean of it poured over her, and she waded through the onslaught of bliss. She let it knock her over and wash all her best intentions away.

He tasted perfect, man and heat and want. Desert sand and library binding glue. Okay, maybe she didn't really know what binding glue tasted like, but all those delicious things they'd done in the library were seared on her brain, and studies had shown that taste and smell were strongly related, so if she recalled the one, the other followed automatically. Wasn't that how the synaesthetes all said it worked?

Also…he had stopped. What?

She opened her eyes to find him staring at her, still with that nipple-perking slow-sugar smile, but now a shadow of concern had drifted over his face. It fell between them. Well, that was not acceptable.

"You went away for a while," he said.

"I'm sorry. I do that sometimes. All the thoughts… Know what? Let's start over. I can do this right." She could. Had she not been trained in this exact thing? Not in sex performance, per se, but in making her body fit her thoughts and making both of those fit her emotions. Forcing the symmetry. Making others believe. She was good at it. Best of the best. Queen of the world.

"Are you worried about the car still? 'Cause I have it on good authority that letting the control rig take us in is perfectly safe."

"No, I'm not worried about the car." Of course she wasn't. She had been in so many cars in so many parts of the world, she couldn't list them, not even with her near-perfect memory. Would saying that sound terribly self-important?

"What are you worried about?"

I'm worried because I married a man who broke me. Because I'm no longer complete, definitely not the girl you remember. I can do so many things I couldn't then, but not the right things. Not the things you would love.

"This is a dumb thing for someone my age to admit, but I just don't have a lot of experience here. With, you know, sex in a car. Or really sex anywhere." There. Bald enough? God, honesty was some uncomfortable shit.

"Second thoughts? Because this doesn't have to happen. Or doesn't have to happen tonight."

"Oh, please, Kellen. I want it. All of it. Swears. I'm just a goddamn freak of nature, okay?" Sudden anger zinged through her body, twining with the electric need he lit in her. Sparks frazzled her extremities; her heartbeat thudded. On the edge of that fury and still holding his gaze, she reached up and nudged her hairpiece off its hooks. She pulled it down into her lap, knowing what she looked like without it. Knowing that the metal psych-emitter net made her nearly bald head look mechanical. Look wrong.

It was that scene in *The Empire Strikes Back*, the original sacred trilogy, where Darth Vader removes his helm and movie-watchers realize that he's not a badass space villain, just a sad, scarred lieutenant whose magic might not be limitless after all. Had Kellen even seen that old movie, down in the piney woods of East Texas hickville? If she referenced it, would he have a clue what she was talking about?

He inspected her head for a long time, finally raising a hand to stroke the fine fuzz at her temples, along her brow line. She resisted the urge to mewl and lean into his touch. Instead she ground her molars and hoped he couldn't see how weird this made her feel.

Even uncomfortable, this was touch. Connection. Kindness. And *his*. She needed it. And feared it.

What if she couldn't stand it? What if she got the emotions wrong?

She had *laughed* when mech-Daniel had tried to kill her. That had been, uh, inappropriate. Wrong. *Wrong reaction. Out of practice, out of bounds, out of chances. Bad.*

"You do know you're still beautiful, right?" Kellen said, wresting her from the self-flagellation of memory.

"What?"

He warmed her all over with a smile, *that* smile. The one she remembered. "Well, I figure you were trying to shock me or somethin', removing your hairdo like that. Just want to let you know that I'm still here. Ain't running. In fact, can I…" He moved his hand back, stroking her head, metal and all.

Holy shit. "Oh, yes, you can," she breathed. "If I were a cat, I would so be purring right now."

He reached half behind his body and tapped something on the control screen. Nothing in the speed or direction of the car shifted, but Angela's seat hummed low and reclined, elongating her body, laying it down for his perusal. His pleasure. "Go ahead, then. Let it all out. I got you."

Let what out, though? What was the right response? What was she...

Oh wow. Just wow. He arced over her, dipped his chin in and kissed her again, long and sweet, working his tongue against hers until it felt like her insides were melting, curling toward him, lava going downhill, trailing clouds of fire. The volcano metaphor wasn't too far off for the rest of it, either, because when his hand dropped to her knee, spread along the sensitive skin right at the back there, and then traveled upward—squirm-inducingly slow and warm and delicious—she could no longer contain the seismic ripples. Her body hummed, vibrated until it was superheated. Molten at the core.

Patient hand beneath her ratty skirt now, persistent, steady. Merciless. If she told him to stop, she had a sense he would. But what a fucked-up thing that would be. She couldn't even let herself think it. Mustn't.

He broke their kiss, pulled it into pieces, separated and sorted. Where before the kiss itself had been a bright point, a supernova in their connection, now there were a dozen or more star points. His mouth at her throat and trailing downward. His hand soothing up the inside of her trembling thigh, bunching her torn skirt up against her hip. The scruff of his jaw, desperately in need of a shave and chafing the delicate skin covering her pulse. His other arm, braced against the car door, holding the rest of his body steady in its exploration.

His teeth trailing there, sharp and dangerous and just for an instant.

She knew why the damsels screamed for a vampire's bite.

Do it, do it. Make it hurt. Make me shatter.

She wasn't aware that she was making sounds until his low "shhhhh" blew in against her clavicle. The slow, sweet stroke of his hand up her leg paused. "You say the word and I stop, sweetheart," he said.

She opened her mouth, only to find that she was shaking so hard her teeth chattered. She struggled, got control of that, but it took a few seconds. Her mind screamed, *Don't you fucking dare stop.*

But out-loud words became an impossibility, because right at the same moment, his hand completed its journey, found her naked slit, and stroked the length of it, basting her with her own desire. His forefinger circled her clitoris, spiraling into a pleasure point so hot, so bright and pure and amazing, she had no control, slammed her eyes shut, and keened, writhing against the poly-skinned seat.

And then, shit how did he do this they were in a goddamned car and no way there was room had he cut off his legs or what because because because his mouth was *there*. Where before his fingers had been. Surrounding her clitoris, forming a vacuum, pulling. Oh holyfuckgoddamn, it was good. So good. So…

No words. Just feeling.

A part of her struggled for a heartbeat, then two,

trying to reconcile thought-emotion-transmission. Trying to instill a passive, pleasant mien and then alter her brain electrics and therefore emotions to match. Autosynchrony. Years of training.

Devolved to blank pleasure in the space between one breath and the next.

His long fingers within her, his mouth on her, he did break her. Apart and into a zillion pieces. And it was fucking glorious.

Synchrony shattered, exploded, paused at apex, and slammed back together in one immolative point of sensation.

She didn't remember reaching, pulling his shirt till the buttons gave, shoving her hands into his hair, or holding on for dear life. She realized it only after the fury passed, only after she could breathe again.

"Holy fuck," she said, and even those spare words came out on a pant.

He chuckled, a low rumble against her pelvis.

"Kellen?"

"Right here, princess."

"I haven't come that hard in ten years."

"Well, don't you know how to make somebody feel special."

"You do rather a good job yourself." The intensity had changed, but all the tension was still there, spooling around them, broidering them into one fused, decorative pattern. "May I touch you now?"

"Uh, yeah. Knock yourself out."

That's when she noticed the shirt, missing buttons. His dark-gold hair mussed. God, he was gorgeous. "Tilt your seat back, like mine," she said.

He did. Climbing over wasn't easy. Especially not

when her whole body felt like electrified pudding. But her will made it possible, found places for her knees to plant, to steady, for her arms, her mouth to settle. Found time to unfasten his jeans, bare his body. Every part fitted to its place, a regression from chaos into perfect order. She needed this, him. She needed, needed to fill herself with this man. Fusion, power, arcing up the nuclear binding energy curve. Meltdown imminent, but she was pegging full power anyhow.

Tilting forward onto him, sliding him into her swollen, aching body. *Welcome. Welcome home, my love.* Every millimeter of invasion lit chain explosions, critical stability failures. Control slipping. Fail-safes shattered. Stars collided. She came again, completely without warning, convulsing around him, clenching him into her.

His face buried in the lee of her neck, his hands spasming, one beneath her blouse, capping her spine, the other spread over her bare ass, stroking her onto him. Did he feel this too, the same bliss she felt? But no, she wasn't transmitting. Was so completely out of control anyhow, any transmission would be a mess. From far, far away, a stern voice told her she was doing it wrong, had failed to identify key brain-emotion causalities.

In that moment, Angela gave precisely zero fucks.

She pushed her rear into the cup of his hand then ground downward, sliding her mons against his pelvis until the ache bled sweet throughout her whole body.

"If my pleasure is what does it for you," she murmured against his hair, "then you ought to be enjoying the fuck out of this. I've already come twice."

A mumble against her throat, below her ear, the bass

burr that clamped itself to her spine and sent shudders through her whole body: "Am fixin' to meet you right there, sweetheart."

She felt it, when he came. Deep, deep. Jolt of tension in his body, hitch in his breath, and the steady thrust upward stilled. She settled atop him, let him work through the onslaught. Pressed a hot, sated kiss against his hair.

In that moment, there was nothing in the whole universe she wouldn't have given to make the last ten years disappear. To delete his hurts, and hers. To have lived this life differently, with him every step of the way. But the universe was not that kind. No take-backsies.

I'm so sorry.

● ● ●

Well, that sure was something. A pure magic something. He hadn't meant to seduce her. He had intended to take this reunion slow, let them get easy with each other. Make sure his heart was safe this time, not used up and tossed. But on the other hand, he wasn't sorry for what had just happened. Not for a moment of it.

Her face was tucked into the curve of his neck. Somehow they had pretzeled their bodies into just one reclined front seat. Probably something was going to go numb soon, but for right now, for this infinite pause, he wanted to hold her.

Her mouth moved against his skin. "Hey?"

"Yeah?"

"You know when you said, back during that holo-conference the night Daniel died, that I had never called you pretty?"

Of course he remembered. He always remembered. "There are reasons why normal humans don't recall every single word they utter."

"Be that as it may," she plowed on, "I might not have called you pretty to your face, but I wanted you to know that I have always thought it. You are beautiful to me."

"Didja now? Well, that's…wait, *pretty*?" He reared back and looked down at her dark head. "Pretty's for spring frocks and lace bloomers and…flowers 'n' shit."

Her laughed burbled, a sound made of pure joy. "Handsome, then?"

"Dukes, caliphs, and corp lords." He feigned offense. "You're killin' me."

"Hot?"

"Tacos."

"Fuckable?"

"I'll own that one."

She steepled one elbow against the seatback, propped her chin on the heel of that hand, and turned those dark-star eyes on him. "You're more than that, you know."

"What you mean?" Moments like these, sometimes it was easier to joke than tussle with embarrassment or confusion. "There's more to life than just being really, really good-lookin'? Not to mention useful between the sheets?"

"We are in a car," she reminded him. "No sheets for miles. And I might know shit about life as a whole, but I am certain there's definitely more to you than godlike looks. All that potential, Kellen. The world is metaphorically your oyster. That fucking idiom was made for people like you. You just have to reach out and grab it."

He raised his eyebrows and flexed long fingers

against her silk-skinned rear. "Talk on some more about grabbing. I like where this part's going."

"I'm being serious here." This was where she'd sigh and roll her eyes. Or where he would have expected her to, once. Only she didn't. She just kept staring. Then she went on. "When I met you, you were the smartest kid in the room. The finest scholar of what you have to realize was a very competitive class of small humans. That's why they teased you at first, the other students. Because of all of us, you were the one who was most likely to run the world. To lead us. If you got rolling, nobody could resist you. Least of all me."

He closed his eyes and flattened back against the body-warm seat. He didn't want to see her face with all that faith shining out of it. "You know what? Them dudes recruited me to the MIST filled my head with similar bullshit. Got me thinking I could make a difference, big'un, help all the folks back home and lots more besides. They had this research core group they were putting together, complete with a place for me. Said I was gonna do cross-species bioalteration work, maybe crack immortality. That was where my research was leading, and holy hell, it was exciting from, you know, a scientific standpoint. Other unspecified magic shit was s'posed to happen too, and poof, the whole world would be peace and glitter and, I dunno, unicorns fartin' rainbows. All's I had to do was drink their Kool-Aid, follow their orders, and jump off a cliff."

"What cliff?" Her face was so solemn, and he couldn't lie.

"They offered me a deal, princess. No baggage. Come

alone, or go on my merry way and wave the daydream goodbye."

Her mouth opened, closed, then opened again, threading faint words. "No baggage, huh? I thought you *wanted* to go to your mom after the hurricane."

He did the head-tilt lip-purse abbreviated version of a shrug. "I didn't, not particularly. Nobody wants to go back to the person who hurt 'em. Nobody wants to stay with the person who can cut them loose without a second thought."

What amounted to abandonment by his mama had hurt for a long time, but a long time ago. There were other parts of his childhood that he'd never get over, but having Mama sign over guardianship wasn't gonna cause him any more sleepless nights. He hadn't been the slightest bit tempted to leave the MIST, not even when Angela had told him about the storm.

"I was worried about my mother and Sissy, sure enough, but Lufkin is pretty far inland and wasn't threatened by that storm. I could have settled my worry without leaving Abu Dhabi permanently. No, sweetheart, when they offered me that deal to drop baggage, they weren't talking about Mama."

Her mouth made a silent O. "What did you…?"

He did shrug this time, beneath the sweet weight of her body. "I told them to fuck themselves in places that would especially hurt. I wasn't going to let you go."

"But then you did."

"Only 'cause you told me to."

Realization washed over her face, painting it pale. "Oh shit, Kellen. Oh holy shit. And that's why you didn't come back, because you were done with them.

Out. I was so oblivious. People have told me all my life how brilliant I am, but now...oh fucking *hell*, was I stupid."

He squeezed her a bit. Would have squeezed tighter, would have squeezed till all her pain went away, but she was a little thing, and dear. "You know what they say, ain't no cure for nineteen. You were just a kid. So was I."

It wasn't like his anger or his sense of betrayal had dissipated. He hated what they'd done to him, and she had been squarely a part of "they." If she hadn't told him to leave, he would have fought those consortium goons. He would have gotten the both of them out of there. Not sure how, but he would have made it happen. Was her goodbye that had sucked the fight right out of him. He hadn't wanted to stay if she didn't want him.

No, he hadn't forgiven her. But he was willing to look past her missteps, to live in the right now. Because right now felt so goddamn sweet in his arms.

"So I'm working out the timeline in my mind," she murmured. Talking him through her processes, as if they were on a project together. Damn, he'd missed that, the easy back-and-forth. It was less easy now, of course. Patching up emotional wounds wasn't like analyzing modern bit-funk lyrics using the Aarne-Thompson tale type index. Angela, though, she lit up when she was working through an academic process, and it was a beautiful thing to behold. "When we went out into the desert that morning to..."

"Fuck like rabbits."

"Yes, that. Had they already approached you and given you their ultimatum?"

"Yup," he said. "And I'd already told them. Not no, but hell no."

"Zeke sent for me at reveille that same morning," she said. Her voice was soft, small. "They offered me a deal, too."

He pulled a breath in, held it just a beat too long, and then released it into the space between their bodies. He stroked her back, beneath her blouse. There weren't words in him to convince her she didn't need to hair-shirt herself. That both their sins were so long ago.

"The first part of my deal was breaking up with you," she said after a long time. "And the second part...was I had to marry Daniel."

"I figured."

"I worried about you, what you would think. If you'd imagine that I loved him, if you thought about me being with him."

"Thinking 'bout you fucking a fan-favorite vid star night after night? Yeah, that twinged a bit, but I got over it." He hadn't, never had, but telling her that would serve no purpose. She was bent on beating herself up, and he was just a terrible enough person to find some salve in that. So he let her.

"The man I lived with wasn't the one people met in his vids. He was really good at acting." She leaned over him.

Opening his eyes was a reflex. He couldn't help seeing the pain writ large on her lovely face.

"I want you to know that I have suffered for my bad decisions," she said.

"You don't need to—"

"Daniel was not kind to me, and every moment I lived with him was fucking horrible. Not adorable tor-ment, like when I'm naked and you're a half centimeter away and refuse to touch me. Different torment. The bad kind."

He nudged the pad of his thumb against her mouth, tracing her lip. "If you need to say it, I will listen, but don't feel you have to."

A couple of messy tears splashed against his neck. She sniffed, to spare him a worse drenching, but more tears followed. He didn't move to wipe anything away.

"Thank you for that. Someday I will tell you, and I hope you won't hate me for it."

Good lord, what had they done to his gal? He wanted to put his hands around Daniel's neck and squeeze. Nasty little shit ought to be thankful he was already dead.

She sank against his body, fitting herself to the shape of him, atop him but not able to get still. He put his arms around her and asked the car to turn up the heaters. It obeyed, fanning warmth up her legs, beneath her skirt, where he still held her close.

She had more bad memories, he was sure of it, and he reckoned she'd release them in good time. She'd popped the cork on them, though, and this froth was just the beginning of a long pour. He swore, silently, to hold her tight through the whole thing. Let her decant at her own speed.

He stroked her back, the dip there above her perfect ass, and drew a line up her spine, testing the tension between her shoulder blades. She sighed like a kitten purrs.

"I don't hold with revenge, generally," he told her. "Those consortium assholes avenge themselves all over the place till they're sticky with it, and I refused to be a part of them. But if he was living right now, I expect I could make an exception for Daniel Neko."

"Wait." She popped back up onto her elbow and frowned down at him, like lightning had just struck her. "You know about the consortium?"

He had wondered when she'd connect the two. Her handlers, his wannabe handlers. End-of-the-world-blabbering conspiracy crackpots, all of them. Better world, after the end of this one. A world entirely populated with elite humans and the technology that bolstered their luxurious existences. Them same asshats who offered him a place among them. "I told you about the deal they offered, and where I told 'em to poke it. Suspect they're also the planners stuck you and Daniel Ashe together in unholy matrimony. Manipulative sonsabitches sure do like their deal makin', don't they?"

"Maybe," she said, steel in her voice, "but I'm not taking any more of their deals."

●   ●   ●

Reluctant as he was to do so, they had to untangle themselves from each other a few times for bio breaks along the way. Turned out there were lots of ways to get comfortable in a car, ways that had nothing to do with rest. This was about the damndest road trip he'd ever been on, yet every second of it was sweeter than stolen honey.

They took the long way around both Phoenix and Tucson, pussyfooting past what was clearly still a country hunkered down and scared. No public transit in sight, no planes in the air. Whole swathes of burbs turned to ghost towns, emptied by fear or worse. It was unnerving to see ruins this close to the capital.

Two alerts came in: more attacks out west, one of which was thwarted by some force that clearly flummoxed the newsvids and the government press reps alike. Apparently, a whole slew of unidentified intercepts came from space, *from the sky*. A couple of cults had already formed and were praying real hard. Garrett included a short note claiming it was aliens all the way, but he ended it with a smiley. He was likely getting a kick out of all the misreporting, because of course, he knew who was responsible for those intercepts.

Kellen had a good idea who'd helped out, too. He sent along a message of thanks to the queen of the Chiba Space Station. If she was watching over the Pentarc and all the space nearby, he felt a lot better about being eastbound and out of pocket.

As if all that man-made chaos weren't enough, Mother Nature offered her own little fuck-you in the form of an eruption of the Volcán de Colima, right there on the border of Jalisco and Colima. Kellen's butterflies were still hanging on, but widespread evacuations had inflated populations in Guadalajara and, to a lesser extent, Morelia. Infrastructure there wouldn't hold long, especially with these other hot spots taking up a lot of the emergency response resources.

He sent a message to Heron asking when they could get their plane in the air, maybe do a drop or a fetch down there in old Mexico. If the Chiba was shielding them, they probably didn't need Chloe dispersed anymore. Just a half second after he hit send, he remembered the data hole over Guadalajara. That would make getting a mission into the area a lot harder, if it was possible at all. Dangit, logistics.

"Seem to you like the whole world's going to shit?" he asked out loud as the feeds continued to roll in. He only half expected an answer.

"That's the pattern." Angela was chewing on a nutro-crunch, eyes closed, her bare feet, still pink in places from her run through the Pentarc spires in wintered grass, propped on the dash. Yoink had draped herself over the upper part of Angela's chest—that spot she called her boob shelf—like a slightly tubby old-Hollywood fur stole. That growled when he tried to move it.

"Shit has a pattern?"

Angela flexed her eyebrows but remained focused on whatever evil she was reading on the backs of her eyelids. "Yeah. The bad shit pattern. Goes like this: bad shit happens, there's an evacuation, and waves of refugees wash up against the nearest metropolis. Femacities are born. Then, just when the NGOs get set up and people start to settle in as best they may, boom, subgroup infighting or another disaster or a crazy person with a bomb decimates that population. Move, settle, repeat. People don't get a chance to grow deep roots or communities. Sometimes they are sent all the way across the world in these massive refugee-relocation initiatives. Sort of like your Pentarc refugees."

"Now hold your horses," Kellen said. Midmorning sun stung his eyes, and he'd slipped a hat on, low over his face. "We're building a home at the Pentarc, a community."

She opened her eyes. "Do you ever ask them if they *want* to stay? Or do you just assume that Pentarc living has to be better than wherever they came from?"

"In a lot of cases, it ain't assumption. There is literally nothing left. Like that island that went under the ocean.

But if they truly want to go home, yeah, we'll help them get there. Ain't our intention to hold hostages."

"I'm not actually talking intentions or ethics here," Angela said mildly. "Just demographics."

Yoink yawned, opened one eye, then the other. She stared at Kellen reproachfully. In moments like these, the cat didn't even need to use her interpreter net. He could see clearly what she needed. She was an unusually expressive critter.

He pushed his hat back and checked the dash nav. "Looks like we're coming up on Las Cruces. Want to get out and walk around some? Rustle up some food other than compressed kibble for our half-starved feline overlord here? Maybe get you a new skirt ain't ripped all up one side."

"Says the mad ripper himself. You could use a new shirt as well, or at least new buttons." Her dark eyes swept him from hair to boots, and her eyelids narrowed assessingly. "On second thought, why don't you just take it off? I could stand the view, pretty boy."

"We have discussed the inappropriateness of the term," he grumped, but his body was in full howdy in response to her sloe-eyed stare. Damn, woman didn't even have to touch him.

"Right. We agreed on *fuckable*, if I am not mistaken."

He grunted. "In any case, it's colder'n a cast-iron commode out there. I am not going to gallivant around shirtless on the short-hair side of winter."

"That is a goddamn shame. Can we go gallivanting again later on, say in summer, then? Or, you know, any time when you wouldn't have an objection. I haven't seen you bare in years and consider myself deprived."

He held that sentence close for a minute, drawing the warmth of it all around himself. Had she just made plans for summertime, plans that included him? Or was that offhand banter? He didn't want to commit to hope at this point, but she painted their relationship in such bright colors.

A part of him wasn't convinced. He wanted to ask for promises, but even if she offered that boon, how could he possibly believe her?

If it is just for today, tonight, tomorrow, I'd best make these hours count.

The car slowed and exited the highway.

"Did the dragon just go sentient, or do you know where we're headed?" he asked.

"Yeah, I adjusted the itinerary some kilometers back. Flea market downtown with a stand of refrescandos attached. We can tidy up, make sure we have everything we need for the next few days. Stores will be hard to come by once we cross the border." She looked point-edly at his jacket, wadded in a pile in the back seat. "We might need more ammo."

He had no plans to use that gun Mari'd given him. Only reason he hadn't left it back at the Pentarc was the kindness of her gesture, and he didn't want to offend. But if things went sideways with Vallejo, they were both going to need a lot more than one dinky pistol and a few boxes of ammo.

Things went sideways with Vallejo, they were more likely to require a goddamn army.

Though come to think on it, he might know some folks could muster up a fighting force. Might even be core-deep in love with one of those folks right now.

CHAPTER

11

THE FLEA MARKET WAS CALLED BIG DADDY'S, AND IT WAS smack in the middle of town. They shouldn't have been able to park so close. When horrible things happened, though, most folk holed up in their homes and plugged into the news feeds, ingesting disaster porn like it was corn chips. Who could blame them? Kellen had been like that once, for a long time in fact, hoping that just sitting still and not fussing would make the angel of death pass by faster.

They got out of the car and safety-set it so that it cycled air for Yoink but wouldn't respond to a thief trying to boost it. Taking kitty along would be a bad bet in a place like this. Too many ways for that gal to get into trouble, and, being her, she would find every last one.

Angela pointed past the open-air stalls and toward an ugly metal building that promised air-conditioning, full-service cloud ports, and bargains-bargains-bargains. A gaggle of mamas swamped with young'uns watched them walk by but didn't say anything. They were the only people Kellen could see, at least on the outside.

There was something creepy about a sparsely attended flea market, and this one sure wasn't helped by the giant armless statue out front, presumably of Big Daddy himself. The pallid-flesh attempt at paint was peeling, but the color had been tending toward zombie even in its prime.

Inside, a few more shoppers milled aimlessly, but most of the people were vendors who, having arranged their wares on booth shelves and folding tables, now lounged in picnic chairs, gazes glued to whatever was being fed into their wearable coms. News, maybe. More likely porn.

Kellen wandered near a booth hawking preserved meat and injectable magnetic tattoos, but Angela grabbed his hand, and he decided to keep on holding rather than wander. If she'd had some kind of mental block against touching others before, she appeared to have blown through that sucker. She was downright grabby lately. Kellen had no problem with that.

He followed her to a booth in the back corner, poorly lit and offering woo-woo on the cheap: oils, crystals, a vaguely Tesla-looking device that promised to enable cross-dimensional communication with loved ones who had passed on. The thick smell of chem-laced patchouli near knocked him out.

A kid with an electronic money belt watched him, suspicious. Couldn't have been more than ten and had an unsettling way of not blinking. "Red stamps are ten percent off today only."

"What if I want to barter?" Angela said.

"I ain't authorized. You'll need to talk to Dead Fester."

Angela rolled her sleeve back and showed the kid something on her com. Kid blinked rapidly then pushed back her picnic chair and scrambled behind a grungy purple-brown curtain Kellen hadn't even noticed before. It resembled one of those changing-area privacy screens, only this booth didn't sell clothes. After a few seconds, the kid returned.

"Dead said come on back."

Angela still had his hand clamped in hers, so Kellen didn't have a choice but to follow.

The tiny office/changing room had a lot in common with nighttime in the desert. That is to say, it was dark. Also lots more cramped and, um, smellier. Back here, the patchouli stench deferred to what Kellen would swear was Somah solution and ammonia. He did a quick scan for organics transport containers or portable surgical rigs. Didn't see either. Which proved exactly nothing. Unlicensed carvers could still do backroom bioalteration without a proper surgery-in-a-box. He himself had improvised more than a few times.

But the lone occupant of the tiny room didn't seem ready to come at them with scalpels, at least not right away. He was a portly gent wearing overalls and sitting on a giant balloon, his close-shorn pate hooked into at least three wire bunches, all connected to what resembled a noodle strainer. He did not disconnect when his guests entered.

"Thanks for agreeing to a meat-meet," Angela said. "I know it was short notice."

"No worries, Angel. Messaging from your *car* in the middle of the desert and sounding all breathless and urgent—how could I possibly ignore all the story potential there?" He finally looked up. He had this amazing expression, kinda disapproving and awed at the same time. "Now that's a new look for you." He motioned toward the dark scruff that just barely covered Angela's implanted psych-emitter rig.

She hadn't bothered to hook her wig back on, and Kellen hadn't encouraged it. He would always prefer her hair long and strokable, but this style suited her. Mature. Serious. Fierce.

The dude in the overalls slid a pair of sunglasses down his beaky nose and gave Kellen a narrow-eyed stare worthy of the most disapproving librarian. "Who's this?"

Lots of ways Angela could answer that question, but her choice came as something of a surprise. "My partner," she said, squeezing his hand beneath her overlong sleeve. "My lover."

"Yer so-posh husband know about him?"

"Daniel's dead," Angela said, her voice exactly that: dead, flat, no-nonsense. "He survived the attempt on his life in October, but his faculties were severely impaired, and he had to be supplemented increasingly with chems and devices. A second attempt, by way of one of these recent smartbomb attacks, finished the job. He died the day before yesterday."

"So you hired pretty boy here to dance on his grave or what? Not that I'm judging, but some people will want the sordids."

"I've been having an affair with this man since I was fifteen," she said. It was even true, sort of. Not counting that long dry spell in the middle. "I tried to get him out of my mind, even confessed tearfully to Daniel, but you know how it is with true love. We've been sneaking, this man and I, like Romeo and fucking Juliet. Also, I'm probably pregnant, but he doesn't know yet, and I won't know for another six weeks that it's actually twins. Follow-up potential there, if the interest level is high enough."

The dealer stared hard at her for a few more seconds, then said sternly, "Make it quadruplets and we might have a runnable rag piece with options for pickups on major channels, since you are—or were—a big-time senator and all."

"Deal." Angela smiled, that practiced, perfect smile he'd seen so often over the years.

The dude threw his wire-studded head back and hee-hawed. Then he rolled his balloon-chair back, stood up, and opened his arms wide. After the slightest of pauses, Angela let loose of Kellen's hand and hugged the man whose name apparently really was Dead Fester.

When she extricated herself from the big man's embrace, she was half laughing, half crying. She held out a hand, and Kellen approached warily.

What she'd said had had the taint of lies on it, but just enough had been true that he had to wonder. *Was* she pregnant? She'd only been widowed what, seven, eight weeks? It wouldn't be obvious yet. Granted, her husband had been a hot-buttered asshole, but that didn't mean they hadn't been intimate. She'd had a tough note in her voice when she'd spoken of Daniel. A victim's limp fury. Had he been at her unrelenting till the end? Every caretaking cell in Kellen's body—and lord knew he had more than his fair share of those suckers—woke up worried.

He took her outstretched hand, moved to stand beside

her, and nodded to Dead. Truthfully, he had no idea what to think, but in such situations, he'd learned it was best to stay quiet and soak up all information as it came at him.

"Kellen, meet Dead Fester, better known as SwankVid, Ursula Dioda, the GNN, and...did I forget one, Fez?"

GNN. Global News Network. Only the news reporting source of record for three multinations, plus the ZaneCorp. And come to find out the whole thing was run by...one dude in the back room of a flea market? *This* dude, moreover? Fucking hell. Pretty much everything Kellen knew about the way media worked just got stood on its head.

"Well, FanSource as well, but that one is a labor of love and is, I'm afraid, somewhat small." He looked proud as a new mama. "You can call me Fez."

Kellen shook his hand. "Is a pleasure," he mumbled.

"Oh, it really could be," the newsman/gossip-monger simpered. "I am not even kidding. You're chin-droolingly hot. The dirty cowboy thing, right? Yee-fucking-haw."

"Uh..."

"Fez," Angela slid in smoothly, "would you like to guess my truths?"

"Happy to, Angel. Let me see. It's true that you and Pretty-Boy Kellen were teenage sweethearts. Also true that Daniel is dead, and good riddance. True he survived October?"

Angela shook her head and held up one finger, like a little kid counting off maths.

"Ooch, strike one. Okay, the quads are fibs, which

is such a pity. Multiple births are all the rage at the moment. Did you know the English princess-in-exile is *enceinte*? Very hush at the moment pending an auction for rights to live-vid the birth, but how tragic you're lying about your condition. If it was true, the two of you would deliver at around the same time. Actually at the same time if you put a surgeon on retainer or banked the fetus. Are you sure you don't want to run off and get yourself knocked up?"

This conversation was making Kellen uncomfortable. Also more than a tad wistful. If they'd stayed together, he and Angela could have a kid almost as old as wee money belt outside. What would that even be like, being somebody's father? It didn't take long for the possibility to settle itself over his life, in bright colors. Looked... well, not bad there.

"Three for four isn't bad," Angela said, ignoring the question. "In all seriousness, Fez, I'm going to need some amazing spin to pull this off."

"What, bringing you back from the dead? Easy peasy lemon squeezie, Angel. Just you let Uncle Dead sort this one for you. Now, how would you like to debut your luscious new undead self?"

"That's kind of a problem, too. I'm not sure yet."

This was where listening without interrupting could get a body in trouble, but Kellen kept his cool. Even though inside, he was screaming. *Whoa, now. You come back, publicly, you'll go back to that life. Away from me. Ghost out. Fuck. How did I let you do this to me again?*

"Okay, no rush," Fez rolled on. "Can I at least know what you've been up to for the last eight weeks, ever since you floated that pink gown at La Mars Madrid's gala? The print pattern for that dress is selling like penny chems at a dance party, by the way."

"I've been grieving-not-grieving, but Kellen makes all the sads go away," she said. "You could imply that he saved me from the ruin of the Hotel Riu. Very dramatic. He's selfless and heroic like that. Rescues baby goats, for fuck's sake."

Fez rubbed his pudgy hands together. "I am so in love with this narrative! It's going to play huge. Now, when last we spoke, you were talking up the evils of Texas, specifically that vomit bag Vallejo. Do we want to say he's responsible for Daniel's murder?"

The question hung on the air for a long moment. Too long. *Yes. Tell him yes.* Weren't they on their way right at this minute to shovel some good old-fashioned justice onto Damon Vallejo's head? Why deny it?

Was this another surprise she was waiting for the last second to spring on him?

Angela's solemn face had gone one notch solemner. "Give me a week on that, okay? Just tease the resurrection for now. Atheist-girl-Jesus: kind of guaranteed to rile people."

"You got it. Oh! And one thing: did you want me to set up a confessional with Rafa, or…?"

"Already on it."

"Oh, magnificent girl." Fez pressed two hands over the place most folks thought their hearts were located. "I have *missed* working with you. A paltry few people in this biz know how all the pieces fit together, you know? So despite the unfortunate thing you have done to your hair—though I still believe we can soar with this new look, maybe a mix of serious and valiant?—anyway, I just want to say I'm glad you're back in the game."

Something stark passed over her face. Real quick, too quick for Fez to have seen. But Kellen did. It mirrored a dark fury inside his own soul. He couldn't address this bullshit with her right now, not with a professional gossip standing right there and gazing at her like she was made of dark chocolate and rubies.

Both their coms vibrated at the same time, and Fez was too savvy not to notice. He gave them the one-eyebrow well-what treatment, despite the fact that this shit was private.

Angela pushed back her sleeve to read the message, in text form, spooling along the smartskin patch on her forearm. Kellen followed her gaze to where their hands were still conjoined and read her message upside down.

It was short, from Garrett, of all people: Defenses here are holding. God save the queen. The data hole over Enchanted Rock moved. How d'you feel about the beach?

●　　●　　●

All the stress and the terror notwithstanding, this was Angela's favorite part of any plan. Setting up the scenario, placing each block. Careful balance, steady. And then, when the precarious structure was perfect, she would storm in like a toddler with a constructo set and smash the shit out of her design.

Okay, so Fez was on board. One bullet point checked. Her personal design was coming together.

Fez was one of her favorite hooks into the social media universe. She'd met him early on in her marriage to Daniel. At the time, he'd been purely fan sites and celeb gossip, but he'd expanded his reach over the years, as had she. They'd sort of grown up together, professionally. She wasn't about to trust anyone completely, not after the last several months, but she couldn't remember being in close quarters with two people she sort of trusted as much as Kellen and Fez. For a bright moment there, she had felt…comfortable. Home.

Dangerous feeling, that. But also impossibly sweet.

After equipping for their journey into the vasty black of Texas, specifically now to the ocean edge of the state, she and Kellen climbed back into the dragon car, spun up the reactor, and laid rubber out of Las Cruces. The northern and eastern borders of the conflict zone were loosely secured, easily bribed through, but here in the west, this close to the capital, the UNAN security took shit seriously. Angela had thought ahead, though.

Her official identity as a continental senator was toast due to her recent tragic death, but what idiot only had one ID? Not this gal. That had been her second bullet point, even though technically, it overlapped with the first.

Just as senators and diplomatic envoys and superstar celebrities had an alternate gate for most sec checks, so did registered journalists. A group to which she now belonged, thanks to Fez. Her GNN credentials, and matching ones for Kellen, would show up on any data scan and would pass the sniff test if border agents checked in at the GNN databases. Best of all, because their car was a mobile news unit, they could broadcast the clearance and wouldn't even be subjected to face-print scanners.

Hugging Fez didn't begin to repay what he'd just done for her.

She slid into the car with energy crackling just below the surface of her skin, about to explode with the need to share these supercool gizmo gadget details with Kellen. All those spy scenarios they used to concoct when they were kids had nothing on what she'd just pulled off or was about to pull off. She was the Jackal, 007, and Mata Hari all rolled into one. *I am the fire. Fuck yeah.*

What she didn't expect was reality. Kellen in a sulk. Why was he in a sulk? Frustratingly in a sulk, and not anxious to talk about what specifically had ensulkened him.

They rode in silence for hours. Literally hours. Kellen alternately stared out the car windows or asked if she wanted water/jerky/a bio break. They passed the security checkpoint, rolling right through it and broadcasting her superspy GNN credentials, and got waved through. And she couldn't even crow about how perfectly that shit went off.

Finally, unable to take it one second longer, she said, "You're quiet."

He flinched like he'd been sleeping. He hadn't. "Sorry. You need…?"

"Not really anything. Not technically. But seeing as we're stuck in this car together for several hours yet, I thought we could, you know, interact." She waited for the obvious flirty comeback, the absolute lowest-hanging fruit, but instead he stretched his long legs along the floorboard and scraped a big hand over his face.

"Sorry," he said again. "Am being bad company."

Yeah, you are. And you're making me nervous/angry/ sad. Was his problem meeting Fez, being reminded that

Angela had a life outside of the little Pentarc-centric bubble she'd existed in these last few weeks? Could he not handle that? Daniel had opposed her strides toward independence, too. He had never wanted to share his toys. Specifically his main toy, her.

And oh shit, she did not just find a point of comparison between Daniel and Kellen. Yuck. She felt like she needed to bleach her brain for even thinking it.

"Was looking out at the land as we passed," Kellen said in a low voice. "Thinkin' how much has changed. This place used to be my home once. And now it's not."

The air whooshed out of Angela. Oh. Okay. Well, she could see why the landscape might affect him. She had seen it, the scarred leftovers of what had once been pretty, on hundreds of strategic sat feeds over the years. Orbital-bombardment craters, half-rubbled ghost towns, and intentional fire-break controlled scorches weren't new to her, or shocking. Sometimes she forgot not everyone had seen the stuff she had. Not everyone had her emotional callouses. Fuck a *muffin*, she was being insensitive.

She thought about reaching out, touching him. Holding him. But connection was *her* core joy source, not his. He didn't need to be constantly stroked, to be reassured that he wasn't alone or incapable or insufficient. He was stronger than that. Stronger than her.

In the uncomfortable silence, Yoink slunk from her explorations in the back seat, climbed onto the center console, and licked her paw in a desultory fashion, peering side-eyed at her two humans, one and then the other. After a while she nosed Kellen's hand until he moved it for her, and then shoved her needy head beneath it.

When he cricked one finger against her chin, Angela could hear the purring from here. *Traitor*.

A traitor that Angela was suddenly super jealous of.

"I thought you were from *East* Texas," Angela said after a long time. They were still pretty far west. No tall trees or green things yet.

"Yeah, Angelina County. Big pine trees, bigger cockroaches. Everything in Texas is big. You know it has—had—five distinct climatic regions? This here is a cold desert, but we should be heading into coastal lowland as we skirt south of San Antone." He said it wrong on purpose, almost defiantly, owning the mispronunciation. People from this area said a lot of things wrong. *Guadaloop* instead of Guadalupe. *Man-chack* instead of Manchaca. *Blaynco* instead of Blanco. The speech pattern drew heckling from outsiders, and it had been a complete bitch during continental and language integration debates, but they kept on, almost like they were proud of their ignorance. Kind of like how Kellen had always held onto his twang.

"You sound like a tour guide." She smiled when she said it but couldn't help thinking that this wasn't the conversation they needed to have. As freaked out as he might be about the damage his home state had sustained, it wasn't like he'd never seen wrecked landscapes. Day in, day out, he rescued refugees on the cusp of annihilation. He knew how these things went down, what an area looked like as it approached the fail point.

"Just regurgitating facts," he said. "Ain't that what us supergeniuses do? When I was a kid, all's I knew about Texas was that pecan trees are better than pines for climbing. Lower branches make getting a boost up easier. Over in Mustaqbal, though, I couldn't read enough about where I come from. Geography, anthropology, bird-watching guides. You gotta know everything about a place if you're gonna defend it."

"We aren't at war," she reminded him gently. Ooooh, it felt dirty to say that. Had she not just spent a year and a half trying to draw the Texas rebels into a war? And for what? Her own career? Good God. Had that really been her?

"Everything is war, princess," Kellen said in a fire-edged voice. "Just getting up in the morning sometimes works itself into a battle. Humans are by nature warriors, killers. Ain't that what all the old texts tell us? We have dominion over the lesser critters, ownership over the land, all by virtue of how very good we are at killin'. But you figure it is ever possible to own something like this, something so vast?" He stretched an arm out, as if he could finger paint the landscape beyond the car windows. "We have failed as stewards, and in revenge, the land has kicked us out. Fucking look at it. We're all at war, and we're all refugees."

"You're getting scary low," she told him. "And I need you to work through this funk before we arrive at the coast. We don't know what we're going to find there, and I can't have you navel-gazing or waxing philosophical." She didn't mention how root-level terrifying it was to see Kellen—bright, optimistic, sunshine and roses Kellen, for fuck's sake—go on about war and death and failure.

"I'll have your back in Galveston," he said, not looking at her. "You don't need to worry about me being on point."

Angela's com buzzed, and she cringed instinctively. Alerts of more attacks? Another update from the Pentarc? Neither promised to be good news. She tapped, and the message crackled out.

"Lucky cat says sum of luck is proportional to number of belly rubs sustained," Yoink communicated. Angela looked down and saw that the cat had stretched all the way across the console, her head and one paw on Kellen's thigh, her fluffy butt pushed up against Angela. A little fur-covered kitty bridge. "More rubbing is urgently required."

So hard not to laugh, so fuck it, Angela did laugh. For once, she didn't resist the urge. She reached down and stroked Yoink's soft belly. When Kellen rubbed between the cinnamon-striped ears and the purring rose to weaponized ultra-low-frequency levels, Angela couldn't help feeling that this was right. This mission, this plan.

This...family?

CHAPTER 12

NIGHT CAME EARLY THIS TIME OF YEAR, AND DARK HAD settled in long before they got to the Highway 6 Bayou Vista exit, where the world ended. Kellen rolled the dragon close to the onset of the ocean but tucked it far enough back that the water wouldn't be able to get at it.

Behind them lay war-scarred Texas, and ahead roiled a monster. The Gulf of Mexico wasn't just a body of water anymore. It was a water beast that had consumed cities, had murdered millions. When Superstorm Agatha had roared up Galveston Bay, shoving mountains of its bloated, surge-driven self up the Houston ship channel, the beast had grown like one of those old Japanese anime horrors.

And Vallejo had intentionally moved his data-hole electronic-coverage bubble *here*. To the horror that he had created. What a ballsy, blight-upon-humanity little motherfucker he was.

Unless he hadn't. Unless they'd guessed wrong about him being under that dark spot.

Was it sick as fuck Kellen kind of *hoped* he'd been

wrong? If Vallejo wasn't here after all, or somebody else had launched those drones, their quest could continue on. More days, more weeks. More time he could be near her, hold her, touch her, feel her voice on his skin and pretend all this would last. Sure, he wanted this mission to end the way it ought and the killing to stop.

He also, secretly, wanted it to never end.

"So do we check in with Garrett now or what?" Angela, bundled up in that ugly, borrowed peacoat, stood by the hood of the car, pecking into her com. Not that it would do her a lick of good.

"Data hole," Kellen reminded her, coming around the scuffed bumper. "We're on our own."

Yoink hopped up onto the car and settled herself between her people. Close enough to touch, but not actually, you know, touching. Anybody wanting to pet her would have to come to her, on her terms. Saucy cat.

"What? So what are we supposed to do now?" Angela sounded frustrated. "We can't go any further with the car. I mean, I know the dragon is durable and smart and handles terrain like it's on tracks, but I don't think it'll…"

She kept on talking. Kellen reached down and stroked Yoink between the ears. "All right, little general. Hook us up."

The cat got still, channeling information through her amplified neural. Out here on the dark edge of nuthin', Kellen might very well be cut off from the rest of the world and its cloud of information, but he had unique access to a totally different cloud. A moving, breathing one. He drew patterns on Yoink's tiny head, and the metal horns by her ears extruded light in rivulets, forming patterns, drawing a picture. Well, a grid more than a picture. Along its light lines, a few dozen to a hundred blips came online, a pattern of color in the starless night.

"What is that?" Angela asked.

"Critters," he answered. "All them critters under the ocean. Yoink just sent out a hello, and they're answering."

"They're...altered? Like Yoink?"

He didn't dare look at her when he said, "The early ones got microchips I put in by hand. But later on we switched to nanotrackers, and those things self-replicate, get passed on. So we got multiple generations now of tracked, augmented critters with artificial adaptations."

"You did this?" She breathed the voice of judgment, and he wanted to crawl in a corner and pretend they saw this eye to eye. He knew her government's policies on unsanctioned alteration. He knew he hadn't been licensed for any bit of what he'd done. He knew if she was a good little law-abiding senator, she'd haul his ass to jail as soon as they got back to civilization.

But he couldn't deny this work, his life's passion, the thing he loved almost as much as he loved her. He just wished she could understand.

"World's gone hostile to wildlife," he said through tight lips, "so I make wildlife fit back into the world. Skin augmented with capillary action for more effective water collection and heat radiation in coyotes out west, Vectran-reinforced hide for prey animals like that vicuña you rode in with, to keep her and her someday-babies safe from poachers' bullets. Yeah, that's what I do."

She moved slightly, let out a puff of breath that

grazed his shoulder, a ghost touch of warmth. "And these ones?" She pointed to the dance of light on Yoink's holographic grid.

He sighed, feeling like he'd just dodged a judgment bullet. "Well, the yellow ones are skeeters—"

"Mosquitoes? Oh yuck, Kellen. Eliminating them was one of the first major successes of this century. Why in seven hells would anybody want to bring back a population of those?"

"They aren't my favorite, I'll admit, but they deserve to live, same as anybody. It wasn't their fault Zika and Dengue B went nuts, and there were better ways of handling that crisis than wiping out a whole species."

"Better ways? You know, it is possible to lavish too much love on a bunch of blood-sucking disease vectors that don't even know you exist."

"Aw, honey, ain't no such thing as too much love," he said. Accusingly as all get-out.

He hadn't meant to put it like that, but watching his words settle over her face, moonlike in the headlights and bathed in something that looked like shock, it felt like the right way to phrase his impression of the matter. The only way, in fact. He dared her to deny it, to prove somehow that she wasn't a heartless, opportunistic, selfish bitch. That she wasn't gonna leave him high and dry just as soon as she got her vengeance.

Her mouth closed, and she took a visible breath. "And the blue dots?"

Well then. Guess that was that.

"Dolphins," he said. "Special ones adapted to live in the toxic radioactive soup of this particular shithole of a coastline."

That super hurricane had taken out the South Texas nuclear plant when it devoured its way up to Houston, and nothing in the whole Gulf of Mexico had been the same afterward. Most natural marine life was gone or changed. Only the sturdiest stuff endured. And the adaptives.

"These bottlenoses right here are natural echolocators," Kellen said, focusing on the dolphin blips and not Angela's too-beautiful face, "so I asked 'em, via their nanocoms and Yoink's relay, to show us anything under water that is neither ruin nor critter."

If Vallejo had some underwater fortress casting up that data hole, Kellen's network would find it.

"They can tell the difference?" The obvious disbelief in Angela's voice caused him to look up.

"Yeah," he said. "They're smart, princess. Brightest of the bright."

Like us. Only better, since they don't give a shit about nation building or law slinging.

On the other hand, dolphins did join pods for a time, then drift off, joining another one. Loyalty seemed transient for them, as were concepts of home or family. So maybe they were more like her and her class than he'd realized. And maybe Angela wasn't the freak of nature he'd been painting her for a lifetime now. Maybe he wasn't either. Maybe both of them fit into their parallel ecosystems just fine, separate but crashing together like storm-tossed birds for one bright, emotionally excruciating encounter, and then just as suddenly drifting off back to where they belonged, separate, content to live off memories until the next climatic convulsion dropped them into the same biome.

"So is that a real big one or what?" she asked.

"A real big what?" This conversation could go down a gutter fast.

"Dolphin." Angela pointed toward Yoink's still-blinking display.

Holy moly. "That's not a dolphin."

The new blip didn't have solid edges like the nano-tracked animals; it was amorphous, a giant, gelatinous, pill-shaped blob burbling through the ocean. Which didn't mean that's what it looked like for real, just that several dolphins had located it and were transmitting click identifications per his request. It was the size of maybe a dozen adult dolphins, so definitely not a marine mammal itself, not even a collection of them. Pods didn't get that big around here, this close to the shore and in an environment as hostile and uncertain as a string of sunken, polluted cities.

"It's coming our way," said Angela in a voice that sounded like armor being donned, safeties unlocked.

Kellen couldn't look away from the image. Jesus, that thing was huge.

"No," said Yoink. "It is here."

Her display went dark.

•   •   •

Dark night, no moon, clouds obscuring the stars. And something that was supposedly not a dolphin coming right at them. Logic required Angela to run back to the car and grab that gun. She knew how to shoot. Sort of. Okay, she had been in conference with people who knew how to shoot. And they hadn't been any smarter or more athletic than her. If those guys could figure out how to disable a safety and pull a trigger, she sure as shit could do the same.

But her goddamned feet would not move. She just stood there, dry mouthed and frozen. Under cover of darkness, Kellen's hand found hers, and she clasped it. Probably harder than she should have.

Out there, the surface undulated. Something splashed. As if a strange mutant sea creature was surfacing, searching. For prey? For her?

"Dolphins say to be quick. The intruder will move soon, underneath the water. From here, he will go into West Bay and may be harder to reach," Yoink said, her digital voice perfectly calm, issuing as it always did from a com, this time Angela's. "He says thank you for the communication relay and seeks admin access. Enable?"

"No," Kellen said. "You don't let anybody in there but me, little bit."

"Okay."

The kitty pushed her head up beneath their clasped hands, almost as if she were insisting on a pet. Only this time her motives were less adorable and more utilitarian.

Kellen guided Angela's hand to the back of Yoink's neck. He stroked the soft fur further up, between the ears. It took Angela a couple of seconds to figure out that he was using the cat's skull as some sort of input device. No wonder he'd worried, back at the Pentarc, that she would be creeped out by Yoink. The interface certainly was…weird. But also not. Figure Kellen to devise a communication system based on comforting touch. How very him.

Yoink went stiff, growling under her breath.

"Easy, sweet girl," Angela soothed. This wasn't her thing, this caring for others. Usually she enjoyed the expedience of pushing her own emotional experience onto others and expecting them to follow. Or to react within a predicted response radius. She never reached out, not physically. Not intimately. But this was her kitty. Her companion. Her friend. She needed to flay some habits. "I'm not going to let you get eaten by a sea monster. I swear all the best swears."

"Do not swear at all, or if thou wilt, swear by thy gracious self." Kellen's voice, coming out of the darkness and laying that heavy shit on the night air.

She tore her gaze from the rising kraken to stare at him instead. "Shakespeare? We are in mortal danger, and you spout Shakespeare? What the actual fuck, Kellen?"

"Would Wordsworth wiggle your noodle more?"

"Wiggle my…" She shook her head to clear the nonsense out. The nonsense stayed put. "Has anybody ever told you that you are completely inappropriate?"

It was dark, he was facing the water rather than the car, and she couldn't see properly, but he might have smiled. Smiled. Right then.

"All the damn time, princess."

"Look, we're about to get fucking eaten by the ocean, Mr. Inappropriate. Color me crazy but—"

Yoink broke in, upping the creepy factor by a gazillion. "You two. He says you two bicker like childhood siblings or very old lovers and which is it?"

That drew them both up cold. They said in unison, "Who?"

"Dolphins say the sea monster. The intruder. The does-not-belong-here-you-take-him." She sneezed. "Dolphins speak strangely. He is on the sub-sea, sub-fish, sub-*marine*. That one."

The cat didn't have a finger to point, but her holo-emitting head lasers rolled out a light grid, like the one before, and put a single blinking dot on it. Ominous, purple, this dot was a hell of a lot closer than any of those others had been, even the mosquito ones. From the grid, it looked like the intruder was about a hundred feet from where the water started, maybe a hundred twenty from the tips of Angela's toes. And he was talking to her Yoink.

"There was a bridge here," the cat went on. "He says it is good you stopped the car because the drop is deep and do you have wet dresses. Suits. Do you have wet suits? You cannot wade to his sub-marine. The drop is deep. The water is cold danger. Do not drink it."

"Let me get this straight. There is a person out there in a submarine, talking to us, through you?" said Angela.

"Yes. He can communicate over short ranges because the anal openings underestimated dolphins, and I can interpret because I am a fancy cat."

"You sure are that, little bit. Now these assholes, are they on the submarine, too?" Kellen asked.

Angela wondered if she should compliment his ability to translate digital cat translating digital dolphin. He'd always envied her ease with languages, but this was impressive by anybody's standards.

"He says he will explain all. He wants...no, definitely no." Yoink bowed up her back.

"No?"

"No." Beneath Angela's hand, Yoink hiss-growled. Her ears flattened. Likely she was beyond soothing at this point, but Angela tried anyway.

The bright dot went away, and Yoink moved, a dark

blur of fear and fur. In the next instant, her claws embedded themselves in Angela's shoulder—*ow*—points of pain—*more ow*—trembling in echo of the cat's own terror. Yoink was still making unholy sounds, and it was all Angela could manage not to do the same. Holy fuck, those claws hurt, but she couldn't do what instinct told her she must: reach up, grab the cat by her scruff, and yank her off. Logic told her it wouldn't work anyhow. Yoink's claws were hooked in deep. They panged at the slightest movement, even breathing.

"Yoink," Kellen said, his voice firm but not shouty, "that shit command he gave you, don't you pay it no mind. Listen to my voice. Who's in charge here?"

"You are, but he wants—"

"Don't matter. I need you to do a thing for me, okay? Can you slink back into the car and try Garrett on the com? Call us some backup, please, and keep them dolphins in the know? Just keep patching them through on my earpiece, and I'll take it from here. You can do that, can't ya?"

Try Garrett? Hadn't he just said a few minutes ago that they couldn't get communications in or out of this data hole? How was this supposed to work? Tiny robot radio mosquitoes?

Yoink was still growling, but she did pull her claws back, withdrawing them from Angela's shoulder. Ow, but definitely not the worst pain Angela had ever endured.

"So," she said. "The plan."

Kellen frowned at the black ocean. "I hope you ain't thinking about goin' down there. It's a toxic soup hell."

"A toxic soup hell full of answers, though," she said.

"Maybe." He shrugged. "We do have wet dresses.

Bought some swanky ones off Dead Fester, after word came we were headed down to the coast."

"Suits. Wet *suits*. We are completely undressed." She covertly peered at him out of the corner of her eye, to see if he got her joke.

He did, even though it wasn't a great joke. His low chuckle rumbled into the night like a physical thing, linking them together.

"Still, diving right in with no preparation is a shit plan," he said, "undressed and sexy as hell or not. We don't even know who 'the intruder' is."

She pursed her lips and glared, but his compliment stroked her insides. "Oh, don't we just?"

"Could be Vallejo," he said. "Could be some other TPA technocrat shithead. Could be Elvis Presley back from the dead. We just don't know what's out there."

"I called out Vallejo's sins in public. The drones up in the sky right now came from Texas. His guilt could only be clearer if he sent me an I-did-it message."

"So we're just going to swim out to his dungeon like lemmings?"

"For a self-professed animal lover, that was terribly unfair to lemmings." She shook her head. "You asked for a relay. What do your dolphins say about that sub?"

He closed his eyes, tipped his head back, and crossed his arms over his chest. The face of capitulation. Maybe? Or he might have just been listening to the com stuck in his ear.

"They've reconnoitered some and transmitted a bunch of data to Yoink and then on to me. They're saying there's only one living creature on that sub. It's a disaster-porn tourist sub, big and quiet but unarmed."

He opened his eyes and shot her a look. "But I still ain't gonna let you go down there bare-assed and vulnerable."

"I don't need your permission," she reminded him, but she kept her tone gentler than it might have been a month ago. A week ago. "Don't you want to end this?"

He had the strangest expression on his face when he said, "All's I want is to make you safe, forevermore."

Because that's what knights in shining armor do. That's why they trot around rescuing princesses. That's why the princesses love them so damn much.

Something clogged her throat, but she swallowed past it. "Good. You keep those dolphins on the line to Yoink and whatever other badass altered beasties you have swimming around, and let's dive."

He peered straight at her in the light of the headlamps for a while. Unspeaking. Unquestioning. Then he leaned down and kissed the top of her head, where her hairpiece usually hooked on. His kiss was soft, reverent, like she was holy to him and not broken.

"That's my girl," he said and turned to the car.

By the time Kellen returned from the trunk with a double armload of diving equipment—wet suits and pony tanks and jacket-style buoyancy compensators and a gajillion other things—Angela had almost convinced her body that it was okay. She was okay. He was okay. They were going to be okay.

She looked out at the water surface, the slightly darker shadow of a submarine sail poking up through the slate black. The old nightmares tried their bad mojo on her—the water is disease, don't drink it, if you breathe, you die, blah and blah. She blew out a breath, banishing the old fears.

"All right," she said, pushing authority into her voice. "I'm going to swim out to a submarine, force this intruder to take me to Damon Vallejo, and then capture, incapacitate, or kill that motherfucker. I'm going to end this trying-to-kill-me nonsense, on my terms. Right now."

"Damn, that's hot." He set a stack of clothing on the hood by her hip.

"What?"

"You in charge." He half grinned but then shook his head and looked away, as if he wasn't prepared to fess up to the compliment or any implications it might have. As if he didn't particularly like the fact he found her attractive when she was in full scary-ass orders-giving mode. Or did he dislike the fact he found her attractive at all?

But he called me hot. And kissed my head. And dug my fuck poem. Her mind snagged on that and wouldn't let go.

Until, oh wait no, *that* was hot. That. Right there. In front of her fervid gaze, with zero embarrassment, Kellen had started taking off his clothes. Pretty much every sane thought fled her mind in an instant. Danger? What danger? No amount of brain training, personal injury, winter night, or mortal risk could have prepared her for the sight of Kellen Hockley ice-cold and naked in the flood of headlamps.

He was gorgeous and lickable, and sweet cosmos, what did you even call those, those ligamenty doodads that arced from a man's hip to his pelvis? Because *those things*. She wanted to put her fingers in the grooves and trace them straight to paydirt. Followed closely by her tongue.

He calmly indicated the pile of equipment on the car

hood a half second before he pushed jeans down over slim hips. "You gonna suit up or what?"

She bit her bottom lip. Released it. Reminded herself where she was and what she was about to do. And then she said the worst possible thing for a girl to say when she was trying to think about anything other than sex. "Don't we need lube?"

He had one leg of a suit bunched up and was about to start pulling it on, but he looked at her, flashed her the side-eye. "How long's it been since you went in the water?"

She flushed. "Years. I had an irrational fear."

He straightened, giving her all his attention. Putting that entire lean body back on display. "I do remember. Are you going to be able to handle this? We could wait till morning, scrounge around for a dinghy or inflatable or something…"

"No, we're doing this tonight," she said, forcing herself to look anywhere but his bod. With a huff of breath, she tugged her shirt up and over her head and then folded it neatly and stacked it on the hood. "We lived near the ocean, and Daniel disbelieved in fear, had no patience for it, so he put me through dive training until I stopped having stupid panic attacks. I'm good. I was just asking because, you know, wet suits and unintentional hair removal and ouch."

"Ah. These suits ain't neoprene," Kellen said slowly, still distractingly naked and so comfortable with it that her hands flexed toward him, completely of their own accord, longing to touch. "They're smartfabric. They'll filter out the toxins, make it so we don't start glowing in that stew out there, and plus, they'll ventilate once we get on board. Biometric sensors help them regulate temperature, and they smell a helluva lot better than the older kind. But it ain't the suits bothering me right now. You do know fear, as a thing, isn't related to how smart you are, right?"

She picked up the smaller suit. Light fabric, almost slippery and still holding the heat from the car's vents. She couldn't find any device pouches. Was the technology built into the fabric? Like her gloves, just for all-over body protection? Soft too, pliable. The suit smelled like decaf coffee.

She tugged one leg of the suit up under her skirt, then the other. Ooooh. No, these suits were nothing like those things she'd worn during dive training. This was like burrito-ing herself in warm satin. She suddenly coveted a whole closet full of these things. In all different colors. This could become an addiction worse than shoes.

"Of course fear is stupid," she said. "Any time you know intellectually that a thing is safe but you run from it anyway, that is stupid."

"See now, it ain't, though. The difference between bravery and cowardice doesn't have anything to do with brain capacity," he said. "It's more about trust. Faith. That kind of thing."

The smartfabric dive suit slid on a lot easier than older kits, but it still took her a few minutes to get the longjohns up, then step out of the skirt. She folded that item, too, and went around to the passenger side to set her dry things in the car and fetch a couple of items she wanted to take in her dry pack. Yoink watched her avidly but didn't so much as nose her for a pet. Suspicious cat, possibly judging her.

When Angela came back around to the glare of head-lamps, Kellen was already working the diagonal press seam across his chest.

All covered up again. Bummer.

But also, he was watching her with the kind of intensity that made her wonder briefly if the dive suit was electrified. Certainly, when their gazes met, she felt a jolt of something hot and wild sizzle through her body.

"I trust *you*," she told him in a voice that had gone husky. "And those dolphins. Let's go."

● ● ●

The thing "the intruder" had wanted Yoink to do, the thing that freaked the poor kitty out so hard, was to put her furry little body in the water and carve out a diving path for her two humans.

Clearly, whoever was out there in a submarine talking to dolphins didn't know shit about cats and water. Especially this cat. Yoink was cool under most pressure—hell, could fly above the ionosphere deck in that spaceplane without a single complaint. But she was not going into the ink-black, death-filled ocean. Not one hair on her fluffy feline ass.

And Kellen didn't blame her one bit.

Truth was, Kellen wasn't looking forward to dunking himself in there, and he sure as hell didn't want Angela to go in. She never had liked the water, and he watched her closely for signs that it still made her nervous.

He had guessed, based on her tight-lipped remark, that Daniel Neko had been a proponent of the flooding technique of getting over phobias. Not Kellen's favorite process. He didn't want to think of Angela shoved into a fear cage and kept there till she learned to calm herself. He wouldn't do that to an animal and sure as shit not to a person. No less the woman he loved.

But if she said she was good to go now, he had no choice but to believe her. She'd used the t-word again. *Trust*.

Now, he had complete faith in the ocean critters to warn him of any danger, but Angela? She wouldn't know about all that going on beneath the water's surface. All she knew was what he'd told her, what he'd implicitly promised. And she had believed him. She trusted him.

Lord, don't make me a liar. Only let this go off good.

He'd done dive training years ago, for rescue missions, but he didn't go underwater that much, certainly not for fun. He felt like a novice out here, press-seaming a serious-looking suit they'd bought used from one of Dead Fester's buddies. He also felt like a fraud forced to play expert to a suddenly calm Angela.

Come to think of it, a way too calm Angela. Eerily so. Like she'd tucked a tranquilizer meltaway under her tongue while he went back to fetch their gear. She'd just stood there staring while he got changed, and for a minute, he worried he'd have to dress her himself like a doll.

Actually, he thought about that a little too much, the idea of dressing her. And undressing her first. Out in the cold winter night.

Or no, he'd have to haul her back into the warmed-up car, somehow keep the cat distracted, strip her down, reverse-peel the smartsuit up her body, and the whole time manage somehow not to say fuck it to this whole mission and just cover every inch of her skin with kisses instead.

And then she'd snapped out of it. She'd stripped down fast, almost too fast for him to see. Not that he wasn't peeking. Not that he wasn't wishing. Not that he hadn't spotted her nipples perked up like goddamn mountain peaks, chilled candies just waiting for a tongue to swirl 'em.

Way too soon, she was looking let's-do-this serious, snapping their tanks into D-rings, pulling on a BCD, tucking their dry clothes into the back seat. All business, all badass. Thank God she knew what she was doing and all, but he couldn't help thinking sort of wistfully about the warm car and a quick fuck. Or a long one. He wouldn't mind taking his time.

She would mind, though. Focused. She was focused as a space telescope, pinpoint and true. *Brain on, now. Get yo shit together.*

He skimmed through the data streams coming in from Yoink, relayed in her familiar not-quite-language. Mostly they consisted of blip coordinates and a rundown of the animals who'd be looking out for him down there in the ocean.

He and Angela tethered themselves to each other, attached dive lights to their gloves, did a quick buddy check, and laid a line out from the car, still with its head-lights on, in case the visibility was so bad they had to walk it back. And then they dove.

Or, without a boat to dive from, they ended up mostly butt-scooting from the water line right up to where the land gave out. The BCDs were weighted, so when they moved off the broken bridge, they tucked right into the ocean, into darkness broken only by their dive lights.

Murk was a mercy, shrouding the ruins beneath them as they moved, the rotting, swaying shells of buildings or cars or trees. Or people.

Of course, he knew all that was down there. Close by. Ghosts watching them pass.

The water pressed in, burying them alive. Some folk had described night diving to him once as akin to floating in space. Well, he'd done the latter, more than a few times, off the Chiba Station, and it was nothing like this.

The ocean black was impenetrable, a tomb with ancient, unbreathable air. The actual air, the stuff he could inhale safely, came through his regulator, scrubbed and scented but just enough not-right to remind him he wasn't supposed to be here. He wasn't aquatic. He was as much an intruder as the person in the submarine, and the ocean didn't want either of them.

He and Angela headed in the direction of the sea monster/blob/submarine, and it wasn't long before they could make out its strobe.

Turned out the sub floated near the surface, only partially submerged. There was probably some nautical term for the way it sat in the water, but Kellen didn't know. Looked like a sub in a movie, and there were handholds up the side. He climbed.

There were no rails atop the sail, and even though he couldn't see the main body of the craft to check for viewing ports, the anechoic plating indicated this wasn't a typical disaster-porn shallow-depth sightseeing boat. This one was military or had been in a previous life. Strange. But the relayed messages from the sea critters repeated that the sub wasn't armed. How they could tell, he did not know, but animals had better senses than people gave them credit for. Especially when it came to things that could kill them.

Kellen shone his dive light on the top hatch and had just about figured out how to open it when it did so on its own, releasing the seal with a short hiss. Inviting golden light bathed the inside of the sub. 'Course, almost any indoors would be warmer than the chill November sea. He had to keep in mind that sunshine color and cozy-making heaters didn't mean this place was safe. In this case, it meant anything but.

He unhooked the dive tether and headed down first. He didn't wait for Angela to take the lead, because he knew she would, and damn it, he hadn't been just flapping his jaws when he swore he wanted her safe. He was relieved when she didn't argue these small gestures, like going first into possible danger. She left him his pride, at least. He couldn't hope for her to recognize that it was more than pride that made him want to be her shield against the world. That it was, in fact, love.

At the bottom of the ladder, he looked around for hatch controls. Apparently there weren't any, or he didn't need them in any case, because the hatch closed itself, slowly, deliberately, as soon as Angela was clear of the ladder. A light embedded in the wall shifted from red to green, indicating that the seals were set.

There was an exit seal down here as well, and he was just starting to get nervous it wasn't going to open after all when little doors in the wall opened and spigots protruded. He had just enough time to close his mouth before the detox spray pelted him. It smelled like gardenia and vinegar. He looked over at Angela, hoping she hadn't taken one of those sprays directly in the face, and she half shrugged.

"Standard protocol," she said. "Most of the world

is water, and most of the water lately is contaminated. Believe me, I've been in worse detoxes."

Sometimes he forgot how much she'd seen, how hooked into the world she'd become. And then other times reminders hit him smack over the head, unlooked for and raw.

The lower seal undid itself and rolled back, revealing a twisty passage heading forward from the sail. Kellen doffed his BCD and tank, clipped his mask to a D-ring, and stowed the lot at the bottom of the stairs. Angela did the same, though she also unclipped her dry bag and brought it along.

They worked in tandem, wordlessly, like they could read each other's minds. In his case at least, the wordlessness, the waiting for her to descend, the patient comfort he offered at the ready in case she needed it, the stalwart resistance to his own near-overwhelming need to take her in his arms and kiss the fuck out of her the moment the seal engaged—all that was a function of who he was and what he did. He was a caregiver. And he loved her.

He didn't want to speculate on her motivations.

In any given sub, the control room was generally under the sail, so it should have been close, visible from the stark, airtight room they found themselves in. Kellen peered forward down the narrow corridor but didn't see anything looking remotely like a control room ought. Didn't hear anything either, other than the soothing hum of a machine underway.

Big fucker, too. Sub like this ought to have a crew in the dozens, even with a remote rig. But Yoink's relay insisted there was only one person on board, other than Angela and him.

The atmosphere was creepy in here. And too, too quiet.

As if the silence weren't bad enough, the surfaces on this boat were strange, not like any sub he'd ever seen, not even the ones he'd only experienced on VR tours. Space was typically a premium on a submarine, so controls and monitors and storage compartments honeycombed the walls, making every available centimeter also a useful centimeter. This thing, in contrast, was built more like a commercial jet. It did not intend for its inhabitants to make themselves useful. It intended for them to be docile. To passively soak in information or entertainment.

Sleek molded wall coverings in bright institutional white shielded who-knew-what. Instead of amine from the CO_2 scrubbers, the treated air in here smelled like a hotel: plastic and cool and lemon with just a faint underwhiff of industrial cleansers. He half expected a chatbot to appear on one of those white-molded panels and offer him a bath towel or a virtual daytrip to some exotic locale.

"Well, this is unexpected," Angela said, echoing Kellen's thoughts.

"Try freaky," he agreed. Neither of them gave breath to the phrase they both were likely thinking: ghost ship. If nothing on board was breathing, that didn't necessarily mean it never had. "Stick close to me?"

"Oh yeah. I got your six, cowboy," she said, but her voice was light.

He turned and looked, only to find her smiling.

"Sorry, I know, mixed metaphor. But there's no reason you can't be a cowboy *and* a special ops hero. It's my imagination, and we're trapped underwater in a titanium death can, so shut up and let a girl play."

It was on the tip of his tongue to say this wasn't a good time to play, that nothing about this mission was fun. Except it was. Being with her, bickering or bantering or whatever they did as a regular habit, that shit was fun. Not as fun as fucking, but fun. And he had missed it.

He had missed her. Even though he doubted he'd be able to keep her.

She had started a ball rolling with Dead Fester. Coming back from the dead. That's what she wanted, what she was planning: her life before. The life without him. He wouldn't stop her from grabbing what she needed, but he needed to keep his own brain zoomed in on the right now.

He had, what, maybe a day left with her wanting to be with him, pressing up against him, stripping down before his eyes and letting his gaze lick her like a hot candypop? And all he needed to do was make this time count, store up memories.

He would need them later, when she left.

The corridor bent like a serpent and led not to a control room but to a lounge. Weird sucker, too. An oval arrangement of low, cushioned benches and matching glass-topped end tables was sunk into the center of the floor, and dark wood paneling and back-lit cabinetry with curved glass doors ringed the chamber.

Was that…were there liquor bottles behind one cabinet door? And old leather-bound books, their spines stamped in gilt, behind another? Soothing recessed lighting made it sort of difficult to pick out details, but the combined effect was like a teak-paneled Victorian gentlemen's club and a twentieth-century Japanese sake bar got together and procreated. On a submarine.

All along one curved side was a giant picture window, plastene and thick, like the multistory glass wall at the Pentarc. Stark lights speared through the murky ocean beyond, picking out ghosts.

And atop a cushion in the lounge's rim, a lone figure perched primly, one dark-clad knee hooked over the other. He faced away from Kellen and didn't speak when they entered, even though he had to have heard the ruckus they made in boarding. He had fluffy, coiffed black hair and was wearing some kind of neo-chinoiserie sateen smoking jacket.

No shit, a smoking jacket.

And that hair? Could belong to only one man. Damon Vallejo. All alone, no witnesses.

If somebody else had come on this mission with Angela, somebody like that hellcat Mari or even Fan, that shiny, dark beacon of a head would surely present a temptation. Blowing it to red, wet pieces wouldn't take good aim nor even a particularly steady hand. Point and shoot. End of a whole lot of menace in a matter of seconds.

Probably it was a damn shame for the rest of the world and human history that Kellen wasn't a person who could murder on impulse like that. Or that he'd deliberately not fetched the gun earlier when he retrieved his equipment from the car.

"Damon Vallejo?" he said, though he didn't really need the confirmation. That hair was justifiably famous.

"How lovely to be identified, even when you cannot see my face," the mad scientist said. He sipped something amber-gold and bourbon-like from a crystal bulb. "I don't suppose you would like to return the favor? No? Oh well. The place is loaded with indulgences. Help yourself, whoever you are." He gestured to one of the glass-doored cabinets.

Angela emerged from behind Kellen in the corridor, brushing past him, charging hell with a bucket of ice water, right into the center of the room. She planted her feet, arched one perfect, nightwing eyebrow, and faced the evilest villain in the history of evil.

"Spare me the Southern charm, Damon. I know you're all alone on this boat, but I am not, *and* I'm armed. Also pissed. Start talking." She stared her enemy the hell down.

Oh yes, sir, she did. His Angela did.

CHAPTER 13

Damon Vallejo was smaller than she remembered. Or maybe it was just that he was seated and dwarfed by this freaky-ass room that belonged anywhere but on a submarine cruising ruined sunken cities in the middle of the night. Cities that he himself had sunk. He absolutely deserved all the filthy names people could fling at him, but looking at him right now, Angela couldn't figure how naming and shaming would solve anything at all.

Everything to be said to such a human had already been said so many times, the words no longer had weight. Horrible. Shocking. Cowardly. Despicable. Unprovoked. What all his detractors failed to mention was the lively intelligence of his eyes, the smile that made one want to lean closer to hear what wisdom might fall from his lips.

Damon Vallejo was one engaging little monster.

Capture, incapacitate, or kill, she reminded herself. Either way, this threat ends tonight.

He patiently met her eyes and smiled slightly. "Ah, Angela Ne—no, Senator now, right? It has been too long. As you are not the jailer I was expecting, could it be possible you and your bespoke plaything have come to rescue me instead?"

Vallejo set his drink down on the ovate table between them. The liquid amber surface tilted off true about ten degrees. The sub was descending.

"The mech-clone you sold me has been disabled," she said. "And I'm not here to play nice. I'm here to serve justice."

"Too late, dear would-be sheriff, though the role does suit you. Alas for you and role-playing, I've been under the cruel thumb of justice for a long time. Imprisoned by it even." He held up his wrists as if they were weighted by invisible shackles. "And now, because of your afore-mentioned desire for vengeance, you are doomed to share my opulent cell, unless you have some plan to get us out of here. Please say you do."

He was bluffing. Angela narrowed her eyes. "Imprisoned by whom?"

"You ought to know, Senator."

Yeah. She ought to. Why *didn't* she know? What clues had she missed? What was she missing right now? There was nothing worse for a politician, a former diplomat for fuck's sake, than to go into a negotiation without all the facts. Panic wetted the edges of her mind, and she struggled to stay sharp. *Find the nerve corridors, dull the autonomics. Steady, slow breaths. This is all conscious.*

Kellen came around to stand slightly behind her, up on the floor level of the sunken chitchat corral. He probably meant to look imposing or something, but all she could think was, *Thank the cosmos he's here.* She could play hardball solo, but what a nifty thing not to have to.

To know that if she even started to misstep, he would be there. With her and for her. She had never in her whole life done anything to deserve that kind of loyalty, but here he was. Confidence flooded her.

"Why don't you start at the beginning and tell me everything?" she said, clasping her hands together at her waist. She kept her face easy, her expression accessible.

She should have been more specific with her words, though. Vallejo anchored his deal with an initial offer. "If I give you information, you will get me out of here?"

"Maybe." Angela noted that even in a so-called prison situation—which she highly doubted was anything of the sort—he wore his signature boots: pointy-toed snakeskin numbers, dyed black to match his super shiny world-recognizable bouffant hairdo. This man had branding down to a science.

"Ask me a question, and I will not lie," said the liar. His boots might be brand-recognizable, but his beard had grizzled along his jaw, and it hadn't been maintained properly. Parts were coming in white, dusting salt into his pepper. He looked tired.

Angela locked her gaze with his, pushing the force of her personality across the room. She tapped her molars, engaging the psych-emitter. It didn't have a receiver in range, but this was her ritual, her zone. Her comfy place. "Where are the crewmen, your so-called captors?"

"No crew." He spread his hands, palms up. "This submarine is remote-piloted, apparently, and I am confined to this capsule. You will notice how this room is separate from the other areas, such as the corridors. It also boasts significantly lower crush-depth tolerances than the rest of the inner hull compartments, courtesy of that window. Wiring in the walls suggests both bulkheads leading out can be sealed and this module can be flooded. If I attempt to pass through either doorway, alarms screech and threaten imminent catastrophic compression. This is no lounge, Senator. It is an interrogation chamber."

"I'm sorry if this sounds less than sympathetic, but to what end?" she said. The scenario he described sounded stupid, and she highly doubted an entity wealthy enough to put this sub together was so sublimely oblivious. Interrogations that ended with death before the revelation of desired information were generally considered abject failures.

Vallejo took a long breath, held it, and then exhaled through his nose. "To what end," he repeated. "I sleep here, in the lounge, you know. Alone. Day after day. These clothes are self-cleaning, and several months of rations are stored, along with significant quantities of alcohol and recreational pharmaceuticals, in the drawers and cubbies in the wall. We move on a circuit. Crystal Beach to Galveston to Matagorda Bay and back. Day after day, taking me through the ruin. Every time we come up the ship channel, still crammed with the wreckage scoured off Galveston Island, the window clouds over and reveals itself to be a smartsurface. A cursor blinks."

"You think someone wants your confession?"

He shrugged, and though he didn't move, part of him, the energy that always seemed to surround him when he was giving presentations, crumpled. "When I was a guest of your fine government, Mrs. Neko, I was forced to produce mech-clones. N-series infiltrator models, like the one you pretend is your husband. Each one I produced cut another sliver of my soul away, but I did it. Out of guilt, perhaps, for my many sins. Your government offered me atonement in exchange for a secret army of spies. But these new captors? I have no idea what they want from me. They never ask, and they never command. They just show me the ruins, and the cursor blinks."

His hand shook when he plucked the whiskey glass, considered it, and replaced it on the table.

Angela wondered if she ought to laugh or applaud. Or both.

Because she so wasn't buying his story, or at least not his assumptions. True, she hadn't seen another soul aboard this sub, and the automation tech he spoke of was available. She was intimately acquainted with the military capabilities she had, up until very recently, been tapped to command.

Partial truth, then? He could very well not be lying about the remote-pilot rig or its circuitous guilt show. The problem was that there were too many parts to his answer, too many folds in which he could hide the lie. She needed to pare down her questioning. Get specific.

"You're looking pretty comfortable, though, for a prisoner."

He flinched. "A scar does not need to be visible to hurt."

Oh. Damn. She flinched, too.

"We negotiated your release," she reminded him. "My government did. We returned you to the TPA, and we got concessions in the valley. For a short while, it seemed we were approaching peace." Which she had opposed, but she didn't see an advantage to confessing that.

"Oh, little girl," Vallejo said, "this is so much bigger than governments."

What?

Angela sat. Her legs weren't working properly, and it had nothing to do with the swim. He couldn't possibly be referring to what she thought…he couldn't possibly know about the consortium.

"All right." Kellen picked up the questioning, giving her a reprieve. "Second question: Did you send your drones against the Hotel Riu when Angela was a guest there?"

"No." Gaze central, no shift of the eyes, just natural blinks. Vallejo's hands remained still, easy in his lap. He wasn't lying.

Kellen pressed. "Did you write the contract to assassinate Daniel Neko back in October?"

"God no."

"Why did you abduct your daughter Mari and bring her to Enchanted Rock?" Kellen asked.

Surprise flickered over Vallejo's face. He was far too well-trained a performer for it to linger long, but Angela saw it.

He set his drink down. "Two days before I shot the clone abomination that you refer to as my daughter, I fell asleep in this chamber. I woke with a hood over my head, in some kind of lab. Not here. A pea-brain I'd met some years before in Texas, a man by the name of Nathan Grace, was there and told me he could bring me the clone body, which contains technology that I could trade for my freedom. To be clear, that *thing* is not Mari, no matter what it calls itself. I also had a hunch holding it hostage might help me punch a hole in the communication null my captors have placed over me and maybe attract the attention of someone who could help."

Aha. So that's what they wanted. The tech that had been used to resurrect Mari. Tech that could be used to achieve immortality. Ice washed down Angela's back, flooding her spine. Athanatos. The consortium.

It was a moment before she realized Vallejo had just revealed his earlier lie. He'd known what his captors wanted. If he even had captors. Her head throbbed, and she swallowed back sick.

"I don't think Mari would ever willingly help you. She's awful sweet," Kellen said.

"It is anything but sweet, young man. That thing you call by my daughter's name was created out of vindictiveness and venom by an entity more repulsive and unnatural still. But we digress." He turned back to Angela, but he was shaken.

Hell, so was she. She hadn't spoken in some time, a silence that Vallejo had no doubt noticed. He was too clever not to realize what he'd said to demolish her calm. She rebuilt that calm, and fast, but the damage was done. He'd seen her wobble.

He peered at her now, intently, and she could have sworn there was a twinkle in his eye. "The assholes, as I may have mentioned earlier via message relay, have been limiting my communications for a few months now, and I needed a hole through their very peculiar firewall. Lucky me, I happened to know of someone who could create such a hole, given the proper impetus, and my captors would never guess we were allies."

Did he just reduce Yoink to a message relay service? Oh no, he did not. Sure, he might not have any reason to know better, but that characterization of her sweet kitty chafed. She didn't take too well to Mari being described alternately as an abomination and an impetus, either.

"Heron's known all over for blowing up firewalls," Kellen said, pride in his friend lacing his voice. "And I know you two go way back. You could've just asked him."

Vallejo put a finger to the side of his nose in a gesture that eerily echoed something Mari had done back at the Pentarc. "Yes indeed, he is, and I could have, but I think you're wrong about him ever agreeing to help me. The appropriate idiom for such an eventuality references blizzards and hell. Mrs. Neko, wherever did you get this one? Potential is strong, but he wants training."

"Mustaqbal, and he's fucking brilliant. But you're still an asshole," Angela said, drawing the focus back. "By 'proper impetus,' I assume you mean kidnapping the woman Farad loves."

"The thing rather, but essentially, yes."

"And that was your only motivation?"

"And they said you were bright."

Damn it, he wouldn't be caught in a you-said trap. Cagey old slimeball, was Vallejo.

"What tech does she have that they want?" she prodded.

His face went very still, like he was weighing truth against a lie. The words appeared to hurt when he did finally speak. That, more than anything, lent them the weight of truth. "Mari underwent a brain-replication process, transferring consciousness one slice of neural connection at a time from a battered and dying body to a fresh new clone. Imperfect process, flawed process, abhorrent process, but, I suppose, valuable to some."

"You're talking about immortality. Athanatos."

Kellen's words were pincers at the base of her skull. How did he know? How *could* he?

"I am indeed." Vallejo nodded, turned to Angela. "I gather it's one of the several research avenues they are pursuing, so that a certain group of people can achieve unending life spans. But you're Medina's protégée, so you know more about these things than I. Now, are you going to help me escape this tin can or what?"

Words erupted from her mouth before she could stop them. "Wait, what does Zeke have to do with..." But she bit the sentence off. She couldn't finish it. Because she knew.

Oh. God.

What he's always been planning.

Athanatos.

She hadn't seen that one coming. Again. Twice now, blindsided by the stupid little bouffant fuckernibble in boots, but this reveal cut deep. The poison of truth bled along its edge.

Of course Zeke was obsessed with immortality. Daniel had been, too. It was the thing they all talked about, all those consortium assholes, when they'd get together for drinks. For policy wonking. For training. For...

For kidnapping rebel scientists and torturing them until they gave up their research?

God. She wouldn't put it past creeps like Limontour or Daniel, but *Zeke*? She'd never thought of him as assholish, never like the others. He'd been kind to her; he'd been her mentor. He'd arranged her admission into the MIST, had planned her career trajectory, her famous marriage. He had accompanied her on the single worst trip of her life, and he'd been there for her through the storm.

"What does Medina have to do with my imprisonment?" Vallejo finished her sentence. "Surely you jest. He plucked me out of the UNAN detainment personally. He mined me for research, made me build unholy things for the last eight years. I'm sure there are worse devils holding his leash, but he's the face, the jailer they send when they need me to do a trick."

"That makes no sense," Kellen interjected. "You're Texas; President Medina's UNAN. Y'all's governments sort of hate each other."

But Vallejo's right. This isn't about governments. It's bigger.

Angela couldn't form the words to tell him no, it made perfect sense. All the grooves fit; all the cogs rolled. On the surface, sure, Zeke and Vallejo were enemies, on opposing sides of a thing that was conflagrating into war even as she sat here. But…what if they weren't?

What if Zeke had been claiming that Vallejo, and by extension Texas, was behind all the drone attacks to give a face to the enemy, to make the people believe? That scenario suited all that Zeke had told her in private, about wanting a war to boost the economy and his personal popularity. To get *her* into a cabinet position, though it hadn't been about her at all, had it?

None of it had. From the beginning, she'd been played.

"There is no government in Texas, boy," Vallejo said. "The scar that you call Texas contains a raggedy few unhappy people, and a lot of dead ones."

"Then all these drone attacks…"

"We did it," Angela said in a whisper. "The UNAN, I mean. My government. My mentor. My *fault*." She had thought she was luring Texas into doing something unforgivable, into attacking, into justifying the use of military force to defend the homeland. Into war. But in reality, her government had initiated the violence. Zeke had. And he'd let her blame someone else for his sins.

She had done the unforgiveable. Again.

"Now wait one minute," Kellen said. "Don't you go taking responsibility for everything shitty in the world. Damon Vallejo is a liar. And I don't mean white tinies, neither. His word's about as reliable as a hot owl fart. He fucking tried to kill you with his death-bot back at the Pentarc."

Vallejo went white beneath his olive skin. "The mech-clone attempted violence?"

"Bet yer ass-bone it did," Kellen said. His voice was rolling, but the angrier he got, the sharper his voice got, the thinner his accent. He was still deep in dialect, but his voice was hard as diamonds. "Haired out and tried to murder her. Just like you programmed it to do."

Vallejo opened his mouth, closed it. Then opened it again. "I can say nothing to disprove your theory, but I will swear on everything sacred that I have worked my entire career to eliminate out-of-control mechs. I would never use one as an assassin."

Which, actually, Angela could believe. Vallejo didn't have the body language of someone who was lying. At least not this time. And also, there was a thing that Kellen didn't know. About how—and why—she'd acquired mech-Daniel to begin with.

"Yeah, well, you—"

"Kellen," she interrupted before he could foolishly defend a woman who didn't deserve it. "When I left Daniel, Zeke gave me the mech-clone, kind of as a stop-gap, so I wouldn't file for divorce. I'd found out some... things and was pretty off the rails. I don't know how he convinced Daniel to maintain the ruse, and I didn't ask. The mech unit was meant to make things right. Zeke transferred it to me, had it programmed with all sorts of government security subroutines. To keep me safe, he said. It was meant to protect me. He said."

Really to keep her trapped, though. Even without Daniel and his horrible lies, to keep her under the consortium's thumb.

Zeke knew how much she had come to rely on mech-Daniel, how easy it would be for her to assign any flaw in the mech's programming to malicious intent on the part of its creator, on the part of Vallejo himself. Scapegoat the mad scientist. How easy for Zeke, how gullible of her.

He totally would have named his secret backdoor Ashe.

She had been played like a game.

"To control you, more likely," Vallejo said, echoing her thoughts. Strange, though; he wasn't crowing. His voice was surprisingly gentle. "Once more, I wish I had never begun the mech-clone project. They have been no end of evil for me, and now apparently for others as well."

Angela thought of the polling boost Zeke got first from Daniel's death and then later from her own demise. She thought of the president's alligator tears during his acceptance speech on election night. He never had returned her messages after the Riu. Why was that, exactly? Because she was no longer useful to him? Because she had worked herself free, on her own terms?

Because he'd found out how untenable the whole situation was for her and was done with her rebellion?

He'd told her to stay put in the ruined hotel, covered in bits of bomb. So his drones could come finish the job.

That night, the night of the Riu attack, mech-Daniel had given her a drink, but maybe his intention had not been to relax her, as she'd assumed. Maybe it had been to delay her from going up to wait for her transport. Or to drug her so that if she did die a horrible flaming death, at least it wouldn't hurt. In hindsight, it was clear mech-Daniel had known the attack was coming. Regardless of his orders or intentions, he had kept her in the room, in the hotel, on purpose.

And he had contacted Zeke even before she regained consciousness. To report in? To request additional orders?

Poor mech-Daniel, he must have been pummeled with instructions coming from all sides. No wonder his artificial neural ultimately couldn't take it. No wonder he was a junk heap in the Pentarc right now.

She thought of Zeke's unusually close relationship with Daniel, both of whom had spoken at length of human immortality and a golden age. Both of whom were hooked in deep with the consortium. Both of whom had sought to control her.

The child we make together will live forever. Best of the best. You were born for this. Now, smile for the cameras, Ange. That's my good girl. Best.

She'd thought Zeke was better somehow, because he said he wanted all the successes for her, on her behalf, but that had been a lie. The wants were still all his. He never once asked her what she wanted. It just never mattered.

Oh, God. Her entire existence was a series of manipulations stacked one on top of the other, a melting sandcastle of a life, and all in service to the aims of others. She had spent years honing her will, learning to shape it and share it, but it wasn't real. It was the will of her handlers. Fucking *nothing* about her was real.

She wasn't a princess, wasn't a queen. Wasn't a person, even. She was someone else's toy. A piece. A pawn.

Nothing.

●　　●　　●

The woman made of will disintegrated right in front of him. Angela Neko, *his* Angela, who had once held him up when he got low, who'd given steel to his own spine, fell apart like a sugar skull left out in the rain. Kellen watched it happen and couldn't do a damn thing to stop it. He went to one knee behind her cushion and caught her at both shoulders lest she ghost away to nothing. He didn't expect those hands to hold her upright—she was supposed to be the strong one, damn it—but she swayed in his grasp.

Hold on there, darlin'. I got you.

His eyes were drawn to the back of her head, her nape, disappearing into her slick smartfabric dive suit, and his hands, holding her steady. He spotted the tip of a claw mark to the left, and he moved his grasp to avoid putting pressure on a wound that must already hurt. And that's when he saw it. Shoulder strap on her dry bag, the shape of which was tucked behind her shoulder blade. The shape in that bag was unmistakable from this angle.

She had brought Miss Mari's gun. Right there, tucked behind a watertight seal and maybe four inches total from the tip of his thumb. Waiting for him to draw it. He dropped his grasp to her biceps, containing both her tremble and his own need to avenge her hurts, moving his hand further from the gun.

Further from temptation.

He had never seen Angela this broken—she was the fighter who always won, always had—and he wanted more than anything to whisk her off somewhere safe, tend her, and holler "fuck it" to the whole rest of the world.

He didn't need to deal with Vallejo or bring hellfire and justice down on the scientist's tacky, crimped head. He didn't even need to know why Angela had reacted so fiercely to whatever bullshit that pissant had spouted. She could keep her private hells private. He wouldn't push. All he needed was for her to be okay.

Which meant he needed to get her away from Vallejo. Across the low glass table, he locked gazes with the old man.

Vallejo looked more tired than anything but couldn't resist one more villainous eyebrow wag. "So. Rescue, then? How are we coming with that? I presume based on your silence that you have no more questions for me. What do we do now? Access your message relay? Signal Farad?"

When no one replied immediately, Vallejo rolled his eyes, exactly the way Mari did from time to time, and managed to look both impatient and defeated.

Angela still shook beneath Kellen's hands. *God, please don't let her be crying. Not her.* As he prayed, he also got angrier and angrier. Low hum of menace, not out of his control. Not yet. Gettin' there, though.

"Best you know," he told Vallejo, "you are thrumming my very last nerve. I were you, I'd get real quiet."

"Well, if the two of you would just make up your minds. I mean, you come in here demanding information, asking questions, practically begging me to talk, and now you want me to be quiet. Which is it? Or do you need to ask her for directions?"

It was the disrespectful tone on *her* that got him.

Kellen slammed his mouth into a line, pressing, holding. Furious heat blurred in a halo around his body, luring the monster out. *Settle. Settle right now. That ain't me.*

Except it was him. It had always been him. Any pacifist's secret was that his inner monster wasn't leashed by will. It was leashed by fear.

Kellen was scared out of his ever-lovin' mind that if he released even a smidgen of this fury, there would be no going back, no path home from that. Failure to subdue the beast meant becoming the beast.

And he'd seen that beast come out way too many times to risk it. Mama had gone to violence just as easy as she went to backwoods moonshine. Lord, hadn't she just. The skills that made him a natural healer and helper had formed themselves of desperation early on, splinting small bones, bandaging cuts in princess-pink adhesive strips, waiting up late after a head-knocking to make sure Sissy kept on breathing and could come to when he jostled her. No coma, no permanent hurt, just a few anonymous logins at the remote doc, and Mama always apologized in the morning. But those nights had sure stretched long, holding it all together. Through it all, he had kept his temper, his monster, under control.

He hadn't become Mama. Not then he hadn't, and he wouldn't stoop to her level now. Insult, even insult to the woman he loved, was not worth losing himself so completely. Insults were just words. His peers back at school had taught him that.

He took a deep breath, steadied himself, and then rolled his wrist against Angela's shoulder, activating his com.

"Hey, Yoink, you li'l fur-butt, please tell me you got that patch up," he said in a low voice.

At the cat's name, Angela stilled. He squeezed her shoulder, and she reached and covered his hand with hers. Not grabbing for the gun, just making the connection. Her touch warmed him all over, but not with anger this time. The monster-luring heat retreated, dissolved into this other, better warmth, a sweet one like scratch brownies just out of the oven. The warmth of comfort in knowing he didn't fight his monsters alone.

"No, it's me," came Chloe's impossibly chipper squeak through the com. "I mean, yes, the cat is here and she's fine, deep into the process of filling me in on all the details. Something about chatty dolphins and mosquitoes and depth charges and herself being critically hungry and sleepy and lonely and had to be fetched ASAP, which is done by the way, but I gather from all she's downloading that you're in danger and hey, guess what? Did you know our plane was armed with tac-nuke missiles? Shall I blow the shit out of something? Please say yes."

Beneath his hands, Angela sighed. He had no idea what she was thinking or feeling, but right now, it was enough that she breathed. That she didn't run. *Hang in there.*

"Not necessary," he said. "But I do need your help to secure this boat. Can you hook into the fly-by-wire?"

The pause was infinitesimal. And excruciating. At last Chloe chirped in. "Aha! I found those depth charges your cat would not shut up about. Hush, kitty. Well, there you go: all traps have been disabled. Feel free to move around the cabin." Her voice hitched in a half laugh, like she'd just made a joke. "Easy sailing from here on out, Doc. I am right above you and have removed the data hole, so you can even chat with the wide world if you want."

"How'd you...?"

"Same process Heron used on Enchanted Rock. I copied the protocol. Go me!"

Kellen didn't say so, but that was a bit worrying. Heron had blown up the black-ICE over Enchanted Rock by accessing the entire global cloud network. It had been a pretty big deal and had very nearly resulted in Heron's brain death. Chloe had not just done that same thing.

Or had she? Could she? She was sweet and all, but damn if there wasn't something just a tiny bit terrifying about her, too.

"Good work, and thank you. Now, can you give us a tow into port somewhere?" There weren't many intact ports on the Gulf Coast. Not after years upon years of storms and population relocations. "Not Pensacola, not east. We'd like to avoid any continental entanglements just right now. How's Tampico look?"

"High and dry and zero UNAN patrols," chirped the AI. After a few seconds, the boat lurched, but then the golden surface of Vallejo's bourbon steadied, flattened out. They were no longer descending. They were submerged and bookin' it. "Whoa. This boat flies in the water. We hit fifty knots. And just wait till I tell Garrett I got to drive a sub."

CHAPTER 14

THAT THING ANGELA HAD THOUGHT EARLIER, ABOUT HOW having Kellen nearby lent her a quantum of confidence? Well, it was true even when every other wick of her life burned to a nub. He still shone. Maybe he was the only good decision she'd ever made. Well, the being with him part, not what she'd done to him. Not the sending him away part. That had been a mistake.

She couldn't let herself think about what he would say if he knew all her secrets. She didn't want to think about being without him. Not again.

Also, she didn't want to sit here and have a conversation with Damon Vallejo. And even more certainly not about all the things he had so easily understood but that had eluded her for a lifetime. She was supposed to be a goddamn genius. A reader of societies and people, of long-term trends and schemes. A strategist, trained. How could she not have seen?

Vallejo had been quiet while Kellen and Chloe talked, but Angela had been watching him. When Chloe had reported that all traps had been disabled on the boat,

Vallejo had been visibly relieved. He'd closed his eyes for longer than a blink, and the hands that had been nervous, alternately clasping each other and reaching for a drink he did not touch, relaxed.

Now he opened his eyes and caught her staring at him. "Is it even possible you didn't know about Medina's plans?" he said in a low voice.

"Why don't we for the sake of argument pretend I didn't," Angela said. She sounded weary to her own ears and felt it even more so. Truthfully, she was tired. So very, very sick of everybody else's bullshit. What she wouldn't give to be back at the Pentarc North Tower, reclining on a hammock and stroking Yoink's soft fur.

If, you know, the Pentarc wasn't presently under attack. If, you know, it was even possible to go back.

"What do you think Zeke's up to?" This wasn't her best negotiation lead. Her position was too weak; she should not have phrased that as a question that could be countered with refusal to answer. She should have wheedled, or at least given him reasons for playing along.

But exercising all her formidable diplomatic training required more will, more energy, than she could muster right now. She desperately needed to hide, lick her wounds, reassess literally everything she knew about herself. But the reality was she could do none of those things. She was on a sub in the middle of the ocean facing down the most notorious villain of her time. *And shit to do before I sleep.*

Vallejo uncrossed his legs and slumped back against his cushions, looking as defeated as she felt. He raised both hands and shoved them through his coif. It sprang back into place right after, but not without the casualty of a few errant locks.

"As far as I can tell, they're done building out their group of elites, the future of the species, the protected class," he said. "That was the effort I knew most about. My wife, Mageda, was part of phase one. She did a lot of testing and recruiting for the MIST, along with her sister and Zeke and Dan and the old gal, I forget her name. They didn't share details."

His words pushed ice pricks against Angela's memory. She didn't want to hear Daniel's voice in her mind, but she could not excise it. Over and over. *The child we make together will live forever.* She swallowed, got herself together. "So now we're in phase two?"

"I suppose so. They're still collecting the technology to maintain themselves indefinitely, hence their interest in the consciousness-transferral process that was used on Mari. With that technology, they can grow clones of themselves and move into new bodies, probably forever, one body after another. They don't care what that makes them, how it alters their souls. How it ruins their minds."

He was talking about his daughter, and she suspected he wanted to go on, suspected he wanted to explain his thinking and why he had shot her. Fuck that. Angela didn't want to hear it. Nothing he could say would change what she thought of him for betraying his own child. And then she thought about what a hypocrite that made her.

"Was the transferral tech their main interest in you?" she asked.

"Well, they were fascinated by my work fabricating mech-clones, but their requests tapered off over the years. Other than the clone-transferral bit, which wasn't even mine, I honestly can't tell you, Senator. Maybe it was…" He swiped a palm over his face, shook his head. "Unless they didn't want my research at all. It is possible they just wanted Heron's."

"Machine-human integration?" Angela guessed. Or maybe the mind-reading thing he'd tried on her that first day they met. That was certainly fascinating, but she couldn't think how it would feather into the overall master-race plan.

"No," Vallejo said, drawing the syllable out as if she were very stupid or very oblivious. "Weather control. Think about it. If you're planning for a small number of humans to endure forever, you have to deplete the rest of the population, else you get unauthorized inbreeding and other chaos points. Mass populations are impossible to control, so they would definitely need to go or get winnowed down to a manageable number. Phase two."

Oh. Right. Wow. She'd teased Vallejo's involvement in weather control to Rafael Castrejon during their live-emote session an eon ago. The day Daniel was killed. But she'd made that up, thought it was bullshit. It hadn't been. That had actually been someone's plan.

Not Vallejo's, though. Zeke's.

"But you can't just nuke all the little people," Kellen interjected. Angela flinched at his voice, glittering over her shoulder, hard and bright and dangerous. Not necessarily the Kellen she remembered; however, strangely, just as comforting. It reminded her of him and his cattle prod, storming the West Spire and cutting down her enemy. Knight in shining armor. Hers.

He swung his long legs over the back of the cushion and sat on the deck next to her shoulder. She could see him in her periphery now. No hiding from him. She still didn't let go of his hand. She should have. Should have run, gotten small, reduced contagion. Recalculated herself. But she didn't. She just kept hold of Kellen, ping-ponging her attention back and forth between her lover and her enemy and her past.

"Because yikes radiation," Vallejo said, referring to the idea of nuking mass populations.

"And you can't just move your armies in," Kellen went on.

"Because in a postarmy world, all our soldiers now are drones, and nobody can rig the whole thing at once with enough real-time coordination to make those big genocides work properly. Too much scattering."

"So you drown them in hurricanes."

"And crisp them in droughts."

"And burn them in volcanoes."

Every scenario spoken aloud was a new image, both bleak and familiar. She had seen these things happen. Mother Nature, acts of God. But the dirtiest secret of all was there was no God; there was no mother's mercy. There was only the consortium with a horrible plan and too many toys.

"They also play up their rebellions, creating conflict zones," she added, half turning on her cushion so she could look up at Kellen. "Remember when I told you about the bad shit pattern? How every massive disaster follows the same refugee-relocation, more tragedy, more population-reduction pattern?"

"Yeah."

She turned back and met Vallejo's gaze. "That's phase two. We're in it. All those drone attacks right now are meant to start a war with Texas. There's no easier cover than war to hide body count. I ought to know."

She had never felt more certain about a thing in her life. Phase one, collect the worthy humans. Phase two, destroy the extras. Phase three? She didn't know that yet, but she felt pretty fucking certain it would suck.

She swallowed, but she was still dizzy and tracing brain paths. None of her usual tricks worked. This gut-sick roil wasn't something created in her conscious mind. It was brain stem–type stuff, primal and lizardy, and she could not stop it. Couldn't stop anything. *Just a toy. Will live forever. Smile for the camera, Ange.*

Kellen squeezed her hand. "Right. War minister. And there you go being all brilliant, as usual."

She flared her eyes at him, startled. "What? What are you even talking about?"

"I'm talking about stopping this phase two bullshit, right now, before Medina gets sworn in for a third term," he said. "He's launching all these attacks and then blaming them on Texas, right? He needs to be stopped, and weren't you two heartbeats from being the war minister of this continent?"

"Well, yes." Essentially. Maybe. "But that was before I…before Daniel died." Before she'd been removed from all her official profiles.

"But you know where the command codes are."

Fucking hell. He was right. She *did*. She knew exactly how to get there. Darknet, string of sixteen digits, photographic memory. Oh yeah. Her eyes stretched wide, and she had to bite her bottom lip to keep from either laughing like a loon or doing something else wildly inappropriate.

Maybe kissing the shit out of that man right next to her. Because he so deserved it. And she so wanted to.

"We still have the problem of rigging a vast continental drone army," Vallejo reminded them.

Good thing he did, too, because Angela had pretty much forgotten he existed and was so very close to climbing onto Kellen's lap right then. That could have been embarrassing.

"It's not really that much of a problem," Kellen said. "Heron can rig your drones, easy. I don't think there's a max number on his command-and-control, not anymore. And am I really talking to Damon Fucking Vallejo about this stuff?" He tilted his head and thwapped it, as if he expected loose logic to fall out of an ear.

"Look, trust me or not, I really don't care," said Vallejo, "but I'm interested in getting off this boat, and you pair all but promised to release me. I'd help Hitler take over the government if such action guaranteed my freedom."

Yeah, that wasn't a scary proposition. But it did have the ring of truth to it. And he had managed to deliver several not-fibby bits of information. Trust him? No. Let him help her stop Zeke and the consortium? Maybe. Angela thought she might need all the help she could get.

She'd actually believed him when he said he was seeking atonement for his sins.

"As I understand it," Vallejo went on blithely, "Farad has to be able to establish and maintain communications with the drone army to rig it. He typically does so through the cloud or via wireless, I would imagine. And we know the consortium or UNAN or whoever is in charge over there can deploy extremely dense ICE nets. If Farad is plugged in to an entire military database, he won't have the bandwidth to get through their security countermeasures."

"But Chloe can," Angela said. She was starting to feel the shift in energy. A whiff of hope. Her command codes to access the continental drone army, Heron's ability to command it, and Chloe keeping the coms open. This could work.

"Um, but before we get rolling, I need to clarify one thing," she said. "You both know what we're talking about doing here, right?"

In the slice of silence that followed, she met first Vallejo's gaze and then Kellen's. The ambient temperature in the submarine went bone-cold. An unspoken word hung in the air: *treason.*

Her com buzzed, and a digital voice crackled its way out. "The term is *military coup,*" said Yoink. "I am standing by for orders."

● ● ●

Was crazy how much planning went into prepping a massive governmental takeover. Kellen had just spent an hour on the com with his Pentarc crew, working through their plans, assessing capabilities, and getting caught up on the whole nation-under-attack thing. The crew had managed to get the entire Pentarc refugee population down into the protected underground area. Surface structures were being guarded by the Chiba Space Station and its queen, knocking drone-launched missiles out of the sky. Her aim wasn't perfect, though. Some strikes were getting through. Couple of times during their chat, some serious strikes had come in.

During one of those, he lost Rook, who had insisted on

coming down last, after all the rest of the barn evacuated. Little Azul had freaked, apparently, and would only come out from under the trough when Rook nosed her into it. But she'd no sooner gotten into the stairwell than a hit on the wall at the edge of his pen had opened up a hole there. The dwarf goatie hadn't been used to open space and no protections, and he had expected the dirt ground to be where it always was. Fan had watched him fall.

She'd gotten herself to safety, though, and the whole rest of his animals. She'd done good.

Kellen was less certain he was doing the right thing. Heron had been easy to recruit to the idea of a coup. Maybe too easy. Mari, of course, was on board because violence was her happy place, and the mamas—Adele and Fanaida—could always be counted on to support anything smacking of anarchy.

Chloe had fully engaged herself in the challenge, and Garrett backed her.

As a matter of fact, the only person who seemed to be harboring second thoughts of any kind was Damon Vallejo. Which, any way you looked at it, was wrong with a capital W.

When they'd gotten control of the boat, or when Chloe had, Vallejo hadn't gone right to the control room/communications module with Kellen and Angela. He'd chosen to stay behind in that weird oval lounge. Well, fine, so they'd locked him back in. But something about his behavior niggled at Kellen, so when the planning chatter started to seem like it would go on forever, he wandered back to check on Vallejo.

The sight that met him wasn't exactly what he'd expected. Wasn't a complete surprise, either.

Vallejo was crouched over a void in the wall panel-ing, directly below the liquor cabinet. He'd managed to get the stark white molding off, and his hands were deep in the electronics webbing the wall. On his head was a pressure seal, roughly head-sized, rigged with a com with its LED app blazing in front, providing a clearer peek into the tangle of wires and diodes and switches.

The getup made him look even more like a mad scientist than he already had, but it also looked sort of perfect on him, like this was his natural habitat.

As Kellen walked in, he heard voices, tiny and famil-iar. The same conversation Angela was having over in the com room. Sly little fucker had been listening in.

When he noticed Kellen in the room, Vallejo didn't jump away from his tinkering. He looked up calmly, still clutching a pair of slip-joint pliers. "Come to interrogate me all alone this time? I do hope you did nothing nefari-ous with the senator."

"Nah, that's later and all private," Kellen replied. "She's hooked into the coms, powwowing with her con-tacts, setting up meetings and petitions and other stuff. You realize she can holoconference with two people at the same time? Gal can multitask like I ain't never seen."

"Angela Neko is uniquely suited to ruling the world. All you MIST kids were."

"Yeah." Kellen folded himself into a half kneel/half crouch so he could get down on Vallejo's level. "What the hell are you up to?"

Vallejo tapped the light off and removed his impro-vised headlamp. His hairdo had valleys in the sides where the pressure-seal hat had jammed it down. "Listening."

"I gathered that," Kellen said. "How did you patch

into the boat's communications with a mobile com and some wires?"

"Young man—"

"Kellen."

"Fine, Kellen. I have been building speaking machines for longer than you've been alive. Early AI work was all about communication. Besides, if I hadn't boosted my com's signal with this submarine's communications gear, your dolphins might never have heard me, and then where would we all be?"

Kellen didn't know about the geezer, but if the dolphins hadn't felt like chitchatting tonight, *he* would be in a nice warm car sleeping off a shitty day in the arms of the woman he loved. Given such an alternative, he couldn't say he preferred being here instead. Talking to a regretful old genius about how they were about to commit high treason.

"So you heard our planning just now," he said. "Find any weak points?"

Vallejo smiled. "I'm not a tactician on my best days, and I'll be honest, I wasn't listening for strategy. I was listening for her voice."

"You mean Mari's?"

The old man shrugged. "Not because I care about the abomination, mind. Only she reminds me of who I used to be, who she used to be. It's different, listening when she doesn't know I can hear. I'm not trying to get her to do anything in particular; I'm not trying to fit her into any schemes. I'm just listening to the cadence, the accent. Her voice is made of memories."

Huh. Figure Vallejo to have the soul of a poet, underneath all those schemes and sins. It wasn't Kellen's place to judge, but the old dude was looking rough around the edges, like maybe regret had started gnawing at him. If the pattern held, guilt would work its way in soon, and what would that even look like, Damon Vallejo on some kind of atonement spree?

Probably pretty dang beautiful. Though it would be a hard sell to the folk he'd wronged. Especially Miss Mari.

"Look, I been meaning to ask you some things," Kellen said, nudging their conversation closer to where he wanted it. "Things I need to air out real good before I let you anywhere near Angela again."

Vallejo turned away from the disemboweled electrical panel. "Ask me anything you need to."

"Why're you helping us?"

"Easy and already answered. Freedom. That explanation isn't working for you?"

"Not really, considering you tried to kill my best friend's partner."

Vallejo narrowed his eyes. "I'm guessing the friend you're referring to is Heron Farad?"

"The same."

"Ah." He looked down at the pliers. "I have explained my reasons for shooting the clone. And you will note that none of those reasons required me to kill her. I meant to disable her, keep her from running, and lure Heron out into the cloud. I accomplished those things."

"Yeah, I hear you about them reasons, but the fact remains that you shot her. You hurt her. Your own kid. Now how you gonna convince me that my Angela will be safe with you trottin' around free? Give me one reason why I shouldn't keep you locked up in here until we settle in a port."

Vallejo put the pliers on the floor and turned to face Kellen straight on. He narrowed his eyes, but not to make them mean. Maybe just to make them see.

"My own Mageda, my wife, was a member of the Athanatos consortium, just like Ezekiel Medina and Daniel Ashe Neko," the old man said, "and I loved her anyway, so I know how this happens. I know how it feels to love above your station. There's no shame in following a woman to the raggedy ends of wisdom. Or beyond."

"So the shame comes in later, then," Kellen said, "like when you kill a few million people? That when it happens?" Lord, he would never do in politics, in her world. Honesty had too firm a hold on him, and he couldn't make it shut up. Not even when wheedling and soft words would do a much better job.

"For what it's worth," Vallejo said, "the weather-control foglet program behaved unpredictably. It was supposed to have repaired the drought in south Texas."

"Well, if the opposite of drought is Noah-level flooding, you really knocked that one out of the park." It was obvious but needed saying.

Vallejo stared down at his hands, streaked with grease. "You are young yet, but someday, you might look back along the path your life has taken and regret," he said. "The next generation will be the breakthrough, Mags and her cronies insisted, super intelligent, the true immortals. She was so certain. She'd run the genomes, you see, and her data had never been wrong, at least not about something so important. She was what we used to call a control freak, and I indulged her, even when she insisted on growing a clone of our daughter, even when she started experimenting on herself. Fatally, as it turned out. There were so many places in our story where I could have stopped her. Where I could have saved her."

"Is all this somehow supposed to convince me to stop Angela from going through with her coup?"

"I'm not telling you to do anything, Kellen. I'm only telling stories." He rubbed one hand against the other, but the stains remained. "As it happened, Mageda's analysis was off only fractionally. Our Marisa was not the harbinger of humanity's future after all, but Zeke and the others were convinced that *her* child would have been. Angela Neko's, I mean."

Kellen's body wanted to cringe away, wanted to sit smack on the floor and let itself be squashed by the weight of what Vallejo was saying. Those consortium fuckers had run genomes on her, presumably matching her up with Daniel Ashe. Was that why they'd arranged the marriage in the first place? For babies. For her babies.

And those babies had never come. Lots of reasons why folks didn't procreate these days, but with the kind of money and other resources at her disposal, she wouldn't have even had to carry a child. And they wouldn't have taken her wishes into account, anyhow. They could have made it happen despite her. The consortium could have put all the biological bits together in a lab. And all without her say-so.

They could have held that threat over her, forcing her to do their bidding. Even if it hadn't been physical control, it had still hurt her. Incrementally, maybe, over time. God, what would that have felt like?

She'd finally had enough, he guessed. And then what? She left Daniel, threatened to divorce him, and let herself be mollified with a mech-clone replacement?

Something here didn't fit.

Kellen's thoughts tumbled, imagining a whole soup of horrible scenarios. And here the whole time, he'd been thinking while he was off saving people and doing good works, she was living large in California, married to her superstar and unfazed by one ill-fated and ill-advised teenaged love affair. He'd assumed she'd gotten over it all, that she'd moved on and only he'd been stuck remembering instead of living.

But there'd been more to her story, behind the scenes. She'd told him just a little, about some of the things Daniel had done, and he'd known even then that there was more.

He hadn't left her for her own good. He'd left her to their devices. And, lord, they had used her.

CHAPTER 15

MODERNISTS COULD SAY WHATEVER THEY WANTED ABOUT THE efficiency of remote management or the speed of space-planes, but there was something relaxing about this under-water transportation business. Floating. Working. Floating and working. Angela wasn't about to burst out in sea shan-ties or anything, but her schemes were coming together *and* she was hurtling forward through space. Efficient.

No need to think about anything. Just act. Inhabit the moment. Make all the things happen.

She was trained for this, *good* at this. She could see success from here. So why did it look so…empty? Lonely. *Stop it*.

The communications room here was crammed with everything she needed, all the gizmos, and she'd been super busy this morning. She'd arranged to have Rafa meet her physically in Tampico, and he was bringing a style suite along. Fez was prepping a big show, simulta-neously cast to all corners of this continent, an interrupt-level brief. The kind of shot across the bow that Zeke couldn't possibly ignore.

She had reserved a sound stage/transmission suite in Veracruz, just inland. That's where the magic would happen. The reservation was for tomorrow evening, and by then, her petitions would be closing, and she'd have a clearer picture of where her efforts stood, whether the public was backing her. Whether she had told the best lie.

From that point, if everything went well, she'd travel to the Capitoline. She'd crash the goddamn inauguration, while the entire population of this planet watched. She'd arranged ticketing through one of her false identities, but according to Chloe, resources weren't really an issue. The Pentarc crew was loaded, and apparently, Heron was so deep into the cloud that Angela's own dead-girl accounts were available, if she wanted them. Security didn't mean much to him. By tomorrow she wouldn't even be legally dead anymore.

It was all coming together. And it was all falling apart.

What happens after? If this works, if I oust Zeke and stop the attacks, then what? What must I do then? What must I become? What must I leave behind?

No, no thinking. Just planning. Planning was a safe place. *Alone is safe. Even if it sucks.*

One leg bent in her chair, one foot on the floor, swinging her back and forth in an arc while she fiddled with the communications board. She tapped through her petitions, watching the numbers climb. Public petition to impeach an elected official. Public support for independent tribunal to investigate the rigging of national elections. Public petition of no-confidence in President Ezekiel Medina. She'd started with one verified electronic signature, hers. The highest-count petition now contained signatures in the millions. That was the impeachment document.

Protests were gathering in femacities all over the continent. She'd logged on to rally in three so far today, gaunt in her smartfabric dive suit and shorn hair, and more were scheduled for the coming hours. Her fans were amazed at her story, at her seeming rebirth. They marveled at her courage to pursue the criminals, the masters. Immortal, they called her, having no clue of the irony.

She was calling her coalition The People Rise. It was earthy, vaguely menacing, but that was okay. That was the mood among the displaced thousands. She'd thought of something milder, like The People Speak or The People's Voice, but this wasn't really a peaceful movement of people. It was an act of desperation, backed by her personal hammer of justice. She *would* stop Zeke's violence. She *would* do it now. And he *would not* silence her.

This was happening. All of it.

An hour ago, she'd gotten word from the Pentarc. Zeke had tried to contact her through mech-Daniel, and Heron offered to relay the communiqués as they came in. Fine, she'd said. Put them through.

"Angela! First, are you okay? Second, where are you? And third, what are you doing, kiddo?"

"I am alive. Surprise," she responded. "Nice of you to ask. Eight weeks after the fact. Are you sure you don't want to confess anything?"

Such as, oh, let's see: you have been micro-managing my life for the vast majority of it, perhaps? Or that you used me to do your warmongering dirty work? Or that you're causing all those drone strikes, all those deaths, which are happening as we speak?

He played it off like nothing had changed. "The election results were in our favor, and I thank you for all your efforts toward that end. But, kiddo, I'm worried about some vidcasts I've seen. Vids featuring you, today. What's going on?"

"I got clued in, Zeke," she said. "I know Texas isn't our enemy. I know you're behind the drone strikes."

He was silent for a really long time.

"Where are you getting these ideas? Is mech-Daniel functioning correctly? You should run a diagnostic on him."

"Why? Are you thinking of ordering him to kill me again? Using your Ashe back door, maybe?" This time she didn't wait through the pause for his reply. "How about you and I make a deal instead? Call off the drone attacks, effective immediately. Apologize publicly."

He took a long pause before replying, "Or else what, kiddo?"

"Or I will have you removed from office." She moved her com closer to her mouth, to up the resonance in her voice. "Do we have a deal?"

There wasn't any reason to prevaricate or pussyfoot. These were the terms. She had copied the conversation and tagged Fez on it. She had no doubt it would be disseminated widely and immediately with verified identity tags.

Don't fuck with me, Zeke. You know I have nothing to lose.

She'd been waiting for ten minutes now for a response. Of course, it was entirely possible that he didn't mean to reply, that their conversation was effectively over. If he proceeded to ignore her completely from here on, it wouldn't surprise her. Zeke and Daniel and their kind were fond of leaving difficult conversation threads unresolved, dangling like live wires on wet pavement.

He knew how thin her patience thread was. Forcing her to wait must be a fucking thrill for him.

Restless, irritated, and just a little scared, she was just about to go hunting for Kellen, when he came to her.

"Angela?" He always said her name that way, the Spanish way, closer to angel. It made her feel worshipped but always unworthy. Everyone knew real angels didn't exist.

She spun the chair so she could see him. Too tall for a sub, he bent in the doorway, one hand curved over the lintel. The look on his face made her heart double-whump.

"Is everything okay?" Such a stupid question, every time somebody asked it. Of course something was unokay. Else why even ask the question? Yet she had, of him, because of that look.

"Vallejo won't be a danger to us going forward," he said in a weary voice. "I am willing to guarantee that personally."

"You're sure? He's wily."

"Yeah, I'm sure. For one thing, I locked him back in the lounge. I also threatened him pretty bad with some shit he's particularly scared of, but mostly, I think he's just tired of being kept prisoner. Those UNAN detention blocks aren't fancy living, and his captors haven't been kind. Don't mean he won't get up to no good the first second we loose him upon the world, but for right now, I think he's harmless."

He crossed the module toward her. This wasn't a

big sub, and apparently, it hadn't been built with more than one communications officer in mind. Little room, spherical, metal, covered floor to ceiling with electronics. There wasn't another chair, so Kellen went to his knees in front of hers.

She couldn't help herself. She reached for him, drew his golden head into her lap, and stroked it until she was halfway to weeping.

The answer to her earlier silent question hovered right there over his bent body. *What must I leave behind?* If this worked, if she kicked Zeke out of office and ended his secret reign of villainy, she had to become something not-her. Something alone and unassailable and made of authority.

Kellen was her weakness, had always been, and if she let the world know he existed, her enemies would use him against her. They would threaten him. They would use him to put her back into her box and make her shut up.

That weakness, the fault in a dragon's scales, the dry spot on Achilles' heel, was love. Love created loss. Love was baggage.

No wonder the mentors had broken them apart. No wonder she must do it again.

"You're trembling like a guilty thing surprised," he said, his voice half-muffled. "Cold?"

"Am I crazy or did you just whip out Wordsworth on me?"

"Definitely crazy, but then, you always been mad as a hatter."

She smiled. "Loopy as a shoelace."

His hair was fine and soft, even softer than Yoink's

fur. She could stroke it all day, every day. This could be her life.

What if they just ran away? Got a unit somewhere, made her digitally dead again, pretended to be the people they should have been, might have been, if no one else had ever intruded on their lives and destinies. Oh, she knew it wasn't real; she knew why they couldn't. In that scenario, the attacks would continue, people would die, and the both of them would be eaten from the inside with guilt.

But for half a second, a stolen frozen moment under the ocean and on the edge of uncertainty, she indulged the fantasy. It was pretty fucking amazing.

So fucking amazing she wanted to—needed to—share it. With him.

Turned out she could. Com room, right? She knew how to use one of those. She knew how to merge her thoughts with another person's. Show him her feelings. Let him into her head. And at the same time, closet away everything he oughtn't see there, shhhh.

Emotion casting was totally her wheelhouse.

She swept one hand over the communications board. The bulkhead separating the com module from the rest of the sub lowered, slowly. Hissed. Sealed.

"When we were out by the car looking at the ocean in the dark," she told him, making her voice into a lullaby, "I watched you get into your dive kit. I watched your body in the moonlight, and you know what I couldn't stop thinking?"

"That you'd better ought give a man his pride and look away when he's that goddamned cold?"

"That somebody with a gift should carve your

likeness. And I would put it by my bed and go to sleep every night, enchanted by such beauty. And I would never have a nightmare again."

"Y'know, you can spout poetry till your voice goes, gal, but sayin' a thing, even a real pretty thing, don't make it true."

"I know." Her throat was so thick with tears, she could hardly speak. "I am a fantastic liar, though, and just once, I need to show you my best lie, my myth and fantasy. I need to make you believe. Please let me."

●　●　●

He couldn't read her mind, had never been able to, but right then when he looked up, he read her face clear as glass, the expression on it, like a book of fairy tales, a thousand free wishes scattered on the surface of reality. He couldn't see the end of their story and didn't want to. He could only see the beauty of it as it was. And also, he could give her the thing she wanted. He could give her all of him. He could give her his faith.

Tell me your tale, oh princess mine, and I'll quest the world for you.

She pulled him to his feet, and he let her. A helm dangled from the ceiling, a psych-emitter contraption, and he let her secure it on his head. He let her unfasten both suits, first hers, then his, and peel away the smart-fabric until their two bodies were bare and rippled like gooseflesh in the stark recycled air. He let her lay their clothes on the hard floor, a blanket to cushion their fall.

The communications room was close, and cold. But her hands were warm, drawing him down.

He felt those same hands from the inside, stroking

his shoulder, the hard ridge of his clavicle, the wild percussion of his pulse. Warm and sweet as she felt to him, so he felt to her. Touch sensation poured from her fingertips into his skin, then cycled back, one loop connected end to end, that insatiable snake of desire, eatin' its own tail.

"I never plugged in to a holoporn suite, even though of course I had one in my home," she said, painting him with her breath. He could feel the brush of it, and her own urge to taste. Salt on her tongue, swallow of tears. "It seemed so wrong to fuck a stranger, to know what they felt with their hands without ever making an attempt to feel their reasons, you know, the imagery. Holoporn with psych-emitter reception only goes one way. It feels interactive, but it's actually passive. Merely science, no myth."

"Which is why folks still get themselves nekkid and together," he said. "If you could science a thing like love, there'd be no hunting for it, and no wishing. No made-up might-have-been. Folks wouldn't need to put all their souls into it."

She moved over him, fierce. "I can make it more than science."

He had no doubt. Just went on letting her.

With her hands, a molasses-slow loop of want unwinding between their bodies, melding one to the other. With her mouth, closing over his, sleek and hot, both victor and vanquished. And then lower, at his throat: taste of sweat and trace chemical detox, wet of her tongue, scrape of her teeth. The shiver of candy sucked against the soft palate too long, too sweet.

Kellen closed his eyes, no longer able to discern

which touch was his and which was hers. It didn't matter anyhow. He could feel her touch, touching him.

"You're casting all these sensory inputs with that doodad in y'head," he said, lying back against the floor, covered by the warmth of her body. "But I still only feel the surface. Guess there are limits to your science."

She laughed low against his chest, her hand on his hip, moving inward. "Well, the porn stars don't get the kind of training I did, and I haven't really started yet."

"Did you sort of just tell me to hold on and enjoy the ride?"

"Possibly. You did say I was bossy."

"Point."

Her hand had found what it was looking for and sheathed him in delicious agony. He gasped, curling his fingers against her back. Still just the sensory input, but good God, so that was what it felt like. What he felt like, to her. Not just the stroke and friction and surge and ache, but the clasp of power, holding another person's pleasure, literally, in the palm of your hand.

He inhaled, and desire filled his head, seeping into every part of him. Overwhelming desire, amplified on each feedback cycle, each body's need consuming the other. He couldn't contain it all, but at the same time needed more. Needed all of her. All of himself. All of whatever beast was both, and everything.

"Can you feel how much I want you?" she asked in a voice made of promises.

"Yes." And he could. Feel it. Not a rhythm or a slide of moisture on her thigh. This was desire of a different sort, from her mind and memory and soul and hope.

Eyes slammed shut, but he could still see his own

skin, wanted to hold it, feel its texture, test its heat. Wanted to push up into her, fuck her, be her, and simultaneously be invaded by her. He wanted to drown in her, drowning in him. Together. Same. One.

She moved atop him, fitting their bodies together, writhing until the hitch and glide, the heat and hollow, press and piston became one machine, working in perfect synchrony. And none of that shit was endurable for long. Not by either one of them.

Best part of this little science experiment she'd thought up? Was knowing exactly how close she tethered herself to the vast edge of ecstasy, and how easy it was to pull her right over into it.

"I love you," she said, underlining her words with feeling, transforming them into revealed knowledge, cosmic truth. "I have loved you all my life and will never stop. Swears."

Past, present. My woman. The best of me.

Her mind, her soul, her body, she was wide open to him, showing and sharing without compromise. No secrets could remain hidden in a surge this wide, this fierce. He knew her. Absolutely and completely. He had never done anything in this life to deserve what overcame him then, the flood of gratitude, of guilt and joy and hope and, yeah, that other thing, too.

Love.

He came, or she did, or they both did. Who even knew the difference at this point? Everything in the universe slammed together, the inverse of creation, coalesced, held for one hot second, and then imploded on a cosmic scream, narrowing and collapsing like a white-point star to this microscopic perfect moment of density.

"Shh," she said, gathering her composure quicker than he could. "Whoa. I'm getting all these astronomical data points in my head. Hawking radiation and event horizons. Did you know you go deep-science at the point of orgasm, or is this surprising?"

"Had never really thought about it before," he murmured. Their bodies slipped against each other when she laughed. She felt full and sated, and he wanted to wrap her up and hold her safe until the end of everything.

"I need to ask, while we're linked like this, so I can feel your feels…" she began. He braced for it, knew what was coming. His body hadn't caught up with his mind, though, so he didn't tense, didn't flinch when she said, "Why were you so sad when you came in here?"

He wasn't anywhere close to being able to talk about it. Too raw. Too hurt. "Ain't like you were bounce-house happy or anything. Swear to heaven you were just this side of bawling. So let's talk about that instead."

"No. I asked you first."

"Yeah, but—"

Both their coms blanged like door chimes when the party starts. As Kellen's was still tucked into the pouch on his dive suit, which was smack under his bare ass, the vibration was a mite fonky feelin'. Angela tapped hers first. Voice only, no vid. Small mercy.

It was Garrett. "Um, hello. I just got a relay communiqué from Heron, but then, I don't know, it…it cut off. First words were something about a response incoming from the president, and then…shit. Just shit. I think…oh man, I think we lost the Pentarc."

CHAPTER
16

"It's gone," Garrett was saying. "Shit. I'm not finding it on any satellite trackers or anything. Thermodrones are reading a massive heat signature in the area, but they're still too far away for visual. It can't be. I mean, there's EMP shielding all over that thing. And alternate means of transmission. It doesn't go dark. It can't. I just... I don't know what happened. Shit."

"Now settle," Kellen said, burring his voice to smooth out the sharp edges of Garrett's fear. He felt the same panic inside, just couldn't show it. Gone. How could something as massive, as permanent as the Pentarc be gone? "Chloe, you there too, honey?"

"Yes."

Odd for her, a one-word answer. Odd and terrifying.

"Okay, I need you to help Garrett find the Chiba Station. The queen has all kinds of feeds, thousands of them suckers, satellites we don't even know about. Now listen, she's gonna be on the lookout for our home, our people. Let's rally here. We need information, soon's we can get it, but mostly we need to keep our own shit together."

He was saying all these things like he believed them, but a part of him already didn't. That same part knew a life, a mission, a moment this good wasn't meant to last. He had dared to hope for a little more time, and that had not been wise.

He didn't want to think of everyone in there, huddled beneath the hyperstructure. He didn't want to think of them trapped, in the dark, when those spires came down.

But thoughts were sneaky bastards, acid bastards, and once let in, they tended to seek out a wound, pry it wider, and make it burn.

He didn't remember standing up but realized he was when Angela pressed her body against the back of his, wrapped her arms all the way around him. Her face against his spine, like she was breathing for him, feeling for him. She wasn't transmitting anything out of her emote rig right now, just white-noise hum. Comfort in soft bursts. A lullaby of soothing thoughts, like one of those Zen fountain doohickies Dead Fester hawked.

She washed her peace over him. Somehow, maybe by reaching through the psych-emitter link and tweaking his own brain. This woman was magic. Weird magic, sure. But his.

The communication board blurred beneath his hands. This wasn't his forte. Fuck, where was that cat?

Tight against his chest, Angela's wrist-mounted com buzzed.

"Yoink?"

"I am in the plane with Garrett," the cat said. "A bad thing happened."

Safe. Both his girls were safe. It wasn't everything he

needed, but it was something. He could put his hands in these holds and boost himself up.

"Sure has. Load up our blip board, little general. Let's see what we've got."

It took her several long, agonizing moments. Then, "The dolphins are bored. You'll arrive in Puerto del Tampico in less than an hour, and can they go away now?"

"Give the pod our thanks," he said. "And then scan up north, in the desert. See if you can find coyotes out near the Pentarc."

More time. His teeth were wanting to chatter, but he wasn't cold, or at least no colder than normal on this boat. But it felt like something core-deep had lost its heater, for good, and the chill spread, filling him up with emptiness. The only parts of him that lived were the parts touching her.

"Some coyotes, yes," Yoink reported. "They are confused. Also, eagles."

First good news he'd had so far. "Can they do a fly-over for us, over home? Also, anybody among those eagles have a camera on board?"

"Maybe. I will see."

Silence gnawed through the cramped communications room. The bank of lights hummed blue.

"Port in an hour," he said. "We should get dressed." But he didn't move.

"Kellen," she breathed against his back. "We will find them. They're going to be okay."

He wanted to reply. Couldn't. All his energy right now focused on keeping his shit together. Not thinking of the tunnels, of the dark. Of the sick way the refugee camps had smelled in Texas after the storm, after the diseases took hold. Or of Sissy holding on to her boy, hours on and they'd both long passed. Cold.

Things falling apart. Chaos moving in. Once again, the rug pulled out from underneath him, peace and home sliced away like a fruit's rotten part. A dead part. Here he stood through it all and couldn't do a damn thing to stop any of it.

"And if they aren't okay," Angela whispered in that voice she had, the one made of titanium and cold fury, "you rest assured, my love, they will be avenged."

●　●　●

"You look magnificent," said Rafa, straightening the points of her collar, but even his voice was solemn. He knew what was happening, what the stakes were. Apparently Rafael Castrejon was something more than a pretty face after all. He'd been with her from the boat, from that moment she'd stepped off, and he'd been tireless. Someday she would thank him properly for this.

Not today. There just wasn't time.

Cool black satin licked her legs, stirred by the air circulators on the landjet. Vidcasters clustered, maybe fifty in this car. Camera lights heated her dress until it burned her skin. Sweat pooled in the expected places, but she didn't melt.

She wasn't made of sugar. She sure as fuck wasn't sweet.

She might look, as Rafa said, magnificent, but she didn't feel anything approaching magnificent. She felt… nothing. Deliberately, cleanly nothing. She'd scooped out everything vital, everything worthy, everything real, and left it on a submarine docked in Tampico.

The nothing was important. People trusted people who felt things.

Today, she needed everyone to trust her nothing, the starkness of it. To feel its emptiness. She needed it to horrify the shit out of an entire continent of people, and she didn't have much time.

Rafa kept primping, feeding her cues, and Fez kept transmitting on all channels, real-time and balls-out. She'd gone live with all of it, the disrobing and preparing, her steady reaction as news items filtered through, as petition signatures soared, as bombs fell. Not hiding where she was, not hiding her intentions. Nothing was sacred. If somebody on this continent didn't know who she was or where she was headed, that was their own damn fault. No secrets, no lies. Only justice.

Alerts descended like party confetti. The UNAN security corps broke for her all up and down the West Coast, marching and chanting, "*Soy el fuego! Viva la unificación!*"

Refugees took up the call, pointing their wrath squarely at President Medina. Federal warehouses were raided in Quebec. Power grids went down in Oaxaca, and protesters planned their marches by torchlight. *Stop the drones*, they screamed. *Stop the fire*.

Because their continent was burning, only now it wasn't just Zeke on the offensive. Angela and her team had joined the fray. She pushed back. She resisted.

All over the unified nation, locks were coming undone. Hangars emptied themselves, disgorging rows on rows of war machines. They accepted Angela's command codes without question, because that's what machines did. Drones rose, filling the sky, and then exploded like fireworks.

Teamwork. She wasn't alone at all.

"How's it going, Chloe?" she asked, not looking down. "How long can you keep this up?"

"As long as I must," the nanorobotic AI replied with fierce solemnity. "Give me another target."

Because Chloe had learned a lesson from mech-Daniel. Chloe recorded things. Things like Heron's remote-rigging process. And she replicated things, too, all over this landmass, a flurry of self-recursion, learning, mastering command systems in the time it took a human person to blink. She was in satellites and live feeds and entertainment consoles and smartbombs. In helicopters and planes and landjets and drones. If somebody had a free-fae light full of nanites in their dining room or street-corner bodega, Chloe appropriated it and incorporated all those component pieces into herself. Her self grew. Every nano within her reach became part of her, became vengeance. In the skies above soft targets, her intercepts did not miss.

Chloe was out, a pervasive net of thou-shalt-not, standing between Zeke's bombs and her people. Illegal, hysterical, call her whatever you wanted, nobody was sticking this genie back in a bottle.

No secrets. No lies.

Angela, Rafa, and Fez hurtled north, toward the Capitoline, and rioters in Atlanta, Chicago, Vancouver, and Veracruz celebrated the arrival of air support for their cause. Angela's revolution had their backs, and that's all the spark they needed. They stormed government buildings, demanding vote recounts, demanding to be seen. To be heard.

Charleston, Portland, Fairchild, and Beale came

online, Chloe's birds in the air, raining justice. Forcing this government to listen. To pause. Just fucking pause.

"Time consumes us all in fire," Angela said to the camera. "El Presidente, I am coming for you. And I am the fire."

Fez signaled cut. The lights dimmed, but slow.

She hadn't slept in almost a full day, and her emotions had been frayed to begin with. But she didn't have time to pause or rest. He'd heard her warning, Zeke had, and he'd not only thrown it back in her face, he'd upped the attacks, made them personal. He'd brought down the fucking Pentarc.

It hadn't been her home, but it had been Kellen's. And Kellen was as close to home as she'd ever get or ever want. She took attacks against him personally, because he represented everything good in her. She ached for him, couldn't close her eyes without seeing his face in her memory, the stark horror he'd shown in the second he heard the news of his family.

She blinked, seeing the image on the backs of her eyelids, vid from a reconnaissance craft. Part of Northy still rose above the desert, but the other spires were simply gone, heaps of steaming, dust-shrouded bones.

"Do we have enough content?" she asked.

"Yes, we do. Now sit down, honey," Rafa said, taking her hand and attempting to pull her to one of the bolted-down chairs. "You've had a really shitty day."

"We have all had a shitty day," she said. "Loop it. And let's get to work."

● ● ●

Never in all his years would Kellen have expected to wake up, rested but empty, staring into the face of Damon Vallejo, that old asshole himself.

It was a kindly face today, though, no malice writ there, and no danger. He'd been looking at something. A book? When he saw he was being watched, Vallejo folded it closed and placed it on his lap.

Kellen scrubbed a hand over his eyes, knuckling the sleep out. "Where we at?"

"In the air over Arizona. We should be touching down shortly. Your friend Garrett said to let you rest as long as you could."

They'd boarded the spaceplane in Tampico, right after Angela had headed off to spark up her rebellion. Kellen couldn't think how he'd been able to sleep. Dreamlessly, even. He wondered if Garrett or Chloe had altered the air mix in the plane. He wouldn't fuss at them if they had. He was so often on the other side, but sometimes, it felt good to be cared for.

"Pentarc, it's...any word?"

The old man looked down at the book. He stroked the frayed cloth binding.

Kellen sat up, grabbed for his com, and realized it wasn't on his arm. Aw, fuck a monkey, man, he was naked. Or partway so. He'd had the forethought to pull the longjohns part of his dive suit on before climbing out of the sub, but the rest of the smartfabric hung loose around his waist. He fiddled with the flop of sleeve, found the pouch, found his com. "Yoink? What's our status, girl?"

She didn't reply through the com right away. Probably because she was loitering right next to his bunk. At the sound of her name, she leapt onto his lap, sat back on her haunches, and gazed up at him, serious as the business end of a cannon. "Awake is good. We are good. Coyotes are good. They call. Javelinas dig. We will be home soon."

So no word from down below. And the wild things dug. Didn't sound good.

He felt the plane beneath his feet, observed its familiar cramped quarters. He'd been sleeping back in the racks, bunks for folk who needed rest. A haven in the air.

Heron kept a footlocker here full of things he picked up, all over the world, always with his Mari in mind. Trinkets he'd stored up for years, just waiting to give her. Had he gotten a chance to?

God, please don't end it like this.

His voice was far from steady when he asked, "We heard from Angela?"

Vallejo sighed. "Only every five seconds. Her face has been plastered on every channel I could find, all morning long. You were clever to get rest, but I really don't know how she endures. Fine woman. Scary woman. If I were Zeke Medina today, I would be very, very concerned."

"That's my Angela," Kellen said, but it sounded hollow, even to him.

They'd covered this, but the separation still twinged. She needed to get on the vids, get her voice out there, force Medina to stop. And he needed to get to the Pentarc as fast as possible. He needed to find his people. They both had promises to keep.

And it wasn't like he and Angela hadn't spent most of the last decade apart. Only something had changed there in the com room on the submarine. Neither of them had spoken a promise out loud, but he felt like one had been made. His soul had sealed itself to her, whether she wanted it or not.

What he felt wasn't even want anymore. He needed her. Here, with him.

There wasn't a psych-emitter on board the plane, but Kellen looked down and tapped a quick darknet message: By our superior energies and strict affiance in each other, we will kick their asses.

Yoink nuzzled his wrist, directing his hand over her wee head. She didn't purr, just pushed herself into his palm. He did like his gals bossy.

Pentarc gone. Friends, family trapped in the dark, underground. God. This plane could not travel fast enough to chase all the horror from its path.

He wanted to weep. He wanted to grab up that sweet little kitty, hold her against his face, and cry like a baby.

His com vibrated, and he looked down. She'd replied: You quote for shit, pretty boy. We're the good guys.

He would have grinned if his soul weren't so damn sore. Still, the words were exactly what he needed. He could hear her voice saying them. It was almost like she was here. Space apart was physical, and their relationship was bigger than that.

He huffed out a hot breath. "I got a change of clothes in one of these footlockers, gramps. Best you clear out unless you wanna watch me get all the way nekkid."

Vallejo rose, slowly, the book of Mexican poetry in his hands. Probably not his book. More likely Heron's. *Jesus*.

"Gramps," Vallejo repeated, tasting the word. "I had always hoped, thought maybe…a-and I know she's not

Mari, not really. I know she loathes me as I have loathed her. But if you find her… Just find her. Please."

Tears in his dark eyes, he scurried from the racks, out into the corridor crammed with equipment and memory.

CHAPTER 17

DIGGING. THEY'D BEEN DIGGING ALL DAY, IN THE COLD ACRID dust. Kellen had hollered until he didn't have any voice left, and his eyes burned. Probably had particulates lodged in there. Things that eddied in this air ought never be breathed. Ought never touch tears. The world smelled like drywall and burnt hair, and the digging, the searching, the hoping—the sick encroachment of despair—would never end.

At first it was just the three of them—Kellen, Garrett, and Vallejo—on the pile. Chloe was off doing something important and terrifying. They pulled and hauled, unceasing. Kellen caught a look at Garrett's hands at one point, bleeding from every knuckle, with antibac cotton rounds and medical tape binding his fists, but his face was set, his gold eyes swimming, and there wasn't any deterring him.

Kellen didn't have much thought for his own comfort or safety, either. He'd told Yoink to stay back on the plane, though, coordinate from there. She had a facility for cataloging and deploying assets, and she could let him know if anything big happened in the outside world.

She could relay Angela's voice into his earpiece, which comforted him way more than it ought.

When they'd gotten here, both wild and augmented animals had been at the pile already for a long half day. Yoink sorted them according to skills, put them where they'd do most good. As she said, those javelinas sure could dig.

There weren't any towns nearby, not for miles, but somehow, within hours of their plane's touchdown, people around here learned of the hit. And they came. Strangers, with food and kind words and strong silence. Strangers who tied bio-filtering scarves over their faces, checked in with General Yoink. And dug.

Mostly they didn't talk, but sometimes he'd hear a word or two, scraps of conversation making its way down a bucket brigade. Recollections, and some thanks. Some of these strangers had come through the Pentarc and had moved on once they got their legs beneath them, steady. They came back now, out of gratitude. Maybe a hundred of them, and all before sunset, dressed for the desert night this side of winter. They weren't leaving. Somebody drove a ratty RV out onto the sand, and somebody else arranged a row of grills, fired them up, heated water in pots. Campfires sprang up like twilight wildflowers, but the atmosphere wasn't a party. Nobody sang.

They needed more shovels.

The dust and debris were so thick in the air, and with the sun on its way down, he didn't notice a flurry or the one that followed. And when the temblor of voices arrived at his back, he paid it no mind. He was so tired, worn down like old shoes. Hope thinned as daylight died.

"No, his name is Kellen. Kellen Hockley. About so tall, gold hair? He's been here all day."

A surge of movement among the others. He turned.

There, striding across the desert, dressed in plain, serviceable clothes and—hot damn, were those cowboy boots? On *her* feet?—was his woman. His angel.

She saw him right about the same time he saw her, and she lit out across the desert in his direction. Bless her, he hoped she didn't mean for him to run as well. He stood there, and she barreled into him, pushed her slight body against him, buried her face in the hollow below his throat. Which might have been why he found it so hard to swallow.

His arms came around her slowly, but they got tight pretty quickly, once his mind admitted she was real. "Thought you were off rousing yourself a revolution, princess."

She leaned back, looked up at him, blinking against the toxic air and gathering night. "Duly underway. One more bomb falls, and I am crashing his goddamn inauguration, as planned. But right now I need to be here. I need to be with you. Please don't make me go away."

He was sobbing. She couldn't see it 'cause of all the shit in the air, drying out his eyeballs. This was sobbing tearless. He felt the hard, half hiccup rumble in his chest, and she was latched on so tight, she must've felt it, too.

"I'm here," she was telling him. "We're going to do this. We're going to find them. I've got you."

Why could he believe it more when she said it? He'd believed in all sorts of shit over the years, and disbelieved as many times, but never anything as much as, right at that moment, he believed in her.

She rose up on tiptoes but still couldn't reach his

mouth. Tiny thing; he always forgot her lack of height. She kissed his chin. Soft lips, warm.

"I love you," she said. "And I brought help."

He looked over her dark head and saw what she was talking about. The public pod service didn't run out here, but folks had come anyhow. Folks in mass number. Folks with supplies and skills and cameras and vidcasters. They'd brought their cars out here, beaters and fancy-pants sedans, long-haulers and dune buggies, all rolling out over the desert. Her revolution, but not armed with guns or bombs.

They'd brought shovels.

$$\bullet \quad \bullet \quad \bullet$$

She'd thought she would dig, haul, and search until she died from it, just fell over and lights out. But the human body is a terribly efficient machine. At a point, hers just told her it was time. And it was apparently Kellen's time, too. They didn't consult each other, just joined hands, checked in with General Yoink, and retreated to a sleek Audi autocar, low to the ground. She didn't have a clue how it had made it over the uneven scrub brush to get here. It was technological magic, making this day endurable.

Its owner was on a bucket brigade and had left the lock open, on purpose. The car had heat. Blessed, wonderful heat, thawing her half-frozen body. She took off her boots and coat, and Kellen wrapped himself around her in silence, warming her the rest of the way.

She set a timer on her com. Four hours.

There were things she needed to say to this man. Questions, confessions, reassurances. In the past, she might have wanted to tell him all her plans, soak in his inevitable compliments on her cleverness. But this wasn't that kind of day. Nothing that had happened in the last twenty-four hours was about her, yet the events had cut her to the very root, tiny slices that bled in regrets and would never stop.

Which was fine. She was trained to endure horrors that weren't hers, to take on pain she hadn't volunteered her heart to hold.

"Someday," he murmured right before sleep took him, "someday I'm gonna lay you down in a comfy spot, someplace worthy of the queen you are. Fuck all these cars 'n' subs 'n' shit."

If he'd wanted to fuck that night, she could have made it happen. Just being near him ignited parts of her body like that's what they were designed for. She could have comforted him in a thousand ways. Because she loved him, and also because she was trained to see to the comforts of others, emotionally if not physically. But this was Kellen. Comfort for him was holding the things he loved safe. So she let him hold her, and she held him right back.

It was enough.

But in the end, they didn't have four hours.

At 3:22 on her timer, somebody rapped at the car door. When she opened it, a chubby twentysomething girl with black hair and face made darker by the night passed along a message. There was somebody coming from the west, on foot. Running. He kept repeating names, and was she Garrett, Kellen, or Chloe?

She woke Kellen, and they followed the girl out, around the southern edge of destruction.

Somebody had sent out a pickup to fetch the runner, which brought him faster to the main hub of the camp.

"His name is Kellen," she called out, dragging him along by the hand. A tangle of people surrounded the pickup. He clutched her hand so tight her bones creaked, and the crowd parted to let them pass.

The bruise of a cloud over this whole area blocked out any moonlight from the sky, but folks had com lights, a dozen or more of them, camera lights, too, all pointed at the truck. She saw him, the runner. Balanced in a crouch in the dirt-dusted bed, serene and still, searching the crowd for longed-for faces.

Dan-Dan.

He looked like he'd been through a meat grinder. The hands capping his bent knees were worn down to the metal beneath, and strips of vat-grown flesh dangled like party streamers from the cuffs of his long-sleeved poly shirt. All his clothes were stained dark in streaks. Very likely, he had already bled out, and the circulatory mechanism that kept him looking humanlike had died some hours back. There wasn't enough wound glue on this continent to fix what had been done to his face. He looked like a monster, but there was something warm in his ruined face, in his posture, something infinitely kind. It was recognition, one person of another.

"Please stop digging," the mech-clone said. "We aren't down there. We went to the tunnels, westward. There are miles of them, but they're underground, too deep to establish any kind of communications, and I'm afraid we are trapped there currently. We have some injuries, but all our people are accounted for. Your animals, too, Doc."

"Heron?" Kellen said, far too softly and in a voice that sounded like dust.

Angela dragged him the last few feet to the truck. She scrambled up over the tailgate, pulling him along, which must have looked nuts to bystanders and the viewing public, she being small and him so big. But she wasn't going to let him have this conversation with his best friend from ten feet away, with all those people listening. It was a closer moment than that, and there was too much to say.

But first, this bit first. She crouched down in front of the machine, cupped the bloody mess of Dan-Dan's jaw in her hands.

"Thank you," she said. "And if there's even a bit of Dan-Dan in there, thank you, too. You are *good*."

The mech-clone lifted his arms wide, and Angela and Kellen both moved into an embrace. With the thing. Group hug, but without all the silly, fluffy connotations that phrase would bring if spoken aloud. Network hug, rather. Family hug. Home.

"He's still here," Heron said through Dan-Dan's mouth, the quality crispy and metallic through the half-ruined voice apparatus. "His kernel is intact, archived as you instructed him to do. But I have, as Kellen guessed, appropriated this body to dig its way out of the tunnel. It was not an easy process, nor quick. I had lots of time to think of what you all must be imagining for our fates. I'm so sorry for that, for the scare. Now, is there a nodal relay anywhere nearby where I can plug this body in? I'd like to get some heavy equipment where we are, to dig us out. There are some among us who cannot climb."

"The plane's parked right over there," said Garrett as he approached the truck bed.

He'd found them. Angela could have thwapped herself for not messaging him first, but somehow he'd known anyway. He hopped over the side of the pickup bed, almost like gravity didn't apply to him. Angela peered at him wonderingly. Hadn't Garrett been working alongside Kellen at the pile all day? Hadn't he busted his knuckles earlier? She was sure she'd seen him with bloody, wrapped hands. Those hands now were smooth, though, long-fingered. Dainty even.

So there was more to Garrett than appeared on the surface. But that was kind of the story with all humans, wasn't it?

"Excellent," Heron said. "You may fill me in on the rest of it as we drive to the plane, then. I assume you three have been busy."

Angela met Kellen's eyes and smiled slightly. "Oh, we have a few balls in the air. Did you know Chloe could rig a whole army, or am I just the last to know all these fun things?"

●　　●　　●

Rescue and recovery went lightning fast once they got that heavy construction equipment in place. Limitless resources will do that for you. The volunteer camp in the desert stayed together for a little while after, though. Apparently there were rumors of treasure to be found in the pile, and Kellen refused to speak to that. If somebody ventured down there and happened to find a pink-diamond tiara or a priceless Russian egg, well, good on them. He was done with digging.

The reunions played awful sweet. The mamas hugged and hugged him, and Fan went on so fast rat-a-tat-tat that even Kellen couldn't keep up, and his Spanish was pretty good. She said something to the effect of, "All our baby animals are safe, and my preciouses also, and all our enemies must die a giant flaming death, and can you make that happen right this minute?"

He could be off by a word or two.

Adele, nearing eighty if she was a day, didn't run as fast as some others during the evacuation, and she'd had a tunnel collapse on her. She'd regained consciousness while Heron was out running that mech's body eastward. Her head, she said, was still giving her gyp, which Fan said was a leftover Britishism and he wouldn't understand, but basically, although Mama Adele felt like hammered shit, she was on the mend.

The attacks had stopped, but nobody knew if this pause would stick.

The dual houses of Congress had called an emergency session, but plans were still on to re-up Medina as president tomorrow at the Colina Capitolina. Shithead had hired a live band and everything for the party after.

There was some concern for the Chiba Station, which had left its geosynch sometime during the attack on the Pentarc and now could not be located, not on coms and not in the sky. Nobody quite knew where it went, and that worried Kellen a lot. The mech-clone queen of that station wouldn't have left Heron if he was in danger, not if she'd had even a spark of choice in the matter. She was loyal. But there was no wreckage either, and she had a lot of power reserves in the station. Possibly she'd gotten bumped off course or something. He hoped the cause of her disappearance was that innocent. He hoped there weren't orbit-to-orbit weapons in play.

Chloe, that little superstar, had drawn herself back together and was hanging out in Mama Adele's recovery room, determined to keep her whole crew within grabbing distance, even though, without a solid body, she wouldn't be doing any actual grabbing. She'd counted the refugees a dozen times and still seemed unconvinced they were all safe.

Garrett sat right there with her. Of course he did.

She could disperse instantly, whenever they needed it, she said. She knew the pattern for fitting herself back together after such a wide spread. She'd put all her borrowed bits back into the free-fae lights all over the country, but if the need arose, she'd round them all back up. Kellen didn't think anybody would call that stealing.

There was a rough spell among those bright reunions when Mari realized her asshole father had come along. Vallejo had been out there digging in the pile with everybody else, and he looked a lot worse for wear after. His bouffant hairdo was sideways, and tears had left deep tracks in the dust on his face. Knowing Mari, Kellen had thought she might just shoot first and ask questions later. But you know what? That girl had a soul deep as a cenote and a capacity for forgiveness deeper still. She also wasn't scared to admit when she was wrong. And she had been wrong about Vallejo. He didn't have shit to do with her auntie's situation.

She towered over her daddy, but she leaned, put her forehead to his, and said some stuff in a low voice that Kellen couldn't hear. Didn't want to. And that old coot had cried and cried.

Things were afoot. Rebellion glimmered like a too-hot summer on the surface of everything.

And when Angela set up her command center about one hour's flight time outside of Denver, in a little town called Crested Butte, Kellen went with her. Pretty town in the summer, used to be crammed to the gills in winter, back when winter snowfall was predictable and ski trips were a thing. They found a unit low on the mountain and a wide strip of place to park the plane. Then they started hauling shit in. Cameras and support staff. Communications arrays and performance tech. Angela spent a whole day recording speeches in all sorts of languages for all kinds of eventualities.

Including one where she didn't survive tomorrow's inaugural ball.

Kellen didn't think he was supposed to see that one. He probably shouldn't have watched. But damn it, he'd been so sure so recently that folk he loved were gone, he couldn't even wrap his mind around a world without her in it. So seeing that speech was a lot like watching a vid, a made-up what-if, a thing he knew could never happen. Would never happen.

A thing he personally would not allow to happen.

He aimed to be there, to protect her, no matter what. She wasn't getting him into another psych helm. She wasn't running off on him again.

'Course, when he mentioned that, there at the end of the day with hours left before dawn and her team wrapping up and moving out for the night, she just slung him a vixen grin. "Not happening. You can put that thought to bed." She paused. "Now, may *I*? Put you to bed, I mean?"

"Didju just sling a flirt at me?" He wasn't gonna tell

her she sucked at innuendo. If he hadn't been so clued in to her tone and movement, he might have missed her invitation completely.

In reply, she dropped her voice to velvet and rubbed it all over him. "I tried to. Did it hit anything like a sensitive spot?"

Only every single one. "I don't know if you realized when you hired this place, but there is, right above where we're standing, a loft sort of doohicky. And in that loft, there is a giant bed."

Her dark eyes narrowed. "You need to go upstairs. Right now."

"Yes'm. Lead on."

She did, working a wiggle into her stair-climbing that made the going way too slow. Not that he didn't enjoy every single sashay.

She'd crawled into some kind of slinky dress for her latest speech recording, but it didn't take much to get that thing off. Wore her brand-new printed cowboy boots underneath, where the cameras wouldn't be peeking and that he found mighty adorable. There was some discussion of cowgirls and haylofts and shit like that. Private discussion.

He kissed her mouth, and then all the rest of her.

They had to move the cat—who complained, jumped back up, and had to be removed a second time, and then flicked her tail and sulked over to a dresser, where she had a better view—but that bed was all he'd imagined it would be. Space enough to spread Angela's body beneath his attention, to lavish and worship and take time over a thing. It was a coming-home kind of bed, a thank-you-kindly one as well. A please-stay-here-with-me-forever, though in fact those words scared him shitless, and he couldn't force them out. He didn't know, even after all they'd been through, what she'd say to that kind of declaration.

His love was a wild thing, a powerful thing, angelic and immortal and fully beyond his ken. But he didn't want to waste the time tonight trying to figure her all out.

Tonight was about licking their wounds clean, about healing.

There was a time, back in the before, when they'd memorized each others' bodies, every curve and valley, mountain and river. Tonight, they fitted the pieces of their map together till no spaces remained between parts. Fusion and perfect, a laser-cut puzzle put right.

It was okay that the big bed squeaked. It was okay that the cat watched creepily from her perch on the dresser. It was okay that winter roared just outside, and nothing tomorrow was promised.

They held.

Each other, the future, the past, all their hopes and dreams and words.

They held.

And then, long after and with their naked, sated limbs still tangled in sheets, she broke first.

CHAPTER 18

"My love, I need to tell you a thing," Angela said. "And after, if you need to leave and never look back, that's going to be okay. Just in case things don't work out so well tomorrow, I want you to know the truth. Keeping this secret has been so very hard."

She almost said *so fucking hard*, but the tone wasn't right. It might have led to more frolicking, and she needed to get this truth out in the open. It was time.

"Aw, love," Kellen said, pressing a kiss against her hair. "I ain't leaving you. I aim to stick on you like glue all the rest of our lives."

Did he realize he echoed his own words from long ago? From their last day together at Mustaqbal? Knowing him, yeah, he probably did. Boys with eidetic memories were such a pain in her ass.

"I thought I had a problem with that," she confessed. "With forever. I thought, back on the submarine and lots of times before, that loving you was a weakness, my Achilles' heel. I worried that if somebody wanted to get to me, to hurt me, they'd just hurt you instead, knowing that it would kill me."

"That's a hard word, kill." He stroked her back, inscribing it with fire.

"But it's the right word," she said. She desperately wanted to leave it at that. To let him keep on stroking her skin, and then she'd pull him into her arms and they'd make love for a full day straight, like goddamn rattlesnakes. But that plan was like all her other plans, a goal to aim for, not reality to live. And all based on lies.

"Nah, you're stronger than you know, princess," he said.

"Maybe. At least, I think you might be right." Unable to stop herself, she wrapped her arms around his body, fit her palms against the ripple of muscles on his back, and drew in a deep breath. He smelled like fresh-showered man, no cologne or clinging scents. Just him. For half a moment, she held him completely in her embrace, and she actually did feel strong. Strong enough to tell him the truth. "At the pile in the desert, when we didn't know yet who'd survived, when we thought the worst, you were still going. Hell, I was still going. We were still living, functioning, even if the worst *had* happened. Somehow the world itself didn't end."

He didn't say anything to that, but she knew she was right.

"The tragic thing, and the secret thing," she went on, "is I didn't always know that. I didn't always know that losing the thing most precious to me would not, in fact, end me." She paused, gathering up courage as if it were armor. And it was, sort of, but cold. "Kellen, what did Vallejo tell you that made you so sad in the submarine?"

He loosed a long breath that eddied in her hair. "He said the consortium wanted you to get yourself hitched to Daniel because they had run your genomes and thought you two would produce some kind of superkid. It struck me that was just the sort of thing an evil person might hold over your head, to keep you down and to make you miserable for a long, long time. Got to say, it pissed me off some."

Close. Real close, Vallejo. Maybe you really are a supergenius madman. Observant at the least.

She thanked the old man silently for not saying the rest. For letting her do it herself. "Except it wasn't Daniel's genome I hitched mine to."

His hand on her back went still. His breath stopped.

"You were..." His voice like dust.

"Um, yes," she said. "I knew before you left Mustaqbal, but I didn't know how to tell you. I mean, we weren't safe. You said it yourself, there's no cure for nineteen. At least technology was on our side, sort of. Zeke said I could bank the fetus until I, quote, got my shit together, unquote." She had been such a mess, and so alone. For a long time after Kellen had left, she just hadn't been able to function. But he didn't need to know that. Not now.

"That snotfucker," Kellen murmured.

"Agreed, knowing what I know now. At the time, he had all the answers, though. Of course, he never intended for me to come back and retrieve the fetus. What he intended was exactly the thing I did. I married Daniel. I promised to put my super girl genome to work, and we tried. A lot. For a long time. But we never got along on, you know, a personal level—in private, he was the asshole no one ever realized, and cruel besides. I offered to get it over with, in a lab, like civilized people. He, ah, didn't like that idea. Despite his threats, I left him two years ago."

"Right about the time you got the mech?"

"Do you remember every single thing that has ever come out of my mouth?"

"Purt' near."

The accent was really horrible. He hadn't done anything to fix it in all these years. She kind of loved it. Okay, real hard loved it.

"So anyhow," she went on, "Zeke bought mech-Daniel to keep my defection from getting back to the consortium. He swore he was trying to protect me from them, said they would be really angry if they found out I ditched Daniel and put a snag in their horrible Bene Gesserit–type breeding program."

He took his time digesting her confessions, and Angela's body tightened, coiled. Damn. She put her brain training on it, worked the tension out, soothed herself, slowed her breath, thought about where she was and who she was with and what they'd just done together. This was why she'd chosen now, when they were both sunk in such deep postcoital bliss they'd be too lethargic to move. When he would be too sated to grab his pants and run the fuck away, as fast as humanly possible.

She knew Kellen. After all these years, she knew him. He tended his people, his critters, and he would never forgive her for, even temporarily, giving up their child. He wouldn't accept as atonement all the messages she'd sent him over the years, unanswered, all the times she'd tried to get in touch. Her own sense of justice was honed to a fine point, but his was at least as sharp.

She lay there, naked, holding on tight, waiting for the cut.

After the longest time, he said, "So where's she now, our girl?"

A shiver skidded down her spine, but he petted it away. "How did you know it was a girl?"

"Science," he said. "Statistically, when folks fuck as much as we did, they more often conceive female offspring."

"That's…" Well, it was intensely sexy that he knew the factoid, and it almost distracted her from the guilt soup she was stirring, from finishing out her confession.

Because this would be a great time to stop. She could leave it right there. He didn't seem to hate her yet. Not irrevocably. But if he knew the rest of it, he would. He was good, at the core. How could he not loathe what she was?

Buck the fuck up. You did it. You did all of it. Can't just skid to the edge of a confession and then wimp out at the last minute. All the way in, right now.

"Okay, that was distracting," she told him. "And *you* are distracting, in the most amazing way, but I need to tell you one more thing."

"You really don't."

"I do. Please listen."

He went silent. His hand stopped stroking.

She continued. "Two years ago, when I left Daniel…"

"Yes."

"I left him because I went to Tamil Nadu, after the flood water receded. I hadn't been there in a long time, but that's where my father was from, and it's where I went, back when I was nineteen and stupid and things got bleak. Anyhow, because I was there after the flood and it was a place I thought about a lot, I went to the cryobank where…where I left it. Her. The place was gone."

"In the flood?"

"No. Years before. They closed doors, went out of business after the Black November financial crisis in '52. Apparently they sent out notices to everyone who had stored material there and gave them a time window for retrieval, but I never got my notice. Daniel kept it back, because my past, my sins, my…daughter were all things he held against me, held over me, to make me do what he wanted."

"So since he didn't have that whip anymore, you left him."

"Oh, worse than that. I killed him."

Kellen didn't say anything. He was tomb-silent as she told him the rest. How she'd funded the contract. How she'd given Heron the green light to go ahead with the job, knowing that mech-Daniel was with her in Guadalajara the whole time and safe. How she'd written the contract in such a way that it would point to Vallejo, even mentioned him specifically in supersecret subcontract riders. How she'd thought that setting up Vallejo, starting a war with Texas, and using that war to spur Zeke's reelection would all bundle together to save her from the consortium's wrath.

How, basically, she was a worse villain than Vallejo ever could be. *Surprise, you just fucked a murderer and might even love her a little. As a bonus, she's the mother of your might-have-been child. Tell me, how does that make you feel?*

"Were you specifically trying to get Mari to take that contract?" he asked in a voice much tighter than usual. A voice that scared her, but she didn't want to analyze it right now.

He was probably asking how far down the evil-machinator hole she'd gone. And she couldn't really give him a depth estimate. She was still falling.

"I didn't know she was trying to find her father," she said. "So no. When you mentioned her name, I was surprised." Surprised enough to accept Kellen's bargain. To agree to get Mari off the hook for murder. Which, incidentally, had covered Angela's own tracks nicely.

Except for Zeke. He must have figured it out. He must have realized what she'd done. And he knew why, too. He'd gone with her to Tamil Nadu. Both times.

So, fine, she killed his friend, he needed payback. That might explain his attempts to kill her—she knew a thing or two about revenge and respected the clean justice of it—but it didn't excuse all the attacks he'd made on mass populations. It didn't excuse his war-mongering or willingness to be the consortium's god-damn sword of awfulness. She still had plenty of issues with Zeke's behavior.

And her own.

"I didn't set Mari up specifically, but, Kellen, *some-body* was going to take that contract. I didn't know who, but I was leading someone right into capital murder. Right into a life sentence. When you told me that the feds would chase her down and kill her ugly and put it all in disaster-porn vids, I almost threw up. Because you're right, that would have happened. And it would have been because of me."

The horror of it washed over her again. The cold slink of blood circulating right after she made a tough decision, a wrong decision, but did it anyway. She'd known there was no forgiveness for her. But also, there was no going back to Daniel. And he'd never accepted that.

The pain was good now, though. The guilt was good. She had done terrible things, and her motivations and reasons didn't excuse them. Justice might be blind, but it wasn't eye-for-an-eye, not in practice. The things Daniel had done to her didn't confer a right to kill him. She was bad. She could spend the whole rest of her life trying to right all wrongs in this world, and none of it would wipe her ledger clean.

They might have lain for hours in the bed, wrapped around each other, Kellen and her. His heart beat steady beneath her ear. He didn't stroke her back again.

After a while, he moved, shifted their tangled limbs until she rolled to her side, and he faced her. He looked at her, at her chin, her mouth, her nose, her eyes, like he was memorizing her features. He kissed her between the brows.

"I love you," he said. "I gotta go walk off some thoughts."

In almost looking-down-the-barrel-of-winter Colorado, with a foot of new snow on the ground? Right.

She watched him get up and pull his clothes on. God, he was beautiful. And he was leaving. And he needed to. And she deserved it.

She didn't beg him to stay. She let him go. And she cried. And she slept.

●   ●   ●

Kellen wasn't in bed when Angela woke. He wasn't there when she breakfasted. He wasn't there to calm her nerves about today. Yoink had gone, too, sometime in the night. None of this stark aloneness was unexpected, but it did hurt fresh every goddamned second, the constant shriek of a wild violin when all she wanted was silence.

Her team arrived, and the updates started rolling in, and she forced nose from navel. Her hodgepodge rebel media group, led by Fez and Rafa, all crowded around Fez's big portable dinosaur monitor and watched the live-stream inauguration. They could have logged into a holocast and VR'd the whole thing, but cramming themselves around a screen, all pressed up together and munching overnuked popcorn, was a whole lot funner. Plus, it gave them a sense of being on the same side, on the same mission. As, of course, they were.

Astonishingly, Angela, sans gloves or any other biodeterrents, did not catch cooties.

During the middle of the swearing-in, one of the high justices interjected, saying the election was being investigated for irregularities and that going beyond this point could in essence give legitimacy to a fraud. A huge chunk of the in-person audience standing around the cold Denver Capitolina cheered like crazy people. But ultimately the ceremony had continued.

Damn it. That had been one of her potential pause points. If things had gone differently there on the capitol steps, she could have stood down, let time and government take their course.

Fucking justices, going through with it anyhow, despite the petitions and the congressional special session. Now she had to get dressed.

The process of costuming for this ball felt very vintage. And by that, she meant a shitload of work. By the end of it, the sun was about an hour from setting, Angela looked terrifying and commanding—a pretty trick for someone her size—and Rafa was a mess of self-congratulatory and gorgeous tears. She also had a lot more respect for, say, Queen Elizabeth I. Vid makeup and costuming professionals. Cinderella's poor overworked godmother.

The gown was backless, fitted, with a double row of shiny, useless buttons down the bodice, a point-collared, abbreviated Lolita jacket, and LED-backlit ebony Kuba velvet to the floor, worn snug. Whoa snug. Uncomfortably snug. Rafa had literally sewn her into this rig, and she was never allowed to piss again.

"You look..." he began, kissing forefinger to thumb, but trailed off in adorable sobs.

She handed him a hanky, pulled from a pocket that, strictly speaking for a dress this tight, should not have existed. "I know. Magnificent. Now, let's go bring down a government."

●   ●   ●

Entrances are important. All the best queens realize this. Thank the makers, then, Angela had expert guidance. Fez arranged for a helicopter to transport them from the airfield to the wide plain of the Colina Capitolina, in case there was traffic. Which there was. Also, protesters had packed themselves in near the capitol complex thick as fleas, so anybody trying to get to the inaugural ball overland was going to be embarrassingly late.

Angela timed her arrival just after the bulk of guests had arrived but before they'd been admitted to the event. While the privileged class, those who hadn't come in underground via pods, stood in the sec-check line out front, bundled against oncoming winter, her helicopter touched down like a dewdrop, and her team helped her out. Fez and Rafa and the rest fanned out to either side, live-streaming everything, working for good angles and light. The psych-emitter beneath her scalp heated and hummed. Transmitting.

Determination. Beneficence. Resolve. Don't fuck with me.

She walked the full length of the mall alone, beneath the weight of all those gazes. All those expectations and hopes. Hundreds right here, millions across the world. Billions, maybe—Fez was just that good.

The pressure hurt, physically hurt, but it wasn't new. She had been trained for this.

The building towered, a marvel of sustainable architecture and big-area additive manufacturing. It was meant to look vaguely Romanesque, hence the name, but really, it reminded her of an obscenely large wedding cake topped with a nipple and a flag. It was lit by a gazillion light cans of free-fae.

Chloe would have a fucking field day with this thing.

She smiled at the thought, let it wick away some of her nerves, and strode on. The sec-check line was just starting to realize who she was and what that might mean for the evening's festivities. A rumble of whispers begun behind fans and coat sleeves rolled out across the twilit mall. She couldn't see their individual faces yet in the twilight and the weird free-fae shadows, but she hoped they were shitting bricks.

Right on the verge, where the fake grass met faker marble and she struggled not to show her bone-deep chill, suddenly, she wasn't alone.

He was there. Kellen.

In a tuxedo. Black, white waistcoat and tie. No tails. Slim fit.

Holy all-the-fucks. No one in the entire history of hotness had ever worn one of those things and looked so goddamn fine.

He winked and extended an elbow. She threaded her black-gloved hand through it. He was wearing gloves tonight, too. How adorably proper. Made a girl want to peel them off. With her teeth.

He arced his long body over hers, his mouth way too close to her ear, heating up her whole shivery self, and said, "True beauty dwells in deep retreats, whose veil is unremoved till heart with heart in concord beats, and the lover is beloved."

It wasn't forgiveness. Not in so many words. Other, better words were support. Partnership. Care. Him. Love?

She knew she ought to continue forward, but it was so hard not to look up at him and just stare. For hours, she could do this. (No, probably not. Not unless he let her take the tux off, have a nice thorough peek, put it back on, take it off again, and so on. For a long time.)

He was impossible and amazing and heart-stoppingly gorgeous and most importantly *here* and hers, her very own, and for the whole rest of their hike up the capitol steps, right past the dinky UNAN sec-check crimp, that's about all she could manage. The thinking, and the looking. Then her brain caught up and she stopped, paused momentarily, and asked, "Wait, Wordsworth? Again? And also, how the fuck did you get here?"

CHAPTER

19

WELL, HE'D GONE FOR A WALK, JUST LIKE HE'D SAID, LAST night. In the cold. With his brain on fire. Had to stop a few feet out the door and go back to fetch his coat and cat. Yoink didn't much like the snow, but she wasn't willing to let him out of her sight. For once she didn't complain, though, just followed. He walked fast, head down, hands deep in his pockets.

Stuck to the shoveled path between the condo units. Walked. Besieged with feeling.

A baby. Theirs. Gone. For a while just the knowledge, that she'd existed, or even almost did, and he hadn't gotten a chance to know her...well, the weight was too much. Thoughts like that could crush a man flat.

He felt like he'd been tied up and now some giant supernatural prize fighter was taking shots at him. *Whump*, right in the gut. He firmed his muscles up to endure it, but the blow hit hard. Wet pricked his eyes. He shoved a harsh breath out. *Get out of your own brain, you dumb fuck. What, everything gotta be about you? This world's on fire, and here you are, nose in navel.*

Fact was, none of this was about him. He wasn't the only one who hurt.

That time must've been hellish on Angela. She'd been raised all her life to believe that a strong woman did not define herself by her relationships but by her accomplishments. It was a weak woman, a disposable woman, who was only somebody else's wife, only somebody else's mother. That wasn't and had never been her fate. She was meant for better things.

He'd listened when she wove her guilty secrets in the dark, how much she adored fairy tales and bad romantic poetry and pretty dresses and stolen kisses: all things that did not progress her career path. Unworthy things and shameful wants.

She had wanted that baby. He knew it clear as daylight. And he mourned the might-have-been and all her pain.

It must've torn her in two, seeing a possibility play out in her mind's eye and then having fucking Zeke Medina tell her she couldn't have none of it. That she needed to "get her shit together." Eyes on. Focus. Solve for X. That she needed to wipe the bad wants off her soul and become his little bespoke political weapon. Alone, though, or on her own. He couldn't even imagine how abandoned she must have felt, buried by responsibility and with no structure to hold it up. That's what mentors were for, parents and partners, too, but none of hers stepped up.

He shouldn't have left her, no matter what she said, sure as hell not right then. But nineteen, right? They hadn't either of them been fully done yet.

If Angela Neko had grown up to be a killer, and she

had, some others shared responsibility for that. Some others needed punishing. He sagged beneath the prize fighter's onslaught, knowing he deserved all he got. By the time he got down to the road, though, he knew he couldn't just keep thinking. Thoughts didn't fix nuthin'. Some action was required here. He tapped his com, and Mari pinged back, and he requested a voice chat rather than text.

"Hey, Doc," she came on through the com. "You okay? And your scary little senator?"

"I'm…" Not okay. *Whump*. "How's the family? How are you?"

"I'm fucking pissed is what I am," she said, still wet-voiced. Her twang rode her hard, a testament to the tumult she must be going through.

"Your auntie Boo…?"

"Yeah, she's probably gone. Thanks for the rats and stuff. Yer cat's keeping us updated better than the god-damn GNN. But there's something else. Kellen…shit, this isn't a good way to do it, but hang on to something, honey. Mama Adele took a turn. Delayed bleeding on the brain, and nobody knew. We lost her right at dawn."

Whump. Hardest yet, too close to his heart. How long could he stand up? He stopped walking, right there in the middle of the road, with snow seeping through the old leather soles of his boots. He wanted to sit down, right there in the slush, and give up. Let the giant pound him into the earth, stop thinking and caring and feeling anything.

But that wasn't him. And he could not.

"How's Heron taking it?" he asked Mari.

And Fan. She was gonna be out of her mind. Every

cell in his body yearned to get on a landjet and go to them, right now. Screw the government, screw the president, screw all of them.

Except…Angela. She needed him still, now more than she had in a long time. He knew she wouldn't hold it against him if he ran. Practical Angela, she'd see the logic. But they'd moved way beyond logic, into that wild world of trust. He belonged to her now, and he was man enough to know what that meant. This time, if she was gonna go into the fire, he was fucking going with her.

"Oh, I've got Heron," Mari said. "And Fan. And Garrett. And Chloe. We all lean on each other, and somehow, we all keep standing. Even my asshole dad can be a comfort when he really puts his mind to it. We're…talking stuff out. How 'bout you? What you need, Doc?"

"A gun, I think." He'd returned the one she'd given him before he'd left for Texas. He hadn't thought he'd ever want to use something like that. He'd considered himself tested back on that sub, considered himself a victor over vengeance. Had been real proud of himself. For the restraint. Discipline. But that was yesterday, and today looked a mite different.

"You ever even used one?" Mari asked.

"Put a cow down with a .45 once, when the CASH knocker didn't work."

"You planning on a clean slaughter this time?"

"I dunno. Might get messy."

"Tell me what you're thinking."

He told her. The scene that had been playing in his mind since Angela had laid that first revelation on his ears.

"I had a bad thought, Miss Mari," he said. "Pure bad, and I can't stop thinking it. What you just said, well, I think it even stronger now."

"Tell me."

"I keep seeing myself showing up at the inaugural shindig, and I find that fucker. Medina. I hit him bloody till he apologizes, to the country and to my family and to *her*, for what he did, and then I stand over him with your gun in my fist, and I tell him this part's for my other girl, the one she never told nobody about, and I put a bullet in his head. That scene comes on, and fuck, it feels real. Feels necessary. You know what I'm saying?"

She let out a long exhalation, almost a whistle. "Lord, do I, and I feel it right along with you, believe me, but that's your darkthing talking. You gotta shut that thing up."

"I know." Somehow he'd just known she'd get where he was coming from. A killer like her ought to. She called it a darkthing; he called it monster. Tomato, to-mah-to. Maybe it was like God, everybody had one but called it different things. Demons, short fuse, bad temper, darkthing, monster.

"Seriously," Mari said. "I know Senator Neko's about to get her little-dictator on, but not even she can save you if you go down this path. You assassinate the president of the unified continent at his inaugural ball in front of a zillion folks watching, that's a problem."

"I know."

She was quiet for a bit, and he heard voices in the background. Maybe just one voice. Maybe just Heron. That was okay. He didn't have a lot of secrets from his best friend and didn't mind passing this latest along.

Kellen had mostly expected Mari to rat him out anyhow. Those two were tight.

"So we've been scheming and have some plans in the works. For right now, you sit," she said when she came back online. "You just settle and sit, and we're on our way."

There wasn't a click to say when the connection died. He didn't bother to tap the com. He sat, like he'd been told, in a void of snow, bleeding cold through his jeans and fire through his brain.

Yoink climbed up on his lap. He stroked her fur and, in the words of Zeke Medina, he got his shit together.

●　　●　　●

Because the universe has impeccable timing, he had just finished telling Angela about his long night by the road, petting Yoink and thinking, when back behind him, all the air on the mall moved. Swirled. At first Angela thought the disturbance might be her helicopter leaving, but that should have happened some minutes ago. And this flurry was bigger. A lot bigger.

Closer, too, right up in the face of the capitol building, forcing the security line to move the hell aside, Heron Farad's spaceplane landed. VTOL jets blistered the fake grass, ears popped beneath its roar, and eyes blinked against its landing lights.

It was fucking beautiful.

Fez, Rafa, and the media mavens circled, must have gotten a megawatt shot of what came down the ramp. First Yoink, then Mari in a slinky orange dress, followed by Garrett and Chloe, who had done herself up as a cross between the Malawian pop goddess Diva Berenice and

Dolly Parton and was doing a fantastic job approximating a real person, and last but sort of least, Damon Vallejo, whose hair had recovered all the swank.

Angela swallowed back a really uncomfortable wad of emotion. Her instinct was to cover it, fix it, but fuck that. No secrets, no lies—wasn't that what she'd been telling herself? She was transmitting. Live and balls-out, just like Rafa said.

Fine, world, this is me. I feel things. I feel sad sometimes. I feel shitty lots of times. I get angry, I get wild. Tonight I feel…cared for. Backed up. Part of something. A vanguard of the storm.

Liberated. Loved. And I'm not sorry for any of it.

She skipped back down the stairs and approached them, thanked them. When she got to Mari, she whispered to the taller woman, "Is Dr. Farad all right? Back in the plane or taking care of Mama Adele, or…?"

Something shifted in Mari's face. It was slight, but Angela knew faces, knew what bone-deep sadness looked like, even when somebody was trying very hard to stop it. "Nah, not him."

"Your aunt Boo?" she asked. Impulsively she reached out and touched Mari's upper arm and didn't even cringe from the touch. It was okay.

Connection. Family. The opportunity to be a part of something that mattered. Kellen and his people had given her so much. And Angela, her government, everything she stood for, worked for, had only ever taken.

Well, she was going to balance out the scales tonight.

Mari pressed her lips together and swallowed. "We got a lot to talk about, but right now, I'm supposed to tell you that Chloe's completed your checklist, and my daddy's been cooking up a little extra something with Dan-Dan."

Angela leaned forward, and Mari filled her in. Just two sentences, but holy shit. Angela was going to have to *hug* that crazy little genius fucker, Vallejo.

Yoink trotted down the ramp just as Mari was done laying down the details. The wee cinnamon-striped kitty slipped past the rest of them because she had to be first. As she approached Angela, she peered up, laid one ear back, and strutted onward, leading the way.

Back up the stairs, back to Kellen, and then through the wide, three-story doors. There was a reception line, but Angela gave zero fucks. There was a podium, too, and that's where she headed, followed by her people. Her team. Crew. Family. The language really needed a better word for what she had, what surrounded her and made her feel mighty. A support structure human halo of awesomeness? Yeah. Something like that.

At the far end of a massive ballroom packed to the rafters, Mari, Garrett, and Chloe fanned out, settling into the suffocating press of expensively garbed human flesh. Free-fae lights gleamed like tiny blue-white stars, illuminating a similarly glittering guest list. Angela spotted several faces she knew, several she loathed.

Zeke wasn't out of his prep chamber yet, but Angela pushed through the curtains, stared down the security guards behind the stage. When they scanned her, all of her data was in order. She lived. They might have heard the rumor of her demise, but they couldn't very well argue with the fact that she was standing right in front of them. And her security clearance was active and up-to-date. They passed her through, and Kellen, too, though she had no idea what his cover identity was. She didn't even know whether this particular magic, the security clearances, were the work of Heron or Fez. Regardless, they were slick.

The backstage room was small, and Angela slipped soundlessly inside. Yoink followed, then Kellen.

Zeke had been meditating or something opposite the door. He liked to center himself before a major in-person. He was seated in a backless tufted chair in front of a floor-to-ceiling mirror that was also probably smartsurface wired. He hadn't put his public "face" on, and his skin was splotchy, his eyes murky and narrow. Nice suit, though. Red and white, the only two colors all the original member states' flags shared. Savvy Zeke, being savvy.

"All pieces are in place. Would you like to play a game?" said a voice from her com. Yoink, but Zeke wouldn't necessarily know that.

He looked up, clearly surprised to see anyone else in his prep chamber, least of all her. Probably. Good.

"Do we have confirmation of the entire cabinet's attendance?" Kellen asked.

"Yes."

"Key members of both congressional houses?"

"Yes."

"Other guests of note?"

"Official delegations from seven nations, two multinational zones, ZaneCorp, the Holy See, the Jam'iya al-Ikhwan. Headmaster from Mustaqbal. Ofelia Ortega y Mars de la Madrid. Frederic Limontour. There are others."

Angela could feel Kellen more than see him. He loomed at her back, taut, a crossbow wound and waiting. Across the room, she met Zeke's gaze. "Good. Lock us in."

"Now you just wait a second, kiddo, you can't—" Zeke started, but the noise cut him off.

A one-note clang sounded through the building as every exit closed. Locked. Sealed. A building like this, possibly the most secure structure on the face of the planet, had a shitload of locks.

Zeke stood up, but Angela cricked a smartglove finger. The wall mirrors turned to monitors, blurred to life, and he sat back down. One screen showed the senate chamber, empty of power players. As they watched, the lights in the chamber went off, and it filled with haunts and shadows. Another showed blocky buildings, stalwart things with that fuzzy glow of multiple shells of shielding. Which, with another crick, disappeared, replaced on the live feed by stark piles of rubble.

"I have disbanded the senate," Angela informed him coolly, "and either destroyed or assumed control of all UNAN data centers. I have changed the command codes for all remote-operated vehicles in the military databases. No more bombs. No more death. If you disbelieve, you have only to attempt login. Your profiles no longer work."

Chloe had been busy, and so had Heron. Angela flushed with confidence in her team. She hoped they were getting this vid feed back on the plane.

She approached Zeke, one foot in front of the other. Some sliver inside her was still a little girl, waiting for his approval, trying to meet his expectations. Wishing she could shine just a little brighter because that would make her good. Best. And she was not allowed to be less than that.

But the bigger part of her, the grown-up part, realized that was all bullshit. His version of winning sucked, and he could no longer hurt her. She knew her own power. She inhabited her own self now. Owned it, past included.

"You will go out to the podium. Your speech will be broadcast live and worldwide. You will confess that you conspired to start a war against Texas. You will admit that you ordered the drone strikes of the last few days. You will apologize and resign effective immediately. Not to worry—a special congressional session will convene tomorrow to appoint your replacement, all according to Article 84 of the Continental Unification Charter."

She was less than a foot from him, could smell his cardamom cologne and hair pomade. He still sat, and she towered above him. Looked down on him. Wondered what it would feel like to squash the fuck out of him. "And if you do all these things, exactly as I have told you, I will protect you from the consortium's wrath. Just as you protected me, mentor."

He stood, straightened his paisley waistcoat, tucked one hand into his pocket like goddamned Napoleon, and adjusted their relative height. One side of his top lip quivered in an almost sneer. "Little girl, I have resources you know nothing about. Go home, play house with your broken mech and the dumb-hick academy dropout by the door. You say nothing more of this, and I might even let you live."

Unlikely. He must really think she was stupid. Or at least malleable. Sadly, she had reinforced the latter assessment of herself over the years. She hadn't bucked the system, not once. Not until she had up and killed Daniel. That must have surprised the fuck out of some people.

It smarted, what he'd called Kellen just now, though. She transmitted that *feeling*, too, through her psych-emitter.

"Oh, you mean, resources like the data center off-shore backups? Oops." She tapped a smartglove pattern against her thigh, and a monitor showed satellite imaging of an unlabeled building off the coast of Vancouver. It had been evacuated during strikes two days ago, but Zeke wouldn't know that. As they watched, the installation crumbled and fell into the sea. Gone.

He looked a tiny bit startled but recovered quickly. "Look, you are wasting my time. Even as we speak, Damon Vallejo is building a population of impersonator mech-clones, which will serve the consortium's purposes, but mine first. Any time I want, I can replace you, and no one would ever know you were gone. Some of those mechs are here in this hall tonight, and on my signal—"

"Well, see, I know that's a lie," she said. Inside, a shout surged through her chest. She didn't let it out, but she did appreciate the thrill of calling him, to his face, on one of his straight-up untruths. He'd been lying for so long, and every fib had grated on her conscience, but she'd never challenged him.

It felt good to speak up. It would feel even better to roar.

A monitor showed live footage of the ballroom outside. Where, incidentally, her own conversation was also being cast to the guests. On a delay, though; Rafa understood the importance of timing, and he'd asked for producer-level control of the "show" in case he needed to—or wanted to—break in with an inspirational montage or something emotive. Whatever. He was the artist here. She trusted him to build her story.

On the vid feed, Vallejo stood very near the presidential podium, being talked up by some fans. He looked comfy, in his element, happy. Most importantly, not a prisoner. Definitely not under Zeke's thumb anymore.

Mari wasn't right next to him. Best guess, she'd waited in the corridor outside the dressing room, in a generally badass way.

"We can do this without blood," Angela told her former mentor. "Without violence."

Something odd flashed across Zeke's face. Compassion? Care? She knew the expression well, but she'd never completely figured out what it meant. It should have occurred to her years ago that as skilled as she was at altering her expression and emotion, he'd probably had similar lessons. If not the exact same ones. He almost smiled, gentle-eyed, when he said, "No victory is won without blood. I only did what was necessary for the future of our species, and how dare you threaten me. You know nothing about this world, kiddo."

Zeke drew his hand away from his waistcoat, and Angela felt the simultaneous grip of one hand on her arm, above the glove, and the push of metal against her velvet gown.

CHAPTER 20

IT WASN'T EASY TO STILL HIS MUSCLES, NOT WHEN HE COULD see a gun pressed against the midsection of the woman he loved. But Kellen had a surgeon's knack for holding steady, sticking to the plan. Maybe discipline more than knack.

"Whatever you're thinkin' about doing, don't."

Of course, Medina ignored him at first pass. All them power-hungry diva elite folks did. They looked right over him. Kellen had always thought someday their blind certainty that they ran the world was going to come back and bite one of them on the ass. Today was that day.

And his were the teeth.

Kellen stretched out a hand to the long table crammed with cosmetics and tiny boxes. Yoink leapt up, settling her head beneath his palm. The metal horns on either side of her skull lit up, and the blip board unfurled before her, stretching in all its holographic glory until the edges of light brushed Zeke Medina's sleeve.

Lights appeared in the wire-frame representation of the ballroom. One. Two. Three. Medina's gaze flashed to the vid feed on the walls, then back to Yoink's dance of lights.

"You're counting the stars, ain't ya? And then looking at faces. Bet you can guess what all those shiny little suckers are. So go on then. Guess."

Medina's gaze cycled twice more. A sheen appeared at his hairline, one that he couldn't blame on the hot lights alone. "They are guests."

"And what kind of guests?"

"Invited ones," Medina said. He might be scared shitless, but he could still rub some haughty sarcasm into his voice.

"Try N-series ones," Kellen said, and he loved the look of sick horror that settled over Medina's face. "Four of Vallejo's best, right here at your inauguration, so the folks they look like can rest safe back at home. Almost like those particular folks knew this shindig might get dangerous. Now who you think told them that?"

The gun slipped against Angela's skirt. The angle was off now, oblique.

"You don't even know what you're—"

"Now, here's where you're wrong, with all due respect," Kellen interrupted. "'Cause I know exactly what I'm doing. I'm showing you your allies, your consortium, and I'm telling you, straight-up, they have all played you like a fiddle."

"Limontour isn't here," Angela said in a voice that was too small but gaining strength. "La Mars Madrid isn't here. Daniel isn't here. But all of their mech-clone impersonators are."

"And they all have fresh, shiny, new back door access keys," Kellen added. "Do you want to know the word?"

The word that would activate alternate programming.
The word that would disconnect them from the whole-
organic humans who controlled them. The word that
would put all that power in Heron's control. Or Chloe's.
Kellen wasn't super clear on how those two were sharing tasks, but either way, whoever got control of those
death-bots wasn't somebody nurturing kind thoughts
about Zeke Medina.

The hand that held the gun trembled, just slightly.

"You won't do anything," Zeke said. "You can't.
I know who you are, Hockley. You haven't changed
much since you slunk out of the MIST, disgraced, fail-
ing, exposed as a fraud. You weren't good enough for
her then, and you aren't good enough to save her now."

Not good enough. Lord, how many times had he
heard those words? They didn't hurt anymore, not when
the speaker's definition of "good" was shit like how
fast he could ruin a person's body or soul or hope. For
himself, Kellen counted goodness differently. Goodness
was keeping the faith, sticking to his rules, playing fair.
Persisting. Not losing hope. He caught Angela looking
at him, her dark eyes wide and lovely. Goodness was
her, and being with her, and making those scared eyes
dance with laughter.

If he could keep her safe and make her happy, he
would be the most successful dude who ever lived.

"Guess it sucks for you then," he told the president,
"that all us dumb-ass failure sorts got the best death
weapons."

It was gone almost instantly, but he caught the spark
in her eye, the veriest pull at the edge of her mouth. *All
you pacifists have the best death weapons.*

I get you, he told her silently, even knowing she couldn't hear. *I got you*.

"Athanatos," he said.

On the blip board, the white stars pulsed.

Then moved, steady, heading for the podium. Heading for this room.

Medina's hand went lax as he watched their advance from four parts of the ballroom. He moistened his lips but obviously couldn't look away.

"What will they do?" he asked. "When they get here?"

"I really don't know," Kellen said, "but I've instructed them to neutralize the threat. Oh, and I painted a big red dot on your ugly head, designated you a target. So whatever 'neutralize' means to a four-hundred-pound mechanical death-bot with titanium hands and a detailed physiological understanding of how your joints all fit together, that's probably what they're planning. At least in part."

"N-series are very creative," Angela added. "And don't forget, they have complete behavioral profiles of all your best friends...I mean psychopaths."

When she spoke, Medina looked back to her. He was still holding the gun, but his arm had slackened, and the weapon now pointed at the floor. It would be easy for him to raise it up again and shoot her. His other hand still gripped her arm like a vise.

Kellen and Angela both had to be smart here, had to be patient. Much as he wanted to leap over there, place his body between her and any threat, he needed to resist. He had a sense sudden moves were bad in this situation.

"Call them off," Zeke said, looking straight at Angela. "Call them off and I'll tell you where to find it."

"It?" Kellen echoed, and he saw Angela's mouth open, close. Blood fled her face, and he knew what *it* was.

"Don't you listen to him," Kellen said. "Don't you listen to that lying fuck. This is what he does. It's his sick superpower. Our girl's gone, princess. You saw the place. Don't you let him hurt you."

Her gaze flew to his, crashing energy in the stuffy air of a small room. *What if, what if, what if.* He could almost hear her voice forming the words, even though her mouth was closed.

Medina still had ahold of her by the left arm, but she reached the right one out. To Kellen.

He moved to her side, clasping her hand. Yoink darkened her blip board, hopped down from the table, and settled her furry self at their feet.

A trio. A team. A family. Enough.

"Shut up, Zeke," Angela said.

"You can't mean to let—"

"Shut up," she repeated, her voice growing louder, more commanding with every syllable. "I'm done playing your game, being your pawn. It's a shit game, and you've taken it too far. Only this time, you lose. I have all the pieces now, and I am the fucking *queen*."

Which was the absolute hell-yeah-est moment of Kellen's life and also right about the time four hijacked N-series mech-clones burst through the doorway. They disarmed Medina, recited his rights, and wrenched his arms back so tight, his shoulder sockets slipped. Medical knowledge does not necessarily mean an innate sense of gentleness or compassion.

"I thought you were gone," Angela said in a low voice as the mech-clones cleaned up and hauled Zeke off. "Not many people, especially good people, could endure me, knowing what I've done. And I could have distracted Zeke long enough for the mech-clones to arrive. All by myself I could have. I'm kind of a big deal when it comes to giving speeches."

"I know," Kellen said.

She looked up at him, her eyes wide and dark and terrifying. "But I'm so fucking glad you came back."

He couldn't think of a damn thing to say to that. Not poetry or teases or even promises. So instead he leaned down and kissed the hell out of her.

*   *   *

There were a lot of legal and administrative noodles to untangle after taking over a government, after ripping the hat off a conspiracy. It was a long night. Word came in some of those protests had turned ugly. Not all security officers had moved aside like the ones in the Capitolina had, and some had fired on the protesters before they got the stand-down. This coup had not been bloodless.

They went together with the whole family to take Mama Adele home. She was originally from up near Leeds, in England, but her own parents were from Motherwell, in Scotland. A bagpiper played when they put her in the ground.

Mari never got confirmation of her aunt Boo's death, but the land where she'd been staying was wiped clean, as if no building had ever existed in that place. The family went with Mari to Lampasas, smack into a war zone, to gather up her family's treasures, what was left of Boo's home site. But it wasn't really closure. Not like Mari must surely need.

Kellen accompanied Angela to all the other services, too. Six hundred twenty-four souls died to make their voices heard, to make their government stop. There were memorials for a solid month after, and Angela remote-attended every single one. Even if she only stayed a moment, to sign the condolence register, she was there. Only good thing to say about any of that was sometimes the services clustered, like the forty-one who went down together in Atlanta.

And all the while he was there, feeling her feels. The way his brain worked, those folks weren't an aggregate. They were names, individual ones, with faces and lives and families and snuffed potentialities attached. And he would know them all, clear as church bells, until the day he died. Sometimes it hurt to have a perfect memory and internal record of the wrong.

Angela made speeches till her voice went, and then she had an amplifier stuck in her throat, and she went on speaking.

When exhaustion snuck up, the two of them tumbled to rest wherever they found themselves, sometimes with clothes on, sometimes not. They didn't talk much, but that was okay. They were soldered together now, didn't hardly leave each other's sight. Hell, they even bathed together—which, he had to admit, was something of a bright spot in the midst of the rest.

The special session indicted Medina on all counts and promptly chose the education minister, some dude by the name of Wendell Week, to be the next interim president and fill out the term just started. Congress declined to create a war ministry. Actually, they didn't even address the status of arms, not officially. Angela, reinstated as the elected senator from California, still possessed the command codes, and both Heron and Chloe sure had a will to rig them suckers. Kellen guessed if the new President Week wanted to blow something up, *and* it wasn't a terribly mean thing to do, he could always ask nice.

Kellen wasn't sure whatever happened with the mech-clones once his people were done with them. They reverted to the control of their owners, most likely. And that bothered him some, how easy it had been to take them over and then give them back. Like the mech-clones themselves had no say in the matter at all. And legally they didn't, so nobody pushed. Nobody said anything, publicly, about the mech-clone hijacking the night of the inauguration. Narrative spun it that evidence against Medina had convinced his closest advisors he was a warmongering psychopath, so they took him into custody. As good citizens do. Narrative, as always, was about ten percent true, but nobody fought the lie this time. They just wanted it to be over.

Three days after the government changed, Week signed a policy directive countermanding all wildlife and weather adjustment initiatives until studies could be made of unforeseen consequences. The order provided full funding for reclamation and rescue as needed, both people and critters.

The official doc didn't say critters. It said animals.

Kellen celebrated Christmas on a hired plane over Florida. Private jet, slower than Heron's spaceplane, but with way better bunks. Bed even, and long enough for Kellen to stretch out on. Not quite wide enough for two people and a cat to fit comfortably, but he wasn't complaining. Sleep while traveling: that luxury made the day begin to feel festive. Like after the longest night, they really were coming out of the dark.

He gave Yoink a pouch of special-order high-priced tuna, and she reacted with typical Yoinkness. First, she ignored him for an hour. Then, she sniffed the pouch, devoured half, sat on his head purring, and went back to the corridor to polish off the rest of the food, nasty smelling but happy. Any cat—hell, any man—should be so lucky.

Kellen rolled over on that comfy bed, tapped a control on the wall, and shut Yoink and her fabulous stink treasure out in the corridor.

Angela did not by habit celebrate religious holidays, which he remembered from before, so he didn't push. He didn't consider himself evangelical about, really, anything. Live and let live and let some more life happen.

Which made her gift to him that night even sweeter.

Air circulators worked at getting the tuna smell out of the cabin, and the plane roared through the night like Santa Claus's sleigh. She came out of the closet lavatory in a nightshirt with some futbol team's logo splashed across the front. Her hair'd grown some, though it still wasn't long. It framed her face like a halo in black. She climbed onto the end of the bed, perched herself beside his feet, and stared down. He'd seen a very similar look on a deer's face once.

It worried him. That deer had jumped off wounded and never come back. Surely he and Angela were beyond such things now. They had better than love. They had trust. Also, they were on a plane. She wouldn't get far.

"I spoke to Fez today," she said. "My numbers are

still polling really high. We're talking ionospheric, so that's scary and awesome. Also, Wendy sent me a summons to Denver. It's possible he means to offer me a ministry post. Education is empty at the moment. What would you think of that, former classmate of mine?"

"I think someday it might be nice you weren't on pet-name basis with the continental president," he replied. "But in the meantime, minister of education is perfectly you."

"I also got a message from Mari, from the island. They're settling in." She shrugged. "She said I could visit, and Azul misses you."

"They need to let that gal back out where she belongs. The vicuña, not Mari. She wasn't meant to be trammeled in some little island home. I only kept her temporary. Wild things like her were born for bigger lives." He met her eyes when he said it, and she knew what he was talking about.

If he had a home on this world, it was probably there with his people and critters. Home was the living creatures that surrounded a soul, not a place or a building. Which made it all so much worse when it existed in more than one piece. One beloved in one place, and another days away and longing.

Angela broke her gaze to the side. She picked at an edge of printed linen sheet and fiddled with it, like she could unwind all those tight wefts if she just kept at it. "Limontour 'reached out' to me. That's how he talks—such a dick. My skin crawls when I think about replying. You know he'll just take it all back to them, to the consortium. But you know, he's teaching at the Mustaqbal now, at least part time. If I take this post that Wendy will in all probability offer, I'll have to interact with him.

Meat-meets. Maybe with other consortium members. I don't know. I'm not sure I can handle it."

He didn't move, and neither did she, but she was drifting. Like that deer, sinking back into the treeline, back to where she belonged. He pulled her hand off the sheet, and she followed him down into the bed. He could roll her beneath his body and kiss her till she stopped talking. He'd resorted to that before and wasn't too proud. But it was Christmas, and she had things needed saying. Turned out he did, too.

"Well, it sounds like folks got a lot of plates spinning on your behalf," he said slowly. Instead of warming herself along the side of him, she moved over top, straddling his pajama'd hips, hands over his ribs. She had a seat any equestrienne would covet. "What if you just told all them to fuck themselves?"

"What if." But it wasn't a question. She looked down at him, and he had no idea what was on her face. She could be thinking anything. "Would you play a game with me instead? I want to guess your truths."

* * *

For a man as smart as he was, it certainly took him time to figure things out. Specifically, things about himself. She'd been keeping a mental log of his reactions each time the former-Pentarc denizens contacted them. He was dying of wistfulness. Worse, he didn't think she noticed.

Had her gaze really ever been so wide that she couldn't see what was happening right in front of her? Well, if it had, it wasn't anymore. She didn't want to see the mechanical intricacies of the entire world. She just wanted to solve for one variable. This man. Hers.

He raised eyebrows and engaged dimple action, but not with his usual grin in accompaniment. More a one-sided, noncommittal grimace. Still distractingly gorgeous, but she could keep her focus despite it. Practice made perfect.

"Am I going to like this game?" he asked.

Great. He wasn't going to make this easy. "I think yes."

"Does it end with you naked?"

"High probability."

"All right. Bring it."

Precisely what she wanted to hear. "Okay, let me see. Hmm. It is true that you are wearing only these pajamas because the organics-removal unit is broken and we haven't used a laundry in a week, and therefore it is also true that there is exactly one layer of synthsilk between my body and heaven at this moment."

He pushed his head back into the pillow and shut his eyes. Other parts of him responded appropriately as well. She contained an urge to whimper.

"Full points. Go on."

"Also true that you would love to go to Isla Luz for the new year and haven't figured out how to tell me."

His eyes flashed open. "Now hold on—"

"Shhh. Don't interrupt," she scolded, shifting her seat just to let him know what happened when he tried to distract her. "Or was that a denial? Did I get that one wrong? You don't want to go?"

He worked the half grimace again. "No, I don't. Not unless you come, too."

Oh. She stopped wiggling. Because this was important. "Kellen, those people are your family. Wherever they are is your home. These things are important to you, and I don't want to pull you away from them. It was wrong, what our parents did to us, letting us go out there to the MIST and follow other people's visions for our lives. I'm not going to do that to you. I'm not going to drag you around the world forever and cut you off from everything you love."

"I hate to say it, but you suck at this game," he said. "Everything I love is right here. You're getting it all wrong."

She dropped one hand to the elastic waistband of his pajama bottoms and eyed him solemnly. "Okay, what about this? It is true that you'll be proud of me still if I resign my office, refuse the ministry appointment, ask you to marry me, and tell you the only place I want to go is exactly where you are so I can hold you any goddamn time I want and make a bunch of babies with you for the whole rest of my life."

In her entire political career, that was, hands down, the scariest speech she'd ever made. She held the floor, waiting for the blowback. Would he laugh it off? Would he reply with a different speech, telling her she needed to think about…fuck if she knew. Her career, her life, her government, her world? Her role in the future disintegration of the consortium and all their as-yet-unknown evil plans for humanity?

Which part of her guess would he find most objectionable?

He covered her hand with his, low over that ligament she'd ogled on a cold November night. She could feel the push of his blood below his skin, the breath in his body.

And a rumble of…oh yes, laughter. What the actual fuck?

"That ain't a game, princess. That's a candy counter, and I want all of it." He wrapped her hand in his, dragging it from the warm spot below the elastic. "But I'm a selfish shit at heart, and I got to have more than that. I got to have all of you, and you're so damn much, honey. So you go ahead and grab all that, and also the rest. Come with me to Isla Luz for a little while and help me walk them out of the dark. *And* if you want to take that post and go toe-to-toe with the consortium, I'll be right there, too, backing you up. It's all open from here, all those possibilities. Just let me live them with you. Don't make me go away."

She leaned down, walking her hands up his body, till she crushed him. Just crushed. She hovered her mouth above his. "So that is a yes?"

"What are you asking in specific?"

"Marry me. Stay with me. Have children with me."

"And help you take over the world?"

"Well, that's a given."

He raised his head off the pillow and kissed her, hot and hard, and she could not breathe, and that was absolutely fine.

"Yes, little queen," he said before the next kiss incoming. "Fuckin' hell yes. Now, if we're gonna mess up all the clean laundry in private, we'd best be quick before that cat unlocks the door."

She can do that? Angela thought, but only for a second. Because words stopped being as important as touches, and it all sort of went downhill from there. Because love. Because kisses. Because joy and faith and connection and hope and life and infinite possibility. She owned all these parts of herself now, and they were all fucking awesome.

Which was exactly how the game was played.

ACKNOWLEDGMENTS

I have the best crew in the 'verse. Many thanks to my superstar subject-matter experts, critique partners, and beta readers: Claudia Renard, Amy Kalinchuk, Tracy Talbot, Jen DeLuca, Sloane Calder, Paula d'Etcheverry, Christa Paige, and Allen Jackson.

And the muse feeders: my Digital Darlings, Faeries, South Austin ARWA Critique, Thursday Night Starbucks Critique, and SFR Brigade. We rise together.

And finally, thank you to the people who championed and built this book: agent Holly Root and the awesome folks at Sourcebooks, especially Cat Clyne, Emily Chiarelli, Hilary Doda, Rachel Gilmer, Sabrina Baskey, Dawn Adams, and Stephany Daniel.

All those people I just called out? Rock so hard. The Tether series could not exist without them.

ABOUT THE AUTHOR

Vivien Jackson writes fantastical, futuristic, down-home salacious kissery. After being told at the age of seven she could not marry Han Solo because he wasn't a real person, she devoted her life to creating worlds where, goldarnit, she could marry anybody she wanted. And she could wield a blaster doing it. A devoted Whovian Browncoat Sindarin gamer, she has a degree in English, which means she's read gobs of stuff in that language and is always up for a casual lit-crit of the Fallout universe. She has been known to write limericks about old Gondor. With her similarly geeky partner, children, and hairy little pets, she lives in Austin, Texas. She'd love to hear from you: vivienjackson.com.

BREATH OF FIRE

The stunning sequel to *A Promise of Fire* from *USA Today* bestselling author Amanda Bouchet

I am Catalia Fisa, and I do not break. Deep breath in. Long breath out. The Gods are telling me I'm some sort of new Origin, which apparently means it's my job to give Thalyria a fresh start. Griffin crowned me with the symbols of the three realms.

If I'm supposed to be not just a queen but *the Queen*, I'd better start acting like it.

"A heart-pounding and joyous romantic adventure."

—Nalini Singh, *New York Times* bestselling author, for *Breath of Fire*

For more Amanda Bouchet, visit:

sourcebooks.com

DROP DEAD GORGEOUS

Brooding London vampires meet *Bridget Jones*-esque snark in Juliet Lyons's second Bite Nights book

Mila Hart's first experience with the vampire dating site V-Date.com is a complete disaster—her date is wanted for murder! But things turn around when she's rescued by dashing vampire cop Vincent Ferrer. Dangerous and devastatingly attractive, he's just the undead hottie Mila was hoping for.

Haunted by his past, Vincent can't risk falling in love again—even if Mila charms him more than anyone he's ever met. But when the killer from Mila's date seeks her out, Vincent is the only one who can protect her. Protecting his heart is a different story...

For more Juliet Lyons, visit:

sourcebooks.com

HER DARK HALF

New York Times bestselling author Paige Tyler
delivers pulse-pounding paranormal romantic
suspense in the X-Ops series

Coyote shifter and covert operator Trevor Maxwell has a
lot on his plate. His former director was killed, and it's up
to him to track down the killer. The job is difficult enough,
but after his boss pairs him with Alina Bosch, a distractingly
beautiful CIA operative, it's damn near impossible.

When the daughter of a DCO VIP is kidnapped, all hell
breaks loose. Suddenly Trevor and Alina are thrown into a
much more dangerous operation, and they'll have to trust
each other to make it out alive.

"As fresh and fun as the first."

—*Booklist* for *Her Rogue Alpha*

For more Paige Tyler, visit:
sourcebooks.com

UNDISCOVERED

After centuries in darkness,
the Amoveo dragons are rising

A long time ago, Zander Lorens was cursed to walk the earth stripped of his Dragon Clan powers. Now Zander relives his darkest moment every night, trapped in a recurring nightmare. By day, he searches for a woman who may be the key to ending his torment.

Rena McHale uses her unique sensitivity as a private investigator and finder of the lost. By day she struggles with sensory overload, and by night her sleep is haunted by a fiery dragon shifter. Nothing in her life makes sense, until the man from her dreams shows up at her door with a proposition…

"Bewitching, haunting, and deliciously carnal."

—Night Owl Reviews Top Pick for Unclaimed

VIKING WARRIOR REBEL

Second in a hot paranormal romantic suspense series featuring immortal Viking warriors by author Asa Maria Bradley

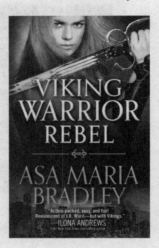

Astrid Irisdotter is a Valkyrie, a fierce warrior fighting to protect humanity from the evil god Loki. She's on an urgent mission when everything goes hideously sideways. Undercover agent Luke Holden arrives on the scene just in time to save her life—and put his own on the line.

Luke may have saved her, but that doesn't mean Astrid can trust him. Tempers flare as they hide secret upon secret from each other, but Astrid's inner warrior knows what it wants…and it will not take no for an answer.

For more Asa Maria Bradley, visit:
sourcebooks.com